About the Author

PHILLIPA ASHLEY writes warm, funny romantic fiction for a variety of world-famous international publishers.

After studying English at Oxford, she worked as a copywriter and journalist. Her first novel, *Decent Exposure*, won the RNA New Writers Award and was made into a TV movie called *12 Men of Christmas* starring Kristin Chenoweth and Josh Hopkins. As Pippa Croft, she also wrote the Oxford Blue series – *The First Time We Met*, *The Second Time I Saw You* and *Third Time Lucky*.

Phillipa lives in a Staffordshire village and has an engineer husband and scientist daughter who indulge her arty whims. She runs a holiday-let business in the Lake District, but a big part of her heart belongs to Cornwall. She visits the county several times a year for 'research purposes', an arduous task that involves sampling cream teas, swimming in wild Cornish coves and following actors around film shoots in a camper van. Her hobbies include watching *Poldark*, Earl Grey tea, Prosecco-tasting and falling off surf boards in front of RNLI lifeguards.

@PhillipaAshley

Also by Phillipa Ashley

The Little Cornish Isles series

Christmas on the Little Cornish Isles: The Driftwood Inn
Spring on the Little Cornish Isles: The Flower Farm
Summer on the Little Cornish Isles: The Starfish Studio

The Cornish Cafe Series

Summer at the Cornish Cafe
Christmas at the Cornish Cafe
Confetti at the Cornish Cafe

Summer on the Little Cornish Isles

The Starfish Studio

Phillipa Ashley

avon.

Published by AVON
A Division of HarperCollins*Publishers* Ltd
1 London Bridge Street
London SE1 9GF

www.harpercollins.co.uk

This paperback edition 2018

1

First published in Great Britain in ebook format by
HarperCollins*Publishers* 2018

A catalogue record for this book
is available from the British Library

ISBN: 978-0-00-825341-7

Set in Birka by
Palimpsest Book Production Limited, Falkirk, Stirlingshire

Printed and bound by CPI Group (UK) Ltd, Croydon, CR0 4YY

To my wonderful readers,
Thank you for sharing in my stories.

Author's Note

Where are the 'Little Cornish Isles'?

The Isles of Scilly are one of my favourite places in the world – not that I've travelled that *much of the world, but I've been lucky enough to visit a few locations renowned for their stunning coastlines, including Grenada, St Lucia, Sardinia, Corsica and Southern Australia. There are some beautiful beaches in all of these places, but I think the white sands and jewel-like seas of St Mary's, St Martin's, St Agnes, Tresco and Bryher are equally, if not more breathtaking than any of those exotic hotspots.*

From the moment I first glimpsed Scilly from a tiny Skybus aircraft in September 2014, I was smitten. From the air, the isles look like a necklace of emerald gems fringed by sparkling sands, set in a turquoise, jade and sapphire lagoon. (Just remember that we're in the chilly Atlantic, thirty miles west of Cornwall and that it can rain and the fog can roll in. Take your wellies, walking boots and umbrella as well as your bikini!)

Within half an hour of setting foot on the 'Main Island', St Mary's, I knew that one day I had *to set a novel there. However, if you go looking for Gull Island, St Piran's, St Saviour's, Petroc or any of the people, pubs or businesses featured in this series, I'm afraid you won't find them. They're all products of my imagination. While I've set some of the scenes on St Mary's, almost all of the organisations mentioned in the series are completely fictional and I've had to change aspects of the 'real' Scilly to suit my stories.*

On saying that, I hope you will find stunning landscapes, welcoming pubs and cafés, pretty flower farms and warm, hard-working communities very like the ones you'll read about in these books. I'll leave it to you, the reader, to decide where Scilly ends and the Little Cornish Isles begin.

Phillipa x

Chapter 1

Even the sign outside the gallery made Poppy McGregor's toes curl with pleasure. It was such a lovely name; so evocative and catchy. Who could possibly resist popping into a place called 'The Starfish Studio'?

She hadn't known then, of course, that this was the precise moment she was about to fall in – and out – of love. She couldn't see into the future, which was probably just as well or she might never have set foot inside the studio at all.

It was too late now. The sunlight glittered on the granite walls, dazzling her. Set back from St Piran's pocket-sized harbour, the Starfish Studio had already cast its spell, luring her onto the weathered veranda with its baskets of cards and giftware.

Her boyfriend, Dan, appeared at her side. 'You're doing it again,' he grumbled.

'Doing what again?' said Poppy, her eyes transfixed by the faded bunting looped around the veranda roof.

'You've got that dreamy look on your face. I expect this means we won't be able to leave St Piran's without another set of bloody coasters and some seashell dangly tat.' Dan picked up a rope garland of shells as if it was radioactive.

Poppy squashed down her annoyance. So far, their week-long holiday to the Isles of Scilly had been relaxing and fun – when Dan hadn't been moaning about being ripped off by coffee shops, boat operators and restaurants. His job as sales manager with a bulldozer company had made him obsessed with budgets and figures. Mind you, she *did* have a scarily large collection of coastal bits 'n' bobs in their small semi in the Staffordshire market town where they lived; their bedroom was already a shrine to the Cornish seaside.

'I only want a quick look. Besides, the artists depend on visitors like us for their livelihoods.' Through the doorway of the studio, she glimpsed bright splashes of colour on white walls.

It was so humid and still that even the bunting hung limply. In contrast, Poppy's own dark brown hair, which she'd blow-dried that morning, had curled into tendrils in the warm, moist air. She'd tried to tame it earlier while visiting the pub toilets and given up. Despite the sunscreen, her nose was pink and her cheeks were dusted in tiny freckles. Oh well, she *was* on holiday. She took a few sips from her bottle of water and stepped a little closer to the door. That cool interior was so inviting ...

'I doubt if you buying a set of coasters is going to keep the whole economy of Scilly going,' said Dan with a world-weary grumble. Sometimes she thought he sounded more like ninety-two than thirty-two.

'I promise you I have no intention of buying any more coasters. You can stay outside and watch the boats if you like, but I'm going to explore.'

Leaving him on the veranda, she stepped inside and sighed with pleasure as the cool air hit her bare arms. An older woman with white crinkly hair tied back with an emerald scarf was sitting behind a cash desk. She smiled and said 'hello' before going back to her tattered paperback. The large ginger cat sitting at her feet thrust its hind leg in the air and washed itself. A faded notice on the wall said that the Starfish had once been a boatshed but had been converted to a studio in the nineteen seventies.

A man with a silver beard was working on a painting as she moved past the sculptures, glass and jewellery. From a faded photo in the window, Poppy realised this was Archie Pendower himself, the artist-owner of the gallery. Judging by the scrawly signature in the corners, many of the works on the knobbly walls appeared to be his. Poppy felt she could almost feel the spray on her face when she gazed at the stormy seascapes. Being oils, the pictures had no glass frames, so she could see the textures and colours in all their glory.

Behind her, she heard Dan's trainers squeak on the tiled floor. Her heart sank as she waited for him to march up and tell her it was time to leave. She was well aware that their ferry to St Mary's was departing in half an hour to take them back to their B&B on the main island. But Dan's footsteps slowed and then stopped.

Poppy sneaked a glance at him. He seemed to be almost as mesmerised as she was, lingering by paintings and showing no signs of being bored. Relieved not to be hauled outside, she carried on exploring.

Although the walls were peeling and the display cabinets showing signs of age, the space still gave her the shivers – in a good way. Alongside Archie Pendower's oils, there was work by other artists and makers. Every nook and cranny was filled with copper fish twisting through metal water, driftwood sculptures, bangles made of semi-precious stones and pendants with silver shells and sea glass in jewel-like colours.

At the rear of the gallery, Dan was now deep in conversation with Archie himself. Archie's deep local burr was mesmeric and Dan's voice was livelier and more animated than she'd heard him for ages.

Clutching a pack of postcards featuring Archie's work, Poppy joined Dan and told Archie how much she admired his work. She hoped she didn't sound like too much of a fangirl but the Starfish Studio seemed to have worked its magic on both of them.

At one time, while she was studying English at university, Poppy had harboured vague dreams about running a gallery. She'd actually spent one of her university summer holiday's earning a bit of cash by helping out in a gallery – more of a gift shop really – at the craft centre near her parents' house. She was well aware that an artist's life was far from the creative bubble customers liked to believe, but she was still in awe of those who made their actual living being creative. She'd always enjoyed dabbling with crafts and spent far too long in the bead shop in her town. She was wearing one of her own creations today: a bracelet inspired by the colours of the sea.

However, when she'd left university she'd got a job as a PR assistant with a building products company and risen to be the communications manager. She still made a few pieces now and then, but work and a long commute meant she had less time than ever for her hobby.

She might laugh at Dan's obsession with budgets and bulldozers, but her own job was hardly creative. On the other hand, it was how she'd first met him: at a construction conference a couple of years before. She'd gone along, thinking that it would be dull as ditchwater and almost decided to miss the final seminar on marketing on the first day. She was so glad she hadn't.

Dan had walked onto the stage and Poppy had perked up immediately. Admittedly, she couldn't remember many of the details of the presentation, but as for the presenter himself – the hour had flown by. He was tall and fit with toffee-blond hair and he reminded her (a bit) of Ryan Gosling. He came across as confident but not cocky, and he really knew his stuff. When she asked a question at the end, he answered it politely and explained his point without patronising her. Afterwards, he made a beeline for her in the hotel bar and while his colleagues were getting pissed, he spent the evening chatting to her. She was impressed by his ambition and his attentiveness. He made her feel special and, by a huge stroke of luck, it turned out they only lived half an hour from each other.

They made arrangements to meet up on a date, and six months later, they'd moved in together. Two years on, their lives were as tightly intertwined as vines and Poppy hoped they would always stay that way: growing closer and building a future together.

'So, how long have you been making a living from the gallery?' Poppy heard Dan ask Archie.

'Too long to remember.' Archie chuckled, caught Poppy's eye and winked. He started to explain to Dan how he'd bought and converted the boatshed into a gallery while his family were young. He mentioned 'while my Ellie was alive' more than once, which must mean he was a widower now, unless the lady at the cash desk was his current partner.

Poppy glanced at her phone and realised it would soon be time to walk down to the ferry. With a smile for Archie, she said, 'I must finish my shopping,' and left him and Dan talking. After swooping on a few 'must-haves', she took her purchases to the counter. The assistant added up the cost on an old-fashioned calculator and put Poppy's money in an old cash tin.

The assistant wrapped the fused glass starfish coasters in tissue paper. 'Beautiful choice,' she said, clucking appreciatively. 'The artist who made these is inspired by sea life on the beaches around St Piran's, you know.'

Poppy smiled to herself. She knew that engaging with customers made the items they'd chosen seem personal. 'Really? I thought I'd seen a starfish like these on the beach the other day,' she said.

'They're certainly washed up from time to time,' said the

assistant, popping the tissue parcel in a paper bag. 'Getting the ferry, are you, dear?'

'Yes, but I think we've still got twenty minutes before it leaves?'

The assistant nodded sagely. 'About that. Anyway, it's only a minute to the harbour and you should hear it tooting from here as it pulls in. Your man's thick as thieves with Archie at the moment. Why don't you carry on having a look round? It's cool in here on a hot day like this.'

Amused at Dan being referred to as her 'man', Poppy picked up her paper bag, which was surprisingly heavy, and smiled. 'Thanks. I think I will.'

While shc waited for Dan to finish his conversation, she drifted around the gallery again. There were many more things she could have bought but she'd already spent more than enough and even if she'd had the cash, there was a limit to the amount she could carry back on the small aircraft taking them home to the mainland. She was probably over the limit already.

She lingered in front of a small painting almost hidden in a niche next to a spiral staircase that was roped off with a sign marked 'Private'. The painting was only six inches square but she instantly fell for it. It showed the studio from the outside, bunting flying, with a ginger cat – like the one by the till – curled up on the veranda. The picture was perhaps 'cuter' than the landscape scenes in the studio, but it captured the essence of the studio perfectly. There was no price on it, but judging by the figures for the larger pictures, she guessed it wouldn't be cheap. The artist may have considered it too twee and deliberately tucked it away in a corner, but it was still a piece of original art and she wasn't going to embarrass herself by asking the cost when she most likely couldn't afford it.

'Well, it's been great to meet you, Archie. Thanks for telling me about your work.' Dan was shaking hands with the artist and smiling in a way Poppy hadn't seen for a while. His job was stressful and demanding. This holiday had clearly done them both good and they'd needed it. She'd been very busy at work too – finding new ways of making drainage sexy was harder than it looked – and they both had a horrible commute through the increasingly clogged, polluted roads of the Midlands. Tiny, remote St Piran's couldn't have been a greater contrast.

The sun made her squint as she followed Dan outside, clutching her bag to her chest, enjoying the weight of the haul inside. She couldn't wait to unwrap them when they finally arrived home, picturing where she'd put the hand-turned wooden dolphin and a cobalt glass trinket dish inlaid with bronze starfish, and deciding who would receive the greetings cards. She couldn't bear to part with the coasters.

'Do you really need more stuff?' said Dan as soon as they were out of hearing of anyone inside the studio. 'Not to mention coasters.'

'You can never have too many coasters.' She glanced up at him, annoyed that he'd guessed what she'd bought, but he was smiling. 'And anyway, I couldn't resist the trinket tray for Auntie Liz's birthday. It's just her sort of thing and you know she'll love the starfish motif.'

He rolled his eyes but amusement lingered around his mouth. She didn't need his approval to spend her own money and his comments on her taste sometimes irritated her. However, he *did* actually seem to be joking this time and his good mood continued as they meandered slowly towards the jetty, admiring the sea and the tiny green fields and the whole exquisite toytown nature of the island.

St Piran's was the second smallest of the inhabited Scilly islands and was divided by a channel from its nearest neighbour, Gull Island. The other coast faced the open Atlantic and a lighthouse that marked the very western outpost of the British Isles. St Piran's took a little longer to reach from St Mary's – the largest of the Scilly Isles – than the other islands and the crossing, though still only twenty minutes, often left people with salty skin, damp clothes and a swirling stomach. However, its isolation appealed to Poppy's soul and might even have captivated Dan.

'Jaw-dropping, isn't it?' he said, coming to a halt at the top of the jetty where day trippers were starting to gather.

'It's breathtaking. I really don't want to go back to work. It'll be hard to return to running campaigns for wall insulation and rainwater products after this.'

'I'm not looking forward to selling bulldozer parts either,' said Dan gloomily.

'Oh, look the ferry's coming.' Her heart sank. It would be at least a year before they would return to St Piran's again, if they could afford the trip. They had a hefty mortgage on their little semi outside Lichfield and interest rates were sure to rise.

'If only we didn't have to get on it,' said Dan.

'Well, we can't afford to stay overnight here, no matter how much we'd like to. I doubt there's any accommodation available anyway and we'd risk missing our flight home.'

He turned to her, a gleam in his eye. 'I don't mean I wish we didn't have to get on it *now*,' he said. 'But one day, I wish we could stay.'

She let out a gasp. 'You mean stay as in *live* here?'

'Yes. I suppose I do. I'm sick of feeling like I'm being torn away and thrust back into the rat race. I'm wasting my life. We both are. All the bloody commuting; I dice with death every day on that M42. The traffic jams, the constant targets at work. Is that really living or just existing?'

Before Poppy could reply, there was a shout from behind. Turning around, she saw a dark-haired man jogging towards them from the Starfish Studio. As he drew near, she did a double take. The guy reminded her in a strange way of the gallery owner, even though he was fifty years younger. His features – the strong straight nose and the chin with its dimple – were just the same. His expression though was serious, as if he was worried about something.

'Everything OK?' said Dan, frowning as the man caught up with them.

'It is now – I was worried I might have just missed you.' He smiled and his face lit up. Poppy felt as if the sun had been switched on.

'Missed us?' she said, unable to tear her eyes from him. His looks were so striking, they took her breath away: he had jet-black hair that brushed his neck. His eyes were almost as dark and the skin of his arms and face was tanned as if he was of Spanish heritage. Her face coloured as she realised she was probably gawping at this extraordinary man.

'My grandpa Archie asked me to give you this.' He held out a stiff paper bag.

Dan frowned. 'We haven't left anything behind.'

'Oh no. It's a gift. He saw your wife admiring this painting of the studio, so he thought she might like to have it. I'm Jake Pendower, by the way.'

Poppy smiled awkwardly as the man held out the bag, but neither she nor Dan made any attempt to take it. She had adored the picture but didn't dare push her luck with Dan.

'Thanks, Jake. That's a lovely thought but we can't pay for it. I'm afraid we've run out of money. You only take cash, don't you?' said Poppy.

'Actually, we do take cards,' said Jake. 'Just so you know.'

'But we've definitely used up our holiday budget and we're ready to get the boat,' said Dan.

Poppy cringed. It was embarrassing to be chased after by this man, trying to sell them the picture, but Dan sounded a bit brusque.

'No.' Jake smiled. 'You misunderstand me. The picture's a gift for your wife. Grandpa noticed her looking at it and thought she might like to have it. With his compliments.'

'Oh, how lovely! Dan – that's so kind, isn't it?'

He shot her a warning glance. 'Yeah, but we can't accept it. You're running a business. You shouldn't be giving things away if you want to make a profit.'

'It's Grandpa's business. It's his decision and ...' Jake gave a wry smile. 'It's not unheard of for him to give pictures away on impulse to people who clearly love his work.' He turned his gaze on Poppy and she melted a little when she realised that, with the sun on them, his eyes were the exact colour of burnt caramel.

Dan shook his head. 'Sorry, mate, we can't accept—'

Poppy cut across him. There was no way she was leaving without that painting. 'Thank you,' she said.

Her fingers brushed Jake's as she accepted the bag from him and drew out the small square painting of Starfish Studio, with its contented ginger cat. The scene was even more beautiful and the colours and light even more dazzling than she'd remembered in the gallery, but it was eclipsed by Jake's amused smile.

'Thank your grandpa for this. I'll treasure it.' She was embarrassed by the heat creeping into her cheeks and her physical response to Archie Pendower's grandson. It wasn't right while Dan was by her side – it wasn't right even if he hadn't been – but she couldn't help herself. She could hardly bear to look at Dan, so she made a play of putting the picture back in its paper bag.

Dan made a big show of checking his watch. 'We'd better get *going*. Thanks for the free picture. You've obviously made *Poppy's* day.'

She cringed. Dan's holiday spirit had clearly evaporated. Maybe he was thinking of their return to work, which was enough to depress anyone.

'It was a pleasure. Hope you have a safe journey home,' Jake said cheerfully.

‘Thanks,’ Dan grunted.

A horn tooted.

‘Don’t miss your ferry,’ said Jake, then let out a small gasp. ‘Oh God. I’ll have to run too. I was meant to be meeting my fiancée at the harbour five minutes ago. We’re going sailing.’

Dan put his hand on Poppy’s back and started to steer her away from Jake as the boat tooted again.

She clutched the picture to her protectively. Of course, Jake had a fiancée and she had a boyfriend. It was clearly time to get back to the real world. ‘Goodbye, Jake. Have a good sail and congratulations,’ she said brightly.

‘Thanks,’ said Jake. ‘Hope to see you again one day.’

‘Poppy! Come *on*!’ Dan was halfway down the jetty now, leaving her to jog to catch him up.

She risked a quick glance behind when they reached the boat but Jake had already gone.

Once they were on board, Dan turned to her. ‘Why did you congratulate him?’

She had to regain her breath before she replied. ‘On g-getting engaged. H-he said he was meeting his fiancée.’

‘Humph.’ Dan turned to look at the view, but a few moments later, his arm snaked around her back and he kissed her cheek. She held on to her purchases while the boat started to rise and fall with the swell. She hoped she’d get to St Mary’s without feeling sick, but even if she did, it would be worth it to have visited the studio.

Dan kept his arm around her and stared out across the ocean, lost in thought.

‘That was fate,’ he said a few minutes later, out of the blue.

She tore her eyes from the view. 'What do you mean "fate"?'

'I don't know exactly, but I wasn't joking: I'm sick of the commute and the daily grind. I want to do something different.'

Taken aback, she pushed the hair out of her eyes as the boat cut through the waves. Dan didn't believe in fate and he rarely did anything impulsive. She was the one inviting strangers they'd met five minutes before to stay with them 'whenever they liked' or blowing their holiday budget on handmade glass coasters. Dan was the sensible, practical sales manager who had the household finances on an Excel spreadsheet and the council bin chart pinned up by the back door.

'That guy – Jake – chasing after us with the painting. I thought he was trying to flog us extra stuff at first, but now, I've been thinking. Maybe we should see it as a sign.'

She gasped. 'A sign? You don't believe in any of that hippy-dippy rubbish. I don't understand.'

He shrugged. 'Not a sign then, but a wake-up call. You love it here and I've never seen a place have an effect on you like this one has. Your eyes lit up like a kid on Christmas morning when you looked around the gallery and you've been, well, kind of glowing ever since that Jake bloke brought us the painting. In fact, you've perked up since we set foot on the island full stop and, I must admit, this holiday has made me think too. I've not been happy at work for a long time.'

'Really? I know our lives aren't perfect, but I didn't realise you were unhappy.' She squeezed his arm, and a pang of guilt struck her. She'd been mooning over a stranger – even if only for a few minutes – and her own partner had been hiding his unhappiness. She hugged him. 'What's the matter?'

'I don't want to waste the rest of my life selling front idlers and bottom rollers. Do you really want to spend the rest of yours telling people how wonderful your firm's soil pipes are? You're creative. You love your beady stuff and you worked in that gallery in your uni vacation. You could have your own place one day.'

She laughed, amused by his confidence in her. 'Helping out at the local craft centre for a few weeks a decade ago doesn't qualify me to run a gallery.'

'Maybe not, but you know more than most people would and that old guy – Archie – he clearly makes enough to live from the studio. And he looks so content with life. So ... comfortable and at ease in his own skin. His grandson seems very pleased with life too, and not short of cash: did you see the watch and trainers he was wearing? He must make a living somehow. It seems as if everyone on the island is doing well. We should look at buying a business here. I already run my part of the business and you know how to market stuff. You could upskill your beadmaking too.'

She listened, half in amazement and half in sheer terror. What had got into Dan?

'The jewellery, it's relaxing and fun, but bead bangles won't pay the bills. Unlike soil pipes.' She laughed, but inside she was thrown by his enthusiasm for such a venture. 'Don't take this the wrong way, but this doesn't sound like you ... you normally like everything to be ... so planned out.' She'd been going to say 'safe' but didn't want to destroy his dreams, even if she was slightly horrified by them.

'I can see my life ebbing away like the rainwater down one

of your drains. I don't want us to grow old and have regrets. I'll be on the way to forty before I know it and I want a change. I love Scilly. Let's do it. It would be a great place to bring up a family too, wouldn't it?'

She almost squeaked in astonishment. A *family*? It was the first time she'd heard him mention children for months and months. She'd always thought – hoped – they would have them one day, but this reference to them was stark. This was getting serious and had caught her totally off guard. She wanted children, but giving up her job? Selling the house and moving to such an isolated place, however idyllic, was a huge change. Did she have the courage?

He squeezed her hand. 'Do we dare do this?'

Her stomach rolled over, and it had nothing to do with the swell. Moving to Scilly would be the most incredible opportunity and surely she'd be mad to let it pass her by?

Chapter 2

Almost three years later

Jake cursed as the baggage carousel chugged round yet again. He could have sworn he'd seen the same bright pink suitcase three times already, yet he was still empty-handed. His flight had reached the stand over forty minutes ago and there was still no sign of his bags. It looked as if his precious luggage – with his whole life inside – might have been left behind in Auckland.

Wait ... there it was!

A large padded rucksack with its distinctive green tag finally appeared through the plastic flaps. He'd been about to call his parents, but now they'd have to wait to find out their only son was alive and hadn't been eaten by a crocodile or zapped by killer jellyfish.

He dived into the scrum of people at the belt. *Yes*! He was almost within touching distance of his camera bag. If he could just push the bald-headed sumo wrestler ahead of him out of the way ...

Sumo-man swung a massive wheelie case off the belt and slammed it into Jake's legs. He stumbled; his phone flew out of his hand and clattered onto the tiles.

'Argh.'

'Sorry, mate,' the man grunted. 'What a game this is, eh? Bloody cattle class. I'm never going Down Under again, I can tell you.'

'Yeah,' said Jake, diving for his phone before it was crushed under the wheels of a trolley topped by a cuddly kangaroo.

Damn. His bag had gone again, obscured by the crowds of people.

Jake held up his hands in frustration. He couldn't care less about his clothes, which were in a wheeled holdall somewhere else on the carousel – if they'd arrived at all. That stuff could be replaced, but his two professional Canon cameras, tripod and an array of specialist lenses filters could not. He'd spent years building up an arsenal of camera equipment that would be impossible to assemble again. Thank God, he'd kept the memory cards in his jacket and emailed most of the best shots he'd captured while he was on assignment.

There was no way he was going to be able to push through the melee now to reach his bag in time; he'd have to wait until he could make his way through. Rubbing his knee, he limped to a quieter spot near the travel money centre and heaved a sigh of relief. His phone screen was cracked but still functioning.

His heart almost stopped when he saw the text. It had come through along with a dozen others, but it was only the message from his mother that brought him out in a cold sweat.

Jake. Where ARE you? Call us please. It's about Grandpa.

He dialled his parents' number and held his breath, waiting for the news he'd dreaded for some time now, but hoped would never come.

'Jake!'

'Mum. What's up?'

'Where have you been? We've been trying to get you for the past day.'

'Flying halfway round the world. I only got your message a moment ago. I'm in the baggage hall at Terminal Five. What's wrong with Grandpa?'

'We didn't want to worry you while you were so far away ...'

His pulse rate rocketed. 'Oh Jesus ...'

'Don't panic. He's not dead. He's had a fall and fractured his hip.'

'What? Is he OK?'

'Yes. Fine. Considering. It was almost two weeks ago and he's feeling a bit better now, but at his age it's going to take a long time for him to fully recover,' said his mum.

Jake was torn by relief that Grandpa Archie was alive and horror that his beloved grandfather had been hurt. No wonder his mum had sounded a bit odd in her most recent email. It was typical of her and his dad not to want to alarm him and to save the news until he was safely home. 'Poor Grandpa. How did it happen?' he asked.

He heard his mother's sigh of exasperation over the phone. 'He slipped over while he was painting on the harbour. They had to airlift him from St Piran's to Cornwall for an emergency operation. Once he'd been discharged from the hospital, we managed to persuade him to spend some time with your dad and me.'

'I'm glad he's OK, but I'm sorry to hear about his accident. I'm getting the train straight to Truro now, if you can pick me up later this afternoon? I can see how he is and spend some time with you all.'

There was a pause. 'Of course, we can collect you, darling, but you can't stay here long.'

He glimpsed his camera bag on the carousel through a gap in the thinning crowds. 'Can't stay? Why not?'

'Because we need you to sort out the handover of the studio to the new tenants.' His mother sounded desperate. She had a demanding job as a senior nurse in the day surgery unit of the local hospital and his father ran a building firm and was *always* working. Jake guessed things had been tense at home because of Archie's arrival.

'What new tenants?' he said, stalking his bag like a panther as he moved towards the belt.

'The new people who've taken over the Starfish Studio, of course. I did mention it in my email. Never mind ... Archie's rented the gallery to a young couple. Running the place has been too much for him and Fen for a good while now.'

'It won't take long,' his dad piped up, and Jake realised he must be listening on speaker. 'And with our jobs and your grandpa to care for, we'd be ever so grateful if you could help out.'

'Help out *how*? Sorry, Mum, I'm not quite following you.'

'By going to St Piran's tomorrow. I know you hate the place, and we wouldn't ask if we weren't desperate, but now you're back and you've got some time off, we thought you wouldn't mind.'

Jake stopped dead in his tracks. 'St Piran's? Tomorrow? I've only just got back in the country.'

'We know, darling, but it will only take a day.'

'Or two,' his dad added. 'A week, tops.'

'You'll be back home with us in Cornwall before you know it.' His mum was using her soothing 'nursey' voice. It was the one she saved for her patients and 'difficult' conversations with the family, thereby instantly raising everyone's blood pressure. Jake was anything but soothed.

'Hang on, I have to get my camera kit,' he said.

He jostled aside a red-faced father wearing a hat with corks and grabbed his camera bag with his free hand. Muttering an apology, he lugged his bag to safety and put the phone to his ear again.

'S-sorry, M-mum. I'm s-still here.'

'Jake? What's going on? You sound very out of breath.'

'I j-just rescued my k-kit from the carousel.' He rested his bag against his bruised knee. 'Mum, did you *really* say you want me to fly off to St Piran's tomorrow?'

'Yes, love. We've booked you onto the afternoon flight and Fen's expecting you. You don't mind, do you? I know it will be hard, but it's been almost three years since you-know-what now, not that it makes things much easier, of course. Like I say, we wouldn't dream of asking you if it wasn't urgent, but you'd be doing us – and more importantly Grandpa – the biggest favour in the world.'

Jake opened his mouth to reply, then shut it again. He stared at the phone screen before dragging a reply out of the depths against every urge to say: *'No chance on the planet am I ever setting foot on St Piran's again as long as I live.'*

'If you really need me, of course I'll help.'

He felt his mother's sigh of relief down the phone. 'Oh, thank goodness for that. We'd half feared you'd say no. I'm glad you can help. And let me say, you facing up to St Piran's might even turn out to be a good thing for everyone.'

Great. Bloody great. Jake was still muttering to himself when he stepped onto the quayside at St Piran's harbour. From Heathrow, he'd caught a train straight to his parents' place, where his grandpa was recovering, and spent the evening catching up with them. The next day he'd whizzed by his own flat, repacked his rucksack and camera bag, and the following morning taken the first helicopter to Scilly.

Although the last thing he'd wanted to do was spend his 'break' on St Piran's, he'd kept his true feelings hidden, for his grandpa's sake. Besides, it surely wouldn't take long to hand over a set of keys, show this Poppy McGregor and Dan Farrow the basics of the Starfish Studio and then escape.

It was hard to believe that only two days previously, he'd been in Auckland after a six-week photography expedition to some of the remoter parts of New Zealand and Australia. He'd been looking forward to spending some time at his own place in the coastal village of St Agnes, a few miles from his parents' home in Perranporth. His flat and attached studio was more of a base than a home these days, as he'd spent most of the past few years travelling the world on professional photography assignments or leading tours for keen amateurs.

He'd filled his time with travel and work, worried that if he stopped to think about the terrible events of that summer's day on St Piran's, almost three years before, he might crumble and break apart. But even Jake couldn't keep working forever and finally he now had a couple of months free before he jetted off on his next project. Going to St Piran's wasn't how he'd imagined starting his break but he wasn't intending to hang around.

There was only one other passenger on the boat as it docked at the harbour, a guy with an Eastern European accent who said he was helping out behind the bar at the island pub, the Moor's Head. He didn't speak much to Jake, which was a relief; at least one person here didn't know his 'tragic past' and wasn't going to offer their sympathy.

The barman hurried up the slope towards the pub, while Jake took a more leisurely pace, steeling himself for the next few days. Halyards clanked, gulls squabbled outside the fish shed and he could hear the distant chug of a tractor in a field somewhere. From the harbour, he headed straight for Fen Teague's cottage. As Grandpa Archie's near neighbour and closest friend, Jake knew she'd have been waiting to see him ever since she'd heard he was coming over on a 'mercy dash', as his mum called it.

Fen's place was one of a row of old fisherman's cottages, perched on the road that led from the harbour to the tiny village that was St Piran's only real settlement. He had the presence of mind to duck as he entered the sitting room of her cottage, straight from the road – the only road – on St Piran's.

She'd obviously been watching for him because she gave him a bear hug as soon as he got through the door.

'Hello, Jake! How was your journey? My, you look thin! Worn out too but very brown. Now, let me make you a nice cup of tea.'

'Hmm. Lovely.' Jake let Fen's comments wash over him and hugged her back. He'd known her his entire life and it was best to bend like a willow in the wind as far as Fen was concerned.

Fen brought in the tea tray and placed it on the coffee table. Jake winced as she stirred the pot vigorously as if it was a cauldron of witch's brew. He'd seen at least three teabags go in. He'd obviously turned into a softy since he'd left home, more used to delicate herbal teas or artisan coffee, but builder's strength was how his grandpa had always liked his cuppas.

While Fen splashed milk into two faded Cornish-ware mugs in the kitchen, he turned his attention to the painting propped up against the gateleg table under the window. Even though the work was only half finished, it was still a beautiful picture. It showed the tiny harbour of St Piran's on a late

February afternoon with a storm threatening. The contrast of spring sunlight on the boats and the looming clouds was so striking and evocative that he could almost feel the keen wind tugging at his hair and taste the salt on the air. The picture had all his grandad's trademark deftness of touch and eye for light and colour, but the ugly splodge of yellow paint across the bottom corner disturbed him. That definitely wasn't Archie's style.

Fen joined him in the cottage sitting room and set the mugs down on the old Ercol coffee table.

'It's a shame about Grandpa letting go of the Starfish,' he said, looking at the picture again. He was still fixated by the yellow scar of paint.

Fen put her hands on her hips and rested her fingers on the edge of the canvas. 'Archie is eighty-two, Jake. You have to expect these things. He's already had a good innings. I knew the studio was getting too much for him, but I must admit I never thought your grandpa would actually sell it,' said Fen.

'I suppose the fall finally helped him make his mind up ... Was this the picture he was working on when he fell?'

'Yes. Pity about that smudge. Apparently, Archie's brush marked the canvas when he slipped over on the wet cobbles of the harbour. He said he was trying to stand back and get a better view, poor thing. Still, I suppose it's lucky he got away with a broken hip ...' Fen's face crumpled. 'It's a long road to recovery when you're getting on like your grandpa is and I know he's better off with your mum and dad but I do miss him. It's been two weeks since his fall and I was hoping he'd come home soon.'

'I'm sure he misses you too. In fact, I know he does.' Jake put his arm around Fen's bony shoulders. She'd never had any spare meat on her lean frame after a lifetime spent working in her market garden on St Piran's and, until recently, helping Archie with the studio. In her late seventies now, she was still on the go all the time. However, Jake didn't recall her being quite this thin – but then again, it had been two years since he'd last seen her. Or was it longer than that? Jake racked his brains. It had been March – so just over two years – when he'd last made it back to St Piran's to visit his grandpa, and even then, he'd only stayed a couple of days. Apart from the pleasure of Archie's company, he'd been desperate to leave as soon as possible and he didn't feel any different now.

'Did he say he misses me?' Fen's sharp green eyes searched his face. Jake wished he hadn't lied.

'Not out loud, but I could tell.'

Fen looked unimpressed. 'Hmm. But he didn't say when he might be home?'

'I'm sorry, Fen, but no. You're right that it's a long road to recovery and he had that bout of pneumonia after the op. He's much better now, but I think the fall has shaken him. You know he's always been as fit as a fiddle until this. They did get him up and walking quite soon afterwards, but I guess being properly mobile takes much longer.'

He let Fen go. She picked up her mug and took a sip. Jake left his alone.

'It's not like Archie to sit around indoors for five minutes, let alone for weeks. I'd hoped he'd be back to the studio by now, but I suppose your parents are enjoying fussing over him and he doesn't like to leave. Maybe I should go and see him again. He kept telling me not to go to the time and expense and that he'd be back soon.'

'I'm sure he will,' said Jake, feeling that he was stretching the truth again. Archie was living temporarily in the ground-floor room converted from the garage that used to be Jake's. He'd been sitting in a chair, his legs covered by a rug when Jake had visited. Jake had been shocked by his grandpa's frail appearance. His bright blue eyes had seemed watery and dimmed, and his beard – Archie's pride and joy – was unkempt. Apparently, he'd refused all offers or attempts to have it trimmed and shaped. From what Jake had seen of the situation, it was Archie who didn't want to leave ... or do anything much at all. Who was Jake to judge? His grandpa might finally be feeling his age and have lost his confidence.

'I took some of his paints over when I saw him in the hospital after he'd had his op. I haven't seen him since then, though I've called him a few times. He's not keen on talking on the phone and I didn't like to badger him ... *Has* he been using them?' Fen asked hopefully.

'Dad set his easel up in his room, by his chair.'

'That's a good sign.' Fen nodded in satisfaction and took a noisy slurp of her tea. She smacked her lips. 'Good brew that, if I say so myself. Archie would approve. I suppose your mum likes that scented muck everyone drinks these days.'

Jake smiled, glad to have a chance to change the subject. The easel had been bare of any work and, according to his parents, the box of paints remained unopened and untouched. 'You can rest easy. Mum had to get in Grandpa's own personal supply of "normal tea". He wouldn't touch her Earl Grey.'

Fen chuckled. 'I'm glad to hear that, at least.' She pointed to Jake's untouched mug. 'You should get yours down you before it goes cold.'

Trying not to gag, Jake swallowed a large gulp of rusty liquid while Fen went to fetch the biscuit barrel. He loved her almost as dearly as Archie but he still couldn't stomach her tea.

'Mum wanted me to come back to help get the studio ready for the new tenants,' he said, accepting a homemade fairing from the plate she held out. Her biscuits were a lot more palatable than her tea. 'They're meant to be arriving tomorrow afternoon on the *Islander* ferry from Penzance,' he added.

Fen sucked on her teeth. 'You'll be lucky. There's heavy seas forecast tomorrow. Word is, the *Islander* may not sail ... Are they aware of the state of the studio?' Fen's voice wavered and Jake felt sorry for her. He knew she felt bad about not being able to keep the studio so spick and span these days. She'd worked for his grandpa for decades, but she, like Archie, couldn't cope with running the business full-time any more even before his fall.

'Don't worry. I heard that the studio needs a bit of an upgrade. The agent gave me all their details and I've emailed to tell her and her partner that Grandpa had let things slide a little, but she hasn't replied, apart from to say they're still coming.'

'The mainland agent who put the details on the property website must have used an old photograph. I'm not sure this Polly will recognise it.'

He suppressed a smile. 'Poppy. Her name is Poppy McGregor and his is Daniel Farrow.'

Fen screwed up her nose. 'Fancy name. Not sure I like this thing for naming people after flowers. Daisy, Lily, whatever. Reminds me of my gran's day. How old is she?'

'Mid-thirties, I think. I really haven't had time to find out any more about them. All I have are the agent's and solicitor's emails. Archie had already given the go-ahead to the tenancy agreement before he had his accident and you know yourself how hard it's been to find someone to take it on. I thought it best to let it go through and explain about Archie when they get here.'

'They'll have a shock. Maybe they'll turn around and sail straight home when they see it.' Her voice tailed off.

He patted her arm. 'I'm sure it's not as bad as you make out.'

'You haven't seen it yet,' she muttered.

'I'll take a look after I've finished here. Stop worrying. No one could have done more to help Grandpa than you and, I promise you, he will do his very best to come home as soon as he's able.'

She nodded and a sudden rattle drew their attention to the doorway. A large ginger cat, almost of fox-like proportions, wriggled through the flap and sauntered into the sitting room.

'Aww. Leo's come to see you!'

Jake smiled at the cat, who did what cats do: ignored him.

Jake loved animals, but Leo didn't love him. Jake had had the scratches and bite marks to prove it ever since Fen had taken Leo in five years before. Leo tolerated his humans; Fen and Archie were his favourites and Leo had allowed Harriet to stroke him. But Jake had the feeling that if Leo had been a tiger, he'd have eaten Jake for breakfast without a second thought.

'I hope you don't mind that Grandpa asked me to deal with the new tenants and help them settle in. Mum and Dad have enough to do with the business and caring for him. I think he didn't want to worry you with having to sort it all out, but that doesn't mean I'm not grateful for everything you've done in looking after it while he's been away – and in the past ...'

'Don't worry. I'm not offended.'

Leo allowed Fen to stroke the fur between his ears. His eyes narrowed into slits, which might have been pleasure but could just as easily mean he was planning world domination.

'I've done my best with the place, but since Archie's been on the mainland, I haven't really had much cause to go to the studio. I wasn't really sure these new folk would actually turn up and, to be honest, I haven't liked to go in there, with your grandpa being away. I'm a silly old devil, but it upsets me to see the place without Archie. I keep wondering if he'll ever be back.'

'Of course, he'll be back,' he soothed, wondering if he was actually being kind to Fen by making so many sweeping and optimistic statements. 'And we didn't expect you to have to sort it out for the new tenants. That's why I'm here. I'll sort out grandpa's paintings and tidy up a bit so there's room for the new stock the new tenants will want to buy in.'

'And they definitely plan on living in the attic flat above the studio?'

'Apparently. It comes as part of the lease and they'll want to save money, so I doubt they'll rent anything else on the island, even if they could find it.'

'That'll be cosy.'

Jake thought of the studio room above the gallery, with its open-plan sitting room/kitchen/bedroom and tiny shower room. It was where he'd stayed many times – and once with Harriet. It was fine for one person, or for a couple for a short time – or a couple who were crazy about each other's company and prepared to share everything. He and Harriet had been at that stage when they'd slept in the studio, but Jake had the impression that Dan and Poppy were long-term partners.

Jake would be staying in his grandpa's cottage while he was sorting out the handover, which he was grateful for. He'd have rather slept on the beach than in the bed he'd once shared with Harriet. The memories of the three good years he'd enjoyed with her were now tainted by the bad ones of their final month together. Their bond, once so strong, had started to unravel before the weekend on St Piran's that was meant to give them some private time away from distractions and help them both focus on each other and resolve their differences.

Instead their stay on the island had finally ended in the most terrible way imaginable. Coming back to St Piran's had brought the memories flooding back in vivid detail. All because of a lapse of judgement on her part, which he had contributed to, however indirectly.

It was all too much. His skin prickled, his throat was thick, he could hear the waves slapping the sides of the boat, hear himself screaming. The floor shifted like the deck of a yacht on a swell or like water. He was going to sink and drown ...

'What's the matter? Jake?' Fen was at his side, holding his elbow. 'You've gone white as a sheet.'

'I'll be OK ...'

'Rubbish. You're swaying. Sit here.' With Fen's help, he lowered himself into the chair. 'Quick. Get this down you,' she ordered.

He gulped down the cold tea and almost gagged, but he covered it just in time. Luckily, the tea revived him and the room stopped moving. He felt solid floor under his boots.

'Are you all right? You look awful.'

'Fine. I had a bit of a bug before I left and, on top of the jet lag, I just felt a bit light-headed. Nothing that some sleep won't cure. Thanks for the tea.' He pushed the mug away from him. 'You were saying something about the new tenants and the flat above the Starfish?'

She blew out a breath. 'Yes. It'll be a big test for two strangers, moving out here. They've not run a business before, have they? And they're coming from the city.'

'I think they live in a market town, but you're right, they've never done anything like this.'

'But they've signed up for it now, so they can't back out.'

'I'm sure they won't,' he said more confidently than he felt. Even though he hadn't been up to the studio yet, he *was* worried about what the new tenants would think of it. If it was as dilapidated as Fen made out – not to mention his parents, who had said they were shocked by the state of the place when they'd last visited a few months previously – he wouldn't blame the new arrivals for claiming the place wasn't as advertised and they were heading home.

Maybe they already had heard on the grapevine somehow ... Poppy McGregor clearly didn't share her partner's enthusiasm, judging by the email the property agent had forwarded to Jake.

Don't worry, I'm coming. Let's face it, I've no choice now, ha ha. :(:(

Let's face it, I've no choice now ... It wasn't very professional for a business email, but maybe Poppy was the quirky type. And the 'ha ha' and double horrified emojis had rung a few alarm bells. There was quirky, and then there was bonkers and impossible to deal with. Jake didn't want any hassle. He simply wanted to hand over the Starfish Studio to Poppy and Dan and bugger off back home to see his family and his own flat.

Personally, he thought the two of them were nuts to leave civilisation and come to the back end of beyond, but maybe they had wide-eyed dreams of starting a new life away from the rat race. Maybe it had been her partner's idea to move and now she'd burnt her bridges, she had no choice but to go along with his lunatic scheme. Shit. He *really* hoped they wouldn't cause him too much hassle. They'd signed the lease and technically couldn't back out now, but the Starfish was in a state ... In twenty-four hours, could he make a difference? If the *Islander* ferry was stuck in Penzance he might have longer ... unless, of course, Poppy and Dan decided to take the plane or helicopter.

Fen broke into his thoughts. 'Do you want a hand sprucing the place up? Will you be going in there this evening?'

Jake smiled. She had enough on her plate keeping her own place from falling down without labouring at the Starfish.

'That's good of you, but I don't think there's a lot I can do this evening. I plan to get an early start in there tomorrow. Think I'll go up to Grandpa's cottage now and settle in, if you don't mind.'

She eased herself out of the chair. 'Course not. I'm here if and when you need me. Plenty of bleach and rags here too, if you want them. I put some milk and butter in the fridge and left you a fresh loaf and a pot of my hedgerow jam. I knew the shop would be closed when you got here and wasn't sure if you'd have time to get some food in Hugh Town. I don't know what they've got left anyway. If the supply boat can't make it tomorrow, the mainland and the off-islands will be running short of everything.'

He hugged her warmly. 'That's very kind. I'd probably have starved without you.'

Her face creased in pleasure. 'If you want anything else, just pop in.'

'Thanks. I'll do that.'

He was halfway out of the door when she called to him from the kitchen. 'Oh, and Jake, there's a crate in the store-room at the studio. I came across it the other day when I was looking out some papers.' Fen came back into the sitting room, drying her hands on a tattered tea towel. 'I thought it was a delivery of frames until I saw the envelope stuck on the side.'

Jake lingered on the doormat, twitching with anxiety to have some time to himself. 'Oh?'

'Envelope had your name on it. Didn't Archie mention it when you saw him at your mum's?'

'No, he didn't.'

'I wonder if he had a premonition something was going to happen and thought he might not come home at all ...'

She crushed the tea towel between her hands and Jake could have sworn her eyes glistened. A shiver ran up his own spine. That was all he needed: a letter from his grandpa that might have been intended to be read after his death. This visit was getting more emotionally tough by the minute and he intended to quash any thoughts of that nature, if he possibly could.

'No.' He reached out and touched her arm. 'Thanks for telling me. I'll take a look.' But he might not actually open the envelope, he decided.

'Good luck.' She pecked him on the cheek. 'And remember, I'm only five minutes away if you do need me.'

Jake got the impression that Fen didn't want him to call her, even if she did want to help him. She probably wanted to wait until he'd had the chance to calm down after seeing the place.

'Thanks.' Jake smiled but started to hurry out of the door when he felt pressure against his legs as something wound its way between them. 'Ow!'

Stars swam and he felt sick as he tried to steady himself after smacking his head against the stone lintel. He held on to the doorjamb for support and, wincing, he opened his eyes. Leo had teleported right under his feet and tripped him up. The cat stared at him, as if to say 'what the hell is up with you, human?'

'You won't win,' Jake murmured. 'I won't give in. I've faced down much bigger beasts than you.'

Leo walked past him, tail in the air.

'You see,' Jake muttered, ignoring the sickening throb in his forehead. 'I told you you'd break first.'

'What's up?' Fen walked into the sitting room. 'Hit your head on the beam. Damn thing. Mind, I always told Archie you'd grow too big for St Piran's.'

'Leo got under my feet. Didn't even know he was there.'

'He's like that. I have to watch out myself. You'll live, though?'

'Yeah.' Jake glared at Leo, who had his tail to him, looking up at Fen.

Fen tutted. 'Leo can't help it. He's a cat.'

Leo strolled up to Jake, staring up at him innocently.

Fen beamed in delight. 'Aww. Bless. Puss has come to you. You're highly honoured.'

Jake leaned down. Maybe Fen was right. Archie loved Leo,

so maybe he should make an effort. Then Leo lifted his tail and sprayed a stream of urine over Jake's legs.

As Fen shrieked in dismay, Jake shook his damp and stinking leg and sighed. Then again, maybe some rifts were too deep to heal.

Chapter 3

'Feeling a bit queasy, love? Still, not long to go now.'

The man opposite Poppy sank his teeth into his pasty. He had dirt under his fingernails and pastry crumbs in his scraggy greying beard ... and oh God, was that a diced carrot nestled among the whiskers? He reminded her of Mr Twit from the Roald Dahl books. Mr Twit crossed with one of the Hairy Bikers.

The smell of meat and pastry hit her and her stomach clenched. She clutched the sick bag tighter. She'd have given her right arm – no make that Dan's right arm – to be beamed onto dry land. Still, not long to go, according to Mr Twit. Surely, she couldn't throw up any more?

'We'll be rounding St Mary's in three-quarters of an hour, give or take. Things will calm down a bit then.'

'*Still* three-quarters of an hour?' she said. 'B-but the isles look so close.' At least they had seemed close ten minutes previously when she'd staggered back, for the third time, from the washrooms into the ferry's café. The low islands – reminding her of black beetles – had appeared on the horizon for a few seconds before vanishing again as the ship plunged into the trough of the next huge wave.

'Give or take. We'll be passing the Eastern Isles and St Saviour's soon and if the tide's right we could be there in half an hour, but we can't go through the lagoon today. Tide's not right. We have to sail round and come into St Mary's the long way.' Mr Twit was obviously a multi-tasker, chewing and talking at the same time, while crumbs sprayed from his mouth and settled on her jeans.

The boat juddered as a wave smacked into it. 'Oh God ...'

'You do look green round the gills, girl, but it'll soon be over. Bet you've had no breakfast, either. Why don't you get something down you? I can get you a pasty if you want? You're in luck. Café hasn't sold out of them today.'

At any other time, she'd have laughed at being called a 'girl', which didn't happen that often now she was thirty-three. But right now, smiling was out of the question, as was laughing, sitting down, standing up, talking or basically existing.

Mr Twit thrust the pasty under her nose. 'Here, have a taste of this.'

'No ... thank ... yeuerghhhh!'

Poppy had just enough time to open the sick bag before she threw up in it, narrowly avoiding Mr Twit's trousers, though looking at the stains on them, a bit of pebble-dashing might not have made any difference. And anyway, right now she didn't care about anything apart from getting off this rollercoaster ride from hell and onto dry land.

When she'd finished retching, she glanced up, hoping that wasn't dribble on her chin, or worse. 'God, I'm so sorry,' (she wasn't) 'I couldn't help it.'

Mr Twit grinned. Mercifully, he'd finished chewing his pasty so his mouth was empty. 'Better out than in, I always say. Been a bit lively on here, even I'll admit, though nothing to what it's like in the winter.'

'Really?' She dug a tissue from her coat pocket and wiped her mouth.

The man grinned. 'Oh, yes. Was on here once in a March gale. Struck us halfway across. Even the crew were queasy. Had to shut the café, so I never got my fried brekkie. I love a slice of juicy black pudding, me. Hey, you're looking a bit iffy again. Shall I fetch you a bottle of water?'

After a moment's hesitation, she nodded. Mr Twit couldn't do anything unspeakable with a bottle of water and she didn't know if she could manage to queue at the café desk and pay for the water without barfing. 'Thanks, I'll just go and freshen up in the washroom first.' She also needed to dispose of the sick bag and find a fresh one – if they hadn't run out. Otherwise, there was always her tote bag. 'Let me give you some money,' she said, reaching for her purse.

'Don't you worry. It's my treat. Welcome to Scilly.'

Mr Twit patted her on the back, and although she didn't know him from Adam, and had been revolted by his pasty munching, she didn't mind.

Ten minutes later, she made it back to her seat, where Mr Twit had a bottle of chilled Cornish spring water waiting. He handed it over and refused once again to let her pay for it.

She sipped the water and felt slightly better. On a scale of one to ten – ten being 'Death, come quickly' – she was now at level eight. At last, there was something positive to take from this whole experience. She'd agonised over a lot of horrendous decisions over the past few weeks, but one thing was clear. She was *never* setting foot on a boat, of any kind, *ever* again.

'Thanks. That's helped.'

'Best take it outside if I were you, get a blow of fresh air now we're near to land. The sun's out and you'll find the ride more comfortable now we're between the isles. I'll come outside with you and point out some of the sights, if you like? Take your mind off things?'

He held out his hand and she shook it limply.

'I'm Trevor, by the way. Not the best start to your holiday, is it, love?'

She managed a weak smile. 'I'm Poppy McGregor and um … I'm not on holiday.'

St Mary's quay was a scene of organised chaos. The *Islander* crew were already unloading bags and freight, including, Poppy presumed, her own worldly goods – or at least the ones she'd been able to pack into half a dozen crates. These had been loaded into a small shipping container in Penzance by the removals company the previous evening. The removals people and the onboard crew had assured her that the crates would be transferred onto the St Piran's freight boat, the *Herald*, and shipped over to the island that same afternoon.

If she was being honest, Poppy would almost have given

all her stuff away if she could only have got off the ferry, but now she was on dry land, she was looking forward to unpacking her own things and settling in.

She spotted a board that was chalked up with the names of different 'tripper' boats and water taxis that ferried people around the various islands. However, she didn't even want to think about how she was going to get to St Piran's yet. She certainly had no intention of finding a lift over until her stomach settled, so she slung her backpack on her shoulders and headed towards civilisation.

Beyond the harbour, a higgledy-piggledy line of buildings was Hugh Town, the tiny capital of St Mary's. She could only see the backs of the pubs, shops and cafés, all hugging the long sweep of pale beach that curved around a small headland. The clouds were low and grey and the rain reduced to a half-hearted drizzle.

Poppy had a good imagination and a creative soul, but no matter how hard she tried, the scene before her didn't look anything like the white sands and turquoise waters of her last visit to the isles – or anything like Archie Pendower's paintings. Today, Hugh Town could have been any small harbour town on a wet and windy day, but nowhere was at its best on a miserable day like this, especially after the journey she'd had.

She'd soon feel brighter after a cup of tea and a good night's rest in the little flat above the Starfish Studio. She couldn't believe she was finally going to sleep in the very place she and Dan had dreamed of since that sunny day almost three years previously. The Starfish was the place they'd given up their old lives for. The place that Dan had persuaded her to make *her* dream too – before abandoning it and her for another woman a month before they were due to move.

Even though Dan had sounded so passionate about the idea on their journey home, she'd fully expected his holiday enthusiasm to evaporate, but it hadn't – in fact, it had crystallised into an active plan to start a new life by the seaside. They'd spent the following two years searching for a business to run on the islands or, failing that, in Cornwall. They'd registered with every property agent and even visited a few places but none had been suitable. Then, around nine months ago, one of the Scilly agents had tipped them off that the lease on the Starfish Studio might become available.

Apparently, Archie Pendower and his assistant were finding it too much to run the gallery and gift shop and Archie wanted to concentrate on his painting alone. It seemed like fate, of course, so she and Dan had jumped at the chance, signed the contract and enrolled on courses on how to run a business while they worked out their notices in their jobs. Neither of them had been back to Scilly since, because they knew one hundred per cent that they wanted the gallery. They'd studied the terms of the lease and had an accountant friend look over the books. The figures only just added up, but that was because the owners had 'let the business slide somewhat', said the agent, but 'all it required was a fresh injection of enthusiasm and a quick spruce-up'.

They'd realised they'd have to tighten their belts and be as self-sufficient as possible while they got the gallery up and running. They were never going to be rich from their new lifestyle, but they considered that the price of moving to paradise and the Starfish Studio also came with the major bonus of an attic flat above the gallery, which was included in the rent. As they studied at the photos on the agent's website, Poppy realised that must be where the roped-off staircase had led to on her brief visit while on holiday on St Piran's. The flat was small, just one sitting-cum-dining-cum-bedroom with a kitchenette and teeny shower room, but that was fine with them both. It all sounded perfect.

At the weekends, Poppy had been visiting dozens of galleries, spoken to the owners and started to make contact with the artists who supplied the studio, as well as exploring new ideas. She wanted everything to be handmade locally or in Cornwall. She envisaged the studio building up a new portfolio of original paintings, sculpture, ceramics, glass-work, metalwork, woodwork, jewellery and textiles. She hoped that Archie would also want to sell some of his paintings in the studio. Everything was beginning to come together and she was starting to get excited about her new life. The dream might have started as Dan's, but it was now *their* dream.

At the start of April – one month before the move – Poppy finally handed in her notice at work. It felt stomach-churningly final and she knew some people thought she was mad, while others were envious. Coming home that evening, she had stopped off at the supermarket to buy a bottle of champagne. She guessed Dan would probably be feeling the same as she was: terrified, liberated and wildly excited. She'd walked into the house to find him already home ... sitting at the kitchen table with his head in his hands, tears streaming down his face.

She'd abandoned the fizz and thrown her arms around him. 'Oh my God. What's happened? Is it your parents? Your sister? Has someone died?'

Instead of letting her comfort him, he'd pushed her away and looked at her like a scolded child, as if everything was her fault.

'No,' he'd said, his voice cracking with misery. 'No one d-died ... I'm sorry, Poppy, but I can't do this.'

Her blood had run cold. 'What do you mean, you can't do this? It's scary, I know that. Especially tonight, when we've handed in our notices ...'

Dan lifted his head. His Adam's apple bobbed. 'That's the thing, Pops, I didn't hand in *my* notice.'

'What? We had a pact. We'd do it together. I gave in mine ... Dan, you're nervous and scared. I can see that, but we've gone too far down the road now. I've told everyone I'm leaving. We sign the contract on the studio tomorrow. We can't back out now.'

'We have to. *I* have to.' He wiped his knuckles across his face and his voice hardened. 'I've made my decision. I'm not going to Scilly. I can't. It's not the move, Poppy. Oh God ... I don't know how to tell you this, but Eve said it was better to be cruel to be kind.'

She jumped up in alarm at the mention of Dan's boss. 'Eve? What do you mean? What's Eve got to do with this?'

Dan had stood up and backed away too, as if he was scared of staying too close to Poppy. Then he folded his arms defensively. 'I'm not coming to Scilly. I'm moving in with Eve. I'm sorry, Poppy, I've tried to fight this, b-but I love her.'

Now, squashing down a fresh wave of anger, Poppy shrugged her backpack onto her shoulders and marched off towards the town. She hurried up the cobbled street past a pub called the Galleon Inn and headed for a tea shop. The idea of a walk in the fresh air and, when she'd recovered, a cup of tea and something plain to fill her battered stomach, was very tempting.

She could check out the town's facilities at the same time and pick up a few supplies from the little supermarket. Only as much as she could carry, of course, but she'd have to get used to that. Maybe she could have some food delivered once she got to know people. She already intended to start a little kitchen garden and maybe find a small patch of land to grow some of her own food. That had been one of Dan's better ideas and, if she kept things simple, she hoped she could manage to grow a few things. She'd never grown a vegetable in her life, of course, but she'd have to learn. There were a *lot* of things she'd have to learn.

After a toastie and a coffee, she was feeling ready to face the short boat trip across to St Piran's. She'd washed her face and brushed her hair in the tea room toilets and added to her returning colour with a touch of make-up. Seeing herself after getting off the boat, she'd been a bit shocked. Even with some blusher, she still had nowhere near the glow she'd had that summer when she'd first visited St Piran's, and the weight she'd lost after Dan had left showed in her face. Her hair was shorter now too, but just as curly, and there were dark circles under her blue eyes. After so many sleepless nights recently, and a boat trip from hell, it was to be expected. But today was the start of the rest of her life, she told herself, dabbing on some lip gloss.

Several people had struck up friendly conversations with her in the tea shop and while she'd queued in the little supermarket, and she was feeling much more optimistic and even ready to face another *very* short sea journey to St Piran's. Having found out the time of the late afternoon ferry, she headed to the quay where the boat was already moored. The boatman was at the top of the steps.

'Want a hand with your bags? The steps are slippery so be careful.' His voice was amused but warm. 'I don't want you suing me, do I, if you break your leg?'

She smiled. 'No, you don't.' She handed him her supermarket carriers and stepped aboard the boat.

Aside from half a dozen birdwatchers, swaddled from head to toe in khaki and weighed down by camera equipment, chattering excitedly and pointing out seabirds wheeling overhead, she was the only other person on board. She pulled the zip of her funnel-neck top even higher and tried to disappear into her hood. If she pretended she was on a cruise between the South Sea Islands, maybe she could kid herself she'd arrived in paradise.

The *Islander* was preparing to sail back to Penzance, and passengers were standing on deck looking down on the smaller St Piran's passenger ferry. Poppy felt strangely calm. She'd made her decision: onward not backwards. Towards the devil rather than back across the sea, not that she could possibly have faced it anyway.

She'd been sucked into a whirlpool of shock and dismay and the moment the news about Dan was out, everyone thought she wouldn't actually go to Scilly, from her parents, to her best mate, Zoey, and all her former colleagues. Zoey was a real city girl, addicted to her fast-paced marketing job with a Birmingham insurance company and the buzz that came with it. Moving to Las Vegas would be far more Zoey's thing than shipping off to a remote island.

Absolutely no one expected Poppy to follow through with her plans – least of all Dan. She remembered his reaction when she'd told him she was going it alone a few days after he'd dumped her.

'You're not going on your own?' he'd said, sneering. 'You'll never cope on your own.'

Which had made her all the more determined to go, no matter how terrified she was. She would rent out the house in case it all went pear-shaped. It was only small and wouldn't bring in much once the mortgage, costs and agent's commission had been taken into account, but there would be a small amount left. As Dan had moved in with Eve, he agreed, and so, here she was ...

'Have you come over on the *Islander*? I heard it was a bit lively on there today,' the boatman said, taking her fare.

'Lively' to Poppy meant a packed club on a hot Ibiza night, or the encore of the headline act at Glastonbury. It didn't mean three hours of puking in the middle of the Atlantic. But she managed a smile. It was a small community and she wanted to make a good impression.

'A bit.' She smiled.

'Are you on holiday?' the boatman asked her, pointing to her overnight bag.

'Not really. I'm starting a business on St Piran's.'

His brow ceased but then he nodded. 'Ah, yes. You must be Poppy. We've all heard about you.' He sucked on his teeth. 'You're very brave to take on old Archie's place. Shame he had to give it up, but that fall has really taken the wind out of his sails. He must be missing his studio and the boat, not to mention Fen, but I expect he's being well looked after by his son and daughter-in-law on the mainland.'

'Fen?' Poppy had no idea who Fen was and she'd only met Archie once, that day at the gallery. She hadn't spoken to him since. All negotiations had been done through a Scilly-based rental agent and by email with Archie's grandson, Jake Pendower. She could still picture the smiling eyes, the light behind their dark intensity.

'Fen Teague. His lady friend.' The boatman winked. 'Though no one knows for certain ... You're sure to meet her when you get to St Piran's. She's been looking after the studio while Archie's away. *Supposed* to be looking after it. Fen's not exactly a spring chicken herself and he had a fall and broke his hip a couple of weeks ago.'

'Really? I didn't know that.'

'Not had much luck, the Pendowers. Poor old Archie was widowed when Jake was a lad and then there's the thing with Jake and his fiancée.'

‘His fiancée?’ Poppy asked, remembering Jake’s comment about going to meet her.

The boatman grimaced. ‘Yes. Terrible it was. The whole island felt Harriet’s loss.’ He sighed. ‘Welcome to Scilly, anyway. I guess you won’t want a return.’

‘Not today,’ she said, still reeling from the news that Jake’s fiancée had died. She’d been about to ask the boatman more, but he’d moved on. When had this tragedy happened? How? If it was recent, dealing with Jake Pendower was going to be very difficult. The poor guy – his fiancée was probably a similar age to Poppy herself ... After this bombshell, she wondered what else awaited her on the other side of the water. She had no idea that Archie had broken his hip, or that Fen was in charge of the studio or that terrible luck seemed to stalk the Pendowers like some malign spectre.

God, what if the studio itself was cursed? Let’s face it, she was hardly arriving under the happiest of circumstances herself. When the boatman had said he’d ‘heard all about her’, she’d been dreading him asking where her partner was ... Still, she’d have to get used to answering, especially when she met this Fen, who was expecting her and Dan to turn up. Why hadn’t she just come clean and told the agent and the Pendowers that she’d be alone? Then again, did it really matter to them? It was her decision to make the move on her own.

After the boatman had collected the birdwatchers’ fares, the boat inched away from the quay and puttered across the harbour, past the *Islander*, which loomed above her. Jake’s loss wasn’t far from her mind. Even though she didn’t know him at all, it was always shocking to hear of the death of someone, especially someone so young, but as she began the final leg to St Piran's, more immediate and practical thoughts loomed larger and reminded her how isolated she was.

If she wanted to travel to the mainland, she'd have to fork out for the plane or helicopter – not that she'd be leaving St Piran's for a while. She'd burnt her boats and sunk her savings into the Starfish and her new lifestyle. She had to make a go of this. She *would* make a go of it – she wouldn't give Dan or the Temptress the satisfaction of limping back home.

The boat bobbed gently as it headed out of the harbour. Poppy's tum bobbed in sympathy and she gripped the edge of the bench. Please let me make it without throwing up, she begged silently. She could see St Piran's with its ancient church tower. She was nearly there.

The hailer from the cabin crackled into life as the skipper addressed them. Poppy sank back into her hood, closing her nostrils as the stench of marine diesel filled the air and spray spattered her face.

'We should be at St Piran's in twenty minutes, give or take, landing at the Main Town jetty today. We leave from the Lower Town jetty this afternoon, so don't forget or you'll be spending longer than you wanted on the island. It might be a bit spicy today, so hold on to your hats. If we do need to evacuate the vessel for any reason, the emergency exits are here, here and here.' The boatman waved his arms in the general direction of the grey waters of the harbour and the open sea.

Poppy huddled down into her jacket. Setting out alone on

an open boat to a remote island and a new business that seemed to attract disaster, she was half wondering if she should take the emergency exits right now and head straight back to the Midlands.

Chapter 4

Jake almost fell into the studio. He'd had to push very hard to persuade the outer door to budge at all because the wood must have swollen in the damp of a Scilly spring. Archie hadn't been back to the studio since his fall, and the building had been shut up a lot over the off-season. Archie tended to use the rear entrance into his work area.

Sunlight streamed through the door and made the scale of the problem clear. The Starfish Studio was almost unrecognisable and he had around six hours to sort it out. Leo sauntered past him and jumped up onto the window ledge, mentally rubbing his paws together and thinking: 'I'm looking forward to watching this.'

Jake walked deeper in, wrinkling his nose at the musty smell of damp and wincing at the peeling, discoloured walls and dusty display plinths, half of which were bare. Fen had confessed to him that over the past couple of seasons, some visitors had found the studio shut when it was advertised as open. The artists who supplied work had expressed dismay at the conditions their work was displayed in. Although big fans of Archie, some had already decided not to send any more work to the Starfish and its cases and walls were growing bare. He wondered if Poppy and Dan knew the full story? He sighed. No matter how much he loathed the task, it was now his job to let them know.

First, he had to clear away the crates of paintings Fen had mentioned.

Steeling himself, he walked into the work area at the rear of the gallery. The large worktable was a snapshot of the time before his grandpa's fall. There were drawings, and tubes of paint scattered on the table and a half-finished canvas on the easel that already provided a great framework for cobwebs. Everything was in place, waiting for its owner to return at any minute, but, of course, he never had and now it was frozen in time.

The crates of pictures Fen had described were lined up at one end of the work area and he found the one intended for him almost immediately, as it had an envelope taped to the top, addressed to Jake, in Archie's spidery handwriting.

Jake sighed. He wasn't sure why Archie had left the paintings for him now, unless as Fen had suggested, Archie *had* had some premonition of the accident.

Jake's fingers hovered over the envelope, a whisker away from tearing it off and opening it. Maybe it was a simple gift that Archie intended to give him, but in his heart, Jake didn't believe that. Archie had never made such a gesture before ... No, Jake was convinced that the paintings inside were meant to be a legacy and opened after his grandfather's death. No matter how good an innings his grandpa had enjoyed so far, the thought of him slipping into a chair-bound twilight when his life had been so vibrant filled him with despair. Archie wasn't young, his parents had reminded him, but Jake wasn't ready to face up to the loss of another of the people he loved. Not yet. Not ever.

'And anyway. I don't have time to open it now. Not with this place in such a bloody state,' he declared to Leo.

Leo made the feline equivalent of 'Yeah, whatever, human,' and went back to washing his paws.

The morning flew by and Jake was sweating and starving after all his work. He'd carried the crate over to Archie's cottage along with the other boxes, which Archie had intended to remove from the studio. Then he'd opened the windows and hunted down a couple of portable electric heaters to try and dry out the atmosphere and ease the smell of damp in the studio and attic flat.

The work had been tedious and hard, but it had given him something to take his mind off being back in a place that held so many memories of Harriet. He'd even put Radio Scilly on loud to try and drown out any negative thoughts. It was mid-afternoon when he finally took a break from trying to get the studio into a state that wouldn't make the new tenants take one look and head for home.

He popped back to the cottage and tucked into more of Fen's loaf and butter and a coffee made with the dregs of an ancient jar of Grandpa's Nescafé. There hadn't been much else that was edible in the cottage, but there was plenty of beer in the old scullery and he'd availed himself of a couple the previous evening before he'd gone to bed.

Despite the alcohol, he hadn't slept well, as worries over his grandpa and unhappy memories had played on his mind. He'd been as astonished as Fen that Archie had decided to rent out the Starfish Studio on a long-term basis. It had always been a haven for Archie to work in and somewhere to sell his own art and that of other local artists and makers.

The studio was only yards from the cottage that Archie had lived in with his wife, Ellie. The boathouse had been lying derelict for a while and when the owner had finally decided to sell it, his grandparents had snapped it up because Archie's paintings had long outgrown the cottage. By then, Archie's reputation had been growing and he'd realised the boathouse would make an ideal gallery space for his own work, close to the main 'thoroughfare' of St Piran's where people arrived and departed.

Jake's dad, Tom, had left the island after school, trained as a builder and started his own small firm. He'd met Jake's mum, Susan, who was a nurse, when they were both in their early twenties, and they'd stayed in Cornwall, where there was more work for them and wider opportunities for Jake. Although his parents had never moved back to Scilly, they'd taken Jake there to see Archie as often as they could. Jake had spent many of his school holidays with his grandpa too while his parents were busy at work.

It was on Scilly with Archie that Jake had developed his passion for photography. Archie said Jake had inherited his creative genes and encouraged his grandson to make a living from his boyhood hobby. So, after he'd left school, Jake had gone to Falmouth University and gradually built up his own reputation as a nature photographer of some considerable talent.

He tried to get back to St Piran's whenever he could and knew his visits were eagerly anticipated. Archie wasn't alone. Since Ellie Pendower's death, Fen had helped Archie to manage the gallery shop, running it alongside her own little small-holding. In recent years, she'd begun to find the long opening hours in the season too much and things had been going downhill slowly but surely.

According to his parents, all his grandpa had wanted to do in recent times – and probably all he'd ever wanted to do – had been to paint. In fact, since his family had been off his hands, he hadn't cared much what he sold as long as he could afford to live. After Jake's grandma died, even with Fen stepping in, he'd showed little interest in the retail side of the business. He had a reputation for paying his bills in paintings and Jake knew that half a dozen hung on the walls of the local pubs, both at the Moor's Head on St Piran's and the Driftwood on Gull Island, one of his favourite haunts.

When he'd finished his photography degree at Falmouth and started to go on assignments around the world, Jake had still found the time to visit Archie as often as he could. He'd brought Harriet here not long after he'd met her and a few times more ... the last being to celebrate his engagement to her with a party for family and friends.

He never brought her back again.

He pushed the memories and Archie's letter to the back of his mind, determined not to have any distractions from the task at hand as he hurried back to the studio. Time was running out ...

He couldn't do anything about the discoloured walls, which were no longer a suitable backdrop for the artworks, or the peeling display plinths. He'd attempted to rearrange some of the stock – what there was of it – and rescue one or two pieces that had fallen off their plinths. Thank God the artists couldn't see the place now, and their precious work scattered around like junk. All of the stock was on sale or return and he wondered how long it would be before their goodwill evaporated and they came to reclaim it.

Still, that was the new tenants' problem. He didn't mean to sound harsh, but he couldn't take on the responsibility of the place. He wanted to keep in the background as much as possible during the handover so the new people would have to hit the ground running.

Having decided he couldn't do any more in the gallery space, he went up to the flat, where he found Leo stretched out on the bare mattress. The heaters and fresh air had already made some improvement to the damp odour, but the mattress was a sorry sight. Jake assumed that Poppy and Dan would be bringing their own bedding on the *Islander*, so perhaps that didn't matter much. However, Archie and Fen had used the flat to make cups of tea, prepare food and use the bathroom and there were still coffee stains all over the worktops and the fridge was none too clean.

With Leo as supervisor, he cleaned the bathroom and had

almost finished scrubbing the metal sink when he heard a warning toot through the window of the flat.

'Damn. Not already!' Jake swore.

Leo glanced at him and his eyes narrowed. Jake was convinced he was sneering.

Jake peered out of the window and saw the ferry pulling into the harbour.

Damn. Poppy and Dan were sure to be on that boat. Should he go down there and meet them? It might be a good idea to prepare them for the shock of the studio – in a cheery way, of course. He would be positive and optimistic but realistic.

He hoped that Poppy and Dan were friendly and tolerant – and didn't chuck the first piece of artwork that came to hand at *him*.

Chapter 5

Fresh butterflies took flight in Poppy's stomach even before the boat nudged alongside the quay on St Piran's. She could see a couple of people waiting on the quayside. None of them was an older woman, however, so she didn't think Fen had turned up. There was, however, a vaguely familiar face. One that, as the boat came to a halt, Poppy recognised. The young guy about her own age was thinner than she remembered and had his hands shoved in the pockets of his jeans. He wore a dark blue hoodie and his mouth was downturned.

At the same moment as she spotted him, he seemed to recognise her ... Had he remembered her from three years ago? She smiled at him and waved. He lifted a hand in greeting and managed a brief smile, although she had the feeling he was confused.

He walked towards her as she stepped off the boat and the boatman handed her the carrier bags.

'Hello ... you must be Poppy McGregor.'

'Yes, that's me. How did you guess?'

'You're the only one not dressed in head-to-toe khaki and you don't have a beard.'

It was obviously meant to be a joke but delivered without any humour so she wasn't quite sure how to respond. 'Oh ... oh, I see what you mean.'

'I'm Jake Pendower, Archie's grandson.' He held out a hand.

She shook it. 'I remember you. We met briefly three summers ago. Your grandfather sent you after me with a painting of the studio. It was a blazing hot day and I – we – had been in the studio. That was the day we decided to move here, if we possibly could,' she said and took a deep breath. Now was the ideal opportunity to tell him about Dan, but she couldn't quite bring herself to say the words. It had been a month ago and she should be used to it by now. This was her new life, where she could start all over again, with no one even thinking of her as part of a couple. *Go on, say it*, she told herself, *tell him* ... but Jake was speaking.

'Yes. I do remember ...'

By the pained look on his face, she thought he didn't seem that pleased at being reminded of their encounter. In contrast, Poppy's recollection of Jake was way more positive.

He was still as striking – more so in fact – with those dark expressive eyes that seemed to hold as much back as they showed. She recalled the way, even back then, his expression had changed from intense to amused within seconds, but there was something different about him. It wasn't so much the barely visible silver threads in his hair or the faint lines on his temple, but the hunched way he stood with his hands deep in his pockets. Something had sucked the life out of Jake Pendower or dimmed his light.

'I'm sorry, I hadn't connected you with the new tenants.'

He lingered on the quayside, seemingly unsure what to do next. She was the stranger, yet Jake appeared to want her to take the next step.

'I heard from the boatman that your grandfather was poorly.'

'From Winston?' Jake said, nodding at the boatman who was a few feet away on the quayside, loading steel beer kegs from a trailer into the back of the boat.

'Yes, but I don't know the details. I'm sorry to hear he's ill,' Poppy said carefully, unsure as to how serious Archie's condition actually was.

'He had a fall a couple of weeks ago, but he's on the mend now. That's why you've got me ... I'm looking after the handover while he convalesces at my parents' place in Perranporth. We should have warned you, but I've been working away and Grandpa hasn't been up to dealing with stuff.'

'It's OK. As long as someone's here to show me the ropes. My circumstances have also changed a bit.' She bit the bullet. 'You've probably noticed that I'm on my own ...'

'I did wonder when you got off the boat alone,' he said in a softer tone.

She steeled herself. 'The thing is that Dan and I have gone our separate ways. Quite recently, actually, and I probably should have told your grandfather and the agent, but there never seemed a good moment.' She hesitated as he listened, holding her gaze with his intense one. 'It's not easy explaining to people that you're not part of a couple any more.'

He pressed his lips together, then spoke quietly. 'I do understand ... more than you know.'

Poppy winced inwardly, guessing that Jake was alluding to Harriet's death. She waited for him to say more, but instead he summoned up an awkward smile.

'Well, maybe it's easier that I only have to explain the other piece of news to one person, rather than two. You see, some other things have changed since you were last here. I'm afraid the Starfish Studio might not be quite the way you remember it.'

This sounded so ominous that she didn't know how to reply. Jake must have seen her panicked expression.

'Don't worry. The building's still standing. Everything's in working order, but I only arrived yesterday and the place hasn't been aired since Grandpa left it. It hasn't been open much over the winter and spring and he must have been using it to sort out and store some of his work, but I've shifted that and started to get some fresh air flowing. The damp climate had affected the atmosphere ...'

She had that sinking feeling again, but the last thing she wanted was for Jake or anyone to think she was a clichéd urban snowflake. 'Don't worry. I thought the studio might not be exactly the same as I imagined it. I'm sure it'll be fine.'

'I just wanted to warn you before you stepped over the threshold. I'll be around for a little while yet, so I can help you ... if you want me to, seeing as you're on your own.'

'Thank you, but I don't need any favours,' she replied.

He flinched. 'Of course not. I'll keep away, of course, if that's what you want.'

She cringed. She hadn't meant to be rude, but his words had reminded her of Dan's sneering contempt when she said she was going ahead with their plans alone – yet Jake hadn't been laughing at her. Damn, why was she still so edgy? 'I'm still getting used to taking this step on my own,' she said quickly. 'Or taking it at all. I'm happy to accept all the help and advice I'm offered.'

Jake shrugged and she realised the damage had been done already. 'It's OK, and anyway, as I said, I'll be out of your hair soon, but Fen and the agent will be on hand to answer any questions. She's Grandpa's friend.'

'I think I might have met her too, on the day we visited the studio. Crinkly hair and colourful clothes? In her mid-seventies?'

'That would have been her, though she's almost eighty now.'

They heard a clang behind them. The boatman had hoisted a beer keg off the boat and into the quay. There was a toot and a couple of passengers climbed on board.

Poppy glanced round and her hand flew to her mouth. 'Oh God. I've only just realised. Has my stuff arrived? It was loaded onto the *Islander* in a packing crate.'

Jake frowned. 'Not as far as I know. Did the *Islander* crew say they'd send it on here? They should have done and they're normally very efficient, although nothing has been delivered to the studio yet.'

'They told me everything would be brought over when I

boarded and I asked again before I got off the boat and they seemed to think I was worrying over nothing. They said the St Piran's freight boat would bring it, but I don't think the ferry has any space for cargo?'

'Not much, though they will take things to and from St Mary's if they have space. Like the beer kegs to and from the pub … We have to get our priorities right, don't we, Winston?' Jake called to the boatman.

With a grin, Winston walked over. He was about fifty with a pot belly, thinning salt-and-pepper hair and a gold earring.

'Can't have the pub running dry, can we?' Jake said. 'You've already met Poppy McGregor, haven't you? She's going to be running the studio.'

'Pleased to meet you,' said Winston, shaking Poppy's hand. 'Again.'

'You too.' Poppy smiled.

'Poppy was asking after her stuff. Do you know when the *Herald* will be here with the freight? I'm out of the loop where timing's concerned?' said Jake.

'I was told it would be here by now …' said Poppy, crossing her fingers and wondering how she was going to get to grips with the names, functions and schedules – or lack of them – of all the different inter-island boats and ferries. There appeared to be dozens of them, all with their own mysterious routes and purposes.

Winston gave a sharp intake of breath. 'I hate to bring bad news, but I've just heard on the radio that the *Herald* has engine trouble. She's under repair in St Mary's and nothing major is getting across to St Piran's from the harbour today.'

'Oh. Oh f—' Poppy resisted the urge to swear and say that if there had been room for half a dozen beer kegs, why couldn't her crate have been squeezed onto the passenger ferry.

'When do you think the *Herald* will be operating again?' Jake asked.

Winston shrugged. 'Her skipper was trying to make arrangements for another boat to bring the freight over. It might be this evening or it could be tomorrow.'

Poppy groaned. 'All my bedding, clothes and bits and pieces were in the shipping crate. I haven't even got a spare pair of knickers with me!'

Jake and Winston exchanged glances.

Poppy squeezed her eyes shut in horror. Why, oh, why had she said *that*?

'I'm afraid that's island life for you,' said Jake, clearly struggling to hold in his laughter.

Winston grinned. 'Not to worry. Your stuff should be here by the weekend.'

She gasped. 'The *weekend*? Shit. Sorry – but what am I supposed to do without clean clothes until then?'

'I expect Fen can lend you a pair of her drawers,' said Jake, his shoulders shaking with laughter.

Poppy squeaked. 'It's not funny!'

'I'm sure it isn't. It sounds very serious, but take no notice of Winston. He's having you on. The skippers will sort it out between them and I bet the whole lot will get here first thing in the morning.' Jake smiled and, despite her indignation, Poppy glimpsed the sunlight behind his eyes for a moment.

'Joking apart, don't worry. Fen and I will try to loan you anything you need tonight – um ... most things anyway.'

'I'll ask around at the quay in St Mary's and give you a bell,' said Winston, still smirking.

'Thanks.' Poppy forced herself to sound cheerful. 'I told myself to be prepared for glitches like this, but I can see it's going to take a lot of getting used to.'

'This is only the start of it,' said Jake and Poppy was sure he wasn't joking.

'*Oh*. I see what you mean.'

If Poppy hadn't been carrying her shopping, she'd have dug her nails into her palm to try and avoid blubbing when she followed Jake inside the Starfish Studio. Jake had warned her not to expect too much, but he'd been right when he said things had changed. In fact, she was finding it impossible to equate the damp, cold space around her with the vibrant gallery she remembered. The photos on the agent's website must have been years old.

She put her bags down. Jake went in ahead of her, so she couldn't see his face and maybe that was what he wanted. 'I'm sure it can be sorted out and if you really feel that the place isn't as advertised then I know my grandfather wouldn't want you to feel forced to stay.'

'I'm staying,' she declared and her words echoed off the walls. Oh, the walls ... they weren't the cool white backdrop she remembered; they were discoloured, chipped and peeling. That was only the half of it. Most of the display plinths were empty and the stock that was left was hardly appealing. Oh

God, was that a collection of crocheted toilet roll dollies by the cash desk?

Jake followed her to the loo roll dollies. He winced. 'Sorry. I should have cleared those away. They must have been made by one of Fen's friends and Grandpa obviously didn't have the heart to chuck them out. Or maybe Fen sneaked them in when he wasn't looking as a favour to her mate. They're not really in keeping with the gallery, are they?'

'I don't want to be a snob,' said Poppy. 'Or offend anyone *but* ...'

'It's your gallery and you have to have your own vision for it. You can't stock every piece that someone offers you and if that means ruffling a few feathers, then so be it.'

He switched on the lights. Despite it being only five p.m., the place seemed dull and the overhead strip light only served to highlight the shabby walls and fittings.

'I can see I'm going to have to redecorate.' She was thinking aloud.

Jake moved by her side. 'That sounds like a plan.'

'And I think we're going to need new stock.'

'Definitely,' said Jake. 'I can help you sort through some of Grandpa's paintings,' he added more brightly. 'There were several boxes of them in the work area and I wasn't sure which he wanted to put up for sale. Shall I phone and ask him for you?'

She swung round. 'Yes. Thanks. I very much still want to sell your grandfather's pictures. It's wonderful and, after all, the studio's reputation was built on Archie Pendower's work.'

'I think that's what he was hoping,' said Jake and gave her

one of his searching looks. 'Have you had much experience of running a gallery before?'

'Does it look like it?' said Poppy, then softened as she realised Jake wasn't being sarcastic. 'Some. I worked in a small studio at a craft centre during one of my uni vacations, but that was a long time ago, as you've probably guessed. I dabble in jewellery making as a hobby, but I'm not a professional. My last job was managing the PR for a building products company, so promoting gloss paint is as close as I've come to selling art recently.'

Jake's eyes crinkled. 'At least you're honest. Some people might have turned up, thinking they know everything about the business. I doubt the gallery trade has changed that much and if you've a realistic idea about the business and you're ready to learn, that's most of the job done.'

She was sure he was being kind but also hoped he was right. 'I've being doing lots of research over the past few months since we decided to move here. I talked to a lot of gallery owners and artists. I've already emailed half a dozen of the people who supply the studio and told them about my "exciting new plans".' She placed air quotes around the last few words with her fingers.

He paused by the desk where Fen used to ring up the purchases. The same vintage calculator sat on the table, although the digital screen was dead. 'Um, what did they say?' he asked.

'Only two of them bothered to reply and said they'd have to think about it. That was months ago and I was going to phone them all back and find out why they seemed reluctant, but things happened at home and, since then, I've spent all my time trying to sort the fallout from me and Dan splitting up.'

'That's understandable and I'm not surprised the artists didn't respond if they'd seen the way this place was going.' He picked up her shopping from the floor by the doorway. 'It can wait until tomorrow after the journey you must have had. I heard the *Islander* was almost cancelled. Why don't you come up and see the flat? It's basic but I've – er – had a bit of a tidy-up this morning, so there shouldn't be too many shocks.'

Dreading what awaited her, Poppy followed him to the spiral staircase that she'd seen on her first visit. The rope barrier hung from the hook on the wall, the 'Private' sign resting on the lowest step. Passing the sign reminded her this was her space now and only she had the right to pass the barrier and enter the flat above. It also reminded her that she should have been exploring the studio and flat with Dan at her side. They ought to have been sharing the disappointment of finding the gallery in disarray and reassuring each other – together. She wondered what his reaction might have been. He would probably have been angry and grumpy and possibly have demanded that Jake cancel the lease and they head straight home. Or maybe he would have jollied her along and been positive. She had no way of knowing and now never would. Everything she'd thought she'd been certain of where Dan was concerned had been blown to smithereens.

'The flat's small but it is cosy, or it will be,' Jake said.

It didn't take long to take in everything, from the dated

but clean kitchenette to the ageing sofa where the plumped-up cushions were lined up neatly. The curtains were tied back from the windows, flooding the attic flat with light. The sun lit up every fading furnishing, chipped cupboard and peeling wall. The sight of her humble new home combined with the efforts a stranger had gone to, to make it welcoming, was almost too much. What finally tipped her over the edge was the double bed, stripped bare apart from the sagging mattress.

She bit her lip, but it was too late to stop tears forming in her eyes. She not only felt miserable, she also felt mortified in case she blubbed in front of Jake.

'It'll be f-fine,' she said, unable to hide the crack in her voice. She dug a tissue from her coat pocket and blew her nose noisily. 'It's been a very long day. A long few months in fact.'

'Why don't you sit down and I'll put the kettle on? My throat's dry anyway, after clearing all that dust from downstairs.'

'Thanks,' said Poppy and sat down on the bed next to her. The springs made an alarming noise as if one was going to pop through the mattress like in a cartoon. Seconds later, the bed lurched sideways and she felt herself tipping over.

'Oh my God ...'

She tried to get up but it was too late. The bed collapsed onto the floor with a loud crunch as the leg gave way. Poppy found herself lurching sideways down the mattress, fully aware it was happening but unable to stop herself. A second later, she'd dropped the few inches from the mattress onto the floor and was face to face with the tufts of the rug.

She'd been slightly winded by the shock of rolling off the bed but nothing hurt so she knew she was completely uninjured. Her descent had happened in such comedic slow motion that it was almost funny. In fact, it *was* funny and the tears that had bubbled out only moments earlier now turned into laughter. She rolled onto her back, her body shaking.

Jake loomed over her, his brow creased in horror. 'Christ. Are you OK? I'm so sorry.'

She opened her mouth to answer but had a fit of the giggles as his face, almost six feet above her, bore an expression of complete disbelief.

'Oh God.' He looked so horrified Poppy laughed even more.

'I'm f-f-fine. It's just ... well it's s-so f-funny. The bed c-collaps-sing ...' Her sides hurt from laughing.

'No. It's not funny. It's terrible.' Jake dragged his hands over his face and groaned. 'I'm so sorry. This bloody place. It's not only a dump, it's downright dangerous as well.'

She managed to stop giggling for a few seconds and pushed herself up to sitting. Tears wet her cheeks.

Jake held out his hand.

'No. I'm fine. Please don't worry,' she said, but he clasped her hand anyway and she half clambered and was half pulled to her feet.

He let go of her hand. 'I knew the place was a mess, but I hadn't realised it was this bad. Look at that bed!' he cried.

She glanced at the mattress. One leg had snapped clean off, hence her undignified fall to earth. 'It could have happened any time. Good job it wasn't in the middle of the night,' she said, with a giggle.

Jake wasn't amused and his embarrassment only made her smile more. He'd obviously been terrified of showing her the place, which somehow made her feel better about how shitty it was.

'It's not good enough,' he declared. 'None of it is. I wouldn't blame you if you decided not to stay,' he said.

'Oh no. Absolutely not.' She fired back the words so hard and fast that he looked taken aback. 'I'm staying. Even if it kills me,' she declared.

'I hope it won't do that. The sofa is safe enough. I've tested it,' he muttered. 'I'll get the coffee.'

She took his advice on the sofa. A few minutes later, Jake handed over a mug and sat next to her.

'I'm sorry the place doesn't meet with your expectations ... I'm sure Grandpa and Fen hadn't noticed or fully realised how much it had gone downhill ... My parents are working full-time and now caring for him. I probably should have come over sooner and made more of an effort, but I've been away in New Zealand.'

'Stop feeling guilty,' she said, feeling sorry for him and wondering what he did for a living. She glanced around her again. 'The flat's fine and I can see you've tried to make it look welcoming. I mean you *have* made it welcoming. I'm digging a deeper hole, aren't I?'

He shook his head and a crooked little smile touched his mouth. 'I'd had no actual idea it was this bad, but I might have guessed. I had promised to come and visit Grandpa at Christmas and I could have checked it out then, but ... well, I let other priorities come first.'

She wondered what those priorities were, but certainly wasn't going to ask. 'A lot of things haven't lived up to my expectations lately, so in the grand scheme of things, this isn't massive.'

Her words surprised even herself. She probably sounded far more confident than she felt, but Jake's offer to let her off the tenancy only made her more determined to stay. Then again, how the gallery would ever be ready for a grand launch in less than a month's time, she had no idea. She planned on opening over the late spring bank holiday weekend at the end of May when there would be plenty of holidaymakers around and her family and Zoey could get away from work for a longer visit.

She savoured her coffee and checked out the furniture again. It might be old but it was perfectly useable and, anyway, beggars couldn't be choosers.

'I'm glad that the studio comes with accommodation though it might have been a bit *too* cosy if Dan had come with me. Especially knowing what I know about him now. We might have done away with each other.'

Jake smiled. 'You'd definitely have been getting under each other's feet. It's going to seem a lot better when you've got all your own stuff around you.' He hesitated. 'Take a look at the view out to the west.'

They took their mugs to the window.

Wow. The sun had come out while Jake had been showing her round and the space was now flooded with light. The flat had windows on all four sides: one at either end of the gable and two large Velux lights in the roof that gave views of the sky. The glass was sparkling and she guessed Jake had cleaned the windows earlier that day. His efforts had paid off because what greeted her made her breath catch in her throat. She wasn't that high up but the elevation was enough to reveal a sensational vista over the beach towards the open sea on one side and the harbour on the other.

'You can watch all the comings and goings at the harbour and jetty from here,' he said. 'And that way, to the west—' he pointed with his free hand '—there's nothing until America. Unless you count the lighthouse and a few Stone Age ruins.'

Poppy gazed beyond the headland that marked the western extremity of St Piran's, to the other low islets floating in the sea. In the far distance was little more than a large rock with a white lighthouse on it. She could feel the warmth from the late afternoon sun through the glass against her skin.

'That's the Bishop Rock.' Jake pointed to the west. 'In Grandpa's younger days, he said it was manned and people used to hitch rides with the supply boat to shout hello to the keepers. He painted a picture of it in a storm – it's in the gallery downstairs.'

'I can't wait to see that. I'm not surprised he was inspired by it. Imagine living out there with only the seals and gulls for company. Are the seas round here dangerous?'

He hesitated before replying. 'If you don't respect them, they're lethal. There are literally hundreds of shipwrecks. Some of the Spanish Armada foundered round here way back.'

'Really?'

'So they say. You should visit the figurehead museum on Tresco if you like that sort of thing. They all come from wrecks.'

He said it almost sarcastically, so she guessed he considered the museum a touristy thing to do. She hadn't actually been to the museum on her previous trip, however, and resolved to go there soon but not to let him know.

The floorboards creaked as he moved away from the window but she stayed where she was. She craned her neck and looked the other direction to the harbour where a few yachts and workboats were moored. The sea looked calm within the harbour but she had an inkling of how wild it could be from her journey here.

'If you want to have a little time to yourself, I'll make myself scarce. I have some calls to make, so when you're ready, come over to the cottage. You can't miss it. It's right there.' He pointed to a stone house about fifty yards up the beach facing the harbour. 'I'll sort out some bedding and a few other things you might need and I'll arrange for the bed to be repaired as soon as possible.'

'Thanks. I'll manage for now on this floor mattress.'

She glanced at the bare mattress again and thought of the shoddy state of the gallery beneath her feet. Great light and amazing view or not, she still had a huge amount of work to do to get her home and business up and running. Jake must have noticed the anxiety on her face because he spoke gently to her.

'Look, you've taken a huge step and had a rough time. It will get easier, I promise you.'

'I'm sure I'll settle in when I get to know people,' she said, embarrassed by his sympathy.

'I meant that being on your *own* would get easier. At least, you'll come to terms with it.' He sounded bitter and as if he really did understand her. Whatever had happened with his fiancée must have caused him terrible pain.

Chapter 6

Jake cursed silently as he jogged down the stairs and out of the studio. That was all he needed: the new tenant turning up on her own and almost bursting into tears of horror when she saw the studio. And – deep joy – a bloody collapsing bed.

He didn't blame Poppy for being upset at what had greeted her. In fact, he'd have probably felt exactly the same. Even if she hadn't been on her own, she had every right to be annoyed and dismayed about the condition of the gallery and flat. The fact that she'd just made a life-changing step only made things ten times worse.

He'd recognised her within a few moments of her stepping off the St Piran's jetty. He'd had no reason to connect her with the new tenants, of course, as he'd never known her name. His reaction, after the initial surprise, had been a mixture of memories – good and bad. The bad ones had nothing to do with her, and yet he couldn't entirely separate them.

He walked the short distance to Archie's cottage, turning over the contrast between that summer's day and now. Poppy was imprinted on his mind as a bubbly, thoughtful woman whose enthusiasm for life he'd once shared. She still came across as warm, if understandably a little defensive at times, and she was every bit as attractive, with her soft brown curls and those blue eyes, but her face was pale, probably as a result of a rough crossing on the *Islander* and sleepless nights before that.

He'd no idea what had happened between her and Dan, although from his five minutes' acquaintance with the man, he'd have bet his new Canon on Dan having been the guilty party. Poppy seemed like a decent person to him. She also had a sense of humour, from the way she was giggling when she fell on the floor. She'd definitely need that over the coming months.

He'd half wanted to take out his camera and photograph her, which had been a bizarre thing to think. The comment about her knickers had made him smile to himself. He also remembered her reaction when he'd run after her with Grandpa's painting on that hot August day that seemed like yesterday but also a century ago. Even then he'd felt a connection with her and had warmed to her instantly.

Grandpa Archie had noticed her looking at the painting and drawn his own conclusions about her. Jake couldn't help being reminded of that day. He'd only popped in on his way to meet Harriet at the St Piran's boatyard, where she'd gone on ahead while he told Archie where they were taking the yacht. The *Hotspur* had been bigger than the dinghy that

Archie now owned; obviously, he'd sold it after Harriet's death.

Once again, the events of that day slammed into him.

'I'm in a hurry, Grandpa. Harriet's waiting for me. She's getting the Hotspur *ready to sail and I don't want to let her do it all herself.'*

'If you're heading that way, run after that couple who were in here. Pretty young woman with brown hair and a pink T-shirt. She's with that chap in the orange shirt. You can't miss them. Give this picture to the girl. Not to him, mind, he's a bit of a know-all, but I can see she fell in love with it.'

Jake took the hastily wrapped picture. 'You're a big softy, Grandpa.'

Archie's eyes twinkled. 'I know, but that's why you love me.'

Jake had grabbed the picture and fled out of the studio past Fen, who told him to be careful on his sailing trip. He'd caught up with the 'girl' he now knew to be Poppy and the 'know-all', Dan, and handed over the painting.

He'd never forget the delight in her eyes or Dan's assumption that he wanted payment for the picture. Jake had teased him a bit, the prat. Poppy had wished him a happy sail and congratulated him on his engagement. Her words were etched on his mind forever, along with the events that had followed.

Poppy had assumed, as any polite and generous person might, that he and Harriet were living in a state of pre-marital bliss.

It couldn't have been further from the truth.

Everyone on St Piran's had thought the same as Poppy, and why wouldn't they? He and Harriet had put on a great show of hiding the darker undercurrents of their relationship. Even his grandpa and Fen hadn't guessed the real truth.

The short break on St Piran's was meant to be a last-ditch chance to try and save their relationship. They'd both said and done some deeply hurtful things in the weeks leading up to that last trip, but they'd both agreed to try one last time to work things out.

They'd never had the chance, and no one but himself would ever know what had really happened in those fatal few minutes before Harriet had lost her life.

Once Jake was out of hearing of the studio, he called the local 'jack of all trades' to fix the bed, then popped in to see Fen, to reassure her that the new tenant had arrived and to explain that she was on her own and he was helping her settle in.

'Poor girl,' said Fen. 'Do you think I should go over and see how she is?'

'Why not let her settle in for this evening?' said Jake, suspecting Poppy might need a rest and some time to wallow in misery before she dusted herself off and came over to the cottage – *if* she came over. He didn't mention the non-delivery of her stuff, or the collapsing bed or Fen would have been round the studio in a flash, fussing over Poppy and fretting over the state of the flat and studio. 'I think she's shattered after the journey and she hinted she wanted to get an early night.'

'If you think she's OK ... How did she react when she saw the accommodation?'

'Fine. She seems to be made of strong stuff to me. Why

not pop over in the morning after she's had a good night's sleep?'

'You're probably right. Thanks for showing her round. I couldn't have stood it if she'd taken one step inside and burst into tears.'

'Like I said, she seems to know exactly what she's doing,' Jake fibbed, pecking Fen on the cheek by way of goodbye. 'So, don't worry.'

Making his excuses, he strode off to Archie's cottage, calling his grandpa on the way to reassure him that Poppy had arrived and all was well. Archie made no mention of the crate of paintings addressed to Jake, so he decided not to let on he'd seen it.

Back at the cottage, he went straight upstairs to the spare room where he was sleeping. He had to edge round the crate in order to reach the airing cupboard. Grandpa Archie didn't have much need for spare linen, but there was a faded but clean set on the shelf. He put the cover on the hardly used duvet from his bed and borrowed his grandad's duvet for his own bed.

For a few mad seconds, he'd debated about offering the spare bed in the cottage to Poppy while he slept in Archie's room, but dismissed the idea straightaway. There was no way he could make an offer like that without it seeming like he was coming on to her – and he assumed the last thing she wanted was any man within fifty feet of her, if, as he guessed, Dan had dumped her.

He found an old-fashioned bar of soap and a towel and smiled as he made up the 'emergency kit' for Poppy, thinking it was a shame there was nothing he could do about her missing knickers. As a final thought, he went to fetch a clean T-shirt from his overnight bag to add to the kit. She could use it as pyjamas or wear it tomorrow as she saw fit.

After today, he decided to keep his distance unless she asked for him. She certainly didn't need a bloke hanging about, let alone one who'd shown her an ailing business and a shabby flat with collapsing furniture. While he'd been embarrassed to show her around the Starfish, he hadn't been embarrassed by the sadness she was obviously trying to hide. The loss of Harriet, though horrendous, had made him far more compassionate towards other people's emotions. He admired Poppy for sticking to her guns and deciding to pursue her plans without her partner. That took a lot of guts.

When he came back into the cottage sitting room with the T-shirt, Leo was lounging on the bundle of bedding, washing his paws.

'Oi, Leo. Get off!'

Leo flexed his claws as if he was admiring his manicure.

Jake clapped his hands loudly, hoping Leo would shift without him having to intervene. 'Poppy might be allergic to cats and she won't want her sheets covered in fur. She's had enough trauma today without you adding to it,' he said before realising that he was actually trying to debate with a cat.

Ignoring him, Leo lifted his hind leg and decided to give himself a more thorough bath.

'Urgh. Do you mind doing that in the privacy of your own home? Or Fen's? Come on, shoo.' He dashed forward, ready to scoop Leo off the bedding, but the cat dropped deftly to his paws before Jake reached him and strolled off towards the open door, tail in the air.

After Leo's departure, Jake realised that Poppy might need a toothbrush, so he went back up to his room and dug out an unused travel toothbrush and toothpaste from the bottom of his washbag. Before he left the room, he couldn't help glancing at the crate again. It was like Pandora's box: begging to be opened so he could discover its secrets. Yet if he opened it, would he regret what he'd unleashed?

Chapter 7

A warm and furry presence wound its way around Poppy's legs as she stood in the doorway to Jake's – or rather Archie's – cottage.

'Oh! What a gorgeous cat! He's *huge*. Is he yours?' She rubbed the top of Leo's head, feeling the thick fur between his ears.

'No, he belongs to Fen and Archie. Or rather they belong to him,' said Jake, eyeing Leo warily. 'He switches between their two cottages, depending on who has the tastiest morsels, I guess, but at the moment, he prefers Fen's, obviously, because my grandpa's away.'

Leo purred and let Poppy carry on stroking him.

'Wow. You're highly honoured. He won't let me do that. We're not the greatest of pals, though I've known him from a kitten, but I haven't seen much of him lately. Fen adores him and my grandad even let him into the studio. I think he was a stray.'

'Well, he's adorable. He must be the biggest cat I've ever seen.'

'Hmm. Personally, I think he's half sabre-toothed tiger. His teeth and claws are sharp enough. Come in.'

Once inside, Poppy homed in on a plate of mashed potato and prawns on the coffee table. Tempting aromas wafted under her nose and her stomach rumbled. She was reminded that she hadn't eaten since her tea shop lunch.

'I've interrupted your dinner. I fell asleep in the chair and when I woke up, it was pitch dark. I almost fell over the bed trying to find the light switch. I only popped in to collect the bedding, but I can come back after you've finished.'

'No. Don't be silly. I mean, don't be sorry. I've got everything ready for you. Over there on the armchair. Leo! Get off!'

Leo had jumped onto the duvet, which had been folded up.

'You're not allergic to cats, are you?' Jake asked.

'Not me. Dan was, so we couldn't have one. He didn't like animals much, anyway, so it was convenient.'

Jake lingered in the middle of the sitting room. He made no attempt to hand her the bedding. Poppy spotted an open bottle of beer on the floor next to the sofa.

'Shall I take the stuff and get out of your way so you can finish your meal?' she said.

'Wait. Did you say you've been asleep since I left you?'

'Not the whole time since you left. I – um – had a few calls to make to my parents and sister and friends, to let them know I was OK. I also managed to get my laptop working with the Wi-Fi too,' said Poppy.

No way would she let Jake know that she'd actually gone back down to the gallery and decided it was even worse than on first sight. It had been all she could do not to take to Facebook with a pity post and share some photos of the broken bed. Just in time, she realised any comfort she might get from her friends' sympathetic comments would soon evaporate. She'd only end up feeling embarrassed and some of her family and 'mates' would feel justified in having warned her she was completely nuts to take on such a project alone. Even worse, Dan might get to hear of it, and she'd rather jump off a cliff – or get back on the *Islander* – than let him think he'd won.

Instead, she'd made a brief but cheery call to her mum, glossing over the truth, and a ranty warts-and-all one to Zoey, both of which had made her feel much better.

'So, you haven't had any dinner?' Jake asked.

'No, not yet.' Damn, she wished she hadn't admitted she hadn't eaten, but it was too late. 'But I can rustle up beans on toast with what I bought from the Co-op.'

'You look like you need more than beans on toast after today.' He paused. 'I've made a fish pie. There's plenty if you want to share. I'm no chef, but it'll save you cooking – or opening tins – on your first night. It's getting late.'

She hesitated. She hadn't expected Jake to be sociable; she'd already come to the conclusion that he was a very reluctant host at best, only dealing with her because there was no one else, but she *was* hungry and in need of company.

Leo appeared at her feet, nudging her bare leg with his nose. He gazed up at her as if to say 'if you don't eat it, I'll have your portion'.

Her stomach rumbled loudly. 'I'd love some pie, but only if you're sure you have enough and I wouldn't be bothering you.'

'Well, I wouldn't have asked if you were.'

Wow, that was clear enough. Poppy believed him.

He tempered his brusque reply with a quick smile. 'I'll fetch you a plate. I can reheat mine in the microwave. Would you like a beer? Or a bottle of cider? Grandpa kept the pantry well stocked.'

Half an hour later, Jake went to fetch them each a second bottle of beer and cider. The fish pie had been delicious and it had been served with samphire, which Jake said he'd foraged from the dunes at the end of the beach. Poppy had never had it before, but it tasted lovely, sautéed in some butter and lemon.

'I have to admit that was a lot better than beans on toast,' she said, sitting on the sofa next to Jake. A fire was glowing in the hearth and the cider was easing the tension from her limbs.

'I hope so. Things always seem better when you've had a decent meal, not that I'm claiming my cooking is decent …' said Jake.

'It's decent enough for me. I must say, I'm feeling a lot more positive than when I first arrived.'

'Thank God for that.' He sounded very relieved. 'Tomorrow, I'll introduce you to Fen, if she doesn't pop round first. She's a lovely lady and a great friend to Grandpa, but she's bound to make a big fuss of you. You'll have to be firm if you feel she's interfering too much.'

'Thanks for the tip, but I'm sure I need all the help I can get.'

'You'll find most of the islanders are desperate to say hello. A new face is always welcome in a small place like this.'

'I'm looking forward to it, but I'm not sure I'm that fascinating.'

'I think you might be a lot more fascinating than you think.' Was that a hint of amusement on his face? He took another swig of the beer. 'I don't want this to sound patronising, but you're brave for coming out here after what's happened. I'm not sure I could do it.'

She laughed. 'I'm not sure whether to be flattered or worried by that.'

'Flattered. Totally. Me and my big mouth.' Jake squeezed his eyes shut and shook his head in embarrassment. 'I'm sure you'll be fine and I'll give you all the help I can while I'm here. If you want it. If not, just tell me to keep my mouth shut.'

'I will. Um, how long do you plan on staying?' she asked, trying to make the comment sound as neutral as possible. The last thing she wanted was Jake thinking she wanted to rely on him in any way, even if she was enjoying his company.

He hesitated. 'I don't know yet. I'm a professional photographer and I'm booked to lead a tour to Cambodia and Vietnam in the autumn, but I've got a load of stuff to catch up on at home on the mainland before then and I want to spend some time with Grandpa and the rest of the family.'

So, he was a photographer. Poppy had had no idea, but she wasn't surprised he did something creative, considering his background. 'Cambodia and Vietnam? That sounds very exotic,' she said.

'Oh, it is. Leo would be well at home. There are panthers, sun bears, leopard cats and even tigers. I've been once before and it was incredible, though even a few years can make a huge difference to the habitats of these animals and make them endangered.' He spoke faster, his voice infused with passion. 'The place I *really* want to go is the Amazon. Have done ever since I was a kid. There are birds, invertebrates, jaguars and giant anacondas.'

'Wow. They sound less than friendly.'

He laughed. 'The animals are fine unless you harass them and then it serves you right.'

'How long have you been a photographer?' she asked, keen to keep him talking, and loving the way he came alive when he spoke about his work.

'I've taken pictures professionally since I left school. I studied at Falmouth University and managed to make a bit of a name for myself. I'm very lucky to make a living doing what I do.' His eyes were bright and he was far more animated and at ease.

'Do you only take pictures of wildlife or do you do portraits and press stuff? I used to run a PR department and I had to book the photographers,' she added, thinking of the briefings she'd had to deliver on how to capture the perfect rainwater pipe or a toilet waste in a new office block. She couldn't imagine Jake doing that.

'Nowadays, all my work is natural history or landscape related, although I did some portraits when I was starting out. I'd much rather be outdoors than in a studio, even though I could probably make more money with commercial jobs. I get commissioned by magazines and travel companies and I run small group tours.'

'Do you have a base in the UK at all?'

'I have a small flat in Cornwall with a studio in an outbuilding. Harriet and I shared it until she died, but I don't spend much time in it these days. In fact, my mate Ryan is on permanent flat-sitting duty while I'm away. I had to sleep on my own couch the last time I was home.' He laughed. 'He has more of his stuff in the place than I do now.'

Until she died. So the worst had happened to Jake's fiancée. Poppy was upset for him but relieved that he'd mentioned her death in the course of conversation. She was sure she'd have found out soon enough on the local grapevine, but she'd much rather hear it from Jake. There was also no way she was going to destroy the moment by asking him for any more detail.

'It sounds like a dream job,' she said, steering their chat in a more positive direction.

'I don't make a fortune, but it's plenty to live on. I get paid well for doing what I love and that's way more than most people can say these days.' He smiled.

'It has to be better than writing about building products. I think the last straw was the day I had to compose my eighth feature on soil drainage systems in a month.'

Jake laughed. 'The Starfish is definitely a big change from that.' He hesitated and looked at her closely. 'So, what made you decide to run a gallery? Do you like art? Or was it your partner's dream?'

'I loved Art at school, and I was going to do it for A level, but Mum and Dad persuaded me to stick to more academic subjects. Like I mentioned, I do enjoy making jewellery in my spare time – just as a hobby,' she added hastily, in case Jake asked if she was going to sell some of her creations in the shop. 'And I've always loved visiting galleries. Big ones like the V&A and small ones like this one. When Dan showed an unexpected enthusiasm to run our own place, after we'd visited that day you met us ... to be honest, I was amazed at first. Not to mention terrified. Be careful what you wish for, if you know what I mean.' She'd perfected the gallows humour lately.

'I know what you mean ...' said Jake softly, then waited for her to continue again.

She wrinkled her nose. 'But I'm here now and, whether I like it or not, I have to make this work for financial reasons, if nothing else. At the moment, Dan and I have agreed to keep our semi in Staffordshire and use the rent to cover the mortgage. He's moved out and lives with his ...' Poppy had to stop herself from saying something extremely rude about Eve. 'With his new woman, but I don't know how long that will last. He may want to sell our house at some point.'

'You can tell me to mind my own business, but I take it you didn't ask him to move in with this woman?'

'You'd be right. We were all set to come out here together. I'd quit my job and I thought he'd quit his and then – boom – one night he came home and told me he'd been having an affair and was moving in with her.'

At the memory of that bombshell, Poppy had to take a few deep breaths of the Scilly air as her anger resurfaced and made her feel almost sick again. The past few weeks had been the longest, most miserable ones of her life ... but now she had to make the best of things, like thousands of other people whose partners had dumped them for the sales director of a bulldozer firm.

'Jesus. Did you even suspect he was playing away?' said Jake.

'No ... I'll admit the last few months were fraught but I put it down to him worrying about coming here. We decided to let out our house to cover the mortgage and found tenants who were ready to move in as soon as we moved out. I was doing long days at work and our spare time was spent packing up and selling stuff we didn't want to leave in the house or couldn't bring with us. Dan was snappy and tense because he was away a lot with his job and on a business course at the local college.' She sighed before she went on. 'At least that's where I thought he'd been ... now I know better. I was blind and naive.' She clammed up. She'd said far too much already to a man she'd only known a couple of hours.

'At least you're here. In spite of him.' Jake pulled a face, as if he thought Dan was a bad smell under his nose, which brought a smile to Poppy's face.

'Dan didn't think I'd come here at all. In fact, after we split, he burst out laughing when I said I was still going to run the gallery. He said, "you'll never make it on your own", which makes me even more bloody determined to run the Starfish. I want to show him how wrong he is, that I don't need him and I can make a success of my life without a bastard like him!'

Her mouth snapped shut again. Her heart beat faster. She cursed herself. Despite thinking she was more relaxed, the anger had boiled over again. The raw hurt was still so close to the surface.

'You must think I'm completely mad,' she said, trying to make light of her rant. 'I suppose I'm still letting Dan rule my life in a way. Yes, even though it was his idea to move here in the first place, he never expected me to follow it through and that's partly what's driving me on.'

'I don't think you're mad at all. From what I remember, Dan didn't seem too impressed with the gallery. Mind you, he did think I was trying to get money out of him.'

'Serves him right! He could be a bit stingy,' said Poppy, recalling her suspicion that Dan might have been jealous of her reaction to Jake. A reaction that, unfortunately, hadn't diminished now. When he laughed, and the light flared again in his expressive brown eyes, she got goose bumps on her arms.

'I may have wound him up a little ...' Jake winced but was also smirking.

'Good!' said Poppy.

'So, did you go along with his idea of buying the studio to please him or did you really fancy a change?'

'I'd definitely thought about what it might be like to pack in my job and live and work somewhere idyllic like St Piran's. I think everyone daydreams about "what if ..." at times but I was taken aback when he actively suggested it. Deciding to move to a remote island to run a gallery was so unlike him. He convinced me that he thought his life was slipping by and that his job was boring and stressful. He was a sales manager for a company that makes those giant bulldozers.' She rolled her eyes. 'Eve, the woman he was shagging – is still shagging – is a director of the same firm. Now the earth obviously moves for them both.'

Jake, who was mid beer, spluttered.

'Sorry!' He wiped foam from his mouth as he laughed. 'It's a good sign that you can joke about him even though you've had a shitty time of late. If you want my opinion, he's a loser. I'll let you into a secret. I thought he was a bit of a prat and Grandpa called him "a know-all".'

Poppy gasped. 'I had no idea.'

'My grandpa really liked you, though, which is why he sent me after you with the painting.' He waggled his empty bottle. 'Want another?'

'I shouldn't and I ought to be getting home ... I mean to the Starfish. Then again, I'm not sure I can sleep yet after dozing off earlier.'

Jake smiled. 'I'll take that as a "yes".' He took the empty bottle from her hand. 'Back in a mo.'

She heard him open the door to what must be the pantry and the pops as he undid the caps. She glanced around the sitting room. It was small but cosy and the fire glowed invitingly. It had been strange to hear Jake's view of Dan, and she didn't think he was merely being kind. 'A bit of a prat'. 'A know-all'. She stifled a giggle as Jake re-entered the sitting room. She really hadn't seen her ex in this way until he'd dropped his bombshell about Eve, but she now knew he wasn't the person she thought he was.

'Here you go. Out of cider, I'm afraid, so we're onto the lager.'

'Have I drunk the bar dry?' she asked, covering her maudlin thoughts with a smile.

'Impossible. There's enough crates of bitter in there to stock the Moor's Head and Driftwood Inn combined – Grandpa's favourite haunts. I'm sure you'll be seeing a lot of them.'

They sat for a while longer, as Jake told Poppy more about his job and some of the exotic, beautiful and downright dangerous locations he'd worked in.

'What about here?' she asked. 'Don't you find Scilly inspiring?'

He took an interest in his beer bottle for a few seconds before answering. 'I used to. In fact, it was coming here as a boy that first inspired my interest in photography. The landscape and wildlife, in their small-scale way, are the equal of anywhere I've been.' He took a drink. 'But I'm afraid I've fallen out of love with the isles. They let me down ... maybe not in the way Dan let you down, but enough that I can never feel the same about them that I used to.'

'Oh.' Goose bumps prickled Poppy's skin again, and not in a pleasant way. 'I'm sorry ...' She thought back to the boatman's comment about Jake's past. If there was ever a good moment to find out what happened, it was now. 'Does this have anything to do with your fiancée?'

Jake gazed at his beer bottle for a few seconds before replying. 'I'm afraid my fiancée died ... unfortunately, on the same day that I first met you.'

'I'm so sorry.' She didn't know what else to say.

'It's a total coincidence that the accident happened that day. I shouldn't have mentioned it. I'm sorry.'

'No. No wonder you remember meeting us that afternoon. Seeing me again must bring back terrible memories.'

'Actually, our meeting brings back the only good memories of that day ...' he said gently, although she thought he was just trying to make her feel better.

Should she ask more or leave it? After Dan had left her, while a few mates like Zoey, who she known since uni, had been brilliant, others would have crossed the street to avoid her. Anyone would think she had the plague rather than a cheating louse of a partner. Maybe they hadn't known what to say to her or were scared that rejection was catching.

She decided to be bold. 'You don't have to tell me. Not if it's too painful. It must be so awful and I didn't mean to bring it all up, but if it helps to talk, then please go on.'

He hesitated for a few seconds then let out a sigh.

'You'll find it out soon enough from somebody else, so it's better coming from me. I was on my way to the little marina when you saw me. Harriet, my fiancée, was meeting me and we were going sailing. Grandpa has a small sailing dinghy that he uses a lot ... but he and my parents kept a larger boat before that. Nothing fancy. A second-hand twenty-seven-foot Westerly Centaur.'

He glanced at Poppy as if the description ought to conjure up a detailed picture in her mind it was, but she hadn't a clue.

'It was like some of the ones in the harbour, only not as grand ...' he explained. 'There was an accident while we were out on the water. The boom hit Harriet and she fell overboard. I was there. The boat was moving fast, and by the time I'd got back to her and got her on board …' He paused and took a breath. 'By then it was too late.'

Poppy knew that Jake must have heard every word of horror, comfort and concern in the book. So she just listened, though her whole body had gone cold. Losing Harriet in front of his eyes must have been a horrific experience. Worse than what had happened to her and Dan by a million miles.

'I don't know what to say,' she said.

'That's OK because there's nothing you *can* say and I shouldn't have spoiled your evening by telling you. You've had a rough time yourself and you don't need to share in anyone else's drama.'

'It's not a drama, it's real, and I am very, very sorry.'

'It was almost three years ago now and I ought to be moving on. I am coping better now and I guess it's time. Grandpa obviously thinks so.'

She wasn't sure what Jake meant by that, but she wasn't about to ask.

He finished the last of his beer in two swift gulps. Poppy still had half a bottle left, but she'd gone off it anyway.

He picked up his bottle and her previous empties and stood up. 'I'll get rid of these.'

'I've had enough too,' she said, taking the hint that Jake wanted her to go. 'I need to make an early start.'

'Finish your drink and don't rush. I'm not trying to get rid of you.' He smiled. 'Honest.'

It was a good attempt at making her feel welcome to stay,

but Poppy wasn't fooled. She was sure Jake regretted revealing as much as he had.

'Can I help you wash up?' she said, trying to offer a distraction for them both.

'No. Thanks. Chill out here until you're ready to leave.'

'Actually, I'd better get a move on. Tomorrow will come around soon enough. Thanks for the food and beer.'

'Do you need a hand carrying the bedding over to the studio?' he asked.

'Oh. I'd almost forgotten that.' She was certain he was only being polite with his offer. Despite his kind words, there was visible tension in his body. 'No, I'll be fine, but thanks for the offer anyway.'

Jake handed her the duvet and bedding, which she squashed to her chest. He piled a small carrier bag on top. 'There's a few essentials you might need in there.' His voice became serious. 'At least, the essentials I could find in the cottage.'

She closed her eyes in shame, realising he was referring to the knickers. 'I didn't expect you and your grandpa to supply everything. I'd have been a little worried if you had.'

Jake managed a smile. His arms relaxed by his sides. Either the joke had rebroken the ice or he was more comfortable now she was leaving.

He opened the front door. 'See you tomorrow, then.'

She was barely off the threshold when the door was shut firmly behind her. She walked onto the cobbles of the harbour, clutching the duvet and bag to her chest, and risked a glance behind. The light went out in the sitting room of Archie's cottage.

It was a clear night with an almost full moon, which fortunately lit her way to the Starfish Studio, otherwise she'd have had to use her mobile as a torch. She'd forgotten about the lack of street lighting. The masts of the yachts in the harbour clinked together and she could hear water slapping softly against their hulls.

Shivering, she pulled the zip up higher on her hoodie. Jake had been through a horrendous ordeal: seeing his fiancée disappearing under the waves and not being able to do anything. How terrifying that it could happen in such an idyllic place: a place he had once loved and that had inspired his whole career. No wonder he wanted to leave.

Once she reached the studio, she deposited everything on the veranda while she fumbled the key into the lock in the darkness. She probably didn't need to lock the place but it was a habit that would be hard to break.

In the darkness inside, two yellow eyes glowed back at her. She flicked the light switch and blinked as Leo strolled up to her feet. His orange fur was bright against the starkly illuminated walls.

'Leo! How did you get here without me seeing you? You sneaky little devil. Well, you can't stay here,' she said, holding the door open for him to escape.

Leo blinked, so Poppy made a grab for him, but he shot up the spiral staircase. The cat must have followed her out of Jake's cottage all the way to the studio and sneaked past when she opened the door.

'I'm not chasing after you all night!' she called. 'You're here until morning now.'

She collected the bedding from the veranda, locked the door and struggled upstairs with her bundle. She was glad that, earlier, she'd dragged the mattress onto the floor of the sitting area, because she was too knackered now. Leo was lying on the middle of it, as if he owned the place.

'Looks like it's you and me,' she said, laying out a sheet, pillow and the duvet next to him. 'And to be honest, Leo, I'd rather share with you than Dan any day.'

As for sharing with Jake ... she was ashamed the thought had even entered her mind for a nanosecond. Without Dan around, she felt able to admit to herself that she fancied him like mad, but Jake was clearly oblivious to any other woman and still grieving for Harriet. Poppy decided that the sooner he left Scilly, the better, for his sake and hers.

Chapter 8

Jake turned off the lights and went upstairs to bed. Leo wasn't in the cottage, so Jake assumed he'd slipped through the cat flap in the rear kitchen door and gone back to Fen's. He had to smile to himself at Poppy's reaction to the cat. She really liked Leo and the feeling was mutual, judging by Leo sticking close to her all evening.

Jake had been almost jealous of the way Poppy ran her fingers through Leo's fur as he sat next to her on the sofa. As they'd chatted, he kept imagining himself in the same position and then telling himself off for having such rogue thoughts. She did look lovely, though, with more pink in her cheeks now she was safely on dry land and had had a few hours to rest.

While waiting for her to arrive, Jake had set up his laptop and worked on the images he'd taken in New Zealand, selecting the best for the magazine that had commissioned him. He didn't want to be caught out by Poppy in the middle of eating his dinner, so he'd prepared the fish pie but waited before turning on the old electric oven. When there was still no sign of her at past eight o'clock, he'd wondered whether to call at the studio to see if she was OK but decided she might have needed more time to herself. He'd also had to start cooking his dinner.

He'd taken another swig from the bottle and smelled the fish pie, starting to bubble in the oven. If you'd asked him earlier today, before Poppy had arrived, he'd have been relieved not to have any more contact with his new tenants. So he was surprised to find he felt quite disappointed that she hadn't shown up.

His heart had started beating quite quickly when she'd finally turned up at his door and he remembered now how suddenly important it had seemed that she'd accepted his offer of dinner. They'd laughed together – he'd enjoyed her company and looking at her.

'Actually, our meeting brings back the only good memories of that day …'

This was true … If only she didn't remind him of that day at all.

And he'd meant it when he told her that things were getting better for him but recovering from grief – and guilt – was painfully slow. Three steps forward and two back on a good day. Climbing up a ladder out of the pit of despair and emerging into the light before slithering down a great long snake back into darkness. He didn't *want* to stay in that dark hole. He wasn't actively trying to stay there – was he?

He'd never even intended to talk to her about Harriet's death, but he'd realised that if he didn't, someone else would and he couldn't bear that. Even so, he'd said so much more than he'd planned to ... He could kid himself that the beers had given him the courage to tell Poppy the bare facts about Harriet's death, but he also knew that he'd instinctively felt she was someone he could talk to. Perhaps it was knowing they were two lonely souls and in their own ways, strangers on St Piran's, but for different reasons.

He switched on the lamp in the bedroom of the cottage, stared at the packing crate of paintings again. Goodness knows where Archie had found it; it looked like it might once have been used to hold goods from a ship. Most things were recycled on the islands, so it might have had several former owners before Grandpa. It was roughly the size of the modern cardboard packing crates that removals people used, except it was made of old pine. The lid had been tacked down with small nails to keep the contents secure.

He'd need pliers to open the lid, he thought, when he examined it more closely. The envelope addressed to him had been placed inside a plastic bag – one of those zip-lock sandwich bags – and taped to the top with parcel tape, which was yellowing.

Should he at least open the letter, to find out what his grandpa wanted to do with them?

He stared at the crate again.

If only he'd never found it or come back to St Piran's, he wouldn't have been tempted to open it. He *shouldn't* open it if Archie really had intended it to be read after his death, but ...

He peeled the parcel tape from the top of the crate, removed the plastic bag and took out the envelope ... Why not read it now, while his grandpa was alive? What point was there in waiting until someone was gone to say the things you needed to say? He loved Archie and his grandpa loved him. Why not face up to what was in the letter *now*?

He thought back to his conversation with Poppy about Harriet – and hers about Dan – it had been a day of unexpected revelations ...

Jake opened the envelope and carefully drew out the contents.

There were two sheets of blue writing paper, covered on both sides in his grandfather's elaborate flowing style. Archie had been brought up in an era where neat handwriting was considered more important than the words you actually wrote. School had stifled his creativity, he'd said, and he'd left the moment he was legally able, at just fifteen. Initially he'd worked in the boatyard next to the studio, which, of course, had still been a boathouse then, and learned to repair and paint the boats. However, art had always been his first love and he'd managed to teach himself to paint and had sold a few pictures until he'd taken the plunge to become a full-time artist. Now, here he was, approaching the end of a long life, about to reveal who knew what to his only grandson.

The paper trembled as Jake started to read.

Dear Jake,

If and when you open this, I'll have gone to that great gallery in the sky. Actually, I'll probably be in St Piran's churchyard, if they'll have me. Doubt they'll let me in to

the posh seats though, I've not been an angel, as you may find out over the next few months.

Don't grieve for me, Jake. I can't bear the thought of you crying over me. God knows, you've shed enough tears since you lost Harriet. Sorry if me saying that makes you angry or upset, but you know, it's been a while now since the poor girl went, and life is very very short. After I lost my dear Ellie, I was the same. I went into a dark place nothing and no one could bring me out of. I neglected your dad and never thought how much he might be hurting too. You can ask him if you like ...

Jake shook his head and dropped the letter on the bed.

He *had* tried to get over Harriet's death. Who had the right to tell him how long he should grieve for? Of course his grandpa knew grief; he had been married to Ellie for twenty-five years when she died from a sudden brain haemorrhage and, yes, it was awful and tragic, but at least they'd had time together and started to bring up a family.

Jake's dad, Tom, had said very little about his own mother dying. It wasn't something they discussed, and why would they? Jake hadn't known her, sadly, and his father probably found it too painful, especially if Grandpa had withdrawn from him. Maybe Jake should ask his mum more about that time: although she obviously hadn't known his dad then, he might have talked to her about it. She'd been amazing with him when Harriet died. Three years had enabled him to realise how wonderful and supportive both his parents had been, and many of his friends.

He read the first few lines again.

I've not been an angel, as you may find out over the next few months.

What the hell did that mean? And did that mean he wouldn't find out now, because Grandpa Archie was still alive? He'd like to say 'very much alive', but he wasn't so sure.

'Oh, Grandpa ...' He heaved a sigh. Archie had every right to leave the letter. It had been Jake's own choice to open it now when it was never intended to be read until his grandad had passed away. Jake had also guessed correctly that the contents would rip open his own freshly healing wounds. He might have known Grandpa wouldn't mince his words.

It was too late to put the genie back in the bottle though. He scanned the next few lines, willing himself to stay calm.

I love your dad and you, and your mum. I've been blessed to have a wonderful loving family, but you are my greatest joy, Jake.

'Shit. Grandpa. Don't do this to me.' Despite his efforts, Jake's eyes stung and he had to force himself to read on.

And so, I've decided to leave you some of my favourite pictures. Now, I can see your face. Hear you cursing. Why me? You know why. Because you always understood me. We're kindred spirits. We're both creative, and no matter how much I love your dad, he won't understand like you do. These aren't my best work – I've never flattered myself than any of my work lived up to the actual power of the real place or how I wanted to express it – but they're pictures that mean a lot to me. I've had them kept back from sale for a while now.

They're of places that I love the most. Places that have made me feel happy – and sad – places that have reminded me of people I love. I know you've fallen out of love with St Piran's and the isles and I understand why. Harriet lost her life here: now you see only darkness and misery in the midst of beauty. That's sad, Jake, and I want to help you feel differently about our home again.

I'm not sure if my plan will work, and I'm sad to think I might be causing you pain, but I have to try. Please take a look at the pictures. You'll know why I chose them. Smile and laugh, and cry if you have to. Honour Harriet's memory and then try to move forward, holding her in your heart – and me too if you can. Think of me with affection and forgive me. And, if you can, forgive our Little Cornish Isles.

With love,

Grandpa x

Jake made no attempt to stem the flow of tears. He'd learned long ago it was pointless. He laid the letter on the bed before his tears wet the paper and walked into the bathroom. He blew his nose and washed his face, knowing he'd probably have to wash it again before he'd finished his blubbing.

He went back into the bedroom, clutching a handful of loo roll, lay on the bed and closed his eyes. He was already a wreck after reading the letter. What fresh wounds might be uncovered if he opened the pictures? He definitely wasn't ready to open the crate yet and look at the paintings.

After a couple of minutes, he folded the letter in four and slipped it in the top pocket of his camera bag. He knew he wouldn't be able to sleep for a while so he went downstairs and switched on the TV to try and blot out his thoughts.

Chapter 9

Poppy was woken early by Leo pummelling her stomach with his giant paws. Waking up next to a strange furry beast on the floor of a new place had been weird. What was also weird was finding that she was wearing a strange man's T-shirt.

Leo scooted downstairs, so Poppy followed and let him out. He trotted off up the hill towards the row of cottages where Jake said Fen lived.

Poppy sniffed the air, which was mild and moist with a tang of seaweed. Hazy clouds hovered above the horizon, but it promised to be a lovely day if and when the sun came out. A few people were already about and, from the harbour, the sound of someone trying to start an outboard motor cut through the quiet. Already, she felt how different this spot was, to what she'd left behind and she reminded herself: today was the first day of the rest of her life.

She dressed quickly, grabbed some toast and decided the

priority was to find out when the rest of her stuff was likely to arrive. Winston had said he'd give Jake a bell about the situation, but Jake definitely hadn't heard from him the previous evening. Poppy was reluctant to come across as an uptight townie, but she also didn't want to rely on two strange blokes to sort out her worldly possessions. She checked the inter-island ferry schedule on the local website and found a number for the *Herald* freight boat office in St Mary's. No one answered, so she crossed her fingers and hoped that meant the crew were already on their way with her stuff.

She headed down to the quay to see if she could find out more and saw an elderly lady in a bright kaftan and a poncho heading straight for her. Recognising Fen, even from three years previously, Poppy hurried to meet her by the harbourside.

'Hello! You must be Poppy.' Fen held out her hand. 'I'm Fen Teague. Welcome back to St Piran's.'

'Thanks. It's lovely to meet you again. I remember you,' said Poppy. She shook Fen's slim hand and smiled at her warmly. After yesterday's bleak arrival, she was determined to be positive from the outset and show everyone she was ready to face all the challenges of island life. 'And if you're wondering where Leo was last night, he managed to get into the studio and spent the night in the flat. I didn't like to pick him up and turn him out.' Poppy didn't confess she'd been too tired to chase Leo around the place and too wary of his claws and teeth to manhandle him.

Fen smiled. 'Ah, that's where he'd been. When he strolled in this morning, I assumed he'd decided to stay at Archie's.

He doesn't really belong to me, nor Archie for that matter. He sleeps and eats wherever the whim takes him.'

'Unfortunately, I'd nothing much to feed him, though I put down some water in a dish and found a few Dreamies in a packet in the kitchenette and left them out. They'd gone by morning when I let him out first thing.'

'Thanks for being kind to him. He must like you.' Fen sighed. 'I only wish I could persuade him and Jake to get on better. Leo always had the run of the Starfish until Archie's fall, but I don't think Jake enjoyed having Leo supervise him when he was clearing it up.' Her face became anxious. 'How *is* the studio? I've been so worried about it being closed up while Archie's away. I have checked it a couple of times, but you know ...' Her voice wavered.

Poppy felt so sorry for her that she decided to gloss over her disappointment. 'It'll be fine with a bit of work,' she said breezily. 'I'd expected to make a few changes and, anyway, Jake had already started to sort the place out.'

Fen's shoulders relaxed in relief. 'That's a weight off my mind. I'm happy to help you all I can, of course. My days of working full-time in there are over, too knackering now, but I'm happy to step in on high days and holidays.'

'Thanks. I plan on being there all the time once I've er – done a few small things – but I'm sure I'll need an extra hand now and again, so it's great to have some experienced back-up. Actually, I'm so glad we've met. I was wondering if you kept a list of all the stock in the studio? And a contact list for the artists who have exhibited their work in recent years? I had a root around yesterday but couldn't find anything.'

'Oh dear.' Fen put her hand to her mouth, then she brightened. 'Hold on. There might be a list in the drawer under Archie's worktable. Have you checked in there?'

'Is that the large table at the rear of the studio?'

'Yes, but the drawer could be locked.'

'It is, and I couldn't find a key with the main set.'

Fen's brow creased. 'Well, I should have a bunch of keys at the cottage somewhere ... At least, I think I do. I'll try to hunt them out and bring them down later.'

'Great.' Poppy crossed her fingers but tried not to let her hopes rise. Fen sounded less than confident. 'I was on my way to the quayside to see if I can find out more about the freight boat. My stuff was stuck in St Mary's last night because the *Herald* is undergoing emergency repairs.'

'Oh no. Poor you. Jake never said anything. I hope the *Herald* will sail later, but I wouldn't raise your hopes too high. The last time there was a problem, they had to send off for parts from the mainland and it was out of action for a week.'

'Oh sh-sugar.' Poppy winced. 'I was hoping to get my things today.'

'I can loan you some clothes and other things to tide you over and you can always stock up in Hugh Town if you have to. You'll find most things there, if you don't mind hopping on one of the passenger launches.'

Poppy nodded. Clearly patience was going to be a virtue on St Piran's, but it was hard not to think with longing about being able to jump in her car and have half a dozen major stores within a five-minute drive. It was also hard to get to grips with the various ferries between the islands: which ones took freight, which ones would carry luggage and which ones only passengers. For the moment, she didn't want to waste any time and money getting another boat to Hugh Town and back for new clothes and other bits.

'Tell you what. Next time I go over to St Mary's, why don't you come with me? I'll show you where to find all you need and introduce you to a few people, not as decrepit as me. We can have a bit of lunch,' said Fen.

'That would be lovely. Thanks. I also wanted to ask your advice. Jake says you have a small market garden. I'm going to need to be more self-sufficient, so I'd like to get some tips on how to find a patch I can work. There's no garden with the studio and I know next to nothing about growing veg, but I'm willing to learn.'

'Goodness, I wouldn't call my bit of earth a market garden. I used to have more land and sold spare produce, but I got rid of the extra garden and now I only have the space behind the cottage. Mind you, that's more than big enough for me. To be honest, I'd be glad of a hand, so I'd be happy to let you work it with me in return for a share of the produce.'

'Really? That sounds perfect.'

'Wait until you've been out there in all weathers trying to pull potatoes or picking slugs off the lettuces before you sound too excited. Come round after you've got the studio straight and we'll sort something out. I'm on my way to the post office to catch the mail, so I have to go. I'll hunt down the key later and be over to lend you a hand. No, don't say you can manage. You're going to need all the help you can get …' Fen broke into a smile. 'There's Jake. I'll leave you to it.'

As Jake strode towards Poppy, Fen was off up the short steep hill towards the 'town', which Poppy remembered from her last visit contained the post office, general store, bakery, church and a few other businesses that made up the hub of St Piran's amenities. Poppy thought Fen looked fitter than some people from home who were half her age and the vibrant lime kaftan suited her personality perfectly. Even so, Poppy was praying she wouldn't have to share her new neighbour's wardrobe.

Jake arrived and the bright morning light only served to highlight how handsome he was. He was dressed in Timberland boots, cargo pants and a grey T-shirt that showed off his tanned arms. No matter how gorgeous he looked, Poppy had to remind herself to place the mental equivalent of police 'do not cross' tape around him.

Last night, she'd lain awake for a while thinking of his revelations about Harriet and how he'd tried and failed to hide the pain he still felt at the memory of her loss. Until he'd mentioned his fiancée, he'd seemed relatively chatty and happy to spend time with her, but Poppy knew only too well what it was like to function 'normally' in public then fall apart when you closed your door behind you.

This morning, he had his usual serious, intense expression, but when he'd crossed paths with Fen as he made his way over to Poppy, a huge smile had lit his face and he'd hugged her. He also had positive news for Poppy.

'Good news. I was on my way to tell you that the *Herald* should be ready to sail to St Piran's by this afternoon. Your crate is safe on the dockside in St Mary's and they're going to load it along with the other freight deliveries and have your things here before dinner. Winston passed on the message to the skipper and he phoned me. I hope that was OK? Obviously, I gave him your number, so you can liaise now.'

She heaved a huge sigh of relief. 'Phew. That's great. Thanks for passing it on and yes, I can take it from here ... Er, how can I transport the crate from here to the studio?'

'The crew will load it onto that trailer, *there*,' said Jake, pointing to a tractor with a low trailer behind it. 'And they'll deliver it to the door of the studio and help you with any heavy stuff. I'm happy to give you a hand with unloading too, if you like, and help you out with the work on the studio.'

'Thanks. Again. But I totally can't keep relying on you – or other people's help – all the time.'

He shook his head. 'I'm afraid if you really want to make a success of life here, you'll have to rely on your neighbours. With only sixty permanent residents on St Piran's, there's no other way. You'll have the chance to repay people soon enough.'

'But not you. You'll be gone.' Damn. She hadn't meant to sound so disappointed.

'Yes, I will, but I can stay a while yet ... and I owe you, on behalf of my grandad. The studio should never have been let in the condition it is.' Jake's phone buzzed and he took it out of his pocket. 'I need to check a few things on my laptop and then I'll be back to the studio, so you can put me to work.'

'You honestly don't need to do this,' she said, trying to be polite but firm. Being owed one by Jake wasn't as much fun as it sounded.

'If you really want me to bugger off and leave you, then I

won't be offended, but if you can stand having me around, shall we get to work on the studio?' He hesitated. 'You're in complete control, of course. I'm only here to do your bidding.'

His dark eyes twinkled and, once again, Poppy glimpsed some of the dry humour and sense of fun she'd noticed when she'd first met him. She had no idea what kind of woman Harriet was, but she must have been special for Jake to have loved her so passionately. Then she reminded herself that she was probably romanticising their relationship. No couple's lives were ever perfect and everyone had secrets, as she'd learned, to her bitter cost.

'OK. I accept. You're right, I'm going to need a hand if I want to have this place fully up and running by the May bank holiday weekend. Ideally, I should have been here a couple of weeks ago in time for the gig racing championships.'

Jake nodded. 'Yes, there would have been lots of extra visitors to St Piran's, but there's no use worrying about that. The season is ramping up now and you'll have your work cut out being ready for a launch by the end of May.'

'I'd like to be ready before then, so I can iron out any teething problems before the rush, but it's going to be tough without any decent artwork. The thing is I need to start publicising the launch and letting people know I'm open, so it's a chicken and egg situation.' Even as she said it, the scale of the challenge was becoming clear.

Jake whistled. 'So we basically have a few weeks to be ready to open.'

Poppy noted the use of 'we' but wasn't about to complain. With slight panic rising, team spirit was exactly what she needed now. 'Don't worry,' she said, giving him a stern look. 'I'm happy to crack the whip.'

Jake raised an eyebrow, then smiled. 'I might not regret volunteering in that case. See you later.'

He left, his phone already at his ear. Poppy strode off to the studio, feeling enthusiastic about making a list of all the jobs she wanted to complete, and hoping that her stuff – and Fen's magic key – would soon materialise.

Oh well, one out of two wasn't bad.

Fen phoned after lunch to say that 'she'd turned the house upside down', including shifting Leo from his bed to look underneath, but still couldn't find the key.

Even without the contact list, Poppy had plenty to keep her busy. The Starfish Studio's website was very dated, both in design and content. It became clear that the artists who were listed as exhibiting didn't actually have any current work on show, as she'd expected. However, with Jake's help, Poppy managed to google the contact details of some of them.

She had also weeded out a few 'artists' whose work wasn't going to be part of her 'vision' for the gallery. Diplomatic enquiries revealed that one of them, the knitted loo dolly creator, had returned to the mainland a year before. He turned out to be a middle-aged man called Tim who was taking a 'creative' sabbatical from work and had begged Archie to display his creations. Archie hadn't had the heart to say no and then ceased to notice the 'objets d'art' and had forgotten to get rid of them. Jake suggested sending them to the charity craft market in the church hall.

In addition, Poppy had her own list of names that she'd gathered during her research before coming to Scilly. It contained a couple of Scilly artists and some from mainland Cornwall whose work she loved: a landscape oil painter, an avant-garde ceramicist, a textile artist and a woman who made ocean-inspired jewellery from silver and sea glass.

'I don't want to overload the gallery with stuff. I'd rather have fewer well-chosen pieces than too much tat,' she said, showing the list to Jake.

He nodded. 'That sounds like a good plan. I recognise some of those names. I've phoned Grandpa and he said that you can display any of his pictures already in the studio.' He hesitated as if he was about to say more. 'It's your choice, of course. You're the curator.'

'I like them all,' she said, 'I think you know how much I admire his work.'

'He's an amazing guy. And I hope he comes back home soon.'

'Do you know when that might be?'

Jake sighed. 'Honestly, no. He seems to be healing physically, although a little slower than the doctors had hoped. He's up and about, but he's showing no signs of wanting to come back here.'

'Maybe he's lost confidence that he can take care of himself?'

Jake nodded but seemed none too sure. 'Maybe. He was still very active, sailing round the islands and wandering all over the place to find inspiring places to paint. Perhaps he thinks that he can't bear to be here if he can't enjoy it like he used to. Anyway ... I've been wondering if the key to that drawer is in his cottage.' He abandoned his mug on the counter and grabbed his phone. 'I'll go and see if I can find it so you can finish your list and start contacting the artists.'

Before Jake returned, much to Poppy's enormous relief, two crewmen from the *Herald* walked into the studio to announce the arrival of her crate and began to unload. At the same time, the island handyperson, Kelly, turned up to fix the leg of the bed. Poppy had been expecting a great hairy bloke, so when a tiny woman her own age turned up, in overalls that were three sizes too large, she did a double take. Kelly was a Geordie, with a platinum blonde crop and a risqué line in banter that had Poppy laughing immediately.

After Kelly had reconstructed the bed, she declared it safe by bouncing on it several times.

'That'll do you, as long as you're not planning on doing Olympic trampolining on it or swinging from the rafters,' she said, with a grin.

Kelly offered to do a few repairs to a drooping curtain rail and a kitchen cupboard that was threatening to pull away from the wall.

Poppy lent a hand where she could while Kelly filled her in on various bits of island gossip, most of which had Poppy almost laughing too hard to be of useful help.

Poppy made everyone coffee and while the crew took theirs outside, Kelly stayed inside.

'We were expecting you to turn up with your bloke,' she said.

Poppy decided to dive straight in and be honest about Dan.

'I'm afraid that plan went out of the window. We split up a month ago.'

Kelly swore. 'Ouch. Did he get cold feet about coming here?'

'Not exactly. He ran off with his boss.'

'Bloody hell. That must have been a shock.'

'Just a bit.'

'What a shit. And she must be a cow – it was a *she*?'

Poppy nodded. 'Her name's Eve. Zoey – my friend – calls her Evil Eve and him Dirty Dan.' She thought of Zoey's rants about Eve and couldn't help smiling. Zoey was a tall, stunning blonde who didn't care what anyone thought of her but was fiercely loyal to her friends and although she was single, at present, she had no shortage of admirers. Poppy had met her at university and they'd stayed mates ever since. She and Kelly would get on well, if they met, and hopefully they might one day.

Kelly burst out laughing. 'Well. He's the loser. You've got some balls to come out here on your own, if you'll excuse me, but I know you'll be fine. I joined my boyfriend, Spike, here after I left the Army a few years ago. He's the chef at the Moor's Head. St Piran's is a quirky place, but I love it. Then again, I'm used to making myself at home anywhere. A run-down shack on Scilly is paradise compared to some of the places I've spent the night in.'

'I bet it is.'

Poppy chatted to Kelly a little while longer, about her days serving as an Army maintenance engineer in some terrifying locations and some of the 'characters' on the isles. Kelly invited her for a drink at the local pub over the next week and for a barbecue at the flat she shared with Spike when he could get an evening off.

'By the way, you do know about Jake and Harriet, don't you?' Kelly said in a low voice.

'I know that she died in a yacht accident,' said Poppy, treading more warily. 'Did you know her?'

Kelly nodded. 'I met her a couple of times when Jake brought her to visit Archie. She seemed nice. She reminded me of Kate Middleton a bit. Really slim, bouncy glossy hair, well groomed, posh voice. Friendly though. Jake was nuts about her, anyone could see ...'

'How awful.' Poppy tried to sound politely interested, with a mental picture of a smiling Harriet cutting the ribbon on a new children's hospital. 'He didn't say that much about what she was like.'

'You're lucky he mentioned her at all. Everyone knows he blames St Piran's for what happened and he's only come back to help Archie get this place ready. He'd got some kind of PTSD about it, if you ask me,' said Kelly, 'and I'll bet you fifty quid he's gone by this time next week. I'm sticking around though, and if you want any help, just call. I do mates' rates. Trouble is, everyone I know is a mate.' She laughed.

They heard the crew clattering back upstairs after their break, so Kelly smiled and went back to work. With her stream of banter with the crew, the noise in the tiny flatlet had to be heard to be believed. In addition to the two crew, a young guy and his mother arrived and offered to help Poppy unpack. They introduced themselves as Lisa and Ben Cardew. Lisa must have been in her early forties and owned the Harbour Kiosk, which sold ice creams and refreshments. Ben, in his late teens, helped her out at the kiosk but also ran scuba diving and snorkelling trips to make some extra money.

The crew unloaded packing cases from the rear of the trailer and hauled them upstairs while Ben and Lisa helped Poppy carry the smaller bags and boxes. Even though she'd winnowed down her possessions, she was aghast at how much space the stuff took up in the studio flat.

'Brought the kitchen sink, have you?' one of the crew joked.

'That's coming later,' she said, watching a growing pile of boxes that threatened to rival an Amazon warehouse.

Lisa slit open the top of a box with a pair of scissors. 'If you find you've too much, you can always hold a garage sale,' she said. 'You'll find plenty of people willing to take your spare stuff off your hands. It's like *Bargain Hunt* round here when someone new arrives.'

'That would be good if I had a garage,' joked Poppy. 'But it's still a great idea. When I've had a sort-out, I'll think about it.'

Once several more boxes had been unpacked, Lisa checked that Poppy didn't want any further help, then left her with an invitation to come over to the kiosk and her house for a coffee any time she wanted.

In a few minutes, everyone had gone and the only sounds were the cries of gulls and gentle swoosh of waves slapping the harbour wall outside the window. Poppy took a deep breath and took in the boxes and bags around her, her life packed and parcelled up.

She delved into one of the cases and pulled out a vase and some photo frames that had once stood on the hearth in the sitting room at her little house. The last time she'd seen them had been weeks previously when she'd chosen and wrapped the items with the help of Zoey and her parents. It had been a tough job back then, and she'd been even more emotionally raw than she was now. Unpacking them in the studio at the start of a new life was a far more positive experience. Nonetheless, it was all she could do to hold it together at the sight of these remnants of her 'old' life sitting in this new environment.

Fen turned up as she was fishing a teapot out of one of the boxes.

Poppy placed the red spotted pot on the countertop; Zoey had given it to her when she'd moved into the house with Dan.

'Hard for you?' Fen asked in a gentle tone.

Poppy turned. 'A bit.'

'Jake told me about your bloke running off. It's none of my business, of course, but you're better off without him. Trust me.'

Poppy had heard phrases like this – in respect of Dan – from her mates, but when Fen spat them out with such venom, she had to smile. Maybe Fen had had a similar experience herself.

Poppy picked up the pot. How many morning cuppas had she shared with Dan from it? 'Everything brings back memories, even a teapot ...'

'And now you'll make new ones in a new place. You don't

need to get rid of the pot now you've got rid of that prat of a husband.' Fen patted her arm.

Poppy was touched by the older woman's kindness. 'We weren't actually married.'

'Even better,' said Fen. 'I wish Jake would move on from his memories.' She lowered her voice, as they heard footsteps from the gallery below. 'That sounds like him. He doesn't seem to want to make a fresh start on St Piran's. If it wasn't for Archie's fall, I don't think he'd have ever come back.'

'No?' said Poppy, glad to have the conversation turned away from her own problems but worried that Jake might hear himself being discussed.

'Maybe you'll keep him here a while longer.' Fen eyed her closely.

'He said he's got a lot of stuff to sort out back home in Cornwall. I got the impression he'd be gone within a couple of weeks.'

Fen sighed. 'He'll want to be with his family and that's understandable. He's hardly been back here since Harriet passed.'

'I don't expect him to stay here for my sake,' said Poppy.

A heavy footstep on the stair stopped any more awkward discussion and Jake started talking before he'd even come into view.

'Right. That's another thing done. Not only have your knickers arrived, but I've found the key to the other set of drawers so you can give me my clothes back now.'

'Jake. Fen's here!' Poppy called, her face warming at Jake's joke. Fen might take it out of context. In fact, *anyone* would take it out of context.

Jake emerged, taking the last steps two at a time. He was slightly out of breath but smiling. 'Oh.' He managed to maintain the smile. 'Hello, Fen.'

'What's this about drawers and Jake's clothes?' she asked.

Poppy stepped in. 'Just a joke. Jake loaned me a T-shirt.'

Fen eyed Jake sharply. 'That was nice of him.'

'Not really. It was an old one,' said Jake, exchanging a pained glance with Poppy. Why they were both feeling guilty or awkward about sharing clothes, in front of Fen, Poppy had no idea. The T-shirt was hardly a secret, yet it felt like one.

'Anyway, all's well that ends well. As you can see, all my things have arrived. Thanks for sorting it out, Jake.'

'Well, that's good news,' said Fen. 'I couldn't really have pictured Poppy in any of my old stuff, I have to be honest.'

'You look lovely and I'd have been very grateful,' said Poppy, while relief flooded through her at not having to wear a hand-knitted orange poncho.

Jake was still smiling, however. 'And back to the other news. I've found the key to the table.'

Fen rolled her eyes. 'No wonder I couldn't lay hands on it at home. Are you sure it's the right one?'

He held out the key, which was secured to a keyring with a small silver dolphin. 'This one? It was on its own in one of the slim dresser drawers. I thought I recognised it.'

She peered at the small brass key. 'Looks very much like it.'

'The only way to know for sure is to try it,' said Poppy, eager to find whatever paperwork might help her continue rebuilding a stable of artists.

They all headed downstairs into the gallery and assembled around the large flat low table that Archie used for working, mixing paints and some framing. Fen stood on the far side, glancing around her from time to time with a wistful expression, as if she was recalling the room in happier times. Poppy stood next to Jake as he inserted the key in the lock and wiggled it. Eventually it turned. The drawer had stuck a little with lack of use, but he prised it open. It was stuffed with paperwork. She looked over his shoulder as he leafed through invoices, receipts and manila folders. She spotted one with 'Artist contacts' on the front.

'That looks promising,' she said.

'Hmm.' He handed it to her.

Fen, standing on the other side of the table, gave a nod. 'That'll be it. I remember helping to compile it, though I haven't seen it for a few years.' She spotted some dried-up paint tubes on the table and picked them up, tutting.

Poppy opened the file and saw the handwritten list of names and numbers, with the odd email address added alongside.

Jake riffled through the other papers in the drawer. 'I'm not sure what else might be useful,' he said, pulling sheets and letters from underneath the invoices. 'Oh ...'

Fen glanced up. 'What?'

Jake shoved something back under the other papers. 'Nothing. I thought it was another list of suppliers, but it's only an old invoice.' He shut the drawer and locked it again, before quietly passing the key to Poppy.

He ushered them out of the work area and back towards the main gallery. Behind Fen's back, he caught Poppy's eye, an agonised look on his face. Poppy mouthed 'what?' but Fen turned around and Jake shot her a smile.

'Shall I help you look through this list with Fen?' he asked.

'Thanks.'

After grabbing a coffee, they worked through the list of artists while the little brass key burned a hole in her pocket. Whatever was in the drawer, Jake didn't want Fen to see it.

Chapter 10

By the time the sun had slipped behind the lighthouse in a blaze of pink and orange, Poppy had compiled a wish list of more artists to contact. She whizzed off messages to them, introducing herself, telling them briefly of her plans to refurbish the gallery and that she'd be contacting them in person and inviting them all to see it once work was closer to completion.

Jake and Fen had left earlier, so she set to arranging her possessions into some kind of order. It was surprising how the addition of a few cushions and her own bits 'n' bobs made the place feel homelier, if not yet like home. Once she'd found a place for the photos of her friends and her parents, she was feeling much better.

The next morning, she was in the studio early, clearing it out ready for the renovation work to start. After a thorough clean, the walls would need washing and the damaged plasterwork repairing. The woodwork would need rubbing down before it or the walls could even begin to be repainted. In the meantime, she'd also have to get word around that the launch would be happening over the late May bank holiday, all while convincing the sceptical artists and getting in some stock.

As she took a quick break for a latte from the Harbour Kiosk, just under a month didn't seem anywhere near long enough. Jake had said he'd help, but for how long? Even with offers from Kelly, Fen and Lisa, the buck stopped with Poppy herself and it was clear she'd underestimated how much work would be involved.

She'd no choice though but to get on with it. She started by packing away all the paintings from the walls into boxes before dragging them into Archie's work area. She hadn't opened the drawer of the worktable, figuring whatever was in there was personal to Jake and should wait until he was ready to open it. She could have asked him but it seemed intrusive and, anyway, she hoped he'd tell her of his own accord when he arrived later that morning.

In the end, Jake and Fen turned up at almost the same time, so there was no prospect of opening the drawer while they were together – *if* Jake wanted to. In any case, they were all too busy. Fen had brought a vacuum cleaner and a couple of brooms and they started to clear out as much of the dust and grime from the gallery as they could. It was a fine, breezy day and with all the doors and windows open, the damp smell was lessening. The stone walls had been whitewashed several times over the years but would need some serious filling and repairs and then several fresh coats of white paint.

'I don't want to have too much clutter around. The studio

should be a blank canvas in itself, with the art obviously attracting all the attention,' she said as they all surveyed the now clutter-free space.

'I agree,' said Jake, then hastily added, 'Not that it's any of my business.'

Fen laughed. 'Yes. Tell us to shut up and get lost if we're interfering.'

Poppy laughed too. 'I doubt I'm in a position to do that and you're the ones who really know how to run a gallery.'

'My experience is all second-hand,' said Jake. 'Some of my work is displayed in other people's galleries, so I know what I want from them, as an artist, but Fen and Grandpa are the experts.'

'Times change,' said Fen. 'Poppy will have fresh ideas and that's exactly what's required. That, and enthusiasm and a good way with the customers.'

Poppy nodded. 'I know exactly what you mean. Some of the galleries I've checked out were welcoming, but others were so intimidating. In some of them, you felt you had to curtsey to the woman or man behind the desk.'

Fen winced. 'Oh, I hope no one's ever felt like that when they walked into the Starfish.'

'Absolutely not. You were very warm and friendly. In fact, you reminded me of my nan.'

Jake burst out laughing at the remark. Poppy cringed when she realised what she'd said, but Fen grinned.

'Well, I am old enough to be your grandma. I wish I had grandkids or kids of my own, but it never happened. Mind you, Jake's always been like a grandson to me.'

Jake put his arm around Fen. 'You've always treated me like one.'

Poppy thought she'd just about got away with her comment but resolved to try to engage her brain before her mouth more often.

'I also picked up a tip from one gallery,' she said, hoping Fen would approve. 'I thought of having fresh flowers on the desk. Just a few local ones from the island to bring St Piran's inside the gallery and to give customers an experience of the natural Scilly, as well as buying a "thing,"' no matter how lovely the thing.'

Fen nodded. 'That's a good idea. Most visitors want to feel they're sharing in a way of life when they buy something.'

'That's how I felt when I walked into the studio. I wanted to take a small part of this whole island lifestyle back home, so I could imagine myself being here. I never guessed I'd actually be back.'

'But here you are.' Jake smiled, as if to give her confidence.

'Yes, and there's no way back, so we'd better get to work.'

Jake and Poppy washed down the walls, while Fen wiped the cabinets and plinths. They put the island radio station on and Poppy listened with secret amusement to this insight into island trivia that would be her life now.

Washing the walls was hard work and she was soon hot and a bit sweaty, working in a vest top and cropped jeans. Jake was in shorts and a T-shirt that showed off his muscular arms and calves. He must spend a lot of his time in rugged terrain lugging heavy camera equipment, so it was hardly surprising he was fit. It was pretty distracting, though, and it was all she could do not to sneak a peek as she returned her cloth to the bucket for a fresh batch of sugar soap.

Poppy might have been imagining the fact that Jake slowed right down towards the end of the afternoon, almost as if he was stretching out the second and final wall wash, but Fen didn't budge from her post as builder's mate. She'd made them endless cups of tea and cold drinks and seemed to have got through most of *Fifty Shades Freed,* once she'd finished cleaning the cabinets, tutting loudly that 'it was a load of old rubbish' and that 'Christian Grey must have bloody good central heating in that apartment of his,' while turning the pages at lightning speed.

Jake kept dropping hints that he needed to leave to speak to a photography expedition organiser, but Fen stayed put, so in the end, they both left just after five. Poppy had intended to carry on working, but as soon as her helpers had gone, the energy seemed to drain out of her. Her arms turned to spaghetti and her legs were shaky after a day climbing up and down stepladders and reaching into corners.

Her PR job had involved nothing more than sitting at the keyboard, racking her brain for fresh puns about drainpipes and shower grates, so her new active lifestyle was bound to be a shock to the system. She'd tried to keep fit by joining the health club with Dan but had hardly ever gone. Now she was on St Piran's, she could save a fortune. Who needed the gym when you were renovating an art gallery?

She didn't miss the stressful commute to work in her small car either, being constantly cut up by faster vehicles or wondering when a truck might pull out on her. What bliss it was to simply crawl up the spiral staircase and straight into the shower … A short while later, she'd washed the plaster dust out of her hair and was wearing a casual dress and a pair of flowery Vans. With a large glass of wine at her side, she sat at the small dining table and sent a few pictures of the work in progress to her family and Zoey over WhatsApp.

Thank God the island had decent Wi-Fi. It felt satisfying to be making progress and to have positive news after all the misery of the past few weeks. She hoped the messages would reassure those she'd left behind that she'd made the right decision to make a fresh start.

She opened up her laptop to browse a few of the artists' sites and remind herself of the best features of some of the galleries she'd admired. Checking her emails, she noticed a couple of the local people had already responded.

She sighed. Both replies, from a painter and a fused glass-maker, were lukewarm, to say the least, and the former had said that 'actually, she wanted to drop in ASAP and collect her remaining few pieces' as they clearly 'weren't working in the current environment'. Poppy realised that she was going to have to try harder to convince the artists that the studio was the best place to showcase their work.

She hadn't noticed Leo leap silently from floor to chair to table. He settled down next to her laptop and she ruffled his fur as she scrolled through her Facebook page. She'd have to start up Twitter and Instagram accounts for the Starfish Studio as soon as possible, but she was too tired to do it right now.

For all kinds of reasons, she'd tried to avoid the internet over the past few weeks, especially Facebook where the endless stream of married and settled friends posting smiley photos of themselves enjoying holidays and evenings out had driven her mad. The last thing she wanted was for any friend of hers to be unhappy, but since Dan had left, it seemed that her whole feed was filled with loved-up couples enjoying shared desserts in romantic hotspots or cuddled up with a jug of Pimm's in the their local 'Spoons. It was all the same: smug snuggliness in public places.

She cringed and thought of the album she'd posted of her and Dan at the helm of a motorboat the previous year, in Ibiza.

'Is no one single?' she said to Leo, who'd decided to sit on the dining table next to her. 'You wouldn't be seen dead blobbing whipped cream on another cat's snout, would you, Leo?'

A post appeared in her news feed that once seen was impossible to ignore. Poppy clicked on it and gasped out loud.

It couldn't be.

As she stared in horror at the screen, Leo nudged her elbow and her finger slipped.

'No!'

Poppy – actually, Leo – had Liked the post. Poppy bashed her keyboard in a panic, running through Love and Ha Ha until she finally managed to Unlike it.

She re-read the post and some of the comments, still not quite able to believe what she'd seen until her phone buzzed and broke her trance. It was a text from Zoey.

DON'T look at Facebook. :(

Followed by a string of emojis showing disgust, crying, vomiting and finally, a big hug.

The phone buzzed again.

Will call you as soon as I get out of work. Z x

Poppy dropped the phone on the bed and returned again to the screen. Eve had tagged Dan in a post and, in the accompanying photo, Dan had his arms around her waist, his chin resting on her shoulder and a soppy grin on his face. He appeared to have grown a hipster goatee and a twirly moustache that made him look as if he was off to a fancy-dress party as a ringmaster. Eve was wearing a skin-tight flesh-toned (unless you were Trump orange, that is) body-con dress and pointing to her stomach with nails that looked like they'd been dipped in correction fluid. There was another photo beside it, showing an ultrasound scan of the tiny Dan/Eve inside Eve's 'baby tummy'.

Eve is feeling: Blessed, said the post, which, mystifyingly, had been set on a Facebook background of tropical palms. It was accompanied by a gif of a chubby baby gurgling as it was tickled.

Can life get any better? Expecting a little miracle in October. We are Officially the Luckiest People in the World.

Poppy's head swam and her stomach turned over with a sensation not unlike she'd felt on the *Islander*. Only this feeling wasn't going to vanish once she stepped on dry land. Dan had once hinted he'd like to start a family; in fact, she recalled his words on that very subject the day they'd visited the Starfish Studio all those years before. He'd hinted that St Piran's would be a good place for kids to grow up, with fresh air and a safe environment, and Poppy had agreed. She still did but, of course, it was never going to happen for her and Dan now.

Every time she took a step forward – moving to St Piran's despite Dan's betrayal and scorn; finding the Starfish in a mess but determining to do it up – she seemed to take another step back. She might laugh at the post's cheesiness but the fact remained: Eve and Dan were having a baby together.

It took every ounce of her strength not to burst into tears.

She reached to shut down the laptop when Leo jumped onto the keyboard. He turned around and lifted his tail ready to spray the screen.

'Argh! No!'

With a loud shriek, Poppy snatched the laptop out of the way before Leo did his worst.

'Poppy! Are you OK?' Thudding boots were followed by Jake dashing into the room.

She almost died of shame. 'It's fine. Everything's fine. It's Leo. He was going to spray the laptop.'

'Thank God for that. I mean, bloody cat. It's disgusting, but thank goodness no one's hurt.'

Poppy grabbed a handful of kitchen roll and wiped down the tabletop.

'Would you like some Dettol?' he asked earnestly.

Well, it was better than a couples' cocktail, she thought, unable to hide a smile at Jake's offer. 'Thanks. It's under the sink.'

Jake glared at Leo. 'And don't even think about giving me a shower, Catface,' he said.

Leo turned his back and sauntered off.

'He can't help it. Fen says he's been neutered, but some cats can still spray,' she said as Leo pummelled her favourite hoodie with his claws.

'Well, I hope he has been,' said Jake, adding in a loud voice, 'If not, it would do him good to have his bits removed.'

'I can think of someone else who'd benefit from having his balls cut off,' Poppy muttered while Jake fetched the Dettol.

'What?' Jake looked up sharply from the kitchen cupboard.

She groaned. 'Not you. Absolutely *not* you.'

'I'm glad to hear it.' He smiled and came over and squirted the table with Dettol. 'Are you referring to your ex?'

'How did you guess?' Wrinkling her nose, Poppy wiped the table furiously. 'Actually, I'd just heard that his new woman is pregnant when you came in.'

'Oh. Shit.'

'They posted it on Facebook. With pictures.'

Jake rolled his eyes. 'He probably has no idea you've seen it.'

He had now, thought Poppy in dismay. He'd get a notification that she'd had Liked it, even though she'd now Unliked it. Too late. She should have unfriended him, she thought. Dan hadn't unfriended her either though ...

'I don't know,' she said, not wanting to let Jake know about Leo's blunder. She replaced the laptop on the table and Jake nodded at the screen.

'He hasn't been with this woman very long, has he?'

'He moved in with Eve just over a month ago on the day he told me he'd been having an affair,' said Poppy, still cringing. 'He'd already moved out a lot of his stuff while I was at work because I think he was worried I might burn all his things or throw them at him ... Now it turns out that Eve's five months pregnant, so he must have been having the affair for a while before then. It could have been years for all I know.'

Jake pulled a face. 'That's tough. I'm so sorry.'

She shrugged, fighting back tears as she threw the dirty kitchen roll in the bin. She didn't want Jake to see her face, but she had to get a grip. 'It's life. I'm here now and I'm determined to make a go of things.'

Jake winced and caught sight of the screen. He took a closer look at the offending post. 'Expecting a little *miracle*? Immaculate conception, is it?'

He was so deadpan, she couldn't help but burst out laughing. 'Who knows with Dan. He always did think he was clever.' A thought occurred that didn't make her feel any better. 'He might have *wanted* me to see that post, of course. I'm sure Eve would.'

'From what you've told me, and what I've seen, I'd go with the "clueless" angle, rather than a cunning plan,' said Jake.

Poppy laughed again.

'At least you're smiling. That's progress.'

She caught her breath in surprise. 'It is, I suppose.'

'Because I'm guessing, where Dan is concerned, you've felt like crying far more often.'

Poppy looked at him. She was momentarily lost for words by his gentle tone and his insight into her feelings. But then ... Jake must know more about loss than she could ever imagine.

'It's OK to be angry and hurt sometimes, you know. Most of the time, in fact.' He smiled. 'You don't have to put on a front, Poppy. It's exhausting.'

She couldn't possibly have discussed such emotive issues with any other guy, or even her parents, but Jake had given her permission to be herself.

'Thanks, and you're right. Eve being pregnant is a nasty shock.' She heaved a sigh. 'Dan seemed keen on us having kids initially and I thought that was one of the main reasons he wanted to move here. I must admit that since Christmas, whenever it came up, he changed the subject. I just thought that once we'd got the stress of moving over, we'd think about it seriously again.'

'And what about you?'

'I'd like one – or two – one day, but my one day was probably sooner than Dan was planning. Or not, judging by that post.' She couldn't help thinking about the post again. How long had they actually been having an affair? How long had she been duped? If Eve was five months gone, Dan must have been sleeping with her for months before he told Poppy he was leaving. That thought cut deep, but she tried to put it aside.

'It's not easy, finding someone who shares the things that really matter, or loves you enough to set aside or change their dreams to help you have yours.' Jake's tone was soft as if he was treading on eggshells.

Leo appeared by his side, rubbing his fur along his legs, but Jake didn't seem to have even noticed.

'It's a miracle that we even find one person, let alone that some people find two,' she said.

'Not a miracle. Impossible,' said Jake.

She could tell he was struggling with memories. Should

she ask him more about Harriet? Was it selfish to only focus on herself? Or was it best to wait for him to tell her about his fiancée if and when he wanted to?

Not that there was much time left for that kind of discussion. Once again, she felt a shiver of sadness that Jake would be leaving soon, even though she'd only known him a few days. Then again, she was probably relying on him too much already, like a baby bird needing feeding. Even as she thought about it, she had to stifle a giggle at the image.

'Something funny?' He raised an eyebrow.

'Only Dan's silly moustache. He looks like an extra from *Ripper Street*,' she said, hoping her fib had fooled Jake and he didn't think she'd been making light of his own worries.

He nodded and a smile crept onto his lips. 'I must admit that 'tache is extremely sad. Now, enough of these gloomy thoughts. You might be wondering about the reason I came over. I need to ask you two favours. One, I was wondering if you fancied coming to the pub for dinner? I thought you might be knackered after all that work and not feel like cooking. You must have been up very early and, frankly, I'm so hungry, I could eat Leo. Which will make a change from him trying to eat me.'

She laughed again, while Leo let out a yawn. 'I was up early, and you're right, the pub sounds great.' In fact, it sounded perfect. She was much too tired to cook and would probably have resorted to a bowl of cereal. Strangely, though, she had enough energy to walk to the pub.

'I also thought it would be a good opportunity to meet some of the locals, if you can face it.' He grinned. 'It's Darts

Night. You should catch a bunch of them all at once. Call it a baptism of fire.'

'That sounds nerve-racking, but I do want to get to know everyone. I can't play darts, though.'

Jake nodded. 'In that case, you'll be a massive hit.' He paused and his tone became more serious. 'But, first, there's something else I wanted to ask you.'

'Yes?'

'Do you mind loaning me that key? I think I need to have a better look at what's in Grandpa's drawer. I'm pretty sure I'm going to need a pint after that.'

Chapter 11

Jake pushed the key into the lock.

'Are you sure you don't want me to leave you to do this alone?' Poppy asked him.

He shook his head. 'No, it's fine.' He tried a smile, because he guessed he might need a sense of humour as well as a pint. 'The studio is technically your place now and I can't believe Grandpa had anything to hide but ... wait until you see for yourself.'

Plus, he reasoned, now that Poppy had seen his reaction when he'd opened the drawer the previous day, there wasn't much point in hiding away what he'd glimpsed. It would have seemed a bit underhand. Also, strangely enough, he felt that if there was one person with whom he could share the secrets that might be inside, Poppy might be it. She was a stranger with no ties or baggage linked to anyone on St Piran's and instinct told him he could trust her. She was certainly one of the very few people he'd felt he might ever be able to open up to about the loss of Harriet ... About the terrible moments before she'd been knocked unconscious and fallen into the sea and about the guilt that raged in his mind that he'd never come to terms with – not only surrounding the circumstances of the accident but their whole lives together.

Jake and Harriet. Harriet and Jake. The perfect couple, crazily in love, made for each other: perfect candidates for the kind of smug and thoughtless social media post that he knew had upset Poppy far more than she was letting on. That 'Instagrammable' image was the one that everyone around them bought into, even Fen and Grandpa Archie. Except it wasn't quite true, was it? The impression that outsiders got wasn't the complete picture, just a version that Jake and Harriet had shown to the world while they battled with problems that were too personal to share with anyone else.

But he'd be leaving St Piran's soon, unsure if and when he'd ever return, so those thoughts would thankfully stay buried unless he decided to open up completely to Poppy, but now wasn't the time for that. He had other secrets to uncover first.

He found the drawer easier to open than previously. Poppy stood on the other side of the table, where Fen had watched them the day before. He took out the bundles of invoices and paperwork and laid them on the table. Finally, he pulled out the sketches.

Each was exquisite in its own way and each had his grandfather's trademark style and his passion for the subject shone through every line.

Jake pushed the sketch pad towards Poppy. 'I wasn't imagining it.'

She rested her fingers on the edge of it. 'Oh.'

'Yeah. That's what I thought.'

'It is her, isn't it?'

'Yes. It can't be anyone else. Grandpa is too good an artist not to have captured her perfectly.' Inside and out, thought Jake, seeing the joyous light in the model's eyes and the uninhibited, almost hedonistic, pose.

'It's a beautiful drawing. Your grandpa was – is – a wonderful artist. Even in this sketch, he's captured Fen perfectly.'

'Yes, he has ... all of her.'

She let out a giggle, then held her hand to her mouth. 'Oh God, I'm so sorry. I don't find it funny, really. Fen's a lovely person and she's beautiful in this sketch. She still is beautiful, but it's hard to see her like this.'

'You mean naked? How do you think I feel? She's practically my surrogate grandmother.' A horrible realisation hit Jake in the guts. 'My God. How old do you think Fen is in this picture?'

'I don't know.' Poppy pulled the drawing towards her. 'Fifty, maybe? Possibly a little younger?'

'That's what I thought.' He let out a sigh of relief. 'So, these must have been done years ago, but after my Grandma Ellie passed away.'

'When was that?' Poppy asked.

'Nineteen seventy-three. She had a brain haemorrhage.'

'Your poor grandpa!'

'I know. Her sudden death must have almost broken him and been terrible for Dad because he was only thirteen when he lost his mum. Wait a minute ...' Jake went back to the drawer. He'd always thought his grandfather and Fen were more than 'just good friends' and this pointed to the kind of close relationship he'd suspected. On the other hand, artists and their models didn't *have* to be in a romantic or sexual relationship of any kind, even when the model was nude. In fact, all artists had to know how to depict the human form.

He'd been commissioned to take photos of women of all ages himself – although always or most often clothed. He could honestly say that he'd seen them only as subjects for his camera. It was his job and he'd always separated his appreciation for them from the way he'd felt about Harriet or previous girlfriends.

He risked a glance at Poppy as she studied the drawing of Fen. He liked the way her hazel brown hair curled onto her shoulders, he loved her eyes and her body, of course – and not in a strictly professional way, he had to admit. He liked her tendency to speak first and think later and the way she had tried and failed not to laugh at the drawing. He couldn't stop looking at her when he was with her or thinking about her when he was alone. Like first thing this morning.

He'd told himself these were all normal, natural feelings for a single guy who hadn't felt this way – or allowed himself to feel this way – about another woman for almost three years. Nothing pervy or weird about them, but somehow, because he was leaving soon, they felt wrong, like a betrayal or a voyeurism, and he felt ashamed.

Dragging his eyes from Poppy, he pulled a few more bits of paperwork from the drawer and at the rear found several more sketches. His heart beat faster as he brought them into the light.

'Oh f-f ...'

They were all of Fen, and all nudes. Two seemed to be studio-based, but one was drawn outdoors, Jake guessed. At first, he hadn't been quite sure it was Fen, but a date and an inscription on the reverse left no doubt.

'What?' Poppy asked.

'I'm not sure. I wish I'd never seen these. Any of them.' He pushed the sketches away and they slid along the table.

'May I?' she said quietly.

'I – why not? It's too late to put the demon back in the box now.'

Poppy glanced at the first two sketches showing Fen sitting on a chair in the studio and lying face down on a couch draped with a cloth. Archie hadn't romanticised her. You could tell it was the body of a middle-aged woman, and there were lines on the face.

'They're still beautiful pictures, even if it's a bit of a shock that they're of Fen,' she said. 'I think they're quite moving. You can see the tenderness in every line ... but these ...' Poppy's voice trailed off. 'Oh, I see what you mean.' She'd picked up the last sketch of Fen lying naked in the dunes, with one hand flung behind her head.

It was the one that had shocked Jake the most. His grandfather had clearly spent more time on it, adding in details such as wild agapanthus growing in the dunes behind his model's hair, which was spread out like a mermaid's. In her other hand, she held a shell. Archie had even sketched in a palette, a few inches from her curled fingers, as if he wanted to hint at his closeness to his model. Her lips were slightly parted, her eyes suffused with – God, he dare not even think it …

'She looks blissfully happy,' said Poppy.

'And young,' said Jake. 'Have you read the back of the sketch yet?'

'No.' She turned it over. 'Hmm. I did wonder about the date. She can only be in her twenties …'

'That date confirms it. And there's the title in his own writing. "The Siren Fen, in Petroc Dunes. 1966." Grandpa was married to my grandma, then. She'd only just had my dad. He and Fen must have been having an affair.'

Jake felt slightly sick. His grandpa had always been his idol, even though Jake knew he wasn't perfect. He could be blunt, he liked a drink, to say the least, and he put his painting before almost everything else – not to mention cutting himself off from his own son after Grandma Ellie had died. Now, he knew why. Archie had felt guilty. Guilty about having it away with Fen – God knows how long that had gone on. Oh Christ, had his grandma known about the affair? Was it better or worse if she had?

'This doesn't mean anything, Jake.' Poppy's voice sliced into his unspoken thoughts. 'Fen might only have been his model. His muse.'

'Then why did he write that she was a siren? You know what the sirens did?'

'Weren't they the beautiful women who lured sailors to their doom on the rocks with their singing? You're reading too much into these drawings. The sirens were mythical and I can't imagine Fen ever wanting to cause your family pain. I haven't known her long, but she seems far too kind and considerate.'

'You've no idea what people can be like in this bloody place. You've no idea what some are hiding behind the perfect veneers. No one's ever what they seem!' The violence of his own words startled him. 'Ignore me. That was well out of order.'

'It's OK. I can understand why you're upset by seeing these drawings.' She spoke softly as if she was stepping on hot coals.

He was ashamed of his outburst. 'I shouldn't have reacted like that. Grandpa and Fen are only human and it's their business what they did. Oh God. Should I tell her about these? They are of her and rightfully, perhaps, I should give them to her.'

'Won't she be embarrassed? Especially if ... you know ...' Poppy pointed at the 'Siren Fen' '... they actually *were* in a secret relationship.'

'Yeah. That's true. I'd probably be better off taking them and locking them away in Grandpa's cottage. I don't even know if Fen knows he kept them.'

'Maybe you could ask her?' said Poppy.

'No! I wouldn't dare.'

'Hmm. True. I don't think I could ask my grandma if she'd been having an affair with her neighbour and posed for nude pictures,' Poppy said it deadpan. Jake opened his mouth. He saw her smiling wryly. 'Maybe you're right. I had absolutely no suspicions that Dan was shagging Eve.' She wrinkled her nose. 'I hope to God he's not painting her in the nude and going to post it on Facebook.'

Jake pulled a face, then had to smile. 'I'm probably being prudish, which is ironic considering it's the twenty-first century and I'm meant to be tolerant and liberal. If it wasn't for the fact that I'm worried Grandpa and Fen might have hurt my grandma, I'd say good for him.'

She handed him the sketches. 'I think you're right to lock them away for now and see what happens or what Archie says in the meantime. He might mention them at some point and then you won't have to ask.'

He nodded and put the sketches inside an old folder, wondering if he'd ever dare ask his grandpa about them or even if he *should*. Archie probably never expected anyone to find them, and might even have forgotten they existed, although judging by the pleasure on Fen's face, that might also be unlikely.

'And after you've put them safely away, shall we go to the pub?' Poppy's eyes sparkled. Actually, Grandpa would have called them 'Caspian blue', but they reminded Jake of the deep ocean on the wild Atlantic side of St Piran's. The sea where he'd lost Harriet ...

Jake shook himself out of his memories. 'Best idea I've heard all day.'

'I'll see you in ten?' She grimaced. 'I need to pop upstairs and get ready for my baptism of fire.'

'You look fine as you are to me,' he said, instinctively touching her forearm with his free hand. Her skin was warm but pale, the skin of someone who spent their life out of the sun and the elements. Embarrassed by his impulsive gesture, he moved his hand away quickly. 'See you at the cottage, then,' he said.

He heard her footsteps on the metal stair as he left the studio with the drawings. On the short walk back, his mind was swirling with conflicting emotions. There was realisation that his beloved grandpa wasn't who he'd thought he was and that his feelings for Poppy were moving beyond purely professional.

As he walked through the door and climbed upstairs to hide the sketches, he caught sight of the crate of paintings again. What other secrets might he uncover when he opened *that*?

Chapter 12

The Moor's Head was located on the highest point of St Piran's and it was the centre of island life, along with the community hall and post-office-cum-shop. As Poppy walked up the hill with Jake, he pointed out the combined fire service/ambulance/coastguard station next to the pub and explained that all the 'staff' were people from the island.

'So basically, that's anyone under ninety,' he said as they walked past the station and into the neighbouring pub.

Letting her go ahead, he ducked under the lintel and into the interior. The sun was setting and the lights were on inside, supplementing the final rays that could penetrate the small windows. According to a sign on the wall, there had been an alehouse on the site for over five hundred years.

'And some of the regulars have been propping up the bar ever since,' said Jake with an eyebrow raise. He went on to introduce her to various locals, while others had no qualms about coming forward and telling Poppy all about themselves.

A petite redhead a few years older than Poppy made her way through the regulars, a glass of orange juice in hand and with an obvious baby bump.

'Hi. I'm Maisie from the Driftwood Inn. Welcome to St Piran's,' she said, smiling broadly.

'Thanks,' said Poppy. 'I've heard a lot about your pub.'

'All good I hope? We haven't seen much of Jake lately …'

She glanced at Jake, wondering how he'd take this, but he seemed OK and pretty relaxed with the question. Poppy sensed he must know Maisie well.

Maisie smiled at him. 'Nice to see you back, Jake. How's Archie?'

'He's OK. It's a slow process but you know …'

Maisie nodded. 'We miss him over at the Driftwood. I hope he's on the mend soon. Pass on our good wishes.'

'I'm sure he misses you too. How many paintings do you have now?'

'Plenty, but there's always room for more. They're beautiful. I gave one to Patrick at Christmas.'

'I did hear congratulations are in order. When's the little Samson due?' he asked.

Maisie patted her bump. 'Mid July. Sorry, Patrick's not here with me. He has rowing practice.' She touched his arm. 'Your grandpa told me you'd been photographing whale sharks on the Ningaloo Reef late last year. I think Patrick's been there and I'm sure he'd love to see you while you're here. How long are you staying?'

'I'm not sure yet. I'm taking a break before my next

assignment. Visiting family and helping with the handover of the Starfish to Poppy.'

'I'm glad you're keeping it open,' said Maisie to Poppy. 'We have a community trust on Gull Island that clubs together to renovate some of the properties. Shout up if you need some help with the studio and we'll sort something out.'

This was such an unexpected and generous offer, Poppy wasn't sure how to respond and Jake stayed silent. 'Um ... that's kind, but I'm afraid I don't have the budget for much professional help. I'm going to have to do almost everything myself, with Jake and Fen's help, of course. They've been very kind.'

'Oh, don't worry about the money. We're a cooperative and we all help each other. I'm sure you can repay us somehow.'

Poppy laughed. 'I could use the help, but I don't have that many useful skills to offer in return when it comes to building work itself, unless you count writing exciting articles about spouts and downpipes.'

'That's niche.' Maisie raised an eyebrow.

Poppy laughed again. 'I was the PR manager at a building products company.'

'Ohhh. PR? Great. You could always help with the Gull Island website or the newsletter, then? Or edit some of the small-business sites? God knows, we need the literary inspiration, and if you can make downpipes sound exciting, I'm sure you could work wonders for a pub or B&B,' said Maisie, who seemed to be a ball of energy and ideas. 'We'll find you something to do ... talking of which, I have to go and speak to the landlord about the Low Tide Festival later in the year.'

Poppy already knew that the festival was a big thing for the islands. For just a few days a year, the spring tide – which Poppy had learned had nothing to do with actual spring but meant 'springing' back and forth – exposed the sea bed between St Piran's and St Saviour's. For a few hours, you could walk between the islands almost without getting your feet wet.

'I've heard it's a big occasion,' she said.

'About as big as it gets on St Piran's. If the weather's good, we can have hundreds of people and the Driftwood is planning to do a joint pop-up bar and food with the Moor's Head.'

'What? On the middle of the channel?'

Maisie laughed. 'Yup. Right on the seabed. Why don't you nip over to the Driftwood for a coffee or a glass of wine soon and I'll tell you more?'

'Sounds good.' Poppy resolved to take Maisie up on her offer.

Maisie was about to say goodbye and leave when they were almost deafened by loud barking and shouts from the entrance to the bar.

'Oh God ...' Maisie lowered her voice. 'It's Hugo. Lucky you. Speak soon. Take carc, Jake, and send our love to your grandpa.'

She hurried back to her table as a youngish guy in a Barbour and brogues walked into the middle of the pub.

'Bas-il!' His voice was a bellow. Seconds later, a sleek Labrador shot past his legs and into the bar. The dog ran straight to Poppy, its claws clattering on the boards. Basil sniffed her bare knees.

Hugo groaned and tried to catch Basil's collar but the dog dodged out of reach.

'Sorry! He's a terrible reprobate. Still, lucky he's not windy today. That dog's bowels are a law unto themselves. Costs me a fortune in charcoal tablets.' Hugo rolled his eyes and held out his hand. 'Hugo Scorrier, from the Petroc Luxury Resort. Pleased to meet you.'

Poppy shook his outstretched hand, realising that while Hugo looked like an old country squire, he was actually not that much older than her. She sensed Jake beside her silently laughing at the unnecessary detail about the dog's flatulence problems.

Hugo's tone changed when he spoke to Jake. 'Hello, Jake. Good to see you back on St Piran's again. How are you bearing up these days?'

Jake shook Hugo's hand too. 'I'm OK, thanks.'

'Staying with us long?'

'Not sure. I'm here to sort out the handover of the studio to Poppy while my grandpa's out of action.'

'Hmm. Shame about Archie. Hope the old chap's up and about soon.' He gave Poppy a closer look, the sandy moustache on his top lip wrinkling. 'I thought you were taking over the place with your boyfriend?'

Wow. Everyone really did know her business, thought Poppy, dismayed at being asked this question so soon after she'd walked into the bar. Still, it was probably best to get the pain over with quickly. 'I was ... but we've gone our separate ways. I'll be opening it on my own,' she said, surprised at how confident she sounded. Inside, her stomach twisted into knots.

Hugo winced. 'Ouch. That's very brave. The old place needs a lot of work, if you don't mind me being frank.' Hugo shot Jake a conciliatory smile. 'I really admire Archie's work, but you have to admit the Starfish Studio has been going downhill for quite a while.'

'It's nothing we can't sort,' said Poppy, sensing Jake simmering with annoyance next to her.

'*We*? I thought you said you were on your own?'

'I'm giving Poppy a hand and Fen's helping too, and from what I've seen so far, her plans for the studio are going to totally revitalise it,' Jake said.

She could have high-fived him. 'Yes, we – *I* – have some exciting plans for the Starfish and Jake's a huge help. Until he leaves for his next assignment, that is.'

'Hmm. I admire your enthusiasm. I'll look forward to seeing the results. Well, our guests at Petroc Resort could be some of your biggest potential customers. It's an upmarket place with discerning visitors who're always keen to patronise the local arts scene. I could help you publicise the gallery. Once it's up to scratch, of course.'

'Thanks. Sounds like a promising opportunity,' said Poppy. She couldn't afford to dismiss Hugo's offer, but she had a feeling she'd rather not get too involved with him, either. 'Oh!' She let out a squeak of horror as she felt something warm and wet against her leg. Glancing down, she found Basil back at her feet and gazing up at her with adoration. A glistening trail of drool linked his jowls and the hem of her dress.

'Basil, that's disgusting. I must apologise for my dog's appalling habits.' Hugo whipped a large red hanky from the pocket of his jacket and handed it to Poppy. She took some comfort that it must be clean because it still had the creases ironed into it.

'Thanks, but I think I have a tissue in my bag.'

'No, I insist. Please.' He glared at Basil. 'There's no hope for you, hound.'

By her side, Jake was trying not to laugh. 'I expect he was only being friendly.' Jake ruffled Basil's ears. 'He's a lovely dog. How old is he, Hugo?'

'Almost two now.' Hugo's eyes lit up with pleasure at the praise of Basil. 'I keep trying to train him but it seems hopeless. He does what he damn well pleases.'

Basil snuffled in delight as Jake stroked his ears and Poppy wiped the drool from her dress and knee.

'He's lovely,' said Poppy. 'Shall I wash your hanky?'

'God no, keep it. Least I can do.'

Poppy struggled not to laugh. Hugo sounded like the presenter of a daytime antiques show.

'Anyway, here's my card. Let's meet up sometime.'

Poppy pocketed the card and Hugo moved to the other side of the pub where he seemed to know everyone. She bought a round of drinks while Jake managed to find a table. Once seated, they studied the menus.

'Told you it would be a baptism of fire,' Jake whispered behind the menus. 'But at least you'll get it all over in one go.'

A couple of hours later, Poppy's head was spinning. She must have met the entire population of St Piran's and more characters from the other islands. Maisie's laid-back Aussie partner, Patrick, turned up along with Jess and Adam who ran the Flower Farm on St Saviour's. Even Jake seemed surprised when he heard that Adam, who used to be the island postman, had decided to help run the farm with Jess – and even more so when he found out that Jess's twin brother, Will, had left the farm to travel the world with a Cambridge graduate who'd come to work for him.

All the gossip was new to Poppy, who kept reminding herself that this was the rebirth of her life now. Telling people that she and Dan had split up and that she was running the studio on her own became easier as the evening wore on. Most of the locals were far more eager to share banter and gossip about their neighbours than pry into her background, so she went with the flow, listened politely and laughed.

She guessed the occasion must be harder for Jake, who had to endure an endless stream of questions about Archie, which she could tell he didn't mind – and about Harriet, which she was sure he found painful. He kept his responses to a few brief words, smiling his appreciation of their sympathy and declaring firmly that he was only here for a short time, while steering the conversation onto some of his recent exotic trips. Poppy lost count of the number of people who told him he was 'mad' but sounded very envious of his adventures anyway.

The other major bonus of the evening was that two of the artists she'd contacted and wanted to talk to turned up to the Darts Night.

Rowan Pentire was an up-and-coming ceramicist who lived in a chalet behind the pub. Poppy spotted Rowan while she was queueing at the bar, having recognised him instantly from his website, and bought him a pint. Rowan, in his early twenties, had auburn hair tied back in a ponytail and was wearing flip-flops and a skull-headed toe-ring. He seemed very chilled about Poppy's plans, and happy to go along with all her suggestions for selling his work.

'Do you want to come around and take a look at the space once we've renovated it?' she asked.

'Sure, but I'm cool with whatever you do.'

'I'll email the terms to you. The commission will be forty per cent,' she said, aware that Archie had been charging thirty-five. Even so, forty was on the lower side for a gallery. Most asked for fifty per cent and even as high as seventy. 'But I think it will be a much more attractive environment for your work and hopefully that will mean added sales.'

'Whatever.' Rowan waved his hand airily. 'I'll drop in when I'm next around. I've been working on some new pieces.'

'That sounds exciting. I love your work and the pieces that are already in the gallery.'

'Thanks.' Rowan left to chat up a girl at a corner table.

Poppy heaved a sigh of relief that her first encounter with one of her 'stable' of artists had gone so well. If only they were all that straightforward.

After dinner, Jake introduced her to a group of three people who included the silversmith, Araminta, aka 'Minty', Cavendish who lived on St Mary's where she had her own established studio. Poppy knew from her website bio that she was in her late thirties. Her platinum hair had been dip-dyed aubergine at the ends and cut with an asymmetric fringe, that was a work of art in itself. She wore black jeans, a man's white shirt with the cuffs folded back and had an air of cool confidence that Poppy found mildly intimidating.

Poppy almost drooled when she saw the fabulous silver pendant around Minty's neck with its solid silver starfish and the bracelet composed of tiny silver sea creatures. The bracelet jingled as Minty swept her fringe off her face. Poppy knew from past sales records that Minty's jewellery sold like hot cakes, but Fen had confessed that she had stopped sending pieces to the Starfish a year before because it 'sadly, was no longer the right environment for her work'.

Jake strode right up to her table, with Poppy in tow. He'd warned her that Minty – a local personality with a reputation that went way beyond the isles in arty circles – might be a tough nut to crack. 'Hi, Minty,' he said, with a smile.

Minty's eyes lit up and she jumped up and threw her arms around him. 'Oh my God. I'd lost all hope of seeing you again. You poor boy ...' she said, standing back. 'Although you're looking pretty good tonight.'

Minty's friends, one male and one female, both smiled and eyed Jake admiringly.

'Did you know,' said Minty, who didn't even seem to have noticed Poppy, 'that Jake and his family are descended from sailors shipwrecked on the islands after the Spanish Armada?'

Jake groaned. 'Oh God, no. That's just a myth.'

'What? Is this true?' Poppy burst out.

Minty finally noticed her. 'It's abso-bloody-lutely true. The Armada was scattered by the wind around Scilly. Besides, just *look* at those to-die-for espresso eyes and that hair – like a raven's wing. Jake *must* have Spanish heritage. Archie too. In fact, the Pendowers have lived on St Piran's for generations. Apart from Jake, of course.'

Minty's eyes gleamed wickedly and her two friends seemed completely rapt. Poppy held her breath. Given that Jake had left and decided not to come back because of a boating accident, she thought Minty was sailing close to the wind with her teasing – and that wasn't a pun. But now she came to think of it – and looked at him closely – Jake might very well have Spanish heritage.

Jake laughed uneasily. 'I don't think there's any record of any Armada ships being wrecked off Scilly. Most ended up off Ireland and Scotland.'

'That means nothing. The sailors could easily have rowed ashore from a more distant wreck.' Minty was clearly enjoying herself. 'And anyway, your grandfather's always telling the Armada tale to tourists, so it must have some truth in it.'

Jake let out a snort. 'That's because Grandpa always gets a free pint out of it.'

'You're so naughty, Minty,' said her male companion.

'That's why you like me.' Minty smirked, then her attention switched to Poppy and her eyes narrowed. 'Aha. Are you Jake's new Significant Other?' she asked.

'No!' Poppy got the word out just before Jake. 'I'm Poppy McGregor, the new owner of the Starfish Studio. Jake was going to introduce me because I love your work and I was hoping you'd let us stock your pieces in the gallery again. I've already started renovating it and I have some fabulous plans. I think it would be perfect for your wonderful jewellery.'

Minty's eyes widened. Poppy had surprised herself, but once the words had started, they rushed out in a torrent. 'That's some sales pitch, but I have my own studio ... and with the greatest respect to Archie, Jake ...' she said, 'the Starfish Studio hasn't been a great showcase for my work lately. Or anyone's.'

'But it will be,' said Poppy. 'I can promise you that. Why not come over next week when we'll have it well underway? Have a coffee and a chat and see how it's going.' She had the feeling that if she could get Minty on board, others would follow.

'Have you had much gallery experience?' Minty asked.

'I worked in a gallery during my student vacations.' Poppy declined to mention her own jewellery making efforts. Somehow, she didn't think Minty would be impressed.

'On Scilly?'

'No. At a craft centre in Staffordshire.'

'*Staffordshire*?' Minty made the place sound like some kind of hell. 'The market's a lot different down here. And with respect, I'm guessing that was some time ago.'

Poppy covered her annoyance with a laugh, deciding a charm offensive was the best method of attack with Minty. 'Oh, centuries ago. Actually, it was just within this century. But at least it gave me a good grounding in the way a gallery works. And, of course, I've done a lot of research since then. I've contacted some of the local artists and Fen and Jake have given me some insight into how the market operates for the Starfish and what the opportunities are ...' Minty and her mates stared at Poppy as if they were judging a wonky

Showstopper cake on the *Bake Off*. She ploughed on anyway. 'But above all I'm passionate about my ethos for the Starfish Studio.'

Minty arched an eyebrow. 'Which is?'

'High-quality pieces, carefully curated from island artists. Archie's work will still be at the heart of the gallery alongside talented established artists like yourself and up-and-coming stars like Rowan.'

Jake spoke. 'And of course, I'm going to start offering exclusive limited-edition prints of my own work to Poppy.'

Poppy just managed to stop her mouth from falling open. This was the first she'd heard of the offer, but Minty had fired up her wicked side and she quickly gathered herself and ran with the idea. 'Of course. Jake only allows a handful of select galleries to show his work,' she said, improvising.

'A handful of *select* galleries?' Minty smiled and Poppy cringed at her own words, which were all she could think of on the spur of the moment.

Minty darted a sly glance at Jake. 'Well, if *Jake* has so much obvious faith in you, then maybe I might have to reconsider. I'll certainly come and take a look at your plans, but I'm not promising anything.'

Poppy smiled sweetly. 'Thanks. I appreciate it.'

'So, when exactly are you leaving us again?' Minty directed this at Jake, now that Poppy guessed she'd served her purpose as entertainment for the evening.

By now, Jake must have heard the question so many times, he could have worn a sandwich board saying: 'I'm not sure yet.'

'Let's hope it's a while. I'll make sure I come over while you're still around. It's been way too long.' Minty reached out and patted Jake's hand. 'You poor boy.'

Poppy wondered if Jake was squirming but decided Minty must know him very well.

'Thanks,' he muttered, then spoke more boldly. 'And I can understand your concerns about new owners taking over the studio. I had my doubts when I first heard from my grandpa.'

Just in time, Poppy stifled a gasp at Jake's frankness, but he quickly qualified his statement.

'Now I've met Poppy and seen her commitment to the studio and how hard she's prepared to work, I have total confidence that she'll make a success of it. *With* the support of her artists, of course.'

Minty smiled. 'Like I said, I'm happy to support her. *If* I'm confident the studio is the right home for my work.'

Poppy was rapidly wishing she didn't need Minty's jewellery in the Starfish. She didn't quite know whether she liked the woman or not, though that was irrelevant to whether she exhibited her work, she supposed. Then again, hadn't she declared that her ethos was to only show the work of artists she admired and respected? Hmm. She might have to compromise on that with Minty Cavendish.

Some of the artists she'd known back in the day had been difficult characters, to put it mildly, and you could hardly expect creative types to conform to convention. Her old boss at the craft centre had told her it was part of the job to nurture a stable of artists – even those you longed to tell to 'shove their creations up their arses'.

'I hope you'll call round at the Starfish soon?' Poppy said with a secret smile, fondly remembering her old boss's rants.

Minty was all sweetness again. 'Of course. I'm always willing to give the Starfish a try, if your plans are as good as they sound. Especially as Jake has given it – and you – such a glowing endorsement.'

'Thanks,' said Jake. 'And if you'll excuse us, I want to introduce Poppy to the vicar.'

The bar emptied quickly as anyone who wanted to take their boats home had to catch the tides. Shortly afterwards, Poppy and Jake themselves left, chatting about the people they'd met on the short walk back to the harbour. At the back of her mind, she couldn't stop wondering if it was Poppy's enthusiasm for the Starfish that had swayed Minty – or her passion for Jake.

More importantly, why had he offered to take some new photographs for the gallery if he wasn't planning on staying long on St Piran's and, as she suspected, didn't really want to be here at all?

Chapter 13

Oh God, why had he said that? Jake was still asking himself the question when he made his breakfast the next morning and opened a pouch of cat food for Leo, who had decided to wander in as soon as Jake had opened the door.

'Why *did* I say it, Leo?' he asked, leaning against the worktop while Leo sniffed disdainfully at the dish of food. Jake's feet were bare under the pyjama bottoms he'd thrown on in case anyone passed by the kitchen window.

Leo spared him a brief glance as if to say 'Dunno, mate. Because you're a bit of a plonker like all humans?' before finally wolfing down his Luxury Hare and Badger Potage, or whatever disgusting stuff had squirted out of the pouch.

Jake decided he'd rather have toast than hare and badger so he sawed off a slice of loaf while reflecting on last night's events at the Moor's Head. Before they were halfway down the road from the pub, he'd apologised for saying he would have prints in the gallery without consulting Poppy.

'I'm sorry. It just came out but Minty was being so ... *Minty-ish.* I couldn't resist it.'

Poppy hadn't seemed annoyed. Far from it. She'd seemed happy with the idea.

'It's OK and you don't have to do it. Even the offer was worth hearing to see her face ... I'm sorry. I shouldn't have said that. She's your friend and also I really do want her work in the Starfish.'

'I wouldn't have said she's a *friend* ...' Jake had begun, then decided that it was better to keep things simple where Minty Cavendish was concerned, if that was humanly possible, since Minty's *raison d'etre* seemed to be to make life complicated for anyone she came into contact with. 'And if you do want some exclusive prints, I'm happy to provide some. If my work fits in with your ethos, that is.'

'Happy' hadn't been quite the right word, in hindsight.

Poppy had laughed, and jokingly said she'd consider it: 'But I will have to charge you the forty per cent commission.'

Jake had said 'fine' and they'd parted at the door of his grandpa's cottage, laughing.

He'd watched her walk off to the studio with the moonlight on her back. Her step was light and he could hear her faintly humming a tune they'd heard in the bar once she thought she was out of his hearing. He'd closed the door behind him, still smiling, and fallen asleep with the same tune burrowing away like an earworm at his mind ...

How different things seemed this morning. Leo finished his breakfast while Jake sat at the ancient kitchen table and buttered his third slice of toast. When he'd woken, rain was lashing the cottage windows and the wind was howling. Last night's euphoria had evaporated.

Whether it was the rain or stubbing his toe on the crate of paintings, he wasn't sure. He'd agreed to supply some prints to Poppy ... which sounded simple enough – but wasn't.

He *did* sell signed limited editions of his landscapes and wildlife shots through a handful of high-quality galleries. However, if the prints were to be any use to Poppy they did have to fit in with her 'vision' for the gallery, which meant that, really, they needed to be of Scilly – specifically of St Piran's.

The problem was he didn't have a single shot of the island.

Prior to Harriet's death, he'd had hundreds – *thousands* – of photographs of his family and of Harriet on the isles. Then, a few weeks after she died, in the grip of overwhelming grief, he'd erased every file from his cameras and his laptop. He'd burnt all the memory cards too and started deleting everything relating to the island from the external hard drive. He'd even tried to remove all the St Piran's shots from his online photo storage account. Eventually he'd calmed down a little and come to realise that it would be almost impossible to delete everything he'd ever taken. There were pictures he'd shared on the internet and social media that he had no control over.

Looking back now, Jake realised the awful state he'd been in those first few months after he'd lost Harriet. He must have been trying to deal with his grief and guilt by attempting to wipe out the source of it.

Even if he could find some photos of St Piran's from that time, he didn't want to put them on public display. They would show St Piran's before he lost Harriet, and the way he'd felt about his homeland then wasn't the way he felt he about it now.

The only thing to do was to take some new pictures: could he do that, when that view was coloured by grief and unhappiness? Some people might think that it couldn't hurt to look at a place through a lens, as long as he didn't actually revisit the scene of the accident. He was already here, for God's sake, with the studio, the harbour, the cottage and sea in front of him every day.

Choosing a location and a subject, truly looking at it – interacting with it – was a totally different matter though. While taking pictures, he couldn't help but think very deeply about his subject matter or the way he felt about it. A stone, a wave, the grass – they weren't simply inanimate objects to him; here, they seethed with memories and emotions and Jake worried he might be pulled back into the abyss.

The rattle of the cat flap startled him and Leo entered the room. The cat stalked off, spraying the doorframe on his way out, but his arrival had at least snapped Jake out of his maudlin thoughts.

He went upstairs to get dressed, ready for the day's work at the Starfish Studio. The crate of Grandpa's paintings sat in the bedroom. He wasn't exactly sure what the paintings would show, but he was certain that many memories lay inside, waiting to be unlocked. Everything seemed to be conspiring to keep him on St Piran's: Grandpa's paintings, helping Poppy to renovate the studio, and now, the need to take more photographs. He'd moved so far out of his comfort zone in the past few days ...

Was that wholly a bad thing?

Jake didn't know the answer, so he decided to focus on practical matters and get over to the studio and start work.

After dragging on jeans and a T-shirt, he looked around for some footwear and found one of his new Adidas trainers wedged under the divan. He could have sworn he'd kicked off both the previous evening before he got undressed, but there was no sign of the other.

'Oh, for God's sake ...' He said it out loud, on his hands and knees hunting under the bed. 'Ow!' He caught his head on the corner of the crate as he straightened up.

Feeling sick for a moment, he sat on the bed, rubbing his head. He had to shift that thing into Grandpa's room. It was like the crate in *Raiders of the Lost Ark*: glowing and throbbing with some mystical power. When he eventually did open it, he half expected evil spirits would fly out and melt his face.

Suddenly laughing at the craziness of his own thoughts, he padded downstairs, wondering where the hell the other trainer was. He didn't remember throwing them around the cottage when he'd got in from the pub last night ... Surely it wasn't in the kitchen ... No one could have moved it ... no human anyway ...

'Oh. Shit.'

Leo was back inside now, sitting in a pool of sunlight in

the kitchen, looking distinctly smug. And there was his other trainer, neatly upturned in the centre of the litter tray – and if Jake wasn't mistaken, it was carefully concealing one of Leo's poos.

Chapter 14

'Oh, he's been doing *that* trick again, has he?' Fen nodded sagely at Jake who'd thumped into the studio moments ago, ranting about having found his trainer in the litter tray.

Poppy, who had been arranging some of Rowan's pots on the new display cubes, transferred her attention to the conversation.

'It's a natural feline instinct. He must think he needs to hide it from a predator,' said Fen.

Jake snorted in disgust. 'I'm not the predator. He is.'

'He's only a cat,' said Fen patiently. 'And you've invaded his territory – don't forget that.'

'It's my house!' Jake glared at Leo, who was lounging on a plinth as if he was the prize exhibit.

'Archie's house,' Fen corrected.

'Whatever. He still stole my shoe and used it to cover up his crap. He hates me. No, worse, he disrespects me. In fact, I'd go so far as to say he holds me in utter contempt. And that was after I bought him that hare and badger mush that costs twice as much as normal food. Well, he can make his own bloody hare and badger potage from now on or catch a mouse or something.'

'Oh, Jake, don't get upset. I'm sure Leo loves you deep down and he's only doing what cats do. As for a mouse, he's never been one for dragging in live catches and what's all this about you giving him strange cat food with badger in it? You know he only likes the Rabbit and Tuna Select.'

'It looked like hare and badger to me. I'm sure I spotted bits of bristle and an ear. There might even have been a stripe in there.'

It was no good. Poppy exploded with laughter. Her sides were hurting and tears streamed down her face.

Jake glared at her, then he laughed too. 'I suppose it *is* quite funny. When it's not your trainers.'

'It's h-hilarious.' Poppy dragged a tissue from her jeans pocket to wipe her eyes.

Jake was smiling and put his arm around Fen. 'I'm only joking,' he said. 'Sort of, but Leo definitely doesn't love me. He only loves you and Grandpa. And Poppy ...'

Fen sighed. 'You can't be loved instantly by everyone, Jake. You'll have to work a bit harder to win Leo over. He probably senses you don't like him, so no wonder he hid his business from you.'

'I'll try to understand him more.' Jake crossed his heart sarcastically then dodged out of the way as Fen flicked her duster at him.

Poppy giggled as Fen chased Jake with the duster. Although

he'd ranted about Leo, he'd soon seen the funny side and his sense of humour was catching. Dan would have gone berserk if any cat had put one of his precious trainers in a litter tray and would probably have tried to have Leo rehomed.

After the joke had been stretched as far as it could, Fen shared more tales of Leo's escapades while they worked, with Jake adding a few stories of his own from his wildlife trips. The laughter and banter were a welcome interlude and Poppy felt more optimistic about her future than she'd done for months. Finally, she felt as if she might actually make a go of a move that had seemed madness even a few days ago.

Her optimistic mood grew over the weekend and well into the following week, as the studio gradually started to turn from chrysalis to butterfly. By Friday afternoon it was a sparkling, whitewashed version of the dingy space that had, just over a week before, made her want to get straight back on the ferry to the mainland. With Jake and Fen's help, she'd prepared and repainted all the gallery walls.

Earlier in the week, she had taken a brief break from the work to go to St Mary's with Kelly who had a working boat for her business. Kelly had introduced her to the small DIY merchant on St Mary's and she'd bought a few essentials from there, but she had to manage her small budget carefully, so she decided to renovate the display plinths and shelving units herself.

Most people on the islands tended to keep unwanted items in sheds and outbuildings in case they were needed by their own family or neighbours at a later date. Fen and Jake invited

Poppy to root through the 'junk' stores behind the cottage and Poppy managed to find a few bits and pieces that way, as well as on the isles' online 'swap' site. Some upended old fish boxes, once 'repurposed' with a tasteful pale green paint, had proved ideal for displaying smaller items such as cards and as plinths for larger items.

The existing plinths had been repaired by Kelly who'd also carried out more minor work on some of the windows and the door too. The local electrician had also removed the harsh strip lighting and fitted new lighting that bathed the artwork in a soft, flattering light.

Maisie had sent over the roofer who'd been working for the Gull Island Trust to make a few repairs to the roof. In return, Poppy had promised to set up a website for the roofer and to help redesign the builder's merchant site in return for free delivery of the materials. It was such a different way of working to the cut-throat world she'd been used to, where everything was costed and analysed to the tiniest margins. Profit was far less important than simple survival, and she soon realised exactly why you couldn't manage out here without help from your neighbours and helping them in turn.

The smell of new paint was still strong, but at least the whiff of damp had almost gone. Archie's paintings had been rehung on the walls and the colours of his seascapes really popped against the white backdrop. Poppy had also arranged some of the existing pieces on the new plinths just to give a flavour of how the gallery would look.

She'd decided to open every day from the launch until October half-term to make the most of the holiday season.

After that, the gallery would be closed, apart from by appointment, until the following February half-term, so she'd have to make enough money to tide her over the winter months.

With the gallery shaping up, she set up meetings with potential artists and continued to spread the word about the launch, which was now less than two weeks away.

Fen admitted that Minty's jewellery used to be on show in what was now a dusty and cracked glass case, so Poppy had the broken panel reglazed and polished the glass until it gleamed. She found some driftwood and pebbles from the beach and arranged a couple of pieces from other artists around the natural materials.

'That looks beautiful.' Fen stood beside Poppy as she fiddled with the display.

'Do you think so? It's not too twee with the pebbles and wood?'

Fen tutted. 'It's perfect. Too good for that Minty.'

Poppy turned in surprise. 'You're not a fan of hers?'

'Her jewellery is very pretty – I'll give her that. It used to fly off the shelves until custom waned, but she has an inflated opinion of her own talents. You met her, dear. You must have formed an impression.'

'I didn't really spend that much time with her to be honest.'

Fen raised an eyebrow. 'Lucky you.'

'I admit she was slightly intimidating.' Poppy had to hide her glee at Fen's blunt assessment of Minty. 'But she is a great lure for customers and she's coming around next Friday to see how we're getting on with the "space". Several of the other artists are coming too.'

‘Oh gosh. Not all together I hope?’

‘No. Rowan’s booked in first, with the others later that day. I thought everyone would prefer individual attention and grovelling, so Kay Baverstock is due after lunch and Minty around four. Why?’

Fen sighed in relief. ‘Thank goodness for that. Minty likes to be queen bee and she can’t stand Kay ... Nor most of the other artists in the gallery. The female ones anyway.’

‘Ouch.’

‘And have you warned Jake?’ said Fen.

‘What about?’

‘Minty descending on us, of course.’

‘Do I need to?’ asked Poppy, slightly alarmed.

‘It might be a good idea.’ Fen lowered her voice as if she expected Jake to burst in on them at any moment. ‘Before he met Harriet, they had a thing, you know ...’

‘They? You mean Jake and Minty?’

Fen pursed her lips and nodded theatrically.

‘Wow. That’s ... surprised me. Um ... this “thing” ... was it serious?’

‘Depends what you mean by serious. Minty thought so, but I’m not sure how Jake felt. He broke more than a few hearts on these islands, I can tell you, before he met Harriet.’ Fen gazed at one of Archie’s paintings on the wall. ‘Then again, it seems to run in the family.’

Chapter 15

Jake popped into the gallery on the Saturday morning. Was this the same place? When he'd last seen it, the floor had still been littered with dust sheets and paint tins. Wow. It was obvious that while he'd been busy doing some of his own work at the cottage, Poppy had moved some of the display cases and plinths into the space, hung a few pictures and arranged some of the artworks on the plinths. Stock was still sparse, but wow, it gave a great idea of how the Starfish could – and would – look by launch day.

'Wow. It's almost unrecognisable,' said Jake. 'My grandpa won't believe it when he comes back.'

Poppy blew a strand of hair away from her face. She was glowing after her efforts and her denim dungarees and blue T-shirt were spattered with white paint. Jake thought she'd never looked more gorgeous.

'Still work to do, but I think we're getting there,' she said. 'With a bit of luck, I'll have more to sell by launch day.'

Jake smiled to himself. She'd tried to hide the pride in her voice, but he could tell how happy she was. She deserved to be.

'Thanks for helping me. I'm very grateful,' she said.

'No way. Don't be. The ideas and concept are all yours. You did well to stick it out here after that first day.'

'Did you think I'd leg it straightaway?' she asked, and he knew she was only half-joking.

'I wasn't sure. I think I would have. In fact, I'd have been on the first plane home.'

Poppy laughed. 'I've thought about it a few times.' She pointed to a space on the wall opposite the cash desk. 'I was thinking of displaying your photos there. What do you think?'

Just in time, Jake stifled a groan. He hadn't even started taking the pictures yet and time was racing by. He had to do something very very soon, because not only did he have to take the photos but he also had to edit them and have them printed on the mainland. Even then, he'd have to get the shots emailed to the specialist printing company and sent over by air. It would cost an arm and a leg, but he'd promised Poppy exclusive pictures and that's what she'd have.

'Is everything OK?' She cut into his thoughts, with an anxious look on her face. 'You don't have to take them if you've changed your mind.'

'I haven't. Like I say, it's the least I could do after we let you down over the gallery. You can sell the prints either in the Starfish or online if you like. I won't let anyone else have them. If that's what you want,' he added hastily, suddenly realising he sounded as if he was doing her a favour. 'And if you don't like them when you see them or they don't fit in, don't say yes because you don't want to offend me. I've a hide like a rhino after so long in this business.'

'I wish I had,' she said, then smiled. 'But I'm absolutely sure I'll love the prints. A Jake Pendower Exhibition will be a real coup for the gallery.'

'It might drive people away.' He laughed, unsure if she was teasing him.

'We'll have to see ...' Her voice was tinged with amusement. 'So have you decided what pictures to take yet?'

'I've a few ideas ... but nothing definite. I'd better get a move on, hadn't I?' He kept his tone light but inside he was panicking.

'Yes, you had.' She bent down to pick up a paint tin that had been left on the floor. Jake swallowed hard. Those dungarees were just about the sexiest thing he'd ever seen a woman wear.

He joined her, picking up a dust sheet and folding it as Poppy stacked the tin on the stepladder. She stretched her spine and raised her arms in the air to ease her shoulders.

'I'll clear up tomorrow. I'm too knackered now. Do you want to go for a drink?'

Jake smiled. He had to get out of the studio. Feelings he hadn't expected and didn't know how to deal with had emerged out of nowhere. They went beyond physical attraction. He should really say 'no' and get away from the source. 'I'd love to, but I think I'll go out with the camera. The light's perfect at this time of the evening and there could be a great sunset.'

'Oh ... OK.' She didn't seem too disappointed – he didn't know how he felt about that.

On Sunday morning, Jake was up at first light. He dug into a bowl of cereal while musing about the previous evening. He had gone out with his camera after he'd left Poppy, but the sunset wasn't as interesting as he'd made out. He'd wandered around the island until dusk, half-heartedly shooting a few pictures, but none of them had been worth keeping, so he'd deleted them. He was back to square one.

He needed fresh inspiration for the new pictures; the problem was that he didn't want any. And the even bigger problem was that he knew exactly where he might find it *if* he had the courage to look.

He left his half-eaten Cornflakes, got the pliers from under the sink and went upstairs. He hesitated before opening the crate, then thought of Poppy. She'd made a leap of faith in coming to St Piran's to start a new life so soon after Dan had left her. She'd been brave and bold. All Jake had to do was look at a few paintings.

It sounded simple, but it was with slightly unsteady hands that he prised out the tacks in the lid and lifted it off.

He let out a breath as he pulled out the scrunched-up newspaper covering the pictures. Inside were around half a dozen canvases, each protected by bubble wrap and secured with sticky tape. Colours and shapes were all he could make out through the bubbles. The tape didn't look old, so he guessed that Grandpa had packed them fairly recently.

He lifted out the first one and laid it on the bed, before peeling off the tape from the wrap. Instantly, he was transported back into a different life. One where everything was innocent and hopeful, bathed in sunlight, with the future not even thought of. A world where he'd lived for the moment and worried only about finding a starfish on the beach or whether there'd be pizza for dinner.

The painting showed a boy on the beach. It was obviously him, even though it was a back view. He couldn't mistake the shock of dark hair, the Cornish Pirates rugby shirt he always wore and, of course, his Nikon camera. He must have been around nine or ten and he was taking a picture of his favourite view of the rocks at the northern end of St Piran's and the ocean beyond it.

That view took his breath away, both because of its stark beauty and the memories it evoked – now, not then of course, when all he'd cared about was capturing the scene and showing it to his grandpa.

He could almost point to the spot where the yacht had nearly run aground while he was trying to search for Harriet after she'd fallen overboard. The painting brought back the crushing panic that had frozen his mind while he tried to stop the boat and sail round to where she'd been swept into the waves by the boom. He'd wanted to jump in to save her but he had to control the boat first or she'd have no chance.

Why had his grandpa left *this* painting of *this* scene for him, knowing it would churn up the darkest memories from the depths?

He'd never know unless he found the courage to face the past ... unless that was exactly what Archie had wanted him to do?

He pulled out another painting, before he lost his nerve, and started to rip open the tape.

Jake shrugged his camera backpack off his shoulders and winced. His back and arms ached, and he felt completely drained, not simply from the physical effort of carrying heavy kit around all day, but because of the emotional strain of the past two days.

It was Monday evening, and for the last two days, he'd taken hundreds of shots at each of the locations featured in Archie's paintings. He'd checked them all while he was in the field, but he needed to transfer them to his laptop, choose his favourites and start the post-processing before emailing the finished shots to the printer in Truro. He didn't expect to get to bed before the small hours.

His stomach rumbled and his throat was on fire so he filled a pint glass with tap water and knocked the lot back. He hadn't eaten since breakfast and had probably become dehydrated. He'd managed on only a bottle of water and a takeout coffee all day. Once he'd started his mission, he hadn't dared to stop. He'd been afraid to stop taking pictures in case his courage failed him, so he'd ploughed on, covering almost every path and byway of the little island, from its treacherous cliffs to its balmy beaches.

He'd struggled several times when he'd revisited favourite haunts with his camera. The memories of days spent with Archie, with his parents, on his own and with Harriet had almost overwhelmed him at times, but he'd stuck to his task. He would honour his grandpa's legacy with one of his own – a unique testimony to Archie's influence on him as a photographer. He'd never taken pictures that were so personal to him and, at times, it had physically hurt him to lift the lens and point it at the scenes that held so many memories, happy and sad.

He splashed water on his face, shoved a ready meal in the microwave and opened a beer while he waited for it to ping. There was no time to waste. After a hasty supper, he went back upstairs and looked at the paintings he'd laid out in the bedroom again. He wanted to fix the scenes in his mind's eye before he selected the shots he'd taken to replicate his grandpa's scenes. He started to sort through the best images, ready to whittle them down to the final half dozen or so.

The small thumbnails unfolded on the screen like a banner; thousands of them. Jake scrolled down, reliving again the places he'd visited over the weekend.

He stopped every now and then, picking out the most striking pictures from experience and instinct.

There.

There was the spot he'd taken a photo of a seal on the rocks while his grandpa had painted it. There was the beach where he and Harriet had lit a driftwood fire. There was the very hollow at the edge of the dunes where he'd proposed to her ...

He caught his breath, clicking through some of the later shots. There was the place where he'd lost her, just as wild and dangerous and beautiful as in Archie's painting. He heaved a sigh and moved onwards to the very last of the images he'd taken.

His body relaxed a little and he smiled as he lingered over the final photo.

He only hoped Poppy would like the results.

Chapter 16

On Wednesday evening, Poppy was trying to stay calm. The artists were visiting on Friday and although the studio was almost ready, her nerves were getting to her. There were only ten days to go to the launch and the days were racing by. She was very happy to accept an invitation from Kelly to go to the pub that evening, where her partner, Spike, was cooking in the kitchen.

She hadn't seen much of Jake since their talk about the photographs, apart from their paths crossing a couple of times around the harbour area. He'd been laden down with equipment and it was obvious he was on a mission. She didn't like to pressure him, though her curiosity over what he would produce was running wild. It couldn't be easy for him – revisiting places with memories that might be painful – but it was his decision, so she left well alone.

She met Kelly and they sat outside the Moor's Head, admiring the fiery sunset over a drink and a delicious Thai fish curry. It was a cool evening but bright and far too nice to be inside. With a couple of beers inside her, after a day arranging her display units in the newly painted space, Poppy was feeling a little more mellow. Things seemed to be taking shape in her life at last.

'Jake's still here then. I thought he'd be gone by now, but it's been over two weeks since he arrived,' said Kelly.

'Yes. He's been a big help. I think he felt guilty about the state of the studio.'

'Is he definitely staying for the launch, then?'

'Yes. He's been busy taking some photographs of St Piran's especially for it.'

'So I heard. That's a big deal for the studio. He's supposed to be a big fish in landscape photography.'

'I know *now*. I googled him,' said Poppy, thinking of all the prestigious publications she'd discovered where Jake's photos had appeared since she'd taken the time to check him out. She'd had no idea how well known and regarded he was, which made his offer all the more amazing.

'Jake must like you if he's taking pictures *especially* for you.'

'For the studio, not me,' Poppy corrected. She was torn between amusement and dismay that Kelly was implying Jake had taken the photos because he fancied Poppy. 'I think he's trying to help Archie in a roundabout way. He wants the place to be a success for his grandpa's sake as much as mine.'

'Yeah. Yeah ... that must be it. Of course it's *all* for Archie.' Kelly smirked and Poppy could tell she didn't believe a word.

'Another drink?' she said, hoping to change the subject.

Kelly laughed. 'I won't say no ... Oh, you've got me going now. I can't wait to see these new photos.'

'Neither can I,' murmured Poppy as she headed for the bar.

Poppy didn't sleep well that night. It was probably nerves and excitement at the prospect of meeting the artists on Friday and awaiting their verdict on the new gallery – not to mention the launch party coming up fast.

Her slumbers weren't helped by the wind that started blowing hard as she tossed and turned in her bed. She kept meaning to get up and shut the skylight in the shower room in case it rained but she must have fallen asleep because the next thing she knew the first fingers of light were creeping into the flat and she could pick out the shapes of furniture in the predawn.

There was a strange noise too. A dull roar, like the heaviest rain she'd ever heard, and as if someone was running a bath ... a very big bath ...

'What?'

She sat up and threw off the covers as she realised that the sound wasn't the wind or rain but water. Very fast-running water ... *inside* the flat.

Her hand flew to her mouth. The sound was unmistakable. Her heart thumping, she scrambled out of bed and squelched over the rug towards the source of the torrent of noise. Water was streaming from under the shower room door. She pushed it open and a scraggy wet ball of fur shot out past her legs on a mini wave of cold water.

'Oh my God, Leo!'

But Leo was gone, leaping onto the bed and licking his sodden fur from the safety of the pillows. Apart from being soaked, he seemed OK, so Poppy focused on the immediate problem: the metal mains water pipe to the basin was split in two. Water was pumping out of the pipe at mains pressure, spraying the walls and ceiling. It had already blasted off several bottles of shampoo, shower gel and a large polished pebble from the window ledge, which must have chipped the edge of the cistern cover on its way down. The damage to the loo was the least of her worries.

She cursed and gasped as the cold water sprayed her pyjama vest and shorts, soaking them in a few seconds. The floor was a centimetre deep in water, which was flowing merrily along the floorboards and down the stairs in a mini waterfall.

'Oh no. The gallery!'

Swearing loudly, she slithered down the spiral staircase in her bare feet, almost slipping down the last few steps. Her heart was in her mouth. The shower room was directly over the work area so she dreaded what she might find. How long had the pipe been broken? How long had that amount of water – the equivalent to the bath taps turned full on – been pouring out?

To her horror, water had already pooled around the foot of the steps and in puddles on the uneven tiles of the gallery floor. Puddles were joining up and creeping towards the front door of the gallery. Some water had collected at the bases of the freshly decorated boxes and plinths. Luckily, the pieces of art, sculptures and ceramics were all off the floor, so, on first sight, none appeared to be damaged.

She'd never imagined that a domestic pipe could create such a noise or such a mess. Plasterboard and dust had come down from the shower room ceiling and water was running down the walls towards the light switches.

Electricity and water ... *they don't mix.* In her blind panic over what to do first, Poppy at least recalled that much. She stood on a stool in the workroom and managed to remove the cover and turn off the electricity. Then she located the stopcock under the workroom sink and turned it off. The raging torrent stopped, but the sound of water trickling down the walls and stairs continued.

She paddled back into the gallery and looked around her, feeling sicker by the second. As the morning sun rose, the droplets glistened in the light. If you'd sprayed the floor and far end walls of the workspace and gallery with a fire hose, it couldn't have been any wetter. Several of the canvases and materials on the worktable had been affected and two paintings had suffered and she noticed now that water was running down the freshly painted walls at one end of the gallery and over two framed original oils of Archie's.

She splashed over the tiles, trying to assess the damage. Thank God she hadn't stocked the gallery fully.

She stood on tiptoe and unhooked the pictures, getting drenched in the process. The first thing to do was remove the paintings from further harm. They were heavy but she got them down and put them on the worktable. The water was still leaking out of the pipe but in a trickle not the Trevi Fountain.

She sloshed through the puddles, at a loss as what to mop

up first. A sob bubbled up at the back of her throat as she contemplated the sodden wreck of her new gallery. She'd thought she was doing OK, making a new life and friends for herself, getting the place into shape again, finding suppliers ... and the launch party was only a few days away.

She couldn't pick up the phone to her parents or Zoey and her friends back home. Maybe Dan had been right. It was too big a job for her. For the second time since she'd arrived, she felt like packing her bags and heading home.

Leo brushed against her legs and stared up at her. He probably only wanted his breakfast but Poppy reached down and stroked his ears.

With a meow, he slipped by her towards the door.

Poppy looked around her and thought of Dan's words again, his incredulous face. She couldn't go back and see him with Eve, gloating and cooing over The Bump.

'Sod it! I won't give in,' she said, her voice sounding small in the gallery space. She picked up the mop and slapped it onto the tiles. One thing was certain: there was no way she was going to bother anyone else at five o'clock in the morning. She was going to have to deal with this crisis on her own.

Three hours later, Jake walked into the studio to find her still mopping the floor. He gasped. 'On my God. What's happened?'

'The pipe in the shower room broke,' she said, deciding not to mention that Leo might have had a paw in the disaster, even accidentally.

She was shattered and damp. She'd swept some of the water out of the front door and had lost count of how many times she'd mopped up the water and emptied the bucket, but she had no other means of soaking it up. The gallery floor was now relatively dry and she'd opened all the windows, but the humid air wasn't making it easy.

He shook his head. 'When did it start?'

'In the early hours, I think. The noise of the water woke me up around dawn.'

'And you've been clearing up ever since? Why didn't you call me?'

'At half past five in the morning? There's no way I was going to bother you or Fen at that time.'

He groaned. 'I wouldn't have minded.'

But she would, thought Poppy and didn't add that she would have to manage this kind of problem without him soon enough. Still, it was a relief to have someone else there to help.

'What can I do?' he asked.

She was glad to have an excuse to stop mopping; her arms were already aching. 'Well, I've called Kelly and she's on her way with the plumber to sort the electrics and pipe. For now, it's mainly a mopping-up operation. You can see the damage to the walls and the bottom of some of the plinths ... then there's the flat. I haven't even started up there.'

She stopped for a breath. Jake's arrival had given her a brief respite but also made her realise how tired, wet and cold she was. Until now, pure adrenaline had compelled her to keep on working but the enormity of the damage and clear-up was beginning to dawn on her. She hadn't had time to think about breakfast or even a drink and the lack of food was making her feel light-headed.

He looked around him, shaking his head. 'What a bloody mess.'

'You should have seen it earlier.'

'I wish I had. Can't be helped, so what can I do now?'

She stuck the mop in the bucket and rested on the handle. 'Do you know what I'd really like?'

He frowned. 'What?'

'A huge flat white and a massive bacon sandwich. No, make that two of both those things. Dripping in brown sauce.'

He smiled. 'I can definitely help with that. Come over to the cottage and we'll draw up a battle plan over breakfast.'

After changing into some dry clothes and devouring a huge bacon butty and a pot of coffee at the cottage, Poppy went back to the studio with Jake. Kelly and her plumber friend arrived shortly afterwards and set to work on checking the electrics and repairing the pipework. A substantial chunk of ceiling would need replacing and some walls would need replastering, all taking time and more cost.

'I'll contact the studio insurer,' said Jake, joining her in surveying the damage. 'But pay for the repairs in the meantime because you don't want to wait while they mess about and hold back the cash.'

'Thanks. That's would be a big help because I can't afford to wait for a claim to be settled. I need to get the place open.' A new and unwelcome thought dawned on her. 'The artists are supposed to be coming around tomorrow. I'll need to contact them all to tell them the meetings are postponed. It'll be days before the place is dried out and ready again.'

A few minutes later, she was carrying a damp rug downstairs when Minty walked into the studio. Poppy swore under her breath.

'Wow. What happened here?'

Jake trotted down the stairs. 'A burst pipe,' he said brusquely.

Poppy hurried over to Minty to prevent her coming further inside. 'And we're sorting it out. There are workmen in here, so I'm afraid you can't come in. I was about to call and explain.'

'I saw the mess outside and guessed you might be trying to sort the place out before my visit tomorrow. Actually, I had been hoping you could have seen me earlier. I'm giving an interview to an art magazine later. It's called *Green Eye*. You must know it.'

Poppy had heard of it but didn't want to give Minty the satisfaction of saying as much so she avoided any answer. '*Actually*, the gallery was more than ready for visitors until we had this water leak ... and obviously I can't show you around now, so could we reschedule?'

Minty craned her neck for a better look at the water-stained walls and wet plinths and carpet. She wrinkled her nose. 'For when? Next year?'

'It's not that bad.' Jake's patience was clearly wearing thin.

'We're hoping to be up and running again in a day or so and the launch is still scheduled for next Saturday. So, if you don't mind,' said Poppy, virtually herding Minty off the premises. 'I'll be in touch later today and we can reschedule your visit.'

Minty smirked. 'OK. I have to admire your optimism.'

'It's nowhere near as bad as it looks and we'll be ready for the launch as planned,' Poppy said firmly.

Minty stalked off, leaving Poppy taking a deep breath to calm down before getting on her mobile to phone the other artists who were supposed to visit.

All the windows of the flat were wide open. Luckily it was now a fine breezy May morning and the boards and floors were drying out. The shower room and kitchen vinyl tiles were a write-off though and the hardboard base had been ripped up. Laying new vinyl would be another job for Kelly, but anything in the flat could wait. The gallery was the priority.

After Poppy had made her calls, Fen arrived to help clear up, and Maisie phoned to offer the services of GIT to help repair the ceiling the next day.

Jake joined Poppy as she put down the phone to Maisie.

'At this rate, I'll owe every business on the islands a website or a marketing brochure,' said Poppy. 'I had no idea my writing skills would be in such demand though I'm not sure when I'm going to fit it all in, what with trying to get the gallery back up and running after this disaster.'

'There's plenty of time for that over the off-season,' said Jake. 'It could have been worse.'

She had to smile, even though it was gallows humour. 'How?'

'The flood might have happened the night before the launch.'

'True.' She looked around her, starting to see that they were making headway on the clear-up. Banging and hammering from below was a positive sign that repairs were underway.

Jake spooned coffee into two mugs and added hot water.

He handed her a mug. 'Drink up. I'll take some downstairs to Fen and the builders in a minute.'

Poppy accepted the drink and felt a rush of gratitude, not only for Jake but towards all the islanders. *Almost* all of them. Trust Minty to turn up at the wrong moment. By now, word of the flood must have spread around the whole island, and possibly beyond. She'd have to work doubly hard to rebuild the artists' confidence that the Starfish would be shipshape by launch day.

'Do you want me to lend a hand downstairs or help you sort out the flat?' he asked.

'I think we'd better concentrate on the gallery,' said Poppy. 'Thanks for your help. *Again*.'

'No problem. Technically, it's our fault – mine and Grandpa's. The pipework must have been working loose for ages.'

They heard a rattle from the shower room.

Jake turned his head. 'What was that?'

'The wind?' said Poppy uncertainly. 'I'd better take a look.'

She put down her mug as Leo sauntered out of the shower room door, like a mini ginger panther, and jumped nonchalantly onto the sofa.

Jake frowned at the cat. 'How did he get in?'

'Through the skylight in the shower room ...' She groaned as realisation dawned. 'In fact, I think Leo might have had something to do with the pipe. I found *this* lying on the floor next to it after I'd turned off the stopcock.' She held up the polished stone that had once rested on the shelf above the loo. 'I left the skylight open after I'd had a shower and he must have knocked it over when he climbed in during the night. It could well have dropped onto the pipe and broken the connection. It was just an unfortunate set of circumstances.'

'With Leo at the heart of it all. What a surprise.' He glared at Leo, who narrowed his eyes at Jake as if to say: 'Deal with it, human.'

Poppy stifled a giggle.

'What's so funny?' Jake said, giving Leo the evil eye.

'Not much, but you and Leo *are* hilarious. You've no chance against him, you know.'

'I've worked that out already. That cat is the Dr Evil of felines.'

She laughed again, the tension of the past few hours easing. 'And I do appreciate your help, Jake,' she said, seizing her moment. 'I'm in no position to refuse it, but I don't want you to feel obliged to stick around and give up your free time working on this place.'

'What if I don't mind helping?' he said after a pause.

She didn't know what to say. 'Thanks, but I'd hate to get used to it.'

He looked at her, then out of the window. 'I understand.'

'Don't be offended. It's not personal,' she said, her toes curling with awkwardness. 'Only I've had to manage without Dan – not that he was much use around the house. I mean, I've learned – am learning – to do without relying on someone else.'

'This is friendship,' said Jake. 'Nothing more, nothing less.'

She winced. This conversation was excruciating, and she didn't have any way of expressing how she felt without sounding harsh or ungrateful. 'I appreciate your friendship. I enjoy it ... and when you're gone I'll *miss* it.'

'Me too.' His answer was barely audible. 'And don't worry, I intend to stay at least for the launch.'

'St Piran's isn't so bad after all, then?' she said.

'It's growing on me. By the minute.' Even before he'd finished speaking, he reached for Poppy and pulled her into his arms. It felt completely natural to do the same and she held his waist as their mouths met. The kiss – oh, the kiss – was perfect. It was warm and firm but tender too ... She closed her eyes, wanting it to go on and on and on. But ...

'I'm sorry. That shouldn't have happened.'

She opened her eyes to find Jake standing a foot away, hands shoved in his pockets as if he was afraid of catching something.

'I don't know what came over me. Can we forget it?'

Poppy felt like someone had turned on the cold water again and aimed it right at her. A moment ago, they'd been so lost in each other. That kiss had felt exactly the right thing to do, but Jake was on his way to the door now. 'It's no big deal. Jake ... wait.'

'No. I have to get home,' he called as he trotted towards the stairs. 'I need to email the photos to the printer or they won't be ready in time for your launch. I hope we can still be friends.'

'Of course we can.'

She heard him race down the stairs and watched him stride away from the studio as if the devil was after him.

'Argh.' Poppy sat down on the sofa, stunned by the switchback turn of events. That kiss … wow. She brushed her fingers over her lips, still feeling the imprint of Jake's gorgeous mouth on her own. Still tingling with the unexpected thrill of it … But the way he'd scooted off, she was damn sure that he'd felt exactly the opposite.

Chapter 17

As soon as she woke on Saturday morning, Poppy began reflecting back on the events of the previous two days. The artists were set to arrive later for their rescheduled meetings but her thoughts were once again on that kiss.

'Can we forget it?' Jake had said afterwards.

She'd found that almost impossible to do. She'd kept replaying the delicious part in her mind and then cringing as she heard Jake's horrified apology. What would have happened if they'd taken things further? Why had he kissed her at all, if he didn't want things to move beyond friendship? And what happened next? He'd implied he was staying on at least until the launch, which implied afterwards as well. She'd always known he'd be gone one day, but his comment had given her hope – hope she should never even have allowed to creep into her mind.

Fortunately, she hadn't been alone with Jake too much since the awkward moment. Kelly and a small army of helpers joined her, Jake and Fen to help dry out the studio, make the repairs and repaint the stained walls and damaged plinths. Once things were tidy again, he left once more, citing 'work.'

She was also relieved she'd ordered in a few items of stock from mainland artists, which arrived safely by the freight boat. At least she had some items to display before they arrived. However, the launch was only one week away and if she didn't persuade them to exhibit today, she'd have a half-empty shop. Word was getting round about the launch too. People were peering through the windows, ads and features had appeared in the island e-newsletters and it had been mentioned on the radio. There was no going back.

Due to the flood, she'd been up until one the previous evening, rearranging the few pieces she had. She'd also checked that the skylight was closed – not that Leo was likely to strike twice – and had finally fallen into bed, physically knackered but with a mind whirling like a Waltzer.

How could she be so nervous when she'd done way more scary things at work? Like launching a new green roof system to two hundred sceptical builders at a big exhibition ... and the time she'd been roped in to demonstrate the suction power of a new shower drain by donning a wetsuit and shower cap at the company conference.

Meeting a few artists ought to be a doddle – even if one of them was Minty.

After nibbling at a piece of toast, she got dressed. She took a few deep breaths as she glanced in the mirror. Her unruly brown hair was pinned on top of her head in an updo and she'd changed into the stripy T-shirt dress she'd loved but Dan said made her look like a French onion seller. She teamed it with the purple suede pixie boots that reminded him of 'a nineteen eighties throwback', and almost considered taking a selfie and emailing it to the git.

She was surprised to find her pale cheeks tinged with pink and a few freckles dotting her nose. The dress was less snug than it had been too, and the weight loss must be a result of all the work she'd been putting in to the studio. Pride stopped her from sending Dan the photo, but the thought of pissing him off made her smile anyway.

She could do this. She *was* moving on. If only she didn't think about him and The Temptress *quite* so often. Or what would annoy them or make Dan so full of remorse and regret that he'd jump on the first plane to St Piran's and beg her to take him back.

Which she would rather *die* than ever do, naturally.

She swore and forced herself to focus on the battle to come: charming the artisan sandals off her stable of artists. Fen had hinted she could hang around in the gallery for moral support if required, but Poppy had politely hinted back that this was something else that she needed to do alone. Fen had seemed relieved and gone off on the ferry to see her friends in St Mary's. Poppy didn't know what Jake was doing and reminded herself again that she really shouldn't care, especially after their disastrous (in his eyes) 'encounter'.

Sometime after ten, Rowan sauntered in and handed over a crisp box containing his latest work wrapped in his granny's old copies of *People's Friend*. Nestled among the heart-warming stories and recipes for sponge puddings were beautiful bowls and objects. His work was inspired by waves and had a voluptuous quality that made you want to look and handle it. Poppy selected her favourite pieces and hoped he wouldn't be offended that she hadn't chosen a couple of the more 'experimental' items, which reminded her far too much of a willy and a vagina. Rowan was laid-back about agreeing on a 'wall price' for his work, cool with the commission and was soon heading off to go paddleboarding with his friend at a nearby beach.

Half a dozen other artists drifted in during the rest of morning and early afternoon with samples of their prints, ceramics, glass, wood and textiles. Poppy had stocked up on herbal teas, primed by Fen, and offered homemade biscuits. It was a two-way process. They were here to judge Poppy and the studio and vice versa.

To her relief, everyone seemed to be impressed enough to allow their work to go on display in the renovated space, at least for a trial period. There were some robust discussions about wall prices, especially with one watercolour painter who Fen had warned 'tended to let his ego price his work'. He left, having reduced his prices by around twenty per cent. Poppy thought the paintings were still overpriced, but she'd done her best. She had a reasonable idea of whose work sold pretty well, but no one could predict exactly what the public would actually buy from the new gallery. You just never knew for sure.

The glass artist, Kay Baverstock, caught Poppy by surprise by arriving twenty minutes early. She was short, round and excitable and could have been any age from forty to sixty. She darted around the studio, peering and sniffing at the display plinths like a beagle puppy let off the lead for the first time. She stopped at an empty cube unit and said, 'This one, please,' before placing a beautiful glass bowl on it. Poppy was surprised Kay hadn't also cocked her leg to mark her territory.

The bowl *did* look amazing in the afternoon sun. The light shining through the window splintered the colours – blue, sea green and purple – into coloured shards. Poppy resolved to keep it in that exact spot and listened carefully to Kay's other observations on displaying work in the gallery, even though she hadn't asked for it. After terms had been agreed, and Poppy had asked if she could stock more of Kay's work, Kay stayed for chamomile tea and biscuits, chattering about her work and gossiping about the other artists.

'You're not having anything by Minty Cavendish in here, are you? Cannot stand the woman. Ego the size of Canada and her work is far too twee for my tastes. All those bloody clanking charm bracelets and silver limpet shells dangling down her cleavage. It's so ... predictable. I really have *no* idea how she sells so well.'

'I'm not sure,' said Poppy truthfully. 'Minty hasn't even been to the studio yet.'

'Well, if you do have to show her work, keep it as far away from mine as possible.'

Poppy was getting desperate when Kay was still drinking tea at three-fifty, but fortunately her mobile rang and her daughter asked her to head back to her house pronto to look after her toddler while she took the family guinea pig to the part-time vet on St Mary's.

Kay bustled off, her imaginary tail wagging furiously, and Poppy prayed she wouldn't pass Minty on the way.

Poppy cleared away the mugs and checked the display case she'd prepared for the umpteenth time. She was annoyed with herself for caring so much what Minty thought. One artist's work in the gallery couldn't make that much difference; it wasn't as if people would flock from miles around to buy Minty's jewellery, but it would help to have her work on the postcards for the gallery and the website. Especially when the Starfish Studio online site was up and running ... which was another task to add to her ever-growing list.

Jewellery was a small, high-value item, easy to slip into luggage and popular as a gift with visitors of all ages and sexes. And Minty really was a very talented and skilled silversmith. You could tell she genuinely drew inspiration from her surroundings and she had the local connection that chimed perfectly with the Starfish philosophy.

Instead of being early, Minty must have decided to be fifteen minutes late. Poppy had rearranged the jewellery display again and again, then thought 'sod it'.

'Why am I even wasting my time?' she muttered and shut the cabinet door so hard it rattled.

'Bad timing?' Minty strolled in just as Poppy was repositioning a postcard under the cabinet to level it on the uneven tiles. 'Shall I come back later?'

'I was making some minor adjustments,' said Poppy, straightening up. She smiled and said, 'Thanks for coming,' in her most welcoming gallery owner voice. She would *not* let Minty rattle her.

Minty wandered into the centre of the studio, peering at the walls and plinths. She lifted up Kay's bowl, wrinkled her nose and put it back quickly, as if she'd accidentally picked up one of Leo's poos.

'So, this is it, is it?' she said. 'I must admit I never thought you'd get it ready in time after that disaster with the burst pipes. I heard half the plumbing had to be replaced. Studio finally crumbling to bits, is it?'

Poppy had to remind herself to breathe rather than snarl. Now she knew how the *Bake Off* contestants felt when the judges gave their verdicts on the Showstoppers. Except Poppy's butterflies in the stomach weren't so much fluttering as beating their wings angrily as Minty wandered around the studio, trailing her hand over the new plinths and peering at the walls, like a sergeant major inspecting a barracks.

'Hmm. It's much better than it was,' said Minty, then sniffed the air. 'Even with the *eau de* Dulux.'

Poppy covered her fury with a smile. 'We think it's a fresh and airy space for any artist's work.'

Minty arched an eyebrow and her stud glinted in the sunlight. '*We*?' she said.

'Me. And Fen of course,' she qualified. 'Jake's also emailed Archie some photos and he approves, which is important to me.'

Minty smirked. 'I can see you've tried very hard and I'll admit it looks miles better on the surface, even if underneath things seem ready to collapse. Out of sentimental reasons for Archie and because I like supporting new galleries, I'd be happy to try out a few pieces to see how we go.' She picked up a postcard and frowned at it. 'The commission is thirty per cent, I believe.'

'Actually, it's forty,' said Poppy.

Minty winced again. 'Ouch, that's high for a gallery with no recent record of success.'

'I think you'll find it's on the low side compared to the going rate. Archie's a lovely man, but even Fen agrees he was undercharging. I've put in a lot of time and investment which should – *will* – result in more sales and make this a sustainable business.'

'Hmm.'

This was like being on *Dragon's Den*, thought Poppy, expecting Minty to say 'I'm out' at any moment and not being quite sure whether she'd weep or cheer if she did. Then she remembered the sales figures for the studio and the percentage of them that had been Minty's jewellery. She couldn't afford to throw that away over a personality clash, even if she did feel like telling Minty where to shove her sea glass.

'It's your decision of course,' she said politely, determined to show that while a jewellery maker of repute was important to the Starfish, she ran the gallery, not Minty.

'Oh, go on, then. As a special favour to the Pendowers.' Minty rolled her eyes. 'Though I'm way too soft. My fans are always saying I should move to London and make squillions, but my muse is here on the isles and it's my public duty to help keep the economy afloat.'

'Thanks. I appreciate it.' Poppy ground the words out.

'I'll bring over some stock when I have time,' she said, jingling her bracelets loudly. They were beautiful, thought

Poppy, and the silver and sea glass stacking rings on Minty's right ring finger were to die for. She'd love to have them herself, but she mustn't start buying her own stock.

'Great.' Smiling through gritted teeth, Poppy held out her hand and Minty shook it quickly, possibly in case she caught a disease.

Poppy expected her to leave and, when she lingered, wondered if she should offer the herbal tea. She really didn't want to string this visit out any more ...

Minty's attention was drawn by something hanging off the back of the sales desk chair. It was Jake's faded blue hoodie, which he'd left behind.

Minty's eyes flicked from the hoodie to Poppy and she toyed with a card on the desk. 'How's Jake been? You've been working closely with him over the past couple of weeks. What do you think about his state of mind?'

Poppy thought of Jake. He was sad sometimes, but otherwise he seemed OK, apart of course, from the kiss and its cringeworthy aftermath. She caught Minty observing her closely as if she was a specimen.

'He seems fine ...' she said.

'Yes, obviously, he *seems* fine, but do you think he's getting over Harriet?'

'I've no idea. I've only known him a few weeks and we don't have that kind of relationship. It's purely professional,' Poppy said firmly, even though it was a lie. She felt no obligation to tell the truth to Minty. Besides, her relationship with Jake *was* professional, since he'd begged her to forget the whole thing with the kiss.

Minty smiled. 'Very loyal of you. But I can tell that he likes you. He makes very quick judgements, you know. He's already hung around longer than I'd expected.' Minty laughed. 'I've been wondering whether to tell you this but ...'

Poppy braced herself. Oh God, here we go ...

'I thought I'd give you a friendly hint not to get too involved with Jake. He has a habit of bolting when women get too close or it all gets emotional. You might as well know that, a few years ago, Jake was here during the holidays between his assignments and we got close ... and he was scared of the strength of his feelings and he left St Piran's. And I hear you've already had enough of that kind of thing – men bolting – with your ex.'

Bolting? Poppy almost gasped. With an image of Jake galloping out of the studio, snorting like a Grand National winner, in her mind, Poppy snapped. She was growing used to dealing with island gossip, but Minty had crossed the line. Worse, she'd touched a raw nerve: Jake had run away after their kiss, almost as if he'd found it too much to cope with.

'I'm sure he's changed since then,' said Poppy, sounding far more confident than she felt. 'He was engaged to Harriet after all and from what I've heard – not that I listen to gossip – he seemed to worship her.'

'Yes, but everyone was a-*mazed* when he said they were getting married.'

Oh really, *everyone*, thought Poppy, or just Minty?

'Jake had only known her a few months. Met her while she was running an exhibition and, in a flash, they were engaged. When he brought her here, they were planning the wedding. Poor boy did seem devastated when she died, but look at the excuse it gave him. He hasn't looked at another woman since, as far as we *know*. Of course, he might have been up to anything while he's been travelling around the world.'

'Like I say, it's nothing to do with me. So …' Poppy gritted her teeth. '*Will* you be coming to the Starfish launch day?'

'I'll have to check my schedule, but I'll do my best.' Minty paused. 'Is Jake planning on sticking around until then or will he be off on his wild adventures?' She winked.

'He's said he'll be here, but I don't have access to his diary so I can't say for certain.'

'Oh well, we'll all know soon enough.' Minty laughed. 'Oh, and by the way, has he shown you any of the photographs he intends exhibiting yet? I'm looking forward to seeing what he comes up with. If he actually keeps his promise.'

'Not yet.' Poppy had been thinking the same thing herself. Jake hadn't mentioned the subject again and she hadn't liked to mention it in case he'd had second thoughts – not that she was going to let Minty know that. 'And I know he won't let me down.'

'Good for you.' A sly smile crept onto her lips. 'Oh well. See you next weekend and good luck. With everything.'

Poppy shut the door behind her. It was proving much harder than she'd envisaged not to get too involved with *any* of St Piran's characters although there were some she wished she didn't have to be involved with at all.

Chapter 18

'*Hello-ooo …*'

Poppy sounded tentative calling from the bottom of the cottage stairs. Jake steeled himself to meet her. He'd been so wrapped up in his thoughts that he hadn't even heard the door open.

'OK. Just on my way.'

He thudded down the treads to find her in the hallway.

'Hope it was OK to walk in? Didn't disturb you, did I?' she said. He cringed at how hesitant she sounded. That was his fault, of course, rushing off after he'd kissed her. He regretted doing that so much: not because that kiss hadn't been hot and wonderful … but because he should never have done it in the first place.. Neither of them was in the right place to start a new relationship. Poppy was obviously still on the rebound from Dan, and Jake himself had no plans to stick around on St Piran's long-term. At least, that's what he kept reminding himself every time he was tempted to kiss her again. God, she even looked gorgeous now: slightly flushed and with her hair falling out of its clip.

'I was in the bathroom.'

She laughed. Her eyes sparkled, but then she nibbled at her lower lip hesitantly. 'I don't like disturbing you when you've already done such a lot, but I came to tell you that the artists' day has gone well. I have stock on its way from Kay, Rowan and even Minty.'

'That's great. I'm really pleased for you.' Jake hoped Poppy would hear the genuine delight he felt at the good news.

'I wanted to ask about the photos ... It really doesn't matter if you haven't had time or would rather not. You don't have to actually provide any. Seeing Minty's face when you told her was enough. She's agreed to show her jewellery, though she drives a hard bargain.'

'She certainly does, but you sound as if you've got the measure of her.' He smiled, hoping, possibly, he and Poppy could put the kiss behind them and move on.

'Hmm.' She glanced around her.

Jake's optimism sank a little and he wondered if Poppy wasn't giving him the full story. What had Minty been telling her? Not that there was anything he needed to be ashamed of, but who knew how Minty had painted things. Arghh ...

'I should probably tell you that Minty and I went out for a while,' he said quickly.

'Hmm. She said as much.' Was Jake imagining it or had Poppy's tone hardened a little?

'It was only for a few weeks when I was here visiting Grandpa in between assignments. It was before I met Harriet.'

She shrugged. 'It's none of my business. You don't have to explain anything.'

'But I wanted to. I think it's best you know because what happened between me and Minty might affect your working relationship with her.'

'Maybe ... but you'll be gone soon and I'm sure things will settle down. I guessed Minty felt disappointed or – or something. It's really nothing to do with me and I can handle her. Anyway, I didn't come to talk about her specifically. What I really came to say was that things went well with the other artists.'

'That's good ... I thought it would be OK though. You've done a great job with the studio.'

'We all have. It was a team effort.'

'Yes. It was.'

'I don't want to push you or pressure you ...' she said.

Jake flinched. Was she going to mention the kiss?

'But do you need any help with the photographs? I haven't wanted to interfere, but I was checking if they'd still be ready for the launch and you weren't having any ... problems.'

Jake suddenly hated himself. Her expression and tone were hopeful but wary, as if she expected him to back out of the deal, to *disappoint* her. He knew what Poppy was hinting at: had he got cold feet and changed his mind, like he had when he'd reached for her and kissed her? He could not – and would not – let her down. Dan had done that and Jake wasn't going to.

'Everything's fine. I've chosen the pictures I want and they're being printed. The canvases should be here in good time for the launch party. I'm sorry I haven't said that much about them but I needed some time and space to work out the shots I wanted.'

'OK. I'm glad things are going well – with the pictures, I mean – and I'll try not to bother you again until the launch. '

'No. It's fine. I have time to help while I wait for the prints. I'm happy to help.'

'Thanks. I'd better leave you to get on with your work now.' She sounded cheerful enough and walked out of the cottage with a smile, but Jake sensed that the previous friendly, relaxed tone of their relationship had changed. All because of that damn kiss.

Chapter 19

'Wow, this is ... cosy.'

'You should have seen it when I moved in,' said Poppy as her friend dumped her bag on the sofa and stuck her hands on her hips. It was the morning before the launch and Zoey had arrived on the early helicopter flight. Poppy had been up late putting the finishing touches to the flat to make it welcoming.

'I wish I had a spare room and an en suite for you, but at least you have a great view. Come and look.'

'I'll be fine,' said Zoey, crossing to the window and letting out a loud 'wow'. 'And I agree about the view. It's amazing.' She turned back to the flat. 'Where are your mum and dad? I thought they were arriving for the launch tomorrow?'

'Mum and Dad got the ferry this morning, but they're on Gull Island. They got a special deal at the Hell Cove B&B.'

'*Hell* Cove?' Zoey wrinkled her nose. 'And is it?'

Poppy laughed. 'Not been yet, but Jake says GIT have recently restored the B&B and the cottages there.'

Zoey stared at her. 'GIT?'

'The Gull Island Trust. They're a collective of local people who help restore each other's properties. Everyone joins in. They even repaired my roof in return for a website.'

Zoey shook her head. 'Bloody hell. You've settled in fast. Helping the neighbours, joining a collective. Then there's Jake. He sounds like he has potential ... and it's nearly been two months now since Dan and you split. You should grab the chance while you can. The guy collecting tickets on the ferry said only two thousand people live across all the islands. Jesus, that's less than at our insurance HQ.' Zoey pulled a face.

'Just as well I'm not looking and, besides, it's way too soon after Dan, and anyway, Jake's the last person I'd want to be involved with even if he was staying.' Poppy tried to sound breezy to put her friend off the scent.

Zoey raised an eyebrow. 'Really? Why?'

'His fiancée died in a yacht accident a few years ago and he's not over it. I think any time would be too soon for Jake. I'm not sure he'll ever be ready to get involved with someone else, and even if he was, it wouldn't be me.' Poppy hesitated, wondering whether to tell Zoey about the kiss and Jake's strange behaviour afterwards. Over the past week, he'd popped in to help with a few jobs, alongside Fen and Kelly, but he'd also been absent a lot too, presumably dealing with the prints for the launch and his other work.

'Why not? If you like him – well, you don't owe Dan anything.'

'I know that, Zoey. Sorry, hun, I didn't mean to sound sharp.'

'OK, so you and Jake. It doesn't have to be a big romance. You could just ... sleep with him or whatever?'

'Zoey!' Poppy picked up a cushion and threw it at her friend, who caught it and held it up for mock protection. Then she sighed. 'It's not that simple. Jake is gorgeous, but he's also – technically – a business acquaintance and he's leaving soon.'

'Exactly why you should sleep with him *now*. There isn't time for things to get complicated.'

'Not with me, maybe, but he's carrying so much baggage already, it's really not a great idea. Zoey, can we drop this for a bit, please?'

Zoey looked puzzled. 'If you say so, but I'll check him out over the weekend and give you my opinion.' She held out her arms. 'I've missed you. Big hug?'

Poppy hugged her, a lump forming in her throat. Now Zoey was here at the heart of her new environment, she felt disoriented, almost as if she'd dreamt the past few weeks. 'I tell you what, I think I'd like a large glass of wine. Shall we go to the pub? I'll introduce you to Kelly and a few of the other locals.'

Zoe gasped. 'There's a *pub*?'

Poppy picked up a cushion and threw it at her. 'It's not the end of the world, you know.'

Zoey glanced out of the window. 'No, it only feels like it ...' She leaned forward and peered outside again before letting out a breath. 'Wow. That's something you don't see on Broad Street on a Saturday night. Or any night. Or day.'

'What are you on about?' said Poppy, crossing to the window.

Zoey pointed at Jake who was walking away from the harbour, with a large cardboard container in his arms. 'That. Him. The guy with the big package.' She smirked. 'Could it possibly be ... the gorgeous Jake who you're not the slightest bit interested in?'

Pulling a face, Poppy sneaked a look. Zoey was right. It was a *very* big package. Jake was almost swamped by the cardboard box, which he had to put down on the cobbles for a second and then pick up again. It looked more awkward than heavy. She watched as he headed for the studio, excitement making her pulse rise. He must have the photos in that box. She really hoped he had ...

'Is he coming *in*?' Zoey said in a stage whisper. Poppy hoped not – she didn't want to face Jake with Zoey watching and probably analysing every move.

He stopped outside the veranda, rested the box on the cobbles and glanced at the windows.

'Get down!' Poppy ducked and pulled Zoey's arm.

'Why the secrecy?' said Zoey, rubbing her elbow as they crouched under the window.

'I don't want him to know we've been spying on him.'

'Wow. He must be special.

'Ssh. Stay out of sight.' Poppy batted her on the arm and poked her head above the sill. She needn't have worried about being spotted. Jake had picked up his box and was now heading towards Archie's cottage. If the photos *were* in that package, as she suspected, it looked like she was going to have to wait a while longer.

He arrived later that evening while Zoey was in the shower.

'I've brought the pictures,' he said. 'Do you want a sneak preview or are you willing to trust me?'

When it came to the photographs, Poppy *did* trust him, but she was still wary of getting too close to him, physically or emotionally.

'I know they'll be amazing,' she said.

'Amazing? You have more faith in me than I deserve.' He moved quickly on. 'I thought I'd hang them on the wall and I've brought a screen to cover them until the big reveal. Is that OK?'

'It's fine. I think that the secrecy will add an air of mystery,' she said. 'People love a surprise.'

'I hope so ... Poppy?'

'Yes?'

'The other day. Last week. It was lovely. I enjoyed it. It was ... well, wow, but I just don't think that either of us is ready to start anything.'

'Don't,' she said, already on the edge of tears, with the emotion of the launch. 'Don't say any more. You're right, of course. It's a terrible idea, so can we forget the whole thing for now? I don't want anything to spoil tomorrow.'

'Of course. I'll go and set these pictures up. If you can promise me one thing? Don't look until tomorrow?'

'I can promise you that much,' said Poppy.

He smiled and left her digging her nails into her palm. Until he'd actually spoken about the kiss, she'd managed to convince herself it wasn't a big deal. Now, she knew it was.

Chapter 20

Poppy and Zoey were up bright and early on the big day. Her parents arrived on the first ferry, followed by Fen, and then there was mayhem. Zoey dropped a bottle of wine on the tiles and it had to be mopped up and Poppy couldn't find the notes she'd prepared for her speech and written on the back of an envelope and had to jot down the bullet points from memory.

Her parents and Fen seemed to have made enough nibbles and cakes to feed an army and were laying it all out on tables in the work area. But Poppy's mind wasn't on the food.

Jake's photographs were hidden behind a portable presentation screen used to show slide evenings at the local community hall. After he'd left the previous evening, she and Zoey had gone to the pub, but Poppy didn't feel able to share the intimate details of her conversation with Jake. She wished he hadn't even spoken to her about the kiss ... She'd rather they'd never mentioned it again, and as for saying she wasn't ready to start a new relationship so soon, she'd been angry and hurt initially, but then thought perhaps he had a point. And even if *she* was ready, he clearly wasn't. She definitely didn't need a guy around her who didn't know what he wanted, no matter how much she fancied him.

Can you trust me? His words rang in her ears.

Yes – and not quite – she thought, looking at the blank screen, wondering what lay behind it and how they'd both feel by the end of today.

'So, please raise your glasses to Poppy, our lovely daughter and the proud new proprietor of the Starfish Studio.'

Poppy blushed as her dad lifted his glass into the air to loud cheers that echoed off the walls of the studio. There was clapping and a resounding cry of 'To Poppy!' then everyone cheered ... *Almost* everyone, because she spotted Minty at the back, limply raising her glass about a centimetre and miming applause with one hand. She didn't care. Today was going even better than her wildest dreams. Just about everyone she'd ever met on Scilly – and many who she hadn't – had dropped by to wish her well at some point since the studio had opened for business at eleven a.m. With her family and best friend by her side, she couldn't have asked for anything more.

She was sure they were breaking some kind of overcrowding rule and had no idea how none of the pieces had been damaged yet, with so many excited people milling around and necking Prosecco, but so far everything was going well. Fen, Maisie, Patrick, Hugo, Adam, Jess, Kelly, Ben and Lisa from the kiosk – the list of islanders went on and on, their ranks swollen by curious visitors and many of the artists whose work she was showing. Even Leo was keeping a watchful eye from halfway up the spiral staircase and had been on his best behaviour. The signs of his last escapade had now well and truly disappeared.

Jake was there too, of course, standing quietly at the end of the studio, with an encouraging smile on his face.

'Congratulations,' he mouthed, then joined in with the whistles and cheering. His eyes were bright and expressive; he looked happy – not to mention heart-stoppingly gorgeous in a white casual shirt worn loose over charcoal jeans. His black hair was tousled because he didn't care how he looked and had no awareness that, actually, he was so sexy, she was having trouble framing her words. It was a shame he'd backed off from her just as things were getting promising.

Oh, shit, this was not what she wanted when she was about to give her big speech on the most important day of her life.

Faces looked at her expectantly, waiting for her to speak. She'd made speeches before in presentations and press conferences, but this was different. While she'd cared about doing a good job, today was about her dreams. It was personal in a way that no job had ever been.

She tore her eyes from his before replying to the toast.

'Well, thank you, Dad, for embarrassing me horribly,' she began.

Everyone laughed.

'And thank you so much, everyone, for coming, and to everyone who's helped me get the Starfish open – twice in fact.'

More laughter from those who knew she was referring to the flood.

'Some of you know that it was a massive leap of faith to come out here to the middle of nowhere...' she smiled and many nodded in agreement '... to this stunning and amazing place in the middle of nowhere. Some of you know that I never intended to come here on my own, but I'm so glad I have.'

She fought against the scratchy itch at the back of her eyes and the thick lump in her throat.

'The support and kindness I've been shown – even though I was a newcomer with a funny accent ...'

More laughter.

'... has been incredible. So, thank you and especially to Fen and Jake. But the Starfish isn't about me at all. It's about all the fantastic artists and makers who have agreed to put their faith in the studio and share their work.'

Minty was positively puffing up at the rear of the studio until Kay Baverstock, keeping as far away from her rival as possible, shouted, 'Hear, hear!'

After more applause for the artists, Poppy continued. 'And finally, I raise my glass to the most important artist of all. One who sadly can't be here today but who is here in spirit and will hopefully be back in person very soon. To the founder and the soul of the Starfish Studio.' She lifted her glass high. 'To Archie Pendower!'

After the applause died down and everyone had had another glug of Prosecco, Poppy spoke again. She caught Jake's eye and noticed him making his way towards the front of the crowd.

'On that note, I'm also very happy to announce some more exciting news. Most of you will know Jake Pendower, Archie's grandson, who is a renowned natural history photographer. Or so it says on his website,' she added.

Jake gasped amid the gales of laughter, but he was smiling too, now standing near the front of the guests.

'Seriously, I'm delighted to reveal that Jake has kindly offered to display some of his work in the Starfish. Not only that, but the photos you are about to see are brand-new shots that are exclusive to the gallery. So new, in fact,' said Poppy, focusing on Jake's face, 'that even I haven't seen them yet.'

There were 'ohms' and 'ahs' from the crowd, and Poppy couldn't resist a glance at Minty. Her lips were pursed as if, as Poppy's mum might say, she'd swallowed a bottle of vinegar. Poppy moved next to the screen that had been covering the wall near to the staircase.

'Ladies and gentlemen, I'm pleased to hand you over to Jake Pendower.'

Jake took over while Poppy took a few quiet, calming breaths.

'Thanks, Poppy. I'm honoured to be able to show my photographs in my grandfather's studio,' he began in a steady voice. 'I only wish he could be here to see them, but he is on the mend and I hope he'll be back soon. Probably to give me his very honest opinion.'

'Oh, he will,' said Fen.

Jake smiled at her. 'Some of you will know that I haven't been back to St Piran's for a while ...'

There were sympathetic murmurs from locals and a few

puzzled expressions from strangers, but Jake went on calmly.

'These isles hold many memories for me. I grew up here as a boy and spent many happy days exploring with my parents and my grandpa. Coming back here and seeing the studio being given a fresh lease of life by Poppy has inspired me to revisit some of those places and look at them through fresh eyes myself.'

His words were simple, but knowing what the island and its memories meant to him gave an intensity to his speech that you could almost feel. Everyone who knew him was rapt and Poppy saw Fen wipe away a tear. She was almost trembling herself, wondering what the photos would show.

Jake wheeled the screen away from the wall. 'So, without further ado,' he said. 'Here they are.'

Chapter 21

Poppy's hand flew to her mouth in amazement at the half a dozen canvases hung on the wall. A collective gasp went up and people crowded forward for a better look.

Some of the photos were in full colour, highlighting St Piran's in all its almost Mediterranean vibrancy. They showed aquamarine and emerald waters lapping white beaches, brightly coloured wildflowers and exotic garden plants in hot pinks, corals and reds. Some featured whitewashed granite cottages with blue doors, basking in the late spring sun above a sleepy harbour where families queued for ice creams. They were soothing, comforting pictures that made Poppy feel safe and sheltered.

Then there were dramatic black and white shots of remote beaches and wild headlands of the northern part of the island. Sea foam flew high into the sky from breakers crashing onto jagged rocks. They were stark and disturbing. Even though they'd been taken on a sunny day, the fear and danger leapt from the scenes.

Every photograph was stunning in its own way and captured the island in all its moods – and for those who knew him, even slightly, there was no doubt that they captured Jake's feelings towards the island too.

The guests burst into a round of spontaneous applause, but Poppy was transfixed by two photographs in particular. The canvases had been displayed one above the other and both were of the Starfish Studio. The bottom photograph must have come from Jake's archive because Archie was outside, carrying his easel and workbox with a ginger kitten tugging at his bootlaces.

However, it was the photo above that made her breath catch. It could have been taken only days ago because Poppy was at the centre of the scene, hanging new bunting above the veranda. Jake must have taken it without her even noticing.

People crowded in, in a disorderly queue, waiting for their turn to look at the prints. Poppy tried to speak to Jake, but he was smothered by people asking about the new pictures. Others started talking to her, asking if they could buy the prints and how much they were. Soon, she was swept far away from Jake, answering question after question about the studio until her head was spinning.

Even as she tried to answer, laugh and be the perfect hostess, one thing dominated her mind: Jake had confronted his memories and bared his soul for the studio. For *her*.

She had no chance to talk to him other than mouthing a 'thank you' over the heads of the crowd. More people arrived and the volume of chatter meant she could hardly hear herself speak. Poppy gave an interview live to the island radio station, her heart almost jumping out of her chest. Was she speaking too quickly? Had she said the same thing over and over? Had she come across as warm and friendly and welcoming – or as an airhead who knew nothing about art?

Too late, now, the radio presenter had gone.

Hugo turned up with Basil, who was so excited that his wagging tail threatened to demolish most of the stock. Hugo tied him up outside and bought a bronze sculpture of a dog not unlike Basil.

Minty's jewellery was horribly popular, with people cooing over it, even though Poppy thought it was a bit overpriced. She was here to make a living, so it was all good. She sold two of Archie's original paintings. She knew that it was the Starfish's honeymoon today and she'd never be able to create a big splash like this again.

An elegant woman came up to the desk and bought one of Rowan Pentire's less obscene ceramic bowls. Poppy noticed her because instead of the usual hiking backpacks, she carried a beautiful velvet and leather handbag. It was so sumptuous, shimmering in the light, that Poppy's fingers itched to stroke it. Fortunately, she managed to restrain herself.

'Your bag's beautiful,' she said.

The woman smiled. 'I made it myself. It's inspired by Scilly even though I'm from Northampton. I'm here on holiday, but it's part work, as I'm always looking for fresh inspiration. I'm an artist maker too.' She handed over a card, saying her name was Pippa Day. 'Actually, when I saw the pieces you have, I wondered if you might be interested in stocking some of my bags and purses. I've got some samples with me, but I can pop in another day when you're not so busy.'

'That would be great. We don't have any leather and textile accessories and if you have some inspired by the isles, I'd be interested in chatting.'

'Have you thought of running workshops?'

'Workshops?'

'Art and crafts classes for visitors and local people. You could charge a small amount of commission to the tutor and, of course, it would get people into the gallery.'

'That's a great idea ...'

Pippa's mention of being on holiday triggered off more ideas. Maybe Poppy could offer weekend breaks and holidays with courses. Perhaps she could set up deals with local B&Bs or the Petroc Resort. She could talk to the St Piran's B&B owner, and the Hell Cove Cottages on Gull Island. In fact, she would email all the upmarket and boutique accommodation providers tomorrow. She could even phone Hugo ... Or maybe not.

But the idea of the workshops and holidays had taken root. She'd speak to a couple of her 'stable' who might be interested in leading workshops. She was a bit late to the party now it was May, but there was still time to set something up for later in the summer and start spreading the word on the tourism and craft forums and websites.

Buzzing with inspiration, she was swept off by a couple she didn't recognise. They turned out to be a retired headmistress and surgeon who 'dabbled in their spare time' and wanted to show her their work, saying it was 'just like some of the pictures on the walls, only more upmarket' and 'aimed at a more discerning clientele'. Poppy's heart sank like a stone when the headmistress proudly declared she'd won a prize in her local art group competition for her watercolour of a chihuahua. They showed her some shots on their phones and Poppy managed to cover her dismay by gently but firmly insisting she liked to have diversity in the gallery rather than too many similar artists.

To her immense relief, Jake must have spotted her trapped in the corner by the chihuahua couple. He made his way over and said she was needed urgently outside. The chihuahua artists left muttering, as Jake ushered her towards the work area.

When she was finally out of the melee, Poppy took a few breaths of air. 'I think I've offended that couple,' she said.

He shrugged. 'I'm afraid it's part of the job to disappoint people. You'll get used to it. I have people showing me their shots all the time, sending me emails, and while some of them are great, most of the people simply think they'll get rich quick from taking a few snaps with their fancy new camera.'

She laughed, then became serious. 'I haven't had chance to tell you yet, but the photos you took – they're incredible.'

'You like them?' He sounded surprised. For someone so experienced, she found his lack of ego a big turn-on. Then she remembered she wasn't supposed to be turned on by him. But no matter what had happened between them, she did love his work.

'They're so – *powerful*. I feel as if I could walk straight into the different scenes.'

'I hoped so. I didn't want to dilute the impact by unveiling them before the day. I wanted to see your reaction as well as everyone else's. Thank you for trusting me.'

He looked at her so intensely, she felt a physical spark of electricity between them. Hot and cold shivers ran down her body. This had to stop. Nothing could come of it.

'Thank you for putting yourself out there for me. I know it can't have been easy to revisit those places.'

'I don't mind admitting it was difficult at times, but it was something I needed to do ...' He paused. 'Poppy. Now's not a great time, with all these people around, but I've something I need to tell you,' he said.

She smiled but her skin prickled with discomfort. 'What? I'm a little worried now.'

'Don't be.'

Poppy's mum tottered up, with a glass of Prosecco. 'Oh hello, Jake. I have to tell you that I'm a massive fan of your work. Those prints are wonderful; they gave me the shivers. What a talent you have. I wish I could capture something so dramatic and eye-catching ...'

Poppy winced at her mum's gushing testimony, but Jake took it in good part. She was desperate to ask him what he'd been about to tell her, but he was swept off by a woman from the local news website and dragged into the mass of people again.

'Jake is so lovely and so talented. I had no idea how well known he was.' Her mum lowered her voice. 'I've been dying to chat to him all day, but I also wanted to ask you something. Dad says I have a filthy mind and I don't want to embarrass you ... but are some of those bowls and pots meant to be ...' She lowered her voice. 'You know ...'

Poppy didn't even need to look at Rowan's display area to know exactly what her mum was referring to. She thought she'd carefully selected his more 'abstract' pieces, but if her mum had noticed, she obviously hadn't curated them carefully enough. 'Um ... Rowan is inspired by the natural human form, but his work is very open to interpretation.'

'Hmm. That one.' Her mum pointed to a pale pink dish with crinkly edges. 'Is it meant to be an ashtray or a trinket tray? Not that it would be easy to get your bits and bobs out of it, once you'd got them in ...'

Her dad joined them. 'I thought it was a piggy bank to be honest, only with a very large slot.'

'Dad!' Her cheeks heated up. Parents. What were they *like*?

Her dad grinned and her mum hit him on the arm. 'Debbie, you'll get us thrown out.'

Heads turned in their direction, including Jake's. His eyes lit up with amusement when he spotted Poppy and her parents sharing the joke. Poppy was desperate to get back to him and find out what he had to say, but it was impossible.

Her mum linked her arm with Poppy's. 'You do know that Dad and I are *very* proud of you?'

Her dad smiled. 'You've done very well. We were so worried about you taking this place on after Dan left.'

'He made you so unhappy. I'll never forgive him and he's welcome to that awful Eve. I pity their poor offspring,' said her mum.

Poppy wrestled with conflicting emotions. She felt pride

and love for her parents, who, while a bit embarrassing, obviously loved her and she loved them. She was also sad that they had hidden their real fears from her. 'You never told me you were *that* worried. You said I'd be fine and you'd help me in any way you could.'

'We will. I wish we weren't working full-time or we'd have come over to help you open the studio. Not that you wanted us to.'

'Thanks, Mum, but like I said, there was no need for you to do that,' she said. The truth was, she'd been afraid that if they'd come with her and seen the state of the place when she arrived, they'd have carted her straight back home. 'And anyway, Fen and Jake have been brilliant.'

Her mum inclined her head towards Jake, who was deep in conversation with Kay and Minty. Probably keeping them apart, thought Poppy. 'Jake's single, is he?'

She winced, knowing what was coming. 'Yes, he's single, but he lost his fiancée tragically, so please don't get any ideas in that direction.'

Her mum gasped. 'I wasn't suggesting anything of the kind. You know me.'

'Yes, I do, Mum, and that's why I'm warning you off Jake.'

'I don't need warning off him. Though he is pretty hot, if you don't mind me saying,' she said dreamily.

'Mum!' said Poppy, and then rolled her eyes at the glint in her mum's eye. 'I know you only want me to be happy.'

'We don't want you to be hurt again, that's all, love,' said her father, shooting a slightly less admiring look at Jake, just as Minty batted him on the arm.

'I've had enough of men, so you can rest easy, and Jake will be off on his travels soon. Not that's he ready for a relationship anyways – he hasn't got over his fiancée, Harriet. She drowned in a yacht accident.'

'Oh, how awful,' said her mum, staring at Jake.

'I'd no idea,' said her father. 'Poor lad.'

'Yes, it was horrible for him, but please don't mention it. Now, excuse me because I think that man there wants to buy something.'

Poppy whizzed off, relieved at not having to continue the conversation about Jake.

While Zoey helped behind the counter, wrapping purchases and taking money, Poppy circulated, chatting to artists, locals and tourists until she was almost hoarse. Her mum handed round the nibbles and her dad topped up people's glasses. They'd insisted on paying for the Prosecco and food, despite Poppy's protests, and she was grateful for all they'd done and to have them here.

Fen caught up with her. Her face was very pink and she was slightly wobbly. She waved her glass and some fizz splashed out onto the tiles.

'Whoops!' Fen giggled. 'I never thought I'd see the time when the studio was buzzing like this. I wish Archie could be here to see it.'

She swayed again and Poppy took her elbow to steady her. 'Jake's treated me to the air tickets to visit Archie. If you'll be all right without me for a week or so?'

'*Totally* fine. I can help look after Leo, if you like.'

'Would you? My mind would be at rest if you did, because

Jake and Leo aren't the best of friends. I wish they would be, but some people just aren't cat people.'

'Well ... I don't think of myself as a cat person either.'

'Leo likes you and that's what matters. Oh, excuse me. I can see your dad topping up people's glasses.'

While Fen zoned in on Poppy's father, Poppy scanned the room for Jake. She felt a little light-headed herself, having been up at dawn. She'd hardly eaten or drunk all day and had abandoned several glasses of Prosecco after just a few sips. The canapés had long gone and she was astonished when her parents started asking if they could start clearing up. It was half past three and, shortly after that, the ferry horn emptied the studio of the last remaining day visitors. Only a handful of stragglers remained, plus her parents and Zoey.

The launch party was over.

'It's gone really well,' said Zoey. 'The cash box is stuffed. You'll be rich as the Saatchis soon.'

'I wish! Don't forget I have to pay the artists their commission and the rent for the studio and my food and living costs, which are higher than at home. I need to make the most of moments like today. There'll be plenty of days when we have very few customers, and I'll be shut most of the winter.'

'Hmm. The winter. Do you think you'll come home for some of the time?'

'For Christmas and New Year, definitely, but beyond that, I don't know. I had thought of making some of my own jewellery to sell in the gallery, if I practise and improve my skills. Or maybe I might have to take a temporary bar job back home and live with Mum and Dad. Or I might get some work on one of the flower farms here.'

Zoey let out a squeak. 'A farm? You on a *farm*? You freak out if you have to cross a field of cows, and what about all that muck and having to wear wellies all the time?'

Poppy laughed. 'Luckily, there would be no cows involved, only narcissi, and I don't mind wellies if I have to. The farmers need the help picking the flowers and packing them up from October to Easter. I've also promised to help work on Fen's allotment. If I leave St Piran's for too long, I'd be letting her down.'

Zoey shook her head. 'I think you should stick to the jewellery. I loved the bracelet you made me for my birthday.'

'Thanks, Zoey. Do you think I could sell my pieces in here?'

'Yes. I damn well do! I'll be brutally honest and tell you what I think of them, if you want me to, but I know you can do it.'

Poppy beamed. Zoey had made her believe that she could make and sell her own stuff if she had the time. 'It's definitely something I'll try over the off-season. I'll build up some stock ready for next spring.'

Zoey shook her head, smiling broadly. 'You're amazing. If Dan could see this place now and hear your plans, he'd probably drop dead with shock.'

'Oh, I hope so.'

Zoey sniggered.

Poppy sighed, remembering that ironically, making her own jewellery had once been one of Dan's suggestions. 'I don't want actual harm to come to him, of course. Only lots of temporary agonies like treading on a plug or a nasty rash round the crotch from those awful football shorts he used to wear … and I'd like it if he got lots of fines for encroaching in bus lanes. If his car was wheel clamped and towed away that would be good too.'

'I'd like to cut his lying balls off, personally.' Zoey hugged her. 'This is great to see, hun. You laughing and joking and running your own business. You've got your mojo back, and whatever or whoever it's due to, I'm made up for you. You deserve it.'

'Thanks. I've missed you though.'

'Me too, but now I've seen that the place has Wi-Fi and a decent latte, I will be back, I promise you. Especially if the Spanish pirate is sticking around.'

'Shhh. Don't let him hear you,' Poppy said, wising she hadn't mentioned the rumours to Zoey in the pub the night before. 'That Armada thing is only a local legend. Probably complete crap.'

'Even so. Don't knock it until you've tried it.'

Zoey went upstairs to get ready for the pub, while Poppy trotted down to the quayside to remove the advertising board. A new thought dawned on her. She hadn't seen Jake for quite a while and, come to think of it, she hadn't seen Minty either.

Half an hour later, Poppy had given up on Jake coming back to the studio. In the end, she sent Zoey ahead of her to meet her parents at the pub on the pretext of freshening up and changing into jeans and a top. Secretly she had hoped that Jake would turn up. She'd been desperate to get him on his own in the privacy of the studio to find out what he wanted to tell her.

There was no sign of him, however, and an anxious text from Zoey made up Poppy's mind. She skipped down the steps into the gallery and came face to face with Minty.

'Minty!'

Poppy's pulse took off, but only because she hadn't expected anyone to be downstairs. Minty was the last person she wanted to see.

Minty pouted. 'Hope I didn't startle you but the door was open.'

'You surprised me … erm, can I help you?'

'I think I might have left my sunglasses here. I thought you'd have gone to the pub by now.'

'I'm on my way there now. Where do you think your glasses are?'

'Maybe on the worktable?' She glanced around her. 'Oh yes, there they are.' Minty picked up the dark glasses and smiled. 'I knew I'd put them down somewhere.'

Poppy longed for Minty to get out of the studio. She was itching to get to the pub, relax – and hopefully find Jake.

Minty moved over to the photo display and gave a sigh of appreciation. 'These are fabulous, aren't they?'

'Yes …' Poppy's tone was wary, the way you might approach a poisonous snake. She stifled a laugh at the thought of Minty with a forked tongue just in time.

Minty swung round. 'Have you seen Jake since the party?'

'No. He must have had other things to do. I guess he's at the pub.'

'Hmm.' Minty smiled in a sympathetic way that made Poppy's skin crawl. 'Forgive me if I'm interfering, but I'm not sure Jake will be at the pub.'

'Why not?' Poppy blurted out.

'He took an urgent call while he was at your launch. I happened to be at the cottage with him ...' she said coyly. 'Did you know he's going away on Monday?'

'What? Where?'

Minty winced. 'Ouch. I can't believe he hasn't told you yet.'

'I haven't had chance to talk to him,' said Poppy, going cold all over. 'Or I'm sure he would have.' She couldn't hide her shock, even though Minty was clearly revelling in delivering the news.

'Oh dear. I hope you won't be too disappointed, but I thought I should tell you.'

'Where's he going?' said Poppy, mechanically. She was numb with shock even though she had no right to be.

'Brazil. To the Amazon, in fact. I asked him for how long and he said it was "unspecified". Whatever that means – ha, you know Jake. He hates to be tied down to details. I'm not sure when or if he plans on coming back here. I'm only amazed he's even stayed this long. You look pale. Are you OK?'

Poppy forced a smile. 'I'm fine and I expect he'll tell me *all* about it soon. It sounds very exciting. Now ...' she stepped forward, ushering Minty towards the door as if she was sweeping out a particularly large spider '... I must leave. *Everyone* will be waiting for me.'

Minty took the hint – not risking being pushed out of the door. 'I'm sorry I can't come, but I'm meeting a gallery owner for dinner at the Crab and Lobster at the Petroc Resort. He's flown in from London specially to see me.'

'Great,' said Poppy with a smile as Minty practically fell onto the veranda. 'Maybe he'll sweep you off there too, though that would be a *terrible* loss to the islands. Still, we'll have to cope somehow. Glad you found your glasses. Byeeeeee!'

Minty scuttled off and Poppy locked the door behind her. She took a deep breath, willing herself to get a grip. Jake was leaving on a photography assignment as he had every right to do and as she'd fully expected he would one day soon anyway. She'd only known him a few weeks and she had no right to be upset or hurt or even surprised. So why did she feel as if a dirty great cloud had chased away the sunny skies of her fabulous day and unleashed a deluge of icy rain on her?

Chapter 22

Damn. He was too late.

Jake tried the handle of the Starfish Studio door but it was locked. The windows were dark and there wasn't a sound from inside. Poppy had probably locked up because of all the takings from the launch and, judging by the silence, she and her friend and family must have already gone to the pub to celebrate.

The launch party had been winding down when he'd had to rush back to the cottage to take an urgent phone call. By the time he'd dealt with the fallout from that conversation, over an hour had passed. He'd been about to return to the party when Minty had knocked on his door.

It was now almost seven o'clock.

Deciding it was easier to explain his hasty departure from the party face to face, Jake jogged up the road and was soon walking onto the terrace of the Moor's Head. The place was heaving with locals, off-islanders and tourists, all out in the warm sunshine. Everyone was in T-shirts and shorts or summer dresses, chattering and admiring the jaw-dropping view of tiny green fields falling away sharply to the sea shimmering in the evening sun. Poppy's parents were enjoying a pint and a G&T at one of the tables. Her friend, Zoey, was chatting to Rowan Pentire and the two seemed to be getting on very well.

There was no sign of Poppy, which might be convenient because Jake wanted to get her on her own to deliver his news.

Jake made his way through the drinkers, saying 'hi' to people he knew. He'd almost reached the bar entrance when he bumped into Poppy. She hadn't seen him and her tray of drinks wobbled as he made contact.

'Whoa.' He smiled at the laden tray. 'Found you at last. D'you need a hand?'

She threw him a brief smile. 'No thanks.'

'Sorry I had to rush off from the party. I had to take an urgent call.'

'I know.'

Jake frowned. 'You know? But how ...' Even as Poppy opened her mouth, realisation dawned on him. Oh, shit. *Minty*.

'The Amazon, isn't it? Sounds amazing. Scary but amazing.'

A guy nudged Jake's elbow on his way to the bar. He knocked Poppy's tray and more drinks slopped out. 'I can explain. Let's go somewhere quieter before you lose all of those drinks,' he said.

A frown deepened between her eyes. 'There's nothing to explain, Jake. Why would you think that? I have to get these back to the gang or they'll wonder where I am.'

He wanted to kick himself. He wished now he'd never let slip to Minty that he was leaving so soon, but she'd forced him into a corner. Literally. None of that mattered now that Poppy had clearly lost trust in him.

He walked ahead of her, clearing a path through the drinkers. She looked gorgeous in her denim cut-offs and a white T-shirt that showed off her tanned limbs. Her hair was piled messily on her head and caught up in a clip. He wanted to kiss her and then drag her off to bed despite all his resolve not to think such thoughts.

Their arrival on the terrace was greeted with cheering and sarcastic applause.

'Thought you'd been kidnapped,' Poppy's father joked, rubbing his hands together at the sight of his pint.

'By pirates,' Zoey added, detaching herself from Rowan's side to take two glasses from the tray. She smirked and shot a look at Poppy. '*Spanish* pirates. Maybe ones left over from the *Armada*.'

This was obviously some in-joke between the two friends. Jake decided to run with it anyway, hoping to lighten the atmosphere between him and Poppy.

'We had a narrow escape, but no one's been made to walk the plank, as you can see,' Jake said lightly, while Poppy handed her mum a fresh G&T. '*Yet*,' he added.

He could have sworn Poppy was trying to avoid catching his eye. He really wished he'd been able to tell her about his plans himself.

'I could do with a pint myself,' he said. 'I'm going into the bar, but I'll be back.'

Hoping Poppy would take the hint, he joined the queue inside the pub, letting someone go in front of him and lingering inside chatting to the landlord, but she didn't appear. Luckily, however, as he slipped out the back door to the gents', Poppy was just coming out of the ladies'. The outside of the pub's toilet block was hardly the ideal location, but they were alone – for the time being – and he was growing desperate, so he seized his chance.

'Poppy. I need to talk to you.'

She glanced away from him as if she was searching for an escape route. 'I was about to go back to the terrace.'

'I won't keep you and I know I don't need to explain what happened at the party, but I want to. What exactly has Minty told you?'

'She came around to the studio after everyone had gone to the pub while I was locking up. She said she hoped I wouldn't be too disappointed but she thought she ought to let me know that you were going away for an "unspecified" length of time to Brazil.'

'Oh shit. I was going to tell you about the trip. I only received the phone call from the agency who arranges my assignments while I was at the party. The photographer who was doing the trip has been taken ill and she can't go for the foreseeable future. It's very sad, but I've been asked to step in at short notice.'

Poppy blew out a breath. 'Sounds like *very* short notice.'

'I know and I hesitated before agreeing to go but it's an assignment for an international wildlife organisation who support some fantastic conservation work. We're going to document the threats to the wildlife and indigenous people in a remote area of the Amazon rainforest. I'm meeting up with local environmentalists and a film crew.'

'It *does* sound amazing. I know you've always wanted to go to that area and I'd be off like a shot if I were you. Honestly. You really don't owe me anything and I expected you to leave way before this. You've already done far more than I expected, but I just wish ...'

'That I'd told you first?'

'Yes. I didn't trust Minty's version of events, but I knew the basics about you going on the trip must be true. Are you actually leaving on *Monday*?'

'Um. It's Tuesday actually. Minty got that part wrong. I plan on seeing Fen off on Monday and leaving first thing Tuesday morning so I can spend a couple of days with the family before I head out to Brazil. I had to say yes, seeing as I'm available – technically – and it's important work. At least, I think it is, and the opportunity of a lifetime. I would never have accepted the job under any other circumstances.'

She smiled and his heart broke a little. God, how had he got in so deep so quickly with this woman? He never asked to feel such a connection to her or be so attracted after barely a month. He'd tried not to – but he obviously hadn't tried very hard.

'I wanted to get to you before Minty... but I'm afraid to say she came around to the cottage and virtually had me pinned against the kitchen sink, asking if we could get together again now I was here. I was caught on the back foot and blurted out that there was no point because I was leaving in a couple of days.'

'Oh. *Pinned* in a corner?' Poppy raised an eyebrow. 'Sounds scary.'

'It was bloody terrifying, actually. I was scoping out whether I could make it out the back door and wondering if I'd left it open.'

'Wow. If you can't handle Minty, how will you ever cope with a giant anaconda?'

He smiled, delighted to be laughed at rather than frozen out. 'We'll have local guides with us and the trip's being organised by a professional "fixer" with tons of experience in that region. Mind you, even he might not want to tangle with Minty on a mission.'

Poppy stifled a laugh. Phew, he was getting somewhere at last ... then he was hit with a fresh wave of guilt.

'I hinted to her not to spread the news around. I hoped that I could rely on her discretion long enough to find you and talk to you but it obviously didn't work out.'

She seemed relieved. 'I did suspect something like that might have happened. So, how long is the trip?'

'Six weeks, possibly longer depending on how things go and if we get the shots we need. I haven't told Mum and Dad or Fen yet, so if you could keep it to yourself until I've had chance ... I plan to see Mum, Dad and Grandpa for a couple of days, collect my gear from my flat and then it's straight to Heathrow. We fly out to Rio on Friday morning.'

'Wow. That is short notice. I used to need at least a month for a weekend in Ibiza.'

He laughed, relieved to see her joking, but he wasn't out of the woods yet. 'If Minty hadn't turned up and I hadn't been stupid enough to tell her my plans, I might have left the news until tomorrow morning because I didn't want to spoil a great day.' He softened his voice. 'Or perhaps the news I'm leaving has made your day?'

'It's fine. Now, can we *please* move away from the toilets and go and have a drink in the sun? I'm gagging for a large glass of wine.'

Jake followed her onto the terrace. She'd seemed to accept his apology, but an air of tension between him and Poppy remained even as the laughter and banter flew around the terrace. He'd thrown out his comment about 'making her day' on the spur of the moment. He'd cast out his line, hoping to lure her into admitting that she would miss him – but it had come back empty. He wasn't even sure whether she'd been upset because he was going, or because he'd told Minty first – and not for a moment had she shown any sign of wanting him to stay or asking if he'd be coming back to St Piran's again after the trip.

Chapter 23

'So, you'll be all right while I'm away?' Fen asked Poppy for the umpteenth time.

It was Monday morning and Fen's wheeled case waited by the front door next to Leo, who was licking his paws, blissfully unaware that his favourite person was about to leave him in the hands of a cat amateur. 'It's only a week, but I know Jake's leaving first thing tomorrow. Can you manage on your own until I'm back? Are you sure you're OK with looking after Leo?' Fen said.

'I'll be fine. Don't worry about me or Leo. Enjoy yourself and tell Archie all about the strange woman who's taken over the studio.'

'Oh, I've already done that.'

Poppy laughed but realised Fen wasn't joking. 'Right.'

'All good. Oh, don't forget the radishes and lettuces. Take the ones that are ready and use them.'

'I won't forget. I promise.'

Fen gave Poppy a quick peck on the cheek and stroked Leo. 'Bye, matey. Behave for your new friend!'

Poppy watched as Jake met Fen at the end of the path and walked with her to the jetty. She hadn't seen him the previous day; once she'd surfaced after the party, she'd been way too busy clearing up the studio with her parents and Zoey before it reopened again for business.

They'd spent the Sunday in shifts helping her before they'd caught the helicopter service to Penzance to start their long journey back to the Midlands. Poppy had collapsed in a heap in the evening. She'd been so occupied with the launch and her family that she'd had little time to dwell on Jake's bombshell about leaving so soon, but now she was suddenly alone, the silence and isolation hit her all at once.

What Poppy hadn't told Fen was that when she'd awoken in the small hours, she'd googled the area Jake was travelling to ... Big mistake. Huge. Yes, there *were* giant anacondas, magnificent jaguars and indigenous people whose way of life was being threatened with extinction by loggers and mining companies. Their stories needed to be told and shown to the world. But her surfing had also revealed that the area was infested with drugs gangs, river pirates and 'organ harvesters' – who had absolutely nothing to do with farming.

'Even if he does get eaten by an anaconda, there's nothing I can do about it,' she told Leo who'd taken up position on Fen's favourite cushion as if he knew he had the run of the place now.

'It's none of my business anyway,' she said, refilling Leo's bowl with fresh water. 'Jake didn't even mention whether he was coming back to the island after his trip. *My* business is to build on the momentum of the launch day and firm up the arrangements for the art workshops.'

Leo narrowed his eyes, clearly unimpressed by her pitch.

'I'll just check there's enough hare and badger to last the week,' she told Leo and received a tail twitch in response. 'I wonder if you'd notice if I fed you weasel and oxtail instead?'

She was deep in the back of the pantry when she heard the door open and Jake calling.

'Poppy? Are you still here?'

She put on a cheery smile and carried the tins into the kitchen. 'I'm still here, just taking care of Leo's menu planning. You see.' She held up the tins. 'What do you think for his supper tonight? Quail and haddock or woodcock and lobster?'

Jake laughed. 'Both are far too good for Leo, but if pushed, I fancy the quail.' He shot a glance at the cat who yawned in response. 'I thought I'd come and see if there's anything you need while Fen's away,' he said.

She held up a tin of food and a pack of Dreamies. 'I think there's enough food in there to last a month, if not a year.'

'I meant you personally, not Leo.' He gave the cat a head shake. 'Leo is taken care of better than any human on these islands.'

Poppy smiled, even though she had a sudden end-of-an-era feeling. She'd known Jake for barely a month, but it had been the most dramatic month of her life.

'Fen got off OK then?' she said.

'Yes. She's looking forward to seeing Archie, but I think she's apprehensive of what she might find. When I spoke to my mum last night, she said he's definitely doing better physically and in himself so that's a good sign.'

'It'll be nice for you to see your family before you go.'

'Yes. Mum's looking forward to it. I plan on a day with my parents and Grandpa, then I'm off to London to meet the rest of the crew. There's a film maker and journalist coming too and we meet the local fixer in a small town once we're in Brazil.'

She left the cat food and treats on the worktop, aware that she and Jake were ignoring the elephant in the room: would he ever be back?

'Do you want a drink at the pub before I leave?' he asked.

She thanked her stars she'd already had an answer prepared to any offer like this. Weaning herself off her dependency on Jake had to start right *now*.

'Um ... I can't. I've arranged to go out with Kelly. We're getting the boat over to St Saviour's. There's a Mexican night at the hotel and a bunch of people from the Flower Farm are meeting us.'

He nodded. 'Oh. Right. OK. Sounds like fun.'

'Hope so. If I can avoid the fancy dress part of it.'

'Pity. I'd have liked to see you in a sombrero.'

She grimaced. 'I think Kelly might be handing them out when we get there, along with maracas.'

He made a maraca shaking gesture. 'Sorry.'

The atmosphere was excruciating. It was obvious they both wanted to get the hell out of one another's company, each for their own reasons. Poppy was in agony. Was he expecting her to invite him? He seemed disappointed and she was glad of that but also felt awful for hurting him – *had* she hurt him? If so, she regretted it but she was being cruel to be kind to herself. She couldn't bear to spend a last night with him. She didn't trust her emotions She might get a bit too merry and say something she didn't mean. Like 'So, when *are* you coming back?' or even 'Don't go.' Either would be a total disaster, so it was way better to keep out of harm's way.

'I'd better open up the studio,' she said.

'Sure. I need to be online and on the phone most of the day.'

'OK. See you later maybe.' *Just leave now*.

'I'll pop round in the morning before I catch the boat to St Mary's.'

'Great,' said Poppy.

Jake left. Leo started to pummel Fen's best cushion with his claws. Poppy thought about shooing him off it and removing the cushion for its own safety but decided the cat needed some consolation for being left in the care of an incompetent female human. She could always buy Fen a new cushion as a thank you for all her help over the past few weeks.

She was fine. Really *fine*. She went back to the studio and set up her board. Customers drifted in and out, and she tried to keep her mind on them, but in the quiet moments, her thoughts would keep returning to Jake. No matter how prepared she'd been for him leaving, and annoyed by his comments after their kiss, she'd still hoped he might stay for a little while longer – or at least say he was coming back.

Wearing a sombrero and shaking her maracas hadn't seemed so bad after several shots of tequila. Poppy vaguely recalled singing along to a mariachi band as she fell asleep in the studio that night. She woke up the next morning with a dry throat and a slightly fuzzy head but no regrets at having told anyone how much she cared about them, apart from a slightly shaky call to her mum and a late-night text to Zoey, who'd replied '*Are you on Prosecco or gin? Love u 2. Call you tomorrow.*'

She didn't even know if Jake would keep his promise to call in to say goodbye, or not, after she'd knocked him back.

As the morning passed and the time for the ferry approached, the cloud of gloom descended once again.

'Hello.' Jake's voice at the entrance to the studio snapped her out of her thoughts. Framed against the morning sunlight through the studio window, he looked so darkly sexy, she could believe every tale about him being descended from Spanish pirates. He was wearing dark jeans and a pale green T-shirt, and his chin bore a shadow of a few days' stubble.

The fizzy feeling in her stomach, arms and head left her in no doubt she fancied him to bits, and more ... She cared for him; she might possibly be a little bit in love.

Her heart sank. Who was she kidding? More than a 'little' and there was no 'might' about it. If she could just get through the next couple of minutes without letting him suspect how she felt, she'd be safe.

'Hi there. You travel light,' she said, noting he didn't have any bags with him.

He smiled. 'I left my backpack outside. Don't want to cause any breakages.'

'Good idea because I'd have to charge you,' she said, pointing to the humorously worded sign asking shoppers to be careful in the gallery.

He raised an eyebrow. 'You're settling into this really well.'

'Yes.' They both smiled, but she felt as fragile and transparent as one of Kay Baverstock's glass bowls.

Leo ambled through the open door towards them.

'Watch out for your shoes,' he said, aiming a laser look at the cat.

'Ah, but Leo doesn't see me as a predator.' Poppy smiled, but inside she half-wished he'd never stayed to help her in the first place. It would have made it easier to see him leave now.

He turned his attention back to Poppy. 'Did you have a good time last night?' he asked.

'Yes. Can't you tell?' she pointed at the dark circles under her eyes.

'Glad it was fun.'

'It was.' The pause lengthened.

Poppy picked up a pile of postcards from the desk. She had to do something with her hands. Jake shoved his in his combat pants.

'Poppy ... I just wanted to say—'

She cut him off. 'Thanks for everything, Jake.'

He frowned, but then said, 'I was going to say the same. Thank you.'

'Why would you thank me?' she blurted out, finding it

harder to keep in her real feelings with every second that he lingered.

'Because, I er ... was a bit of a miserable sod when you first turned up. Still am from time to time, but not *quite* so much.'

His crooked, self-effacing smile tied her stomach in knots. Why now? Why suddenly admit to herself that she'd fallen for him when he was leaving any moment? That was why, because he was leaving and she was safe. Almost safe.

'I've enjoyed myself a lot these past few weeks and it's made me realise that I'd forgotten how to let myself do that lately. I'd shut myself off to having any kind of fun.'

'Me too,' said Poppy. 'It's been a lot easier having your help. And Fen's.'

He reached down and ruffled the back of Leo's neck. Leo let him and Jake let out a gasp. 'Bloody hell. That's progress.'

'You see, perseverance pays off.' Poppy kept her tone jokey and light, but her inner voice was willing him to leave in case she did something silly – like cry. What was she like? Had she made no progress at all? She'd only known Jake a month, but this farewell was almost as bad as Dan walking out. Worse, because Dan was a shit and Jake wasn't – or hadn't proved himself to be yet.

She moved behind the cash desk and picked up an art catalogue for safety – from herself mainly in case hugging might be required. She needed to bring this to a close.

'Safe travels. Look forward to seeing your pictures,' she said.

Jake frowned. He was probably wondering why she was

clutching the catalogue to her chest. 'I'll email you the best ones,' he said.

'Can't wait. Now, I think I just heard the ferry hooting.'

He glanced at the door. 'I didn't hear anything.'

'Maybe I was mistaken, but it's almost time.'

'I guess so ... OK.' He didn't smile.

Poppy was teetering on the very edge of losing it. She knew if she even hinted she'd miss him, he might offer to come back to St Piran's again. But he might not and that would break her freshly healing heart all over again. How, how, *how* had she let herself become so attached to Jake so soon after Dan? That wasn't how things were supposed to be. It wasn't being strong or smart, or any of the things the websites said you should be.

Toot.

She almost passed out with relief. 'There, you see. I'm telepathic.'

'Yeah. Sure. I'll be off then.' He walked towards the door.

'Don't get eaten!' she called.

He turned around and smiled. 'I'll try not to.'

And his smile was the last she saw of him. Perhaps the very last she would ever see of Jake Pendower in the flesh. Unless Archie returned and he came to visit him. That could be months or even years, if Jake's recent track record was anything to go by.

She busied herself with the vital task of tidying the immaculate cash desk and fanning out the postcards on the desk. She checked the petty cash yet again, just in case. Thank God that the customers would soon arrive.

Warm fuzziness against her legs made her look down. Leo's furry face gazed up at hers, his eyes almost questioning. She picked him up and he allowed her to cuddle him before half-heartedly attempting to bite her, wriggling free and ambling off up the staircase to her flat. Oh well, at least *he* was sticking around.

After Jake left, Poppy dealt with a steady if unspectacular stream of visitors, with a relative rush at the end of the afternoon. She'd been very glad to keep busy, either chatting to customers or phoning and emailing to try and organise her first workshops and holidays.

Leo sauntered in and out via the front door to the studio when it suited him. He had been dining at the studio, at Fen's and at Archie's, but with Archie's cottage locked up, his choice of eateries was now down to two. Poppy had shut the studio by five and was catching up with some work. She'd left the rear door behind the work area ajar, to let in some fresh air and to enable Leo to come and go as he pleased, but by half past six, he hadn't turned up. She assumed he'd used the cat flap and gone to Fen's, so she closed the studio door and went to see if he was waiting to be fed.

There was no sign of him at Fen's cottage, so she put down a full dish on the tiles and locked the cottage again. He was bound to return to one of his homes sooner or later, and it would have to be Fen's now because she couldn't leave the studio door open all night. By ten o'clock, it was dark, a weather front had moved across the isles and Poppy had to make a dash over to Fen's with a torch to check on Leo. The moment she switched the light on, she could see that the food hadn't been touched.

Either Leo wasn't hungry or he hadn't been home. He hadn't been to the studio either ... A ripple of unease stirred in her stomach. However unpredictable Leo was, he loved his food, and as Jake and Fen had pointed out, he especially loved his hare and badger.

After checking the rest of the cottage, she locked up again and wandered home, sweeping the beam of the torch over the road and the cobbles of the harbour, hoping to see a pair of eyes glinting in the darkness or waiting for her on the veranda of the studio.

By eleven she went up to the flat and stood at the window. A break in the clouds revealed the half-moon for a minute or two shining onto the restless sea. The lighthouse beam flashed a couple of times, but there was no sign of Leo.

Poppy woke before dawn. She'd left the bathroom skylight open despite the squally rain showers that had blown in for most of the night, and had slept fitfully, expecting Leo to climb in off the roof at any moment, but he hadn't.

She scrambled into her clothes, pulled on a waterproof and hurried over to Fen's cottage. The food was still untouched.

'Oi, Leo! Where are you hiding, your furry little devil? Are you really that pissed off that Fen's left?' A mad thought struck her. Dogs had been known to follow their owners hundreds of miles, but Leo would have to have super feline powers to swim from the Alcatraz that was St Piran's. Jake might think he was the Blofeld of the cat world, but Poppy knew differently.

Panic began to set in then. She would never ever forgive herself if Leo had come to harm on her watch. How long should she wait? Should she phone Fen? No, it would worry her unnecessarily and possibly make her return, by which time Leo would probably saunter in to one of his homes, oblivious to the full-scale cat hunt he'd caused.

There was no one she could call who could help in any way. With Fen and Jake gone, she was aware of how alone and isolated she was.

She took a calming breath. Leo was a cat. A cat who loved to roam. That was what cats did. With this cheering thought in mind, she locked up and turned to head back down the road to the studio, planning on making herself a large mug of coffee while she waited for the wanderer to return.

But all the way home, her mind whirled with nightmare scenarios. Might he have got into a fight with another cat or a dog? He wasn't an aggressive cat, only a bit aloof, but a dog could hurt him badly. What about a fox or a badger? She had no idea if there even were any on St Piran's. She doubted it very much.

By the time the ferry arrived a couple of hours later and Leo hadn't shown up around any of his homes, Poppy was frantic. She had no choice but to put on a smile for the customers, although she did start asking casually if any of them had seen a large ginger cat, or if they did, could they please let her know.

Several times, she'd looked up Fen's mobile number on her phone. How long dare she leave it? Her finger hovered over the number when the phone rang out. It wasn't Fen. It was

Jake. He'd only got the first syllable of 'Hello' out when Poppy launched everything at him.

'Jake! I'm so glad you've called.'

'Why? What's the matter? Are you OK?'

'Leo's gone missing.'

'What do you mean. Missing?'

'He didn't come home – any of his homes – for dinner last night and I searched for him until dark and earlier this morning. I'm so worried about him.'

The phone was silent for a couple of seconds. 'I'll come back from St Mary's,' he said.

'St Mary's? What are you doing there ...'

'My plane had mechanical trouble, then there was low fog at Newquay, so later flights were delayed. I was on standby. Someone offered me a bed for the night, so I stayed over. I didn't want to risk coming back to St Piran's and missing the first flight out,' said Jake. 'I was about to walk up to the airport now. But I'll get the jetboat to you.'

'You can't come back now! You'll miss your flight to Cornwall.'

'Let me worry about that.'

She stopped objecting. If Jake thought the situation with Leo was serious enough to return, things must be bad. 'I'll never forgive myself if we can't find him,' she said.

'We'll cross that bridge when we come to it. I'll meet you at St Piran's harbour as soon as I can.'

It was no good. She'd have to close the studio. Leo was more important. She guessed Jake would be along in half an hour at the most in a fast boat. An extra person searching would be a huge help and if Leo still didn't materialise, then Jake could help her make the decision to call Fen.

Having a sudden flash of inspiration, she locked up and ran down to the quayside where Trevor, the local fisherman, landed his catch and where Leo had been known to hang around in the hope of a treat. Her hopes were dashed because there was no sign of him, nor had Trevor seen him. Feeling more and more desolate, she made another round of the immediate vicinity of the studio and two cottages. Jake would be here soon so she wandered slightly further up the hill from Fen's towards the 'town'.

As she neared the crest of the slope, she spotted a man in chinos and a pink shirt ahead, on his knees, with his head in a hedge next to the road. Even from the back she knew it was Hugo Scorrier, part-owner of Petroc Resort. His black Labrador was sniffing around Hugo's feet.

He backed out of the hedge and, spotting Poppy, called over to her. 'Hello. Poppy isn't it? Have you seen Fen Teague? I'm afraid her cat's dead.'

Chapter 24

Poppy's stomach turned over and over as she ran to Hugo. 'Oh God, no! Fen's away. I'm looking after him.'

Hugo parted the hedge. A bundle of ginger fur lay beneath the leaves, as lifeless as an old sack. 'I'm very sorry, but he looks a goner to me.'

'Oh, Leo. Leo. Leo ...' Light-headed with horror, Poppy touched his fur. Her fingers were wet with the dew ... He'd probably been lying in pain for who knew how long. 'He must have been here all night,' she said, fighting back tears.

'Looks like he might have had an argument with a vehicle,' said Hugo, touching Leo's paw. His claws looked rough and his pads were torn. 'Poor puss. It must have been a car or a van – or trailer or quad bike. Something big enough that the driver didn't notice. Damn bad luck though, considering there can't be more than a dozen vehicles on the whole island. I'm very sorry.'

Her throat was thick with despair. She stroked Leo's side

in a way she'd never have been able to if he were alive. 'I'm so sorry, puss.' He couldn't have been gone long because he was still warm. If only she'd found him sooner, she might have been able to save him ... Tears spilled out of her eyes. She'd have to tell Fen. Oh God ... She held her breath. She was sure there had been a tiny ripple of movement under her fingers.

'Leo?'

She was answered with the tiniest twitch of a tail. Then Leo opened his eyes.

'You're alive ...'

He gave a faint purr.

'He's not dead!' She swung round to Hugo. 'We have to try and help him.'

If there was the tiniest chance for Leo, she'd move heaven and earth to save him.

Hugo knelt by her side. 'Come on, old chap. Don't give up.' He tickled Leo's ears and gently touched his paw and was answered by a small snarl, which Poppy took to be a good sign.

She heard someone running up the path and, a few seconds later, Jake was by her side. He could hardly speak. 'J-Jesus. What's happened?'

Poppy had to stay calm for Leo's sake. 'Leo's been run over.'

'He probably crawled under the hedge after a glance with a van or trailer,' said Hugo, stepping back to let Jake take a look at the cat.

Jake snatched in a breath and knelt down by Poppy's side. 'You've been in the wars, haven't you, boy?' He gently stroked Leo's head. Leo purred and Poppy's heart broke a little more.

'We need to get him to the vet's,' she said.

'I think there's a part-time surgery in St Mary's,' said Jake. 'I hope there is.'

'I know Asha, the vet,' said Hugo. 'If I phone ahead, she'll help.'

'Thanks, Hugo. We need to get Leo there as quickly as possible if he's to have any chance,' said Poppy.

'I can give you a lift in the *Kraken*,' said Hugo. 'If we go now, we can catch the tide and be in the harbour in under ten minutes.'

Jake turned to Hugo. 'Thanks, Hugo.'

Hugo called his dog to him and clipped him on his lead. 'You bring the little chap down to the harbour and I'll have the *Kraken* ready for the off.'

Hugo left, followed by Basil, happily wagging his tail, oblivious to the drama happening under the hedge.

Leo was just a cat, thought Poppy, but she would do *anything* she could to save him.

'Help me lift him out of the hedge,' said Jake.

Poppy's hands shook as she stroked Leo to keep him calm. 'I'm so worried about hurting him.'

Jake glanced at her. 'Me too, but we've no choice.'

'I think we need an old towel or something to wrap him in and keep him warm. I'll go to the studio for one.'

'No, let's not waste time.' Jake got up and looked around him. 'Wait a sec.' He climbed over the wall of the B&B opposite. Towels and sheets were flapping in the breeze. Jake tugged a white towel from the washing line, clambered back over the wall and handed it to Poppy. 'I'm sure they won't mind,' he said.

Leo gave a few pathetic meows as Poppy tucked the towel over him as carefully as she could and Jake moved him from beneath the hedge. It was clear that Leo had cut his paw as there was blood on Poppy's hands and on the towel when they moved him. He let out a few yowls, every one of which made Poppy flinch in horror. Never having owned a cat, she was so worried she might be causing more pain and damage to him, but they really had no choice.

With Leo in his arms, Jake hurried down to the harbour, Poppy leading the way. Hugo had the engine of his smart motor yacht already running. Poppy got on board and took Leo carefully from Jake, who untied the *Kraken* before jumping aboard.

'Do you want to sit inside the cockpit with him to keep warm?' Hugo called as he guided the boat away from the harbour.

Poppy sat on the bench seat with Leo in her lap. Jake shut the cockpit door to keep the wind off them all and the boat picked up speed. Basil sat by Hugo's feet, turning his head this way and that.

'He's probably wondering why a cat has been allowed into his boat,' said Jake, obviously trying for a bit of gentle humour to comfort Poppy.

Basil's ears twitched as if he knew they were talking about him.

'You'll miss your flight,' she said.

'I already have,' said Jake. 'But I don't care. I can get another one tomorrow. Or the next day.'

'You'll miss a day with your family. I'm so sorry,' said Poppy. 'And Fen …' She glanced down at Leo, lying almost motionless in her lap, his ginger fur a stark contrast against the white towel. He had made a few sounds during the journey, some purrs and a little chirrup, despite his ordeal and the pain he must be in. 'We need to tell Fen, but I can't face it. I was looking after Leo and it's my fault he's like this. I should have kept him shut in the studio or her house.'

Jake shook his head. 'No. Leo would hate to be kept inside and Fen wouldn't want that. This is his life, wandering around as he pleases. It's just shitty bad luck. You know yourself that there's hardly any traffic. *If* that's what happened.'

'It must be. Hugo's right.'

'Five minutes to go,' Hugo called. 'I've arranged for transport from the harbour to the vet's.'

'Thank you, Hugo,' said Poppy, then turned to Jake again. 'We will have to let Fen know.' The very thought made her feel sick.

'I'll call her later, but let's see what the vet says first. If the worst happens, well …' Jake lowered his voice as if he didn't want Leo to hear. 'I'll break the news myself.'

Five minutes seemed an agonisingly long time, but eventually the *Kraken* arrived at Hugo's pontoon in St Mary's harbour. Poppy carried Leo up the steps to a minibus with the Petroc Resort livery.

'Our driver, Kieran, will take you to the vet's,' said Hugo. 'Please try not to worry too much. If anyone can save Leo, it's Asha. She did wonders with Basil's cruciate ligament. She's a marvel.' Hugo smiled.

'Hugo has faith in Asha. That's high praise.' Jake touched Leo's ear. 'You're in the best hands, mate,' he said, but Poppy thought the reassurance was all for her sake.

'Call me and let me know how Leo gets on and whenever you need transport back to St Piran's,' said Hugo and waved them off in the minibus, which would take them the short distance to the vet's. En route, Hugo had told them that Asha held a part-time surgery on the island, as well as attending to the Petroc Resort's small dairy herd and a few farms on the other islands.

Jake whispered in Poppy's ear. 'I always thought he was a bit of a prat. In fact, everyone thinks he's a bit of a prat, but he obviously loves animals.'

'He thinks a lot of the vet too,' said Poppy. 'I hope he's right.'

Asha was a few years older than Poppy, and almost as tall as Jake with Afro curls tied back with a satin scrunchy. She was already wearing scrubs when she met them at the door and Poppy and Jake carried Leo into a room tacked onto to her cottage, which served as her waiting room and surgery. Poppy hadn't been to a vet's since she was a teenager and she'd taken her rabbit to have its teeth filed under anaesthetic. She'd been anxious enough about going for that procedure, but this was far worse. What if the vet said she would have to put Leo out of his misery? She'd have to phone Fen and ask for permission ... She felt light-headed with horror.

Asha helped them lay Leo on her examination table. Seeing him lying there made Poppy want to throw up, but Asha spoke to the cat calmly and Leo allowed her to examine him. It was clear she'd met him several times before for routine vaccinations and check-ups. Asha checked his claws and limbs and listened to his heart with a stethoscope.

She nodded. 'Definitely an RTA. Don't see too many from St Piran's. Any clue what vehicle?' she asked.

'No idea,' said Poppy. 'Could be anything from a quad bike to a tractor.'

'He would have crawled under the hedge, so he must have been able to move initially, but you say he could have been out there for a night?' Asha asked.

'I'm afraid so.' Poppy was almost dumb with misery. 'I must have walked past the spot a couple of times too.'

'It was almost impossible to see him. Hugo only spotted Leo because Basil sniffed him out.'

Asha stroked Leo, her voice softening as she spoke to the cat. 'Good for Basil. You are an adventurer, aren't you, Leo, honey? I know you love to roam about. Well, I'll do some X-rays, but I think he may have fractured a femur. There could be internal injuries of course, but there's no blood around his mouth, so that's a positive sign.'

Leaving Asha to it, they walked outside and Poppy lost it. She burst into tears. Jake put his arm around her.

'I'm sorry. This isn't helping Leo,' she managed to say.

'Just let it all out. It's the best thing to do.'

'Yes, but Leo's a cat.'

'A cat who loathes me.' Jake smiled at Poppy. 'But if anything happens to him, I'll be crying too. Let's hope that Asha's as good as her number one fan, Hugo, makes out.'

After the X-ray, Asha called to say that Leo had a smashed femur that needed a simple pin and some stitching around his toes where his foot had been grazed.

It was still early in the day and Asha had decided to operate immediately. Jake and Poppy decided it was easier to stay on St Mary's than go home, so Jake took her into one of the cafés and made her have some tea and biscuits even though she wasn't hungry. While they waited, he talked about some of his previous photography trips, presumably to take her mind off Leo. He'd run holidays and been on commissions to photograph the Northern Lights in Iceland, giant tortoises and whales in the Galapagos Islands, gorillas in Rwanda and his most recent trip to an island off the southern coast of New Zealand to photograph penguins and sea lions.

'It all sounds more exciting than writing about drains,' said Poppy, then her phone rang. Her heart was in her mouth when Asha's number flashed up. 'It's the vet.'

She pressed answer and her pulse rate rocketed as she listened.

Jake paled visibly.

She ended the call. 'It's OK. Leo's out of surgery. Asha pinned his leg. He's in a collar, which he'll hate, but Asha thinks he's got a decent chance of a good recovery.'

'Really?'

'We can collect him later when he's recovered more and she'll tell us how to care for him then. I'm so relieved.'

'Me too.' Jake hugged her without warning. It felt natural

to have his arms around her, and after so much anxiety, the warmth and solidity of another human so close was hugely welcome. She made no effort to move away, but eventually – it couldn't have been that long – she did drop her hands and there was fresh air between them again. She didn't want to seem needy; that was the very last thing she'd ever have wanted Jake or anyone to think.

She pulled a tissue from her bag and blew her nose. 'Thanks for coming back and being here.'

He smiled and shook his head. 'Don't thank me. I feel as responsible for Leo as you do. More, in fact, as I've known him much longer.'

'I hope he really will be OK.' A twinge of anxiety tugged at Poppy. Leo was by no means out of the woods yet and would need to be looked after carefully over the next few days and weeks. 'And now, I think, we really do have to phone Fen.'

Chapter 25

Poppy sat on a bench overlooking the harbour beach while Jake called his parents first and told them what had happened. Fortunately, Fen was actually at the house visiting Archie, so they were able to gently prepare her for the news that Leo had been involved in an accident but had had some surgery and would hopefully be on the mend soon.

As expected, she burst into tears and then declared she was immediately coming back to St Piran's. Poppy listened as Jake let her cry and after much persuasion, he convinced her that Leo was out of danger and to wait and see how Leo was faring before she decided to cut short her trip and rush back the very next day.

Poppy took the phone and managed to reassure Fen further and get across how sorry she was that Leo had been hurt while in her care. To Poppy's relief and shame, Fen didn't blame her at all. Poppy promised to phone up at regular intervals with progress reports on Leo. It was a huge weight off her mind. Now all she had to worry about was Leo's recovery.

After they'd phoned Fen, Jake took Poppy to the Galleon pub and she bought him dinner. She begged Jake to let her pay for Fen's flight home, if she wanted to come back early, but he refused. When the discussion became heated, he pointed out that there would be a sizeable vet's bill, which he was also going to settle, but suggested she make a contribution to that. It was several hundred pounds, but Poppy was happy to dig into her savings without hesitation.

It was almost nine o'clock before she could even contemplate leaving Leo at the vet, even though Asha had said she would be monitoring him throughout the night and they could come back to see him – and possibly take him home – the next day. It was still light, as she and Jake walked from the pub to the harbour to hitch a lift back to St Piran's.

It was a beautiful late spring evening, and being Scilly, the air was still warm. The sun was hovering over the horizon, surrounded by coral-coloured clouds. The masts of dozens of yachts were silhouetted against a sapphire sky, resembling a scene from the Caribbean. Poppy was reminded of why she and Dan had wanted to move here in the first place. He wouldn't have dropped his plans to hurry back for an injured cat ...

Back on St Piran's Jake came into the flat and they sat up with a whisky he'd found in Archie's drinks cabinet. Finally, having accepted that Asha wasn't going to call them in the middle of the night, whatever happened, Jake went home and Poppy went to her own bed.

It was with a thumping heart that she called Asha the next morning, but her fears were soon allayed. The vet said that if Leo continued to do well throughout the rest of the day, she could collect him at the end of the afternoon. Poppy phoned Jake with the news and he said he'd go to the vet with her but mentioned again that he 'had a few things to get ready for his trip'.

He sounded friendly enough, but he was also brief and the light-hearted edge of the previous evening was missing. She could have sworn he was eager to be on his own and off the phone as soon as possible. After all, he already had been ready for his trip when she'd phoned him about Leo. He'd been on his way to the airport in fact.

Well, that was fine. *Totally* fine with her. Jake's departure had only been delayed – she knew that. Leo was what mattered ...

She opened the studio and unpacked a couple of new pieces from Rowan. It was a beautiful day, very similar to the day on which she'd first seen the studio. Hungry and thirsty visitors gathered at the harbour, enjoying a drink and an ice cream at the kiosk. A good proportion of them were lured along the seafront to the studio and tempted inside the cool interior. Poppy sold a painting, one of Minty's pendants, two of Kay's glass bowls and one of Rowan's 'ashtrays', along with a variety of postcards and greetings cards. St Piran's was dressed in its summer best and working its magic on the tourists. When an expensively bohemian group of artists from the Petroc Resort turned up and ordered several of Archie's prints to be mailed back to London from the printer, Poppy was grinning from ear to ear.

In her few quiet moments, darker thoughts came back to her. Leo's recovery was replaced with the worry that he might have a relapse and Fen's reaction when she saw him. Jake was leaving too ... Poppy tried not to think about that too much. Every instinct told her to tell him how she felt, but she was too afraid of his reaction. They were friends, but if she asked him if they could ever be more than that, would that destroy their friendship completely? And how could they see each other when he had a home in Cornwall and spent his life travelling the world? She couldn't and didn't want to get in the way of that.

She shut the shop at four, exhausted with the lack of sleep and constant stream of customers – and anyway it was time to collect Leo. He was understandably subdued when they turned up at the vet's, but she was pleased to see that he bared his teeth at Jake as he helped Poppy get him in his carrier. It wasn't easy because he was wearing a cone of shame, but eventually they coaxed him with his favourite treats. His hind leg had been shaved and stitched and Asha had told Poppy to 'let him mooch inside at home for ten days until his stitches were out' and sent them away with antibiotics and painkillers.

'Home' for now was to be the studio, where Poppy could keep an eye on him until Fen returned. However, Jake needed to rearrange his flights to Cornwall and phone his parents and Fen again, so they headed back to Archie's cottage instead. Leo's accident meant he wouldn't be able to spend any time at all in Cornwall with them and would have to get a flight straight to Newquay, collect his kit and then fly off London all on the same day. Poppy felt very guilty about it, but very relieved that he had come back.

They settled Leo in the familiar surroundings of the kitchen where he tucked into some dinner and then dozed despite his cone. Jake poured them both a large glass of wine and went into the kitchen to make his calls. Poppy sat on the sofa, as snatches of his conversation drifted in. With Leo safe and on the mend, she finally had time to realise that Jake really would be leaving now and this time it would be final. She took a large sip of her wine and gradually the tension started to ease. Sheer relief and exhaustion made her feel as if she had no marrow in her bones ...

The next thing she heard was Jake speaking softly to her and she felt a hand on her shoulder. She blinked awake.

'H-hi. I must have fallen asleep.'

'It is allowed.' Jake grinned. 'You must be tired – you never even finished your wine.'

She spotted the half-full glass and laughed.

'I was going to leave you asleep ...' he started.

'No. I'm so glad you didn't. I snore like an elephant according to Dan.'

'That's gallant of him to say so. I bet you don't.' He grinned. 'I thought you'd like to know I've rebooked my flights. I'm leaving on the first one to Newquay tomorrow, leaving me just time to pop by the flat for my stuff and then catch another plane to Heathrow from there.'

Actually, Poppy didn't like knowing this fact at all, but it was exactly what she'd expected. 'I'm so sorry you've missed seeing your family to come back here, and it must have cost a lot of money.' She swung her legs off the sofa to make room for him.

Jake filled the space. The sofa was small and being this close to him was making her twitch. He smelled gorgeous; she didn't know what aftershave he used, but it made her want to take big gulps and say 'ohhh' out loud.

'Don't worry. I spoke to Grandpa after I spoke to Fen. He understands and he knows how much Leo means to Fen. He'd much rather I looked after the cat than abandoned you to deal with a situation like that.'

'I know but ...'

'Stop feeling guilty. Leo's going to be OK, fingers crossed, and I'm not short of cash at the moment. All I've done for the past three years since Harriet died is work. I've taken on every job I was offered that took me away from home and my mind off losing Harriet. The money is important only in that it makes sure I can eat and buy new equipment and help out my family and others when I can. Like now. You've probably worked out I don't spend it on clothes or personal grooming.' He smiled.

'You look OK to me,' said Poppy, then realising what she'd said, added, 'I mean, you always smell nice and er ... clean.'

Jake stared at her. She had offended him. Arghh.

'Sorry, I'm always putting my foot in it.'

'No, I'm not offended. I was thinking the same thing. That you look OK to me too and you smell great. In fact, you look more than OK.'

'I've fallen asleep in my clothes. I bet I have mascara all

down my face after crying over Leo. My hair must be a terrible mess ...'

'True,' said Jake, with a grimace. 'You have panda eyes, your top is covered in cat fur and your hair is a mess ... a beautiful, sexy mess.'

Wow.

'A mess? I wish I hadn't said you smell nice now.' She laughed, but her skin tingled. Something had shifted. The atmosphere had turned in a heartbeat for no reason at all, but wasn't that the way when you were falling – had fallen – for someone? Logic didn't come into it.

'I meant what I said about you being beautiful,' he said.

Her chest tightened. Not because Jake had used the words 'beautiful' and 'sexy', but because his hand slipped over hers. It wasn't a gesture of comfort this time. It wasn't companionship; this touch was something completely different.

I'm not ready for this, she thought, *and Jake will never be*. But what exactly was *this*? Two people who'd been hurt in different ways. Two people who were attracted to each other and had kept their feelings hidden for months.

'Do you really think this is a good idea?' she said, as he took her other hand. 'After last time?'

'I try not to think these days.'

Her heart was beating so fast, she could hardly reply. She'd wanted Jake for weeks and hadn't dared admitted it to herself. He could, and probably *would*, be all kinds of trouble. He was still grieving for the love of his life and leaving, probably forever, tomorrow. She was on the rebound and in an emotional state over the cat ... It was definitely a bad idea but ...

Her lips tingled even before they'd kissed. Then there was wonderment at the strangeness of another man's mouth on hers and another man's hands around her waist. A man she'd wanted to kiss *so* much, however hard she'd tried to deny the fact.

Touching was tentative at first, but it grew in firmness and confidence. They were both exploring, testing each other out. She let her hands slip lower from his waist to the back of his cargo pants. She had her hands on his bum – Jake's lovely arse that she'd admired so many times. She wanted – *had to* – squeeze.

He didn't seem to object. He slipped his own hand lower and kissed her more deeply, darting a warm tongue inside her mouth.

Wow. Her toes curled and hot darts of lust shot through her.

'Think we'd better go upstairs,' he said. 'OK?' He stopped kissing her and looked down into her face, still holding her around the waist.

Poppy slid her hands higher, accidentally on purpose pulling out his T-shirt as she did so. 'Yes. Yes. I wouldn't be here if it wasn't.'

'Only I need to know it's all right with you? I don't want to get this wrong, misread the signals, do something you don't want or like.' He touched her cheek. 'Are you sure you're fine? You're trembling.'

'I'm nervous and - and - I want this. A lot.'

He smiled. 'Me too. Both of those things.'

'Good.'

They virtually ran up the stairs and she was out of breath by the time they reached the bedroom. Jake was breathing heavily too. They kissed again, eyes closed, moving to the bed.

'Ow!' Poppy's eye flew open. Her hip throbbed where she'd hit the corner of a crate.

'I knew I should have moved the bloody thing.'

She laughed, the soreness subsiding. 'I'll have a bruise tomorrow,' she said.

'I think I should check now,' he suggested.

'Perhaps that would be a good idea.'

Jake nodded at her skirt. 'Would you mind if I ...'

'Not at all.'

She was wearing a flirty summer skirt with side buttons. One by one, Jake undid the buttons, his fingers fumbling a little.

'Let me,' she said, teasing the final one from its buttonhole, though her own fingers were trembling too.

Jake parted the material and exposed her hip.

'There's a mark,' he said, kneeling by her side and looking up at her.

'Is there?' She squeezed out the words through a dry throat.

'Yes ... Here.' He laid his finger lightly against the bare flesh of her hip just above the side of her knickers. She stiffened and had to stifle a laugh, but when Jake pressed his lips to her skin, she could only gasp. The breath had been stolen from her body.

'Better?' he asked.

'Getting there,' she said with a sigh.

He got to his feet and held her. He kissed her and then whispered, 'Are you sure about this? I know I am.'

'Yes, I'm sure, but it's been so long for me,' she said. 'I'm probably out of practice.'

Jake smiled. 'It's been years for me too. I've probably forgotten what to do at all.'

'In that case, I suppose we'll both have to make it up as we go along.'

The late evening light cast patterns on the cover and the old brass bedstead. The pent-up desires, the misery and drama of the past few months melted away. There was no yesterday or tomorrow, only this moment and she was going to fall headlong into it and forget about what might come afterwards.

Chapter 26

Jake spooned coffee into two mugs. When she couldn't get her favourite skinny decaf flat white from the Harbour Kiosk, Poppy liked her instant strong with plenty of milk. He knew her better than she thought. After the previous night, he now knew her a *lot* better.

Early morning sunshine spilled onto the kitchen tiles. Making coffee had been his second job after checking on Leo, who allowed himself to be stroked and then tucked into his breakfast. He was now lounging on his cat bed, batting at a fly with his good front paw and no doubt planning to take over the world. He'd probably do a much better job than any of the current lot running it, thought Jake, while he waited for the kettle to boil.

He'd left Poppy asleep on his side of the bed. She'd actually been down to check on Leo in the middle of the night during a break from the bedroom proceedings. Once satisfied that

Leo was dozing contentedly, she'd come back to bed with a happy smile that had driven Jake insane. Phew. He was already knackered before he even started his journey to Brazil, but what a way to go.

Grinning so hard it hurt, he carried the mugs up the twisty cottage staircase. He'd managed to find his boxers without waking her, so at least she wouldn't have too big a shock when he delivered the coffee. Then again, he thought, he hadn't been out of bed that long ...

A thought hit him: would she be getting dressed right now, ready to get the hell out of the cottage and vowing never to see him again? Last night had been ... awkward, funny, sexy as hell. As it turned out, neither of them had forgotten how the whole thing worked. But she was sitting up in bed with the sheet pulled up over her breasts, checking her phone, when he walked in.

'Leo?' she asked.

'Wolfed down his breakfast and plotting world domination from his bed. I brought you a coffee.' He rested the mug on a crocheted coaster on the bedside table.

'Thanks.' She did a double take and her lips parted in surprise as if she'd suddenly realised he was in his boxers and she was in nothing at all. Jake's insides did the funny little thing they had been doing for a while now when he looked at her. That weird tingly feeling ought to have been a warning not to get too deeply involved. It wasn't one he'd heeded though, was it?

He took his own mug to his side of the bed. 'Ow! That bloody crate.' Hot coffee splashed onto his arm and he cursed again. He wasn't sure which hurt most, the stubbed toe or scalded arm.

She scrambled down the bed and rescued the mug while he rubbed his arm.

'I really need to move that thing.'

She laughed. 'You said that half a dozen times last night.'

'I know ...'

Jake collected his coffee and sat on the bed glaring at the crate.

Poppy sipped her coffee, then said, 'Are those the paintings Archie left you? The ones you based your photographs on?'

'Yes. Grandpa left them for me to open after he passed away, but I couldn't resist.'

'Judging by the photos they inspired, I guess they conjured a mixture of memories?'

He nodded. 'You could say that. Some were of me and my parents with Grandpa when I was young in our favourite spots on St Piran's. Others ... were harder to look at and harder to revisit.'

'You didn't have to revisit them. I hope that you didn't feel you had to for my sake.'

'No. I wanted to create something fresh and original for the studio and when I'd opened the crate, I had no choice. Once the idea of recreating Grandpa's scenes took hold, I felt compelled to do it. If that doesn't sound too up myself.'

She laid a warm hand on his arm. The hairs stood on end at the lightness and warmth of her touch. This was dangerous. It hadn't been just sex.

He put down the mug. Had last night been the biggest mistake of his life or the best decision he'd ever made?

'I also needed to confront the memories, to see how bad they really were. I've kept away from St Piran's since the accident happened, apart from one quick visit. That was almost two years ago and I could hardly bear to be here. Every minute was torture and having to hear people's sympathy and keep on answering politely when I wanted to scream and swear – well, I couldn't handle it. But this time, I've stayed longer. I didn't think I would, and taking the pictures, remaking the memories – some of them anyway – I did it, but there's something else now that I can't handle.'

'What?'

He took a deep breath before speaking. 'It's Harriet – her presence. It used to be with me every waking minute and in my dreams, but now …' He hesitated but Poppy's eyes were gentle and encouraging so he went on. 'I'm losing her, Poppy. At first, she was seared on my mind. Every feature, every word, her voice, the scent of her, even the taste, but now she's almost gone. I can't see her colours so vividly or hear her like I used to.'

Like seeing her disappear beneath the surface of the water, even as he held out his hand, as he reached down. He'd caught her and pulled her aboard, dislocating his shoulder in the process. He didn't even notice the pain at the time, it was eclipsed by the agony of knowing she was dead.

'I'm sorry.'

'Are you?' He sat on the bed and rubbed his hand over

his mouth. 'That's the problem. I don't know if I am or not. I don't know if I want to see or hear or feel her that strongly. For a while now, I haven't been able to decide if it's because things are getting better that she's fading. Maybe she has to fade away before ...' He was going to say, before someone else can take her place, but stopped just in time.

Perhaps not quickly enough for Poppy, who, judging by the swallow and the confusion in her expression, had read his thoughts. Damn. You weren't supposed to talk about past partners in this situation, were you? Well, bollocks to that. They were both drawn together by loss and loneliness, and not only because he'd wanted to take her to bed almost from the first moment he'd seen her step off the boat. He could admit that now.

'While I was downstairs, you checked Dan's Facebook, didn't you?'

'No, I ...' Poppy shook her head. 'Yes. I shouldn't have. I couldn't help it. I don't do it so often now, but since he and Eve have been posting about the baby, I can't seem to help myself. I hate looking. I want to stop.'

'You will one day, but you're not ready yet.'

'Sounds as if neither of us is ready,' she said. 'Not quite.'

'Do you love him?'

She hesitated, which was enough for Jake. It had only been two months since she'd split with Dan, a heartbeat of time when you'd once thought you'd love someone for the rest of your life. For eternity.

'I did once,' said Poppy. 'Now, I just don't know ... Does

that sound mad when he left me for another woman and is clearly a massive tosser?'

Jake had to smile. 'Not at all. Plenty of women – and men – have fallen for massive tossers. And keep on loving them. Like I said, you can't just untangle yourself from love, like untying a complicated knot. You might think you're free one day, and then bam, you're pulled back sharply and it hurts every time. You're still part of that person's life and maybe you'll always have the tie that binds you to them. I don't know.'

'I don't want to be tied to Dan forever.'

'You might not be. I don't know ... maybe because he's still here and you can see that he's becoming an even bigger tosser every day, you'll find it easier to cut him adrift.'

'Jake. Last night was great. But, you know, I think I'd find it easier if we said our goodbyes now. Is that OK?'

Her words were gentle but firm. She seemed to be pushing him away. Was she trying to avoid making the parting even more painful? Was that for her sake or his?

He nodded. 'Probably best. I have to get my plane this morning or I really will miss my flight to Brazil.'

She smiled. 'I'll take Leo with me when I leave. I need to open the studio.'

'Good idea. I'll bring his bed and things over with me before I go.'

'I can collect them if you leave the key.'

Wow. She really was keen to avoid a long goodbye and make a clean break. 'Whatever you want,' he said. 'I'll let you get dressed.'

'If you don't mind.'

The fact she needed privacy was another sign to him that last night's intimacy was at an end.

He went to the bathroom and came back to find she was already downstairs. He made them toast, which neither of them wanted, and then she left, after the briefest of hugs, carrying the disgruntled Leo in his basket.

The cottage was eerily quiet inside when she'd gone, with only the crying of gulls on the roof breaking the silence. Jake looked at one of his grandpa's paintings again that had inspired his photographs. It showed the studio, with him standing outside with a fishing net. His parents were next to him, his dad with his arm around his back and his mother smiling, holding a forerunner of Leo in her arms. It was the ultimate happy family portrait. His grandpa didn't go in for sentimentality as a rule. In fact, Jake could never recall seeing work up for sale or public view with such a personal edge. These paintings were obviously meant to be a family album and one that Grandpa Archie hadn't felt able to share while he was alive.

'I get it, Grandpa, that I should count my blessings. I know that's your message and what you're trying to do,' he said aloud to the picture.

Harriet was gone – truly gone – but Poppy was here.

If he did admit how much he cared for her, what would she say? She liked him, he seemed to make her laugh and she'd obviously found him less than hideous or she wouldn't have spent the night with him. And what an amazing night. The memory flooded back. They'd laughed and explored each other, tentative at first, then growing in confidence. He'd felt ... like *himself* again. Ready to make new memories. The problem was that Poppy was still fresh from loss and betrayal. He really didn't think she was ready to start again. Perhaps, one day ...

Chapter 27

Fen arrived the day after Jake left. She shed buckets of tears over Leo but brightened up to find him moving around in spite of the cone. Soon his stitches were out, his collar was off and he was wandering again despite Fen's attempts to keep him inside.

The time crawled by for Poppy in that first week after Jake had gone. The first few days had felt *almost* like when Dan had walked out. The difference this time was a sense of loss without the anger. No matter how many times she'd reminded herself that she never came to St Piran's hoping to find romance or affection, it didn't lessen the fact that she probably had been a little bit in love with Jake ... OK. A *lot* in love with him, despite every effort not to fall for someone so soon after Dan.

She missed Jake's dry sense of humour, his thoughtfulness, even his moodiness. She missed seeing the glimpse of bare skin where his T-shirt had parted company with his ancient jeans, and the sight of his firm arse bent over a tin of paint. She missed his grumbles as he emptied Leo's litter tray or opened the hare and badger. She missed his tenderness as he carried an injured cat to the vet or caressed her bare skin until she'd clutched at the pillows and cried out.

In his emails and WhatsApp messages to her, he almost always asked how the 'Furry Fiend' or 'Ginger Peril' was and whether he'd stolen any trainers lately or flooded the studio. Whether Leo missed Jake, it was hard to tell. He was back on the prowl and up to his tricks. Fen had caught him turning on the new taps in the workroom for a drink of water and he'd chased an unfortunate mouse into the studio and the terrified little thing had shot into the storeroom.

Jake sent photos of himself in canoes, one of a jaguar at dusk, another of some local people with a giant anaconda they'd captured temporarily. He sent shots of breathtaking vistas over the tree canopy and of tropical birds with impossibly bright colours. He emailed heartbreaking pictures of the devastation wrought by mining and logging in the rainforest. Poppy imagined his face, smiling or serious, behind the camera, and where he might be sleeping that night.

He sent a video of a hammock in a hut in a rainforest village. The noises astonished her: eerie shrieks and cries of nocturnal creatures, the buzzing of insects that must be gigantic judging by their voices. It sounded like *Jurassic Park* on steroids.

He told the story of his trip in lots of photos and few words, just as she'd expect, but he didn't mention when – or if – he'd be back home. Poppy didn't even know where he thought of as home. Was it Archie's cottage? His flat in Cornwall? His parents' place? Or was home wherever he happened to lay his head at the time? A hammock in a hut? A tent? A hotel? The Starfish Studio? The longer he was away, the more he seemed to have been an imagined fleeting shadow who had passed through her life.

As high summer arrived on the islands, St Piran's surpassed itself in beauty. Colours popped on land and sea. Thousands of blue and mauve agapanthuses grew wild all over the isles, not to mention in people's gardens. The days were still long, bringing stunning sunsets that set the sky ablaze as the sun sank below the western horizon.

Poppy didn't think about Jake all the time. She didn't have time to think about him all the time because she was too busy running the studio, repaying her favours to other islanders and tending to Fen's allotment when she could. She'd also taken up her jewellery making again in a small way, sending off for some kits and following some online tutorials. She made a necklace and earrings set that she felt was worth putting in the studio at a modest price and was beside herself when a visitor bought it within a week of it going on display.

She didn't have time to make much stock while the season was in full swing but the small success had boosted her confidence and made her determined to nurture her own creative side over the off-season.

She also threw herself into island life, joining in with barbecue nights, karaoke evenings and narrowly avoiding being persuaded to join the St Piran's gig rowing team.

Three weeks after his accident, Leo was sufficiently healed

for Fen to set off again for the mainland to spend a few days with Archie and some of her own extended family, which included a younger sister, nieces, nephews and their offspring. Poppy was petrified that something would happen to Leo again on her watch and shut him in the studio at night, even if it meant he drove her mad, meowing to be let out and pummelling her stomach and chest with his claws in the small hours. He could far more easily have been run over in the day, of course, but she felt happier knowing where he was at night, even if he kept giving her looks that would have frozen over hell.

This time, Leo survived the week, but it was with an immense sigh of relief that a bleary-eyed Poppy met Fen at the jetty after her visit. Families were stretched out on the beach in the sun or sitting with ice creams outside the kiosk. Dogs barked and children shrieked as they splashed in the shallows. The water might look tropical but it was chilly even in summer. Once it was established that Leo was fine and Fen had had sight of him strolling along the jetty as if he was king of St Piran's and been allowed to pick him up and give him a brief cuddle, Poppy asked Fen how Archie was.

'Is he on the mend?' she asked, walking side by side with Fen. She wore cut-offs and a vest top now that her pasty city-girl limbs had finally acquired a honey-coloured tinge.

'He had a setback a few weeks ago but he seems a lot better to me, both physically and mentally.' Fen gave a sigh of relief. 'He's even picked up a paintbrush again. He painted the scene from the window of the house. It was all very Archie – that angry sea and the sun and rain of a summer storm. I could tell he's weaker than he was from the brushstrokes, but the old fire was back, which is what counts.'

Poppy wanted to ask if the family had heard anything of Jake. It had been almost a week since his last WhatsApp message to her and she hadn't seen any pictures on his Instagram account for a few days either. But she didn't want to seem too eager.

'That's a great sign if Archie's painting again,' she said instead. 'I'd like to have seen his new picture. Do you think he'll bring it home with him ... when he comes back?' she asked. Even as she spoke, she was thinking of grandfather and grandson. Would Jake come back too?

'He'll probably leave it there for Jake's mum and dad,' said Fen and sighed. 'Poor Jake. He was in a bad way when he first came back to deal with the handover of the studio.' She then smiled broadly. 'You cheered him up though, and I thought he'd stay for good, I really did.'

'I expect he had no choice, given his job,' Poppy said, dismayed at the way the conversation was going. Fen had a way of getting straight to the point, and even if there was no malice behind her blunt comments, they still touched a raw nerve.

Fen tutted. 'Ah, but Jake *does* have a choice and that's the whole point. He's used his job as an excuse to keep away from St Piran's since Harriet died. We could understand it in one way, but when he stayed away, and as far away as possible, from Archie and his parents, they were very hurt. Archie didn't say as much and he'd never let on to Jake – he realised that the boy needed to grieve in his own way – but I could tell he was cut up and missed him badly.'

'Everyone has to deal with loss in their own time, I guess,' said Poppy, not wanting to reveal her own sense of disappointment where Jake was concerned.

'They do. Archie was racked with guilt when Ellie passed away. I know that too.' Fen's voice trailed off. Poppy held her breath. She thought of Archie's drawings of Fen. Nothing had been mentioned of the sketches since Jake had shown them to Poppy when they'd first been restoring the studio. Jake had thought it better for those memories to be locked away, but Poppy wondered now whether Fen was about to share her story.

Then Fen laughed. 'Anyway, enough talk of people who aren't here. How are *you* doing? Have you managed to set up those workshops and holidays you told me about? Has Hugo helped or has he been as much use as a chocolate teapot as usual?'

Although a bit disappointed not to get to the bottom of Archie's sketches, Poppy smiled. Perhaps it was right that some memories were better left in the past. 'Actually, I have a watercolour taster day next weekend, which includes lunch,' she told Fen. 'The Petroc Resort advertised it on their website and half a dozen people have booked. They're taking a fat cut, of course, but I'll make a little money from it and it will help get people into the studio and spread the word. I've also set up a weekend workshop in October, as part of a holiday package with the Petroc Resort.'

'That sounds good. Will you need a hand on the day? I don't mind cutting a few sandwiches.'

Poppy laughed. 'I'd love that and the locally sourced lunch

is part of the attraction. I'd hoped to offer some rocket and tomatoes from the allotment. With the bread from our island bakery, plus some goat's cheese from the Flower Farm herd, I think I can produce a completely local lunch. I'm going to get organised and promote more regular courses in the spring and autumn next year if these go well.'

'I'm sure they will. I hope so. I want you to make a go of it. You're becoming part of the furniture.'

Poppy was touched by Fen's warm words. 'I'll never be rich, but I will make something from the use of the workshop and sale of the artists' work, of course. Hopefully we'll have repeat bookings and word will spread through the art community.'

Fen nodded. 'Archie used to run courses years back when he had more patience and I had the energy to help organise them. Then he decided to switch his focus to the painting.'

'Will he want to use the studio to work when he comes home?' asked Poppy, suddenly wondering how she'd handle a permanent artist in residence after being on her own for so long.

'You know, I hadn't thought of that ... mind you, the first thing we need to do is get him home at all.'

'Is there any date planned yet? He must miss it terribly.'

'Not yet, but knowing Archie, he'll just wake up one morning and decide today's the day to come home.'

They'd reached Fen's cottage and stood outside on the tiny front garden where a clump of mauve agapanthus flowers nodded their heads in the breeze.

Fen gave her a shrewd look. 'If you're planning on organising these workshops for next year, you must definitely be thinking of staying on yourself?'

'I guess ... yes, I must be. I'll see how the first couple go, but I want to make a go of it here. I want to give it a decent chance. It's been hard leaving my family and friends, but the place has seeped into my soul. If that doesn't sound too weird.'

'Not at all.' Fen patted her arm. 'We'll make a local of you yet.'

The workshop went well, and even though it was exhausting keeping eight demanding amateur artists happy, fed and watered, Poppy was delighted with the additional income and planning to organise more. Three of the attendees signed up on the spot for the autumn weekend course, despite Leo strolling in and managing to knock over their easels like dominoes.

The summer was taking its toll, with every moment taken up with admin, island life or just the logistics of making sure she had enough food. If she was honest, she was putting in more hours than she had in her old job, but the compensations were worth it. The sunsets were the most spectacular she'd ever seen, seals regularly popped up to greet her on her walks and one morning she awoke to find a pod of dolphins frolicking in the sea outside the harbour.

Missing her family was the downside, so she was delighted when Zoey arrived for a visit. She dumped her bags on the floor of the studio and bear-hugged Poppy. She'd come to stay for a week and other than a weekend visit from her parents, Poppy hadn't seen anyone from home since the launch.

'How's it going? Heard from D'Artagnan on his travels lately?' Zoey asked almost as soon as they'd let go of each other.

Poppy rolled her eyes. 'You do know that D'Artagnan was French, not Spanish?' she said, amused.

'OK. OK. But have you *heard* from him? How long has it been now? A month?'

'Six weeks.' Six weeks exactly tomorrow, Poppy could have added, but she didn't dare let on to Zoey that she'd been counting the days. She'd tried not to count them but couldn't help remembering that final moment: the damp squib of it. She'd been protecting herself, but now she wished she'd wrung every last drop of pleasure from their time together, even if that might have made letting him go even harder. 'And I had a WhatsApp message and some photos from him this morning as a matter of fact. An amazing shot of a sloth and an anaconda, and one of a golden lion tamarin. Incredible lighting. I don't know how he does it.'

Zoey seemed unimpressed. 'So, you're really missing him badly?'

'Honestly? I haven't had time.'

Zoey folded her arms and pursed her lips. 'That's being honest?'

'I did miss him for a while. I'd sort of got used to having him around, but that's exactly why I'm glad he's gone. I didn't like waiting for him to leave and knowing I'd miss him. I don't want to miss anyone again. It's too soon after Dan. It's just not ... convenient right now.'

Zoey laughed and sat down on the bed. 'Oh, Pops. Love

doesn't come along to order. It's not a train running to schedule. Unless it's running to a Southern Trains type of schedule.'

'You mean waiting all day for one, then three come along at once and they're not even going where you want them to?'

Zoey smiled. 'Something like that.'

Poppy laughed. 'Well, Jake's train doesn't have any room left for anyone else, and even if it did, I'm not sure I want to climb aboard. In *any* way. Have you seen Dan?' she asked.

Zoey pulled a face. 'Do you really want to know?'

'I shouldn't, but yes. Tell me the worst.'

'My mum spotted him and Evil Eve a few weeks ago, actually. They were coming out of JoJo Maman Bébé with a buggy.' Zoe bit her lip. 'Sorry.'

'No. It's fine. I only wondered.'

'If it's any consolation, they were having a bit of a row. Mum said that he was moaning about the price of the buggy and Eve was telling him not to be such a mean bastard. Or something like that. Mum didn't actually use the word "bastard".'

'That sounds like Dan.' Poppy smiled.

Zoey reached for her. 'Come on, have a hug. It still hurts, doesn't it?'

'No, it's just annoying. It's annoying that I even care what he might be doing.'

'Do you still love him?'

'I don't think so. In fact, no.' In truth, Poppy was no longer sure if she had ever really loved Dan, not in the way she should have, or even in the way she felt about Jake.

'Hate him?'

'Hate's a strong word,' said Poppy.

'A word you used about him twenty times a day until you came here, so if you don't really know how you feel, that's progress. Now, can we please have a glass of wine?'

'How about a G&T? Would you like some seaweed gin? It's been made with local kelp.'

Zoey grimaced. '*Seaweed*? Do I have to?'

'It's part of the St Piran's initiation ceremony. Just like in *The Wicker Man*. We're on the lookout for a virgin to sacrifice to the weather gods.'

Zoey let out a shriek then smirked. 'I'll be safe then. Hand over the gin.'

As the holiday season got into full swing, Poppy determined to make the most of trade while the place was buzzing, but she also hadn't wanted to miss a moment of Zoey's company, so Fen kindly stepped in for a couple of afternoons, and on others, Zoey helped Poppy in the gallery. For the rest of the time, Zoey was happy to take a book to the beach and sunbathe or hang out in the gallery when the weather was wet.

One grey morning near the end of the week, Zoey was inside helping Poppy unpack a new delivery from Rowan. His more graphic 'pots' were proving surprisingly popular with Hugo's well-heeled Petroc Resort crowd. Poppy had lost count of the women she'd heard tittering as they handed over the cash for their purchase, 'for a friend from my book club, of course. I can't wait to see her face!'

Zoey delved into the box that Rowan had dropped off

earlier that morning and held up a crinkly pasty-shaped object. 'Erm. Excuse me, but is this a fanny?"

Poppy took it from her and set it on top of Rowan's display plinth with his other works. 'No, it's a dish. You have a filthy mind.'

Zoey curled her lip. 'Must have because it looks exactly like a fanny to me. Still, if it sells.' She reached into the box and unwrapped another piece. 'And this, I suppose, is a jewellery stand?' Zoey waggled a blue-glazed phallic sculpture under Poppy's nose. 'Well, there's no way any of my rings would fit over *that*.'

Poppy giggled. 'It's artistic licence, and anyway, I don't think it's for rings. You could slide bangles and bracelets over it, I suppose. These sell far better than I expected.'

'I bet they do. All those posh ladies who lunch must live secret lives.' Zoey picked up the 'fanny bowl' from the plinth and tried to push the 'willy' into the 'fanny'. 'The slot is too small. God, whoever made this has no idea.'

'St-stop it. Y-you'll break the willy.' Poppy tried to hold back the giggles.

'That *can* actually happen you know,' said Zoey, whose eyebrows shot up her face as she examined the willy. 'Emma at work's brother had it happen. He had to go to A&E. He said it was the worst pain he'd ever known. Worse than when his Achilles tendon snapped. He said that it made a noise like a gun going off.'

Poppy had to put the 'fanny' down. Her sides hurt and her eyes were streaming. She couldn't speak for laughing.

'I need the loo now,' said Zoey, with a grin. 'Handle that with care, won't you?'

While Zoey went to the bathroom, Poppy wiped tears of laughter from her eyes and checked her mascara in the mirror of one of the display cases. Oh, but she *had* missed Zoey over the past few months. She'd missed sharing a laugh and a drink, consoling each other and dishing the dirt. While she loved the studio and the stunning landscape – and getting away from Dan had seemed the right thing at the time – doubts were creeping in. She'd made new friends of course, but Zoey being here, making her laugh, well, it would be very hard to say goodbye again.

Poppy travelled all the way across to St Mary's airport with Zoey and waited until her flight had been called. Even though she'd settled in well, part of her wanted to get on the little plane with her friend, especially when Zoey hugged her and whispered: 'I miss you, hun. I hate to get slushy, but I really do. I know it's pathetic, but I actually cried after you moved here. I thought Dirty Dan pissing off with Evil Eve would make you stay.'

'Me t-too,' said Poppy, gulping down a sob.

Zoey's shoulders shook under her embrace. It wasn't like Zoey to be sentimental at all and she'd set Poppy off.

They broke apart.

'What are we like?' They said the words together and both burst out laughing.

'It's not the moon, you know,' said Poppy.

'May as well be,' said Zoey, pulling a face.

'I'll be back home after October half-term and at Christmas,' said Poppy.

Zoey nodded. 'Can't wait. Let's do FaceTime later. If I survive this flight. My Smart car is bigger than that bloody plane!'

'Madam, are you getting on this flight or staying the night?' The uniformed Skybus official gave Zoey a stern look and with a final hug goodbye she hurried out of the doors to the awaiting plane.

Poppy stayed right until the tiny aircraft had zipped off the end of the cliff-top runway and over the sea towards Cornwall. Then she took a deep breath, squared her shoulders and headed for the harbour to go back to St Piran's, the studio and her own company.

Soon Zoey's visit was only a memory and another week had flown by. Poppy threw herself into wringing every last drop out of the season and setting up new opportunities. When she wasn't working or socialising with Kelly and the other islanders, she helped Fen in the allotment, although there had been far less time for that than she'd hoped. Perhaps she'd have more time one day – if she stayed on.

Before Poppy knew it, Jake had been gone almost eight weeks, as his trip had been extended. She still missed him. She looked forward to his emails and photographs, although she hadn't heard from him for a couple of days. He'd warned her he wouldn't always have Wi-Fi and it was obvious that communication would be difficult in such remote places, so she tried not to think too much of it.

It was a sultry high summer evening and she'd been over to Petroc to discuss the arrangements for an art weekend in the autumn. The moment she set foot off the boat in the harbour at St Piran's, the heavens opened. The days were long but the cloudy weather had made it seem dark early. Even on the short run to the studio, the rain had grown heavier and was being driven off the sea by a strong wind. You could barely see beyond the harbour wall and St Piran's might as well be the only Scilly isle in existence because every other trace of dry land had vanished into the mist and rain. By the time she reached the studio, Poppy was drenched and ran upstairs for a towel to dry her hair.

Rain drummed on the studio roof and hurled itself against the windows. The temperature had dropped too. She changed her T-shirt and jeans and pulled on an old hoodie. She went to put the kettle on and heard a noise from below. It sounded as if someone was hammering on the door of the studio.

At seven o'clock? Surely, they could see the closed sign. She peered out of the side window, which overlooked part of the veranda, but all she could see was a large rucksack propped up against the wooden step.

Her heart rate shot up and she shot towards the stairs. There was one person who might turn up on her doorstep at this time of night. She must not get excited. Even if Jake was back, she shouldn't feel like this: the sweaty palms, the pounding heart, the *hope*. It was crazy and dangerous.

She stopped scampering down the stairs and slowed her pace. Let him get wet – after all, he'd spent weeks in the rainforest – let her breathing subside, let her appear cool and calm and not the least bit like she cared that he'd come back when she'd lost all hope of him returning to the Starfish ever again.

God, who was she kidding?

She hurried to the door and flung it open.

A wet, dishevelled figure stood on the veranda. 'Well,' he muttered. 'Aren't you going to let me in?'

Chapter 28

In those first few moments, she hadn't even been sure that the bedraggled figure on the veranda *was* Dan, but close up there was no mistaking him. His hipster beard was straggly and his sodden hair was like rats' tails. Rain dripped down his nose and water pooled from his boots onto the decking.

'This must be a shock,' he said in a croaky voice.

Poppy noticed the dark circles under his eyes and realised that the water running down his face might not only be raindrops.

'It is but ... come inside. You're drenched. How did you get here?'

She stood aside so he could walk into the studio.

'I got a plane earlier and then a minibus to the harbour ... and then I had to beg someone to bring me across in one of those yellow speedboats. It cost me forty quid just for a fifteen-minute ride over here!' He dumped his rucksack on the tiles. 'As if I wasn't soaked by the rain, that thing was like riding a bucking bronco on water.'

'You're lucky you managed to get across at all in this weather. The scheduled ferry has been cancelled because of the storm.' Poppy had no sympathy for Dan being forced to pay out for the jetboat. 'What *are* you doing here?'

'I – I don't really know. I just got on the plane from Birmingham and then from Newquay and – here I am.'

He looked around him at the studio and artwork, but the walls might have been transparent. He was physically in the room but absent mentally. Something wasn't right or else why was he here at all?

Poppy touched his arm. 'Dan?' she said softly. 'What's happened?'

He looked at her with an expression of pure desolation 'It's my dad. He's dead.'

She reeled. '*Dead*? I'm so sorry. B-but what about Eve? Why aren't you with her?'

'She can't handle it ... not in her condition.'

Dan sniffed loudly and Poppy choked back a sob herself. She'd liked Dan's dad, Pete, a lot. He could be a bit loud, but he was funny and jolly; in fact, he had far more of a sense of humour than Dan had. They'd often shared a joke and Pete had actually phoned Poppy and told her how upset he was when Dan had first left. It was shocking that he appeared to have died so suddenly.

'My God. What a terrible shock. What happened? He was only sixty.'

'Heart attack. You know he liked to enjoy himself. The fags and the whisky.' Dan heaved in a breath.

'What about your mum?' Dan's mum and dad had split a long time ago and his mother now lived in New Zealand.

'She knows. I had to tell her ... God, that was awful ... horrible ...' He covered his face with his hands.

'I bet it was. Poor you – and your mum, hearing the news from so far away.' Poppy grabbed some paper towels and handed them over, still trying to process the terrible news.

'She was no fan of Dad and they were barely speaking since they split up, but she was very upset. She couldn't stop crying and saying "no, not my Pete", so I had to let her new bloke comfort her and phone back. You'd never think Mum and Dad were at daggers over the divorce terms and virtually throwing things at each other. Anyone would think she still loved him.'

'She probably did. You don't let go of love that lightly, if at all,' said Poppy, thinking of Jake's words to her. Of her own feelings now, about Dan. They were confused too. She was on the verge of tears herself, seeing his distress.

Dan reached for her and she let him cling to her, while she made soothing noises, but at a loss as to how she could possibly comfort him. Maybe she couldn't and he only needed her to be there, with her. Yet the whole situation also felt wrong. Dan shouldn't be here. He was in the wrong place ... with the wrong person.

'I really liked your dad and he was always kind to me. I can understand that your emotions are all over the place, but wouldn't it be better to tell Eve all of this – how you feel?

Won't she be really upset that you've left her and flown out here to see me?'

He stared at the tiles. 'I don't think Eve will mind,' he murmured.

'But she must do!' she cried in frustration. 'How could she not be upset that you turned to me for support when you need it most and not her? I'm sure she can cope better than you think.'

Dan twisted his tissue round and round, his voice racked with misery. 'I've fucked up everything.'

Poppy tried to comfort him, laying her hand on the back of his coat. 'None of this is your fault, Dan. You couldn't have done anything for your dad and Eve needs you now, and the baby.'

'The baby?' he said as if he'd no idea what a baby even was, let alone that Eve was expecting his in a few months' time.

The tiny down on Poppy's arms stood on end. Something *was* wrong. Had Dan had a total breakdown?

'Your dad must have been looking forward to his first grandchild, but you'll still have the baby, Dan. You and Eve.'

She genuinely meant to comfort him. She couldn't wish this kind of pain on him, or anyone, and she was seriously worried about his mental health. The events of the past few months had been enough to tip anyone over the edge, even if Dan had brought most of his problems on himself.

'I'm sorry. I didn't mean to make things worse. I only meant that you and Eve will have the baby to love soon.'

Dan looked up, his face a picture of total misery and despair.

'That's just it. We won't because it's not my baby. Eve's been lying through her teeth to me all along. It's Gabe Hartmann's baby. You know, that tosser MD who runs Vargo's Construction? Turns out he was shagging her too but he wouldn't leave his wife.'

Poppy's jaw dropped. 'I don't understand—'

He cut in. 'It's over between Eve and me. That's why I'm here. I don't expect you to forgive me, but I've made the biggest fucking mistake of my life. I threw away everything that meant the most to me. I need you, Poppy. I still love you.'

Poppy gawped at him, lost for words. Oh God, this wasn't how she'd expected her evening to go at all.

Twenty minutes later, Poppy sat opposite Dan as he sipped a Bacardi-laced mug of hot chocolate while wearing her winter dressing gown and fluffy socks. His wet clothes were drying over the heated towel rail in the shower room. He'd finished sobbing, but she placed a box of tissues by his side just in case.

The phrase 'I still love you' was still too much for her to comprehend. She'd longed for those words once, now she felt sick at hearing them, but this was absolutely not the time to break that news to Dan.

'Feeling better?' she asked.

'I think so.'

'At least you're dry and warm,' she said, realising that she was talking to him like he was a child. Apart from the rum in his hot chocolate, he might as well have been. Her dressing gown just about fastened, enough to cover his decency at least.

'When did Eve throw you out?'

'Two days after Dad died. He was taken ill at my auntie Gill's birthday party. We called the paramedics, but he was dead within half a minute, so there was nothing they could do. It was horrible. I can't believe it. One moment he was Dad and the next he hit the patio and he was gone.' He shuddered. Poppy sat next to him and took the mug from him and held his hand. She didn't know what else to do.

'I really am so sorry, Dan,' she said, devastated at the idea of big, funny, kind Pete losing his life so young.

He burst into tears again and buried his face in her shoulder, clinging to her. She tried to hold it together for his sake and let him have another good cry.

'Sorry,' he said. 'I can't seem to stop.' His hands were shaking as she handed him his drink.

'Don't apologise. I don't know what I'd do without my mum and dad ... but you should let people know where you are. And don't you have loads to deal with? The funeral arrangements? Finances and things like that?'

'Auntie Gill's been helping me sort things out, but there's nothing else I can do until the funeral. I ought to call her and my mum, but my phone's dead. Can I borrow yours?'

'Course you can. I'll give you some privacy. I'll be down in the studio. I'll try and find you somewhere to stay.'

His face fell. 'Can't I stay here?'

Even though she'd already worked out he might ask, Poppy was still dismayed. 'I don't think that's a great idea. For a start, I don't have room. It's a studio flat.'

'Well, I can't stay anywhere else.' He pursed his lips. 'I kind of expected you to put me up in the circumstances.'

'If you'd called me, I'd have tried to arrange something more comfortable,' she said, thinking that she'd also have done her best to persuade him not to come at all or said she wasn't on Scilly. 'I'll help you find somewhere,' she added reassuringly while guessing she was clutching at straws. It wasn't as if St Piran's was bursting with hotels and the few places that existed would be more than likely fully booked in the main season.

'Thanks,' he muttered, with a distinct edge of sarcasm.

While Dan used his mobile to call his auntie, Poppy escaped downstairs to use the landline but also to take a few moments to calm down. She phoned round the two bed and breakfasts on St Piran's and the Moor's Head but all rooms had been reserved for many months. She considered phoning round some of the accommodation on the other islands but she'd need to find a boat to take Dan across. It was unlikely anyone would want to go out onto the rough seas and it would cost a fortune.

The alternative was to try a neighbour, but Fen had gone to visit a friend in Plymouth. Poppy didn't want to let Dan sleep at Fen's cottage or Archie's without their permission, even though she had the keys. She could ask Fen, she supposed ... but somehow, it was too personal and intimate to discuss with Fen. Whether she liked it or not, she felt Dan was still her responsibility.

She walked back into the studio to find him staring out of the window at the rain.

'I couldn't find a place for you to stay, so I'm afraid you'll have to sleep on the floor.'

'The floor?' he said as if she'd told him he had to sleep in the cat basket.

'Yes. The floor.' Surely, she thought, he hadn't been hoping to hop back into her bed? She tried to sound cheery and positive. 'I've got an airbed and sleeping bag, so you should be comfy. Zoey managed on the air mattress for a week and you know how picky she is.' She smiled encouragingly.

'Well, if it's OK for Zoey, I guess I'll have to manage. I can see you're short of space. It's much pokier up here than it looked on the internet. I bet you were gutted when you first saw it.'

'Actually, I was pleasantly surprised and the owners helped me redecorate it. It's fine for one,' she added pointedly.

A squall of rain pattered against the window. Dan stared at the grey sea, where waves slopped against the harbour wall, and the island boat that was safely tied up alongside the quay. 'Christ, look at that rain. I had no idea the weather could be this shit here. It was all so idyllic when we came.'

'The storm will blow over by nightfall,' she said, biting back a comment about it being a good job he'd decided not to come to St Piran's to open the studio with her, then. She kept reminding herself he'd suffered a terrible loss and she needed to cut him masses of slack. It was hardly surprising he had no thought for anyone else's feelings when he'd lost his dad so suddenly, but after so many months apart, she couldn't help thinking that he'd always been selfish and thoughtless, she just hadn't noticed how much until now. 'I'll just go and fetch the air mattress and pump.'

Poppy managed to scrape together two portions of mac

and cheese and found a couple of beers that Jake had brought over before he'd left. She let Dan pour his heart out about his dad, and his childhood memories, good and bad.

He blew his nose again and she handed over the half-empty box of tissues. 'I was wondering if you'd come to the funeral with me.'

She almost dropped the box. 'What? I-I—'

'I know it's a lot to ask, but I need your support. I don't think I could get through it without you.'

'You'll have your family. I really liked your dad and I do want to pay my respects ...' She'd never considered that he might expect her to go with him. Of course, she wanted to help and support him but ... 'I'm not sure I can leave the studio at short notice,' she said.

'Why not? It's your own business, isn't it? You can't be that busy out here.'

'Actually, we are. This is one of our peak times. I'd need to find someone to cover ...'

Tears trickled down his cheeks again.

She was torn in two. 'Look, I want to come to show my respects, believe me, but I'll have to see what I can do.'

By half past ten, they were both exhausted, so she suggested he get some rest and helped him blow up the mattress and make up the bed.

She disappeared into her shower room to change into her pyjamas and he did the same, emerging in only a pair of boxers. Even that was a weird enough sight: Dan in his pants. She tried to avert her eyes as he strolled around the kitchenette, collected a glass of water and took it to his makeshift bed on the floor. The thought that they'd once slept naked together every night made her cringe. He wasn't unattractive; he was fit and lean from his gym and mountain biking habit, but he was now a stranger to her, sexually.

She couldn't help comparing him with Jake who was more naturally muscular. Jake also had a nicely hairy chest unlike Dan, who, if she wasn't mistaken, seemed to have waxed or shaved off the light dusting of hair he used to have around his pecs and down his stomach. Maybe it was to better define his abs or something. She wished she hadn't noticed, but it was hard not to with him virtually naked in the flat. What would Dan say if he knew she'd slept with Jake? She shuddered to think.

And while the thought of Dan in the nude made her shudder, the thought of Jake naked gave her shivers of a different kind.

'Goodnight then,' said Dan, snapping her out of her thoughts about warm, naked bodies entwining in the bedroom of Archie's cottage. How far away that seemed now, how long ago ... though the memories were as vivid as a painting. She could smell Jake, fresh from the shower, and feel his warm skin under her fingertips and his thick dark hair in her hands. She shook the image away.

Dan eyed the airbed the same way that Leo eyed the wrong flavour of cat food when the shop hadn't had a delivery.

'Night,' she said, climbing under her duvet. She switched off the bedside lamp and heard him thumping the pillow and grumbling as he turned this way and that on the mattress.

She lay awake for a while, listening to the rain against the panes and the slosh of water on the shoreline, while trying to process the fact that Dan had landed on her doorstep and what she'd do with him next ...

She didn't know how much later it was when she woke with a start.

'Fucking hell!' Dan shrieked and Poppy fumbled for the lamp. Her heart banged away like crazy.

'What's the matter?' she called. 'Dan?'

The light clicked on and she blinked. He was sitting up, with his hands in the air. Leo was standing on his stomach, hissing.

'What the hell is this thing doing on me?'

She scrambled out of bed, still half asleep. She clapped her hands. 'Leo! Get off him!'

Leo jumped onto the floor.

'How did it get in?' he shouted.

Poppy scooped up Leo and deposited him on her bed. '*He* is called Leo and *he's* a cat, not an "it". Wait ... did you open the skylight in the shower room?'

'Yeah. It needed some fresh air in there. I was trying to be considerate, you know ... you always hated me not opening the window after ...'

Poppy cringed. 'Too much information. Leo must have got in through the skylight. He usually stays at Fen's overnight, but he must have come out through his cat flap. He's only trying to be friendly.'

'He can't sleep here with us.' Dan pulled the duvet up to his neck, presumably to protect himself from Leo, who was no longer interested. Instead Leo lay on Poppy's side of the bed, stretched out all four paws and yawned. His leg had healed nicely, she thought, which was much-needed good news.

'I'm not throwing him out. He must be missing Fen and he'll probably spend the rest of the night on my bed.' She climbed back under her duvet and nudged him gently onto the other side of the bed. 'Shift over, Leo,' she said and for once he obliged.

Dan glared at the cat in disgust. 'I'm allergic to animal fur, you know!'

Poppy was determined that no matter what the circumstances, Leo was staying put. 'Then open another window.'

Chapter 29

In the end, Poppy decided to go to the funeral, not so much for Dan, as for his dad. She wanted to pay her respects to a man she had liked a lot. If she had to go back to the Midlands, she could also spend a little time with her own family who she missed more than she dared to admit. It was the first time she'd been back since opening the Starfish Studio, and she braced herself for an emotional few days.

Like all funerals, the best that could be said, was that it was now over, thought Poppy as she lay awake that night in the spare room at her parents' bungalow. Dan's family had asked her to travel in the lead car and sit in the front row and she hadn't liked to refuse them even though it had felt decidedly awkward. Dan had insisted on holding her hand in the car and as they followed the coffin into the church. Everyone must think they were together again, and a few of his relatives went so far as to tell Poppy how glad they were. Dan didn't try to explain, leaving Poppy in total limbo, wondering whether she should contradict him directly or simply let it go, considering the occasion.

Never mind, she would soon be back on St Piran's. She couldn't leave the studio any longer. There was still almost three months left of the season, even though Fen reassured her that things were ticking over while she was away. She had found a space on the new helicopter shuttle in a few days' time, leaving her a chance to catch up with her parents, and with Zoey and her other friends.

Zoey met her for a drink the next evening in one of their old haunts. They squeezed into a booth away from the bar and Zoey told her about a disastrous Tinder encounter and a promising date she'd had with a personal trainer from the health club who she claimed looked like Aidan Turner. Poppy laughed almost continuously and it felt so good after the gloom of the past few days. Missing regular catch-ups with Zoey and her family was the biggest downside of being on St Piran's and was a serious temptation to move back home.

Zoey soon turned from her own love life to Poppy's.

'Are you OK? Dirty Dan turning up at the studio must have been a shock,' she said.

'You can say that again.' Poppy sipped her cocktail. She was struggling to hear Zoey above the hubbub in the bar from the music and scores of raised voices. It was rammed with people and she wasn't used to the level of noise or crowds of people after the quiet of St Piran's. On one level, she'd missed the buzz; on the other, she found it almost oppressive.

'I'm a bit surprised you came back with Dan for the funeral,' said Zoey.

'It was more for Pete and his family's sake than Dan's, although he was in a terrible state, what with his dad and Eve leaving him.'

'I was amazed when you told me she'd thrown him out but it serves him right ...Oh God, I hope he's not trying to get you back, is he?'

Poppy didn't want to tell Zoey that Dan had said he still loved her. She knew exactly how her friend would react, so she laughed it off. 'There's no chance.'

'I bloody hope not ... and what about Jake? Have you heard from him?'

'Not for the past few days, but he's probably stuck in some remote place in the jungle. I'm not waiting on his every email.'

'Oh really?' Zoey shook her head, then said gently, 'I admire you so much, Poppy. What you've done: making a new life for yourself after what Dan did to you – well, it's amazing. I might sound bossy, but that's 'cos I love you and I don't want anyone or anything to mess up what you've achieved.'

'Don't worry. They won't,' said Poppy, but from the doubtful expression in Zoey's eyes, she wasn't sure she'd convinced her friend completely.

The next morning, she'd only just finished booking her rail ticket south when Dan called to meet her for a 'chat'. Even though she was apprehensive about what he might have to say, she needed to face it head on. Besides, she was leaving the following morning so it was their last chance to talk face to face. How would he react when she told him she was going back to Scilly? Not that it should matter to her; after all he was one who'd left her.

Fen phoned to see how she was. Poppy picked up the call, crossing her fingers that there had been no more cat-related floods.

'Is everything OK at the Starfish? How's Leo?'

'Everything's tickety-boo. And Leo is a little monkey. He brought a dead goldcrest into the studio yesterday and dropped it right on the toes of Minty's snakeskin boots. She screeched like he'd committed a murder in front of her.' Poppy could hear the chuckle in Fen's voice. 'She actually came over to bring some more of her bits and pieces, though it was more like a royal visit. I'm sorry to say they're selling very well and didn't she let me know about it. I half wish no one would buy them.'

'It is a m-mixed blessing,' said Poppy, laughing as she pictured Leo delivering his 'gift' for Minty. 'I can't say I'm sorry I missed her although I've noticed she hasn't been calling in as much since Jake left.'

Fen chuckled. 'Hmm. By the way that Tim – the Phantom Crocheter – was here and complained that Rowan's latest bowl range was obscene, but I feigned all innocent, told him I'd no idea what he meant and asked him to explain. I thought he was going to have a heart attack trying to tell me why Rowan's pot was so rude and then he started to back-pedal like the clappers. Maisie and Jess were here, and they were wetting themselves too and Tim made a sharp exit.' Fen tutted loudly. 'Some people are such old fogeys. The things they get worked up about – a few saucy pots – when there's so much real horror in the world.'

'I know,' Poppy said, she could hardly speak for laughing. The Starfish Studio, she realised, made her smile. St Piran's made her smile. For all its quirky and often frustrating ways, she missed it. 'I wish I'd been there, Fen. I'll be back the day after tomorrow. I can't thank you enough for holding the fort.'

'I don't mind, honestly. Now it's not my responsibility and I can dip in and out when it suits me, I enjoy working in here. It's like having a grandchild you can hand back at the end of the day. Not that I've had any, of course.'

'Well, I'm glad you're enjoying it and thanks again,' said Poppy. She had a pang of sympathy for Fen. She didn't know if Fen had ever wanted children of her own or not; it was wrong to assume that she had. However, judging by those drawings of Archie's, she was convinced that she'd had at least one love affair and that it hadn't ended happily. In that way, she and Fen were kindred spirits. There might be almost fifty years between her and Fen, but they had a lot in common. Fen had a young and generous spirit and Poppy hoped she was that open-minded and fun to be with when she was almost eighty.

'How's your man doing?' said Fen. 'It must be hard for him, on his own.'

Poppy cringed. 'Dan's OK, I think, considering. I'm fine. I'm looking forward to coming home,' she added, just in case Fen hadn't got the message that Dan was definitely not 'her man'.

'Don't worry about the studio. I'm managing and everyone's chipping in.'

'I don't know how to thank you.'

'Oh, you'll be able to too soon enough. We're notching it up on your account, ready for when you come home.'

After saying their goodbyes, Poppy put down the phone and looked around the sitting room. Her parents had redecorated after she'd gone to university but a few traces of her youth remained. A photo of her with her friends on graduation day and a watercolour of a Cornish harbour she'd bought while she was working in the craft centre. The room focused her mind on how much had changed since those days – before she'd even met Dan – but also on her ties to home, the love she had for her parents and how much she missed Zoey. Had she tried to take too many steps, too soon after Dan had left?

In the space of a few minutes, her mood had switched from gloom to hope and back to gloom again. Fen's reports of the studio and island life had briefly set her back on track: she'd been looking forward to returning to the Starfish and kick-starting her new life. Now, she didn't know where home was any more.

The Canalside Café was a cheerful sight with its brightly painted narrowboats chugging past the red-brick cottages and pub. She and Dan had cycled there many times from their Staffordshire home in happier days and Poppy felt it was a place that might lift Dan's spirits and also one where they could find private space to talk.

Lime and willow trees overhung the canal and she noticed that the leaves were tinged with yellow and a few were floating on the water canal. A slight hint of autumn was definitely in the air here in the Midlands, while it still seemed high summer on Scilly.

When Dan turned up, they ordered a coffee and a cake each – although Poppy had little appetite – and managed to bag an outside table next to the towpath. With cyclists, dog walkers and families, the café and towpaths seemed packed to her. It was such a contrast to the studio, where half a dozen visitors constituted a crowd.

They talked about the wake and even shared a few smiles at some of the off-colour jokes and dodgy anecdotes that Dan's elderly uncle had related when he'd had one too many whiskies. Poppy didn't mention that some of his relatives had asked if she and Dan were back together.

'Mum's invited me to fly over to Auckland in November to visit her. She said she'll pay for my ticket,' said Dan.

'That sounds exciting. It'll be a great experience,' said Poppy, pleased that he sounded keen to take his mother up on the offer. With the distance between them, he hadn't seen that much of her over the past few years.

He nodded, then seemed distracted by a narrowboat idling alongside them and people shouting as it manoeuvred into the lock. Poppy gave him time, but the goose bumps were raised on her arms. She had a feeling something was coming ... and that she might not like it.

He turned back to look at her. 'You could come with me, you know.'

Chapter 30

'Thanks for the lift, mate.'

Jake jumped off Trevor's boat and walked briskly up from St Piran's harbour towards the Starfish Studio. He didn't want to get into conversation with anyone before he reached it, so he kept his head down and barely grunted a 'hi' at the couple who ran the kiosk. Never mind, he had a reputation for being a taciturn, moody sod, so they wouldn't be surprised. Thirty seconds later, he was stepping up onto the veranda to find the door ...

Locked.

He tried it again and then realised that there was no stock on the decking. Come to think of it, he hadn't noticed the advertising board at the end of the quay, but then he'd been homing in on his destination like Leo after a fresh dish of hare and badger.

He smiled. He'd even missed Leo while he'd been on his travels, let alone Fen, his grandpa and his family. And as for

Poppy ... the nights had been agony. The days hadn't been quite so bad, as long as he was totally engaged in his subject. However, in any spare moment, she had slipped into his thoughts with her smile and her wicked laugh and her arch comments and her lovely smell and her curvy bum and her toned, tanned legs. And now he was back to try to persuade her that he'd been a total twat and should never have left without telling her how he felt about her ... but first he had to get her to answer the door.

In fact, he thought, peering through the window, it looked as if there was no one in at all, yet it was half past ten; the ferry was about to arrive bringing the first visitors of the day. Maybe she was having a lie-in, although it was unlikely ... unless she'd been out the night before, or unless ... Jake groaned and squeezed his eyes shut. Unless she was having a lie-in with someone else.

'Oh, the wanderer returns!' Jake turned around sharply as Minty skipped up the steps onto the veranda. 'Are you looking for Poppy?'

He managed to dredge up a brief smile. 'Hi, Minty. Yes, I was wondering why the studio was closed.'

'Hadn't you heard? Poppy's gone back home.'

He frowned. 'Home to the Midlands? For a break?' He'd thought it was weird while it was still holiday season.

Minty shrugged. 'Um. A family crisis. I don't know for absolute sure because I only heard it on the grapevine.' She wagged her finger. 'It's naughty of me to speculate. I could be completely wrong.'

'Wrong about *what*?' Jake was riled, even though he

suspected Minty was trying to wind him up – and succeeding.

'No. I absolutely don't want to cause trouble between you two.' The glint in her eyes suggested otherwise.

'I'm sure you don't,' he said smoothly, trying charm on Minty. 'But if you have any clue why she's gone, I'd really appreciate your insight.'

Minty sighed. 'We-ell. She did have a guy staying over. In fact, he answered the door to me a few days ago. I popped over with some new pieces for the studio as they've been selling so incredibly well, but the studio was locked, which is unusual it itself, don't you think?'

'I've no idea,' said Jake, fighting the urge to shout *Who was this man?* 'Poppy isn't used to leaving doors unlocked yet, being a city girl. You say some bloke answered the door ...'

'He did. He was in his boxers, you see, and it was almost ten o'clock in the morning.' Minty virtually purred in delight at delivering the information. 'I had quite a shock.'

'I'm sure you've seen it all before,' said Jake.

'Actually, not enough of it ...' She looked him up and down as if she wanted to lick him.

Jake forced himself to stay calm. 'So, this man? Do you happen to know who he is?'

'He's her ex, apparently. Although maybe not *so* "ex" any more from what he said to me. He referred to himself as "her partner", although I know she's meant to have split up with him months ago. He told me that Poppy was still in bed and he'd give the stock to her when she "surfaced".' Minty did a finger quoting gesture just in case Jake hadn't got the message about the bed. He had, loud and clear.

'And?' said Jake, hating to let on to Minty that he cared so much about Poppy's love life but eager to glean every tiny detail.

'And when I asked him when the studio would be open, he told me he didn't know as Poppy was getting a flight back to Newquay with him and then they were taking the train to Birmingham. He said that his father had passed away and Poppy was going home with him.'

'Shit.' The word slipped out before Jake could stop it. 'Going home for good?'

Minty laid her hand on his arm. 'I honestly couldn't say, but this guy – Dan, I think – said he didn't think she would be back once she'd gone home. He did say that he'd like to try and make a go of things with her again.'

'What?' Jake couldn't stop himself this time.

'I'm sorry if it's bad news, but ex-partners do often get back together. Once you've had that spark with someone, it's hard to put it out.'

'Seems like it,' said Jake, realising a fraction of a second too late that Minty was hinting at their fling.

Her eyes lit up in delight. 'Do you want me to make you a coffee? You've had a long journey and a big shock. I presume you're staying at Archie's?'

'Yes, I am and thanks, but no thanks, to the coffee. I'm knackered to be honest, Minty.'

Her face fell. 'Are you sure? I don't like leaving you like this.'

'Like what?' Jake flashed her a smile. 'There's nothing wrong with me that a hot shower and a good kip won't cure.'

'Both of those things sound fabulous but would surely be better with a friend?'

Well, you couldn't blame her for trying, thought Jake, though he was desperate to be alone to process what Minty had shared about Dan and Poppy getting back together.

'Thanks, but I need to be on my own. And thanks for the information. See you around.'

'Hope so and you know where I am if you need me.'

Jake smiled again even though it hurt his jaw, slung his pack on his back and left her on the veranda.

His mind worked overtime while he let himself into the cottage. Only something major would persuade Poppy to close the studio in mid-season and her ex-partner losing his father was just such a thing. Poppy was a kind and loving person and she'd never turn away even a cheating louse like Dan in those circumstances ... though why the guy had travelled all this way to see Poppy, when he had a new partner, was beyond Jake's comprehension.

Then again ... Dan might have travelled all this way precisely *because* he must have left his new partner. He'd obviously woken up to the fact that he was an idiot to have left Poppy and headed out here to get her back. And Poppy had gone with him – which was understandable but also made Jake feel slightly sick. Why didn't he say something before he'd left? Because it was way too soon, that's why. As he suspected, Poppy clearly hadn't got over Dan and who knew what might have happened if the man had flown out here grieving and vulnerable – and begging her to give him another try?

Damn, damn and damn.

He trusted Minty's version of events about as much as he trusted Facebook news, but she wouldn't have made up Dan being at the studio, or Poppy leaving the island with him. Nor would she lie outright about what the man had said about Poppy. He wandered from kitchen to sitting room, unable to rest even after his long journey.

Dan and Poppy had only been separated a few months and they had been together for years and were obviously committed to each other enough at one time, to plan a new life on Scilly. God knows, after Harriet's death, Jake would have given anything to have her back, no matter what had passed between them before her accident. Poppy might have thought she was over Dan, but he'd often wondered if she was putting on a brave face and was still hurting far more deeply than she'd ever let on to him.

Despite their night together, he and Poppy had never really opened up to each other about their feelings. That was mostly his fault for shutting her out and blowing hot and cold, as his mum liked to put it. He didn't want to pressure her because he'd been worried that she wasn't ready for a new relationship, but after so long away from her, he now knew that it was he, Jake, who'd been afraid to start again. And, of course, if he admitted his real feelings, he'd have to stay on St Piran's to be with her. These past weeks, so far from home and so far from Poppy, had made him realise that he *did* want to be with her and did have the courage to go for it. Now it looked as if he might be too late.

He should call her – better still, he needed to see her face to face.

First, he phoned his mum to let her know he was home.

'Jake. Where are you?'

'On Scilly. At Grandpa's house.'

'What? What are you doing there? I thought you were coming straight to us after you landed?'

'I – needed to come here.'

His mother let out an audible sigh. 'OK. I won't ask, but all's well that ends well because it's perfect you're on St Piran's. We've been trying to get hold of you for ages.'

By ages his mum probably meant twenty minutes. 'Why? What's up.'

'It's your grandpa, I'm afraid.'

'Grandpa?' Jake sat up; his pulse rocketed. 'Oh God, what's happened to him now?'

'Don't panic. He's fine.' His mum sounded stressed out herself. 'In fact, anyone would think he'd made a miraculous recovery overnight. He's coming back to St Piran's. He just decided this morning, booked a flight and demanded that your dad take him to the airport. We couldn't get hold of you until now. He's probably on his way across to St Piran's as we speak.'

Chapter 31

Jake scanned the faces on the deck of the *Islander* ferry, hoping to spot his grandpa before he walked down the gangplank. It had berthed at the quay in St Mary's a few minutes before and the staff had swung into action, tying her up and bringing forklifts ready to unload the freight and luggage she brought along with her passengers.

Excited visitors chattered on the deck, pointing and taking pictures as they got their first close-up glimpse of St Mary's – but there was no sign of Archie. It was just gone noon, and soon the visitors would pour off the boat and into the little Scilly capital or onto the smaller vessels waiting to take them to the 'off-islands'.

After his mum had called, Jake had tried to reach Fen via her sister's landline, only for it to go straight to answerphone. In the end, he'd found Lisa from the Harbour Kiosk who told him that Fen had taken the helicopter the previous morning to attend a funeral on the mainland. Jake's jaw had dropped.

Fen hated the helicopter after one bad experience years before so he was astonished she'd set foot on one now. Lisa had no idea who the friend was but said Fen had been very upset and had left Leo in her care until she returned.

Jake's mind was whirling: with Poppy probably back with Dan, Fen grieving and out of contact and his grandpa about to arrive, he'd landed in the midst of total chaos. However, he had to pull himself together, as meeting Archie was his immediate priority.

He'd booked a place on a private jetboat to St Piran's, figuring it would be easier to have a 'taxi' than have to crowd onto one of the public services. When he couldn't spot the old man from the quayside, he guessed he was already on a lower deck waiting to disembark. He still used a walking stick, so it was likely the crew would give him some assistance to get down from the deck and off the ship. They probably all knew his grandpa anyway. Archie had always loved the *Islander* ferry, preferring the leisurely three-hour cruise to the short flight.

Jake hurried over to the gangway and, a minute later, Archie appeared. One of the crew was carrying his bags.

He was waving away any attempts for assistance. 'I'm fine. Don't fuss. Thanks for carrying my bags, but I don't need any more help,' he told the crew member holding his elbow.

Jake jogged over. 'Welcome home, Grandpa!' he said, hugging him warmly.

Archie squeezed Jake's back. 'It's good to be here.'

'Thanks,' Jake said to the crew member who held the ancient holdall and battered suitcase. 'I'm sure Grandpa appreciates the help, even if it doesn't act like it,' he added quietly.

'A pleasure. See you around, Archie,' said the crewman with a grin and left the bags next to them before disappearing back into the ship.

Archie peered at Jake. 'You look thin, boy. What have you been eating in that jungle? Spiders?'

'They're very nutritious,' said Jake, thinking that his grandpa had lost a bit of weight too but looked miles better than when he'd seen him at his parents' house a few months previously.

Jake slowed his pace while they made their way towards their water taxi, but his grandpa was doing remarkably well.

'I've arranged transport over to St Piran's,' said Jakc, 'Look, the jetboat's already here and waiting. Shall I give you a hand down the steps to it?'

'The jetboat, eh?' Archie's eye twinkled. 'I'm highly honoured. I can manage the steps if you'll carry my bags.'

'Of course, Grandpa. Did you know that Fen's gone to the mainland? Has she spoken to you about it?'

Archie frowned. 'No. Not a word.'

'Lisa says she took the helicopter.'

'That thing? Why?'

'She rushed off to a funeral, apparently. Lisa said it was a family friend.'

'A friend? Oh.' Archie sighed. 'Oh dear. Poor bird. My poor Fen.'

'What do you mean? Do you know whose funeral it was?'

'Not for definite, but I can guess if Fen took the helicopter. Poor poor girl.'

'Who is it?'

Archie shook his head. He seemed downcast.

'Grandpa. What are you not telling me?'

He patted Jake's hand. 'Nothing, boy. I only feel deeply sorry for Fen, losing her friend. I'll call her when I get into the cottage. Now, let's get home.'

Jake decided not to push the topic: his grandpa would tell him more in his own good time and it was obvious Archie was desperate to be back in his own space.

Despite his insistence that he was OK to climb down the steep stone steps, the jetboat skipper kept a close eye on him – much to Archie's disapproval – and helped him on board, citing 'health and safety'. Jake kept a watch at the rear, trying not to fuss but wary of his grandpa's still-fragile condition. His doctors had said he was healing well, but Jake wasn't prepared to take any risks.

On the short voyage to St Piran's, Archie didn't miss a thing, commenting on the restored tripper boat in the harbour, how high the tide was, and noticing that the jetboat had a new skipper at the helm. He drank in every feature, the rocky skerries, the sandbanks glistening with weed, the seals basking in the sun and the seabirds wheeling overhead. Every now and then, he made a remark, but as they neared the St Piran's jetty, Jake noticed him fall silent.

On the quayside, a small throng of people was waiting.

'What's this?' Archie said, pointing to the little crowd who were waving at him. Jake broke into a grin as he spotted Lisa and Ben, plus the landlady from the Moor's Head and Maisie – and wow, with a baby buggy. Jess Godrevy was also there, holding a large bunch of flowers from her farm.

'Welcome home, Archie!' they chorused as the skipper cut the engine.

He shook his head. 'I said I didn't want a fuss,' he muttered, glaring at Jake.

He held up his hands. 'I might have mentioned you were coming back to a few people, but the welcome party is nothing to do with me. They've turned up of their own accord.'

Archie grunted and the crewman opened the gangway door so they could disembark. He agreed to be helped off the boat as the jetty steps were steep and slippery with seaweed.

'Welcome back!' everyone chanted again once he was safely on the stone quay.

'You soft devils,' he said, then saw the baby buggy and his face lit up. 'Is that the little one? Fen told me she'd been born.'

Maisie pushed the buggy forward and lifted a tiny baby out of it, which promptly let out a piercing wail. 'Meet Eloise Jonquil Samson. The newest and –' Maisie winced '– loudest inhabitant of Gull Island.'

'She's very bonny. Like her mother,' said Archie, as the baby grasped his thumb. Jake was sure there was a glint in his grandpa's eye. 'I've missed a lot,' he said.

'You can catch up now. Hope we'll be seeing you in the Driftwood soon?'

'And the Moor's Head,' said the landlady. 'We've a pint of Challenger waiting for you when you're ready.'

'Thanks,' said Archie, smacking his lips at the mention of his favourite local ale. 'You won't keep me away from the Driftwood or the Moor's Head. The beer in those mainland pubs is like gnats' piss. I'm dying for a proper drink.'

Everyone laughed, including Jake. His grandpa sounded far more like his old self than he had for months.

Jess held out the bouquet. 'Great to have you home.'

He kissed her cheek. 'You shouldn't have, but thank you.'

'Shall I drop it at the cottage for you?' she said, nodding at Archie's stick. She'd obviously realised he didn't have a free hand to carry the large bunch of pinks.

'That'd be grand,' said Archie, then shook his head. 'I hear you're back with Adam Pengelly. I don't know why you two ever split up. I could have knocked your heads together.'

Jake cringed, but Jess clearly took the advice on her love life in good spirit and laughed. 'Actually, we're engaged,' she said, holding out her left hand.

Archie looked at the ring and blew out a breath. 'Postmen must be paid well these days. Congratulations. Adam's a lucky man.'

Lisa from the Harbour Kiosk stepped forward and gave Archie a brief hug. 'There's a cream tea waiting in your cottage. Sorry, I have to get back to work now, but we're here any time you need anything.'

'I don't deserve all this fuss,' said Archie. 'But I've also missed a proper cream tea, so that'll be grand.'

'Thanks, everyone,' said Jake. 'Maybe we can get together for a drink when Grandpa's settled in?'

'Definitely,' said Maisie. 'There's the christening to look forward to and I'm sure we'll see you all at the Driftwood to wet the baby's head.'

'Try keeping me away,' said Archie. 'See you all later and thank you for the welcome party. Now bugger off back to work.'

Laughter echoed off the stone as people dispersed to go about their business. Maisie and Jess pushed the baby in the direction of the beach, while the landlady walked back towards the pub at the other end of the island. Lisa was already at the kiosk, putting on her apron ready to serve ice creams to the visitors lounging at the outside tables.

'How's business been at the studio?' Archie asked Jake as they made their way steadily to the cottage. They were almost level with the studio.

'OK, I think. I haven't had chance to ask since I've been back.'

'Your mother said you didn't get in touch with her for a week. She was beside herself.'

Jake winced at his grandpa's admonishment, because it was well deserved. 'I was totally out of contact in a tribal village in the middle of the jungle. The satellite phone stopped working, the radio packed it in and there was no internet.'

'Sounds like the old days on St Piran's,' Archie said tartly. He slowed down and then stopped in front of the studio. 'My ... *the* studio looks smart.'

Jake smiled to himself. He'd been a little nervous of his grandpa's reaction to the revamped building. 'You approve?'

Archie stepped forward. 'If it looks as good on the inside as the out, I do. Is that a new roof on the veranda? And it's been repainted.'

'The Gull Island Trust came to help with the roof repairs and exterior paintwork and I helped Poppy with the interior painting. There's more work been done inside ... a lot more ...'

Archie tutted. 'I shouldn't have let it go downhill. If my

bloody hip hadn't let me down, I'd have helped you do the place up myself. What a silly old fool, I am, slipping over like that. It half killed me to have to leave all the work to you, Jake. I know you hate coming back here.'

'I didn't mind the work. I was at a loose end after my last job in the spring, so I needed something to keep me occupied. I'd been travelling a long time and I don't hate St Piran's. Not now.'

Archie gave him a searching look. '*Don't hate it*. My, that's progress. What's changed your mind, boy?'

'I don't know. Time and ...' Jake shrugged. 'I just had to get on with things. Shall we go to the cottage and get settled in?' He clammed up and changed the subject. His falling back in love with St Piran's was rapidly turning into a falling back out now Poppy had left.

'I'd like to see around the studio. I was planning to get back in there and start painting again,' said Archie. 'Why is it closed? Where is the new woman – Poppy? I'd have thought she'd have been keen to show the place off.'

It was the question Jake had been dreading and he was only surprised his grandpa had waited until now.

'She's not here.'

Archie raised a bushy white eyebrow. 'Where's she got to?'

'I don't know exactly ...'

Archie peered at him.

'I think she's gone home,' said Jake.

'Why? Does Fen know what's going on?'

'She probably does but I haven't had chance to speak to her.' Jake cursed himself for being a coward.

'I'll call her as soon as I'm settled in and I'll ask her what's happening.' He gave Jake the gimlet eye. 'Don't you have young Poppy's phone number yourself? Or her internet? You seem to be on your phones and computers all the time, so can't you contact her?'

Jake squirmed under the interrogation. 'Yes, I do have her number but I only found out today she'd gone and then Mum phoned and said you'd be here. And it's not that simple. I don't want to interfere, Grandpa.'

'I thought you and she were friendly. Fen said as much and you never stopped mentioning her name on the phone.'

Jake smiled to himself. He might have guessed that he couldn't pull the wool over his grandpa's eyes.

'Well, I don't know where she is and I haven't asked her and I don't want to, so can we leave it at that? *Please?* I'm sure I'll find out soon enough. Let's get your stuff into the cottage.'

Archie shook his head. 'I really do despair of you youngsters sometimes. Whatever happened to seizing the day and just getting on with things?' He sighed. 'Come on, let me get home …' His face suddenly changed to dismay. 'More importantly, if you've all been off flying your kites, who's been looking after Leo?'

Jake reassured Archie that Lisa from the kiosk had been looking after him. Lisa had also mentioned that Poppy had gone to the mainland to attend a funeral with her ex when he'd bumped into her on his way to meet his grandfather on St Mary's. It seemed increasingly likely that Poppy might have decided to give up on the Starfish, but until Jake could ask

Fen if she'd heard anything – or swallowed his pride and spoke to Poppy directly – he was going to be left in self-inflicted agony.

How arrogant and bloody stupid it seemed now, to simply think he could turn up on her doorstep and declare undying love without even telling her he was coming or giving a hint of his feelings in his messages to her.

OK, he'd only summoned up the courage to admit them to himself a week ago, and as for deciding to tell Poppy – that had only happened on the flight to the UK. He'd booked an onward flight from Newquay to Scilly while he was in the departure lounge at Heathrow. Everything seemed to be dovetailing – coming together in a perfect way – but not once had he considered Poppy not being there when he came home.

Jake settled Archie in and made a cup of tea while his grandpa rang Fen, but when he came back he found Archie shaking his head at the phone.

'I still can't get hold of Fen. Her sister said she went for a walk a couple of hours ago. She'd expected her back by now.'

'I don't know why she won't have a mobile,' said Jake.

'She says she's managed without one this long and doesn't want to be bothered now. You can't blame her. Though I wouldn't be without my iPhone.'

'I'm sure she'll be back soon; she probably bumped into someone she knows.' Hiding his unease, Jake handed over the tea and sat opposite Archie. He had to confess one of his big secrets now before his grandpa made his way upstairs to the bedroom. 'Grandpa. I need to tell you something.'

Archie frowned. 'This sounds serious.'

'I found the crate of paintings in the studio and the letter.'

Archie slurped his tea before muttering. 'Oh?'

'I moved the crate into the spare room.'

'I suppose you opened it and the letter?'

Jake reached out and touched his hand. 'I know it was wrong, but I couldn't help myself.'

'I guessed you might, but when you didn't mention it all this time, I wasn't sure you'd opened it. It was meant for you after I'm gone. It's all right, boy, don't fret about it.' He patted Jake's arm.

Jake was flooded with relief. 'You didn't really think something might happen to you, did you?' he asked, pleased to have the burden of the crate lifted from his mind.

'I was just being prepared. It seemed the sensible thing to do while I was able. I didn't know at the time I wrote the letter and packed up the paintings that I'd end up in hospital.'

'I was worried about you.'

He patted Jake's arm again. 'Turns out it takes a lot to finish me off, though I'll admit when the accident first happened, I was in a lot of pain, but worse than that, I felt helpless. I had to rely on the nurses to do everything for me and then on your mum and dad. I hated it and I know some people have to accept the help, and it might be wrong of me, but having my independence taken from me was like a bereavement.'

'We wanted to help you. We all want to see you better and no one minded doing what they could.'

'I did,' said Archie fiercely. 'I thought I'd be stuck in a wheelchair or immobile. I didn't know if I'd ever be able to come back home and live in my cottage, or paint where I want to in the open air or sail my boat. I still don't know if I can sail her, but at least I'm here.'

'I thought you didn't want to come home ...'

'I did but my confidence took a knock and, well, I haven't seen as much of your mum and dad as I ought to, so once I'd stopped feeling so sorry for myself, I decided to make the best of a bad job and spend some time with them. I missed Fen and Leo and the isles like a limb, but the plus side of being away – being with your mum and dad – dawned on me too.'

'They enjoyed having you, especially once you were on the mend.'

'Yes, well it was good to see them and catch up. Besides, I don't heal so fast these days and it didn't take much to set me back ... I was glad of the company and the support, no matter how much I grumbled. Once you started mentioning Poppy and working with her on the studio, you seemed more like your old self too.'

Jake caught his breath. He knew that something else might have behind his grandpa's extended 'recuperation' but hadn't been quite sure ...

'Really?'

'At first I was only grateful you were here to help her. I felt so guilty, but I knew I was in no fit state to paint, let alone redecorate the studio. Then I detected more. You sounded happy, Jake. You stopped talking about the place like it was a hell on earth that you wanted to bury or pretend never existed. You mentioned the photographs and I knew that you were on the mend too.'

'I – I think that coming back helped. Seeing it through fresh eyes. Through your eyes, Grandpa.'

'And through hers?'

'Yes. Through Poppy's eyes. She saw things I hadn't noticed or made me look at them in a new way.' He hesitated, only now voicing a feeling he'd had for months. 'She hasn't only made me see the landscapes through fresh eyes but myself as well.'

'And love?'

'Maybe.' He shrugged. 'I don't know.'

'Does she?'

'What?'

'Know how you feel? Know what you've just told me?'

'I doubt it. I haven't told her. In fact –' he took a deep breath '– the reason I headed straight here from Heathrow, rather than calling in at Mum and Dad's, was because I wanted to tell her how I feel before I lose my nerve again. The months I've spent apart from her have made me realise that. Call it perspective ... But now she's gone too.'

'And you won't phone her to find out what's going on?'

'No. I don't think it's right to intrude.'

'You mean you're too scared?'

'Yes. I suppose do. She might want to make a go of things with her ex again.'

'Her ex?' Archie snorted. 'From what I saw of him, the man is a total prat.'

Jake laughed, recalling Dan's brusque brush-off when he thought Jake was trying to sell him something. 'I only met him once, but I have to agree.'

'He kept me talking in the studio and was a know-all. He seemed to like putting Poppy down too. Treats people like they're some kind of business deal he has to win. She won't go back to him, Jake.'

'I hope not, but she's been lonely here, however much she's tried to hide it. I'm not sure she'd made up her mind to stay.'

'So, what are you going to do about it?' said Archie.

'Call Poppy.' Jake surprised himself with the forcefulness of his response.

'Then get on with it before it is too late.'

Jake was about to reply when there a rattle from the front door.

'Leo!'

The cat trotted in and jumped deftly onto the sofa and then onto Archie's lap.

Archie rubbed his head and Leo purred like a drill. 'I thought I'd never see you again, matey,' he said, his eyes bright with moisture. 'But I'm back now and I'm never going away again.'

After a late lunch, Jake left his grandpa to have a nap and went for walk, taking his camera with him. It was a lovely day and he thought he might capture some images while he summoned up the nerve to call Poppy. To his surprise, he realised he wanted to take photos; it wasn't a burden: he'd rediscovered his love of St Piran's since he'd produced Poppy's prints.

He took a narrow track behind the cottage, which led through the modest garden and up through the gorse and bracken onto the small stretch of heathland that covered the central plateau of St Piran's. The island was only a mile by a mile and a half and barely a hundred feet above sea level.

Half a dozen hardy red cattle grazed the heathland and were milked at the small farm. Their milk was made into butter, frozen yoghurt and the ice cream sold at the Harbour Kiosk. They lifted their heads and looked at Jake as he walked past but went back to their grazing. He climbed up to a small cairn, which marked the highest point of St Piran's. A mile across the inky deep-water channel, he could see the low green island of St Mary's and make out the *Islander* ferry at the quayside. Beyond St Mary's, the smaller islands of Gull and St Saviour's were hazy outcrops.

It was a calm late summer afternoon, the light mellow and kind. He took a few pictures of the cloud patterns on the sea but he struggled to get the right shot. Deep down, he knew he was only putting off the moment when he had to make his call.

He sat down on a lump of granite. With his heart beating fast, he dialled her number but it went straight to answerphone.

'Fuck.'

One of the cows lifted its head as he swore.

He left it a few minutes, staring out over the sea, willing Poppy to pick up her phone, but his next two calls also met her answerphone. He stabbed the off button but then thought she might worry something dire had happened to him or the studio if he didn't at least leave a message, so he called back a fourth time and left a message.

'Poppy. It's Jake. Nothing to worry about but I thought I'd let you know that Grandpa's back on St Piran's. I hope you're OK ... Call me if you can ...' He shoved the phone in his pocket. 'Shit.' He could email her or WhatsApp her when he got back to the studio. *But no, this can't be done in a message*, he thought.

A second cow stared at him. A cow with impressive horns.

'I know, I know. Another mad human talking to himself. Bet you get a lot of that,' Jake told the cow. 'Maybe I should go and see her face to face,' he said, then dismissed the idea. He couldn't leave Grandpa until Fen came home. 'I can't just turn up on her doorstep without warning her. What if she's with him – Dan the Man?'

The cow had stopped listening and was munching the grass. Jake sighed. The cow obviously thought it was a rubbish plan too. After another few minutes of staring at his phone, willing it to ring, he pushed himself up and strode back towards the cottage.

'Grandpa ...' Jake called softly as he let himself into the hallway. He didn't want to startle his grandad or wake him unnecessarily.

Jake pushed the sitting room door open a crack and peered round it. Archie's favourite chair was empty.

'Grandpa!' He checked the kitchen before trotting upstairs to see if Archie had gone for a lie-down in his room. There was no sign of him in the cottage, so Jake went back down and out into the garden. A few minutes later, he was beginning to worry a little. Archie hadn't left a note.

He went out onto the harbourside to see if he could spot him, and Trevor saw him.

'Good to see Archie back,' he said.

'Have you seen him, then? I've been for a walk and he wasn't in the cottage.'

'Yes, not ten minutes ago. He went into the Starfish. Do you know when Poppy will be back by the way?'

'No, sorry,' said Jake, as his unease made his stomach clench.

He found the door to the studio unlocked and guessed that Archie had used his own keys. Sure enough, Archie was standing in the work area.

'Grandpa! I didn't know you were up and about or I'd have come back from my walk sooner.'

'I couldn't wait any longer to see the old place and I thought you'd be busy. Did you speak to your girl?'

'She's not my girl, and no. I did try, but she wasn't picking up her phone ...' Jake noticed that the drawer to the worktable was open and then realised that its contents were spread over the table.

'Has anyone been in this drawer?' Archie asked.

Jake winced. 'Yes. We were looking for a list of artists and suppliers and I found a spare key ... so we sort of opened it.'

'I see.' Archie ran his fingers over the paperwork and sheets on the worktable, spreading them apart. 'And did you find anything?'

Jake hesitated. Although he and Poppy had come across the sketches by accident, he did feel he'd pried into a very personal aspect of his grandpa and Fen's lives, but there was no use denying he'd seen the sketches now. 'I did. *We* did. Poppy and I found some old sketches of Fen in the dunes. We didn't know what to do with them because they seemed kind of … personal, so I locked them in the bureau in the cottage.'

Archie sat down on the stool. 'Oh, you did, did you?' he said quietly.

Jake perched on the seat opposite Archie. 'I guessed they were important to you and Fen so I thought it was best to put them somewhere safe. I hope you're not too upset?'

Archie shook his head. 'No. No. I'm not upset. I should have moved them anyway, but I'd half forgotten they were even in there until this afternoon when you told me you'd opened the crate.'

'I'm glad I opened it now. It did help me, even if you hadn't intended me to.'

His eyes lit with hope. 'Really, boy? I wanted you to love St Piran's again, then Fen told me you seemed to be getting on with Poppy and so I also thought it wouldn't do any harm to stay away from the island a little bit longer to give you time together … You falling for Poppy was a bonus I'd never reckoned on.'

Jake shook his head but he couldn't keep the smile off his face either. Grandpa Archie was a crafty old devil.

'As for the sketches, I knew you'd find them one day,' Archie went on. 'Of course, I have a past, Jake. So does Fen. None of us are perfect. Nobody is. I made mistakes, bad decisions – just like you seem to think you have.'

'You don't have to feel guilty; whatever happened with you and Fen is none of my business.'

Archie grabbed his arm. 'I want to tell you! I know you weren't happy with Harriet, not as happy as a couple about to spend the rest of their lives together should be. You needn't hide it, Jake, I could tell from the final time you visited me with her.'

'I ... we were trying to work things out between us.' Jake had never admitted to anyone that he and Harriet had been having problems. A pang of grief and guilt clutched at him. This was a difficult conversation but one that he couldn't, and now realised he didn't want to avoid.

Archie's voice had taken on a passion Jake had rarely heard him use. 'What goes on between lovers should stay between them, but you may as well know, as you've probably guessed, that Fen and I – well, we have been more than friends.'

Jake prickled with discomfort. It felt wrong to hear the details of his grandparents' private lives and he definitely didn't want to be told that his beloved grandfather might have hurt his grandmother. 'I'm not sure you should be telling me this,' he said softly.

'Are you afraid to hear it? Well, don't be. None of us is perfect, but if you're worried that I had an affair with Fen behind Ellie's back, you can rest easy. Fen and I have always had a fondness for each other that went beyond friendship, that's true. We all knew each other at school, you know. Fen and Ellie were in the same class at St Piran's primary school, back in the day when the island had a school. I was couple of years above them. We grew up together.' Archie paused and pulled out a handkerchief from his pocket and dabbed his eyes.

'Don't tell me this if it upsets you,' said Jake.

'Or you?' Archie came back. 'I'm sorry, Jake. I didn't mean

to be harsh but I need to tell you in case I never get another chance, so please hear me out.'

'OK,' said Jake, moved by the intensity of his grandpa's tone.

'I loved your grandma and I loved Fen, but I had to choose one and I chose Ellie. When we left school, and I'd started to make enough to support a family with my fishing and my painting, I married her and we settled down. I still cared for Fen, but I was never tempted to do anything about it, even though she lived so close. We kept the way we felt about each other deep inside and I *hope* Ellie never knew.'

Archie paused for breath before going on.

'I'll admit that after she passed away, I tormented myself for years that she might have guessed I also loved Fen and suffered silently. I hope not. Fen had her own private life, and she and I stayed friends. It wasn't until after your grandmother had been gone a year that Fen and I became close again.'

'That's when you did the later sketches,' said Jake, still uncomfortable with such private details but realising that his grandpa needed to get this huge burden off his chest. He'd probably never told another person how he felt in his whole life.

'Yes. It must have been a shock finding them.' A smile touched his lips.

Jake had to smile too. 'It's OK, Grandpa. I'm a photographer – I've seen racier stuff.'

Archie chuckled. 'But nothing so personal?'

'No. Probably not,' said Jake, recalling the shock of seeing the drawings again.

'I was young once and I am an artist, so I've seen and experienced a lot more than you imagine. Although life drawings aren't my strong point.'

Jake let him pause, then voiced the thing he had to ask. 'There was another drawing, Grandpa. Fen seemed a lot younger in that one.'

Archie nodded. 'Yes, I did that picture of her too and in the same place, but that early sketch wasn't meant for me ... Like I said, nothing ever happened between Fen and I while your grandma was alive. But it's not my business to tell you. It's Fen's.' He leaned forward and put his hand over Jake's. 'What's important and what I'm trying to say is that I know you feel guilty about what passed between you and Harriet before she died and it's held you back from finding happiness elsewhere. You've punished yourself by hating this place and staying away from here and from anyone else you might have found comfort with.'

Jake had to remind himself to breathe. The memories of the weeks before Harriet died were vivid. Part of him was angry with Archie for dragging them up, but his grandpa was right. He had used his guilt as an excuse to cling on to the past and beat himself up. If he'd been able to admit that to himself, he might have fought harder to stay with Poppy.

'You're right. It's been hard to forgive myself. I'm not sure I ever will, but I do want to be happy again. I want to let Poppy know how I feel, but it might be too late. I don't know if we can work things through.'

Archie shook his head. 'Jake, boy, I'm glad my misfortune has given you the chance to see things differently. Move on

– things will never be perfect. If you think they're even half perfect with Poppy, then let her know and don't let her go. Hold on and make the most of every moment. Fight for her.'

Chapter 32

Poppy hitched a lift back to St Piran's on Kelly's workboat and squeezed in between the packs of electrical supplies and roof tiles. It was lucky she'd spotted Kelly and her workmate as she was on the quayside because her phone battery had died hours before in the airport at Newquay.

But – deep breath – she was finally back at the Starfish after a twelve-hour journey by train, bus and plane from the Midlands. She put the key in the lock of the door and her stomach flipped. It was already open. She'd definitely left it locked, but – she let out a sigh of relief – of course, the Cardews wouldn't have bothered to lock it while they were keeping an eye on things. It was only Poppy's city paranoia.

Her anxiety evaporated once she was inside because the studio looked fine – it looked amazing, in fact, compared to the tired and crumbling space she'd been confronted with on that first day back in May.

She headed upstairs to the flat, plugged her phone into the

charger in the kitchen and looked out of the window. It was a still evening, the waves gently lapping the shore next to the harbour and a few people were still around, loading fish off boats. She recognised every one of them and it reminded her of how much she'd missed Fen, Kelly and her friends on the island ... and she'd missed Leo.

As for Jake, she'd tried very hard not to miss him, but it had been impossible. She hadn't heard from him for almost a week now, the longest he'd been out of communication since he'd left. She hoped he was OK.

Her phone went nuts as a string of text messages came through. There were two from her mum and one from Zoey. She picked up the phone, still connected to the wall, and texted her mother with a rapid: 'Home safe, TTYL', just as several messages came through from Jake.

'Where are you? J x'

'Back on St Piran's. R U at home? J'

'Need to talk to you. Call me'

There was an answerphone message from him too. With a pounding heart, she listened to his voicemail.

'Poppy. It's Jake. Nothing to worry about but I thought I'd let you know that Grandpa's back on St Piran's. I hope you're OK ... call me if you can ...'

Jake sounded out of breath and there was a noise in the background like a cow mooing. He was back on St Piran's with Archie? What was going on?

Should she call him? Go around to Archie's?

She texted him: Back at Starfish. No battery. Do you want to come over?

If he was with Archie, it was better that they had their conversation privately.

She hung over the phone, waiting and willing it to beep.

Five long minutes passed before she heard the door open below in the studio and Jake's voice call, 'Poppy? Hello. It's me.'

She flew down the stairs and almost landed on top of him. He looked – amazing – tall, a little tired perhaps, but very tanned. Every instinct told her to throw her arms around him and kiss him, but his serious expression stopped her just in time.

She stepped off the bottom stair. 'You're back.'

Jake hung back. 'You too.'

'I hadn't heard from you for a while ... I was a bit worried ...'

A trace of a smile touched his lips. 'That I'd been swallowed by a giant anaconda?'

'It's not funny!'

Jake stopped smiling. 'No, it isn't. We did have a few hairy moments, but all our comms were out of order and then when I got home ... well, I didn't know if you wanted me to call you.'

'What do you mean?'

He shuffled his feet, awkwardly. 'I heard that Dan had been here after his father had died. I'm very sorry. It must have been a massive shock. I assume he wasn't that old?'

'Pete was only sixty. I liked him a lot. He was larger than life and he loved a drink and a smoke. To be honest, he was a lot more fun than Dan.' She sighed. 'He had a sudden massive heart attack so it was a horrible shock for Dan. He was in a bad way and he wanted my support. I decided to help him.' She'd been about to say she had no choice, but that wasn't true. Everything was in her control.

'I understand,' said Jake, but there was a tension in his body that said otherwise.

'Who told you Dan had been here?' she asked.

He hesitated, then said, 'Minty.' He grimaced. 'And a few other people.'

'Minty! How did she know?'

'She said she'd come over to the studio and that Dan had told her you were going back home with him and he implied it might be permanent.'

'Oh God. Dan ... I never said anything about staying away. I admit I was soft with him while he was here. He was in bits, but there was nothing between us – on my side – other than friendship.' She hesitated. Jake didn't need to know the details of her conversation with Dan at the café ... but he did seem desperate to know she wasn't staying with Dan. Her stomach flipped. Could this mean that ... 'I left in a hurry,' she said. 'But it doesn't matter now. We're both back. How long have you been here?'

'Since this morning ... I came straight round to see you. There are things I want to say to you, but I'll walk out now if that's what you want. I don't want to pressure you, not after the time you've had with Dan leaving and coming back ... He didn't only ask you to go to the funeral, did he?'

'What makes you think that?'

'A hunch. A fear ... Why would he come all this way to see you and ask you for support if he didn't still love you? When

I heard you'd gone back with him, even if I dismissed what Minty told me, the odds on you and he getting back together were strong. I didn't want to pressure you or risk being knocked back. But lately I've realised that some things are worth fighting for.'

Poppy listened in amazement. So, it was true. Jake was opening his heart to her after all this time. She hadn't expected him to be here at all, let alone to tell her that he wanted to be with her. She felt as if she could jump for joy.

'You-you'd better come up to the flat.'

They sat next to each other on her bed. She could hardly believe that he was only inches away after all this time. She could feel the warmth of his body, the weight of him next to her on the bed. She wanted to reach out and touch him.

'So, you and Dan,' Jake began. 'What happened? I feel sorry for his loss, but why did he come over here? I thought he was with Eve. The Temptress.'

She smiled. 'He was, but she was tempted by someone else. The baby's not even Dan's.'

Jake snorted. 'Jesus. I'd say poor Dan, if I didn't think he was a total twat.'

'He said he'd made a big mistake and he wanted us to get back together.'

'And were you tempted?'

'No. It's funny, but despite how much he'd hurt me, I used to fantasise about what I'd say and how I'd feel if he walked in that door and begged me to take him back. Does that sound mad and sad?'

He shook his head. 'Neither. Just sounds human, like

someone who's been hurt. So, when he did turn up, how did you feel?'

'Confused. Angry with him and sorry for him. Disoriented, as if the past few months had never happened. Weird, because he'd invaded my new life. I couldn't cope with him being in the Starfish, a place I rebuilt – *we* rebuilt – from the fragments of my old life.'

'And what about when you went home?' Jake sounded as if he was teetering on the edge of a cliff, afraid to ask the question.

'Just as strange. I felt terrible explaining to Dan that our time had passed. I tried to let him down gently, but I don't think he'd ever have come back if Eve hadn't left him, and even if Dan had decided to dump her, I still would never have him back. He's not the person I thought he was and I'm different too now. I'm stronger and more independent than I ever dreamed. I've come here and gone home again but I'm back. I'm sticking with St Piran's and the Starfish.'

Jake covered her hand with his fingers. The connection was electric after so long apart, so long not knowing how he felt or how she did and now – *knowing*.

'I don't love Dan any more. I care about him and I'm sorry for him, but only as a friend. I can't be the prop I once was. You know when you wish for a thing so hard until it hurts and then when you get it, it's too late? You've moved so far on, you don't feel the same? It's like that with Dan. I've moved to another place, in every sense of the word.'

He took her other hand. 'I ... do know the thing about wishing for a thing so hard it hurts,' he said softly. 'The pain of losing Harriet was so strong that I'd have given up everything to have her back. I wished it was me, a thousand times. For her parents' sake, for my sake. If I was dead, I wouldn't have to bear the pain. But I don't feel like that now.'

She held his hand. 'I'm glad, Jake.'

'I need to tell you something else too. Grandpa had guessed, but I've never told anyone else ...' He faltered momentarily before going on. 'Things weren't perfect between me and Harriet when she died. We'd both been having doubts about getting married. That afternoon on the yacht, we were rowing about trivial stuff to do with the wedding. Who would sit where and whether various people should have been invited at all. It was a niggling little row at the start, but it escalated. You know, the way arguments develop when there's something bigger underneath?'

'I know. The stuff you've kept a lid on – the things that really matter – come to the surface,' said Poppy.

'Yes. Exactly that. What you don't know – what no one knows – is that we'd both been having doubts and Harriet had confessed to me that she'd had too much to drink at a work conference and she'd had a one-night stand with some guy she met in the bar.'

Poppy gasped. 'Oh my God.'

'Obviously I was shocked to the core. It was about a month before the accident. She swore it had meant nothing, that she'd been under a lot of stress and worrying if we were doing the right thing. She also promised me that it would never happen again and we should try extra hard to make a go of things. So, I forgave her – because I did love her – and we tried to move on. The doubts niggled at me, of course, and the trust was lost and I think she wasn't sure either.'

'I know the feeling. Doubts eat away at you, you blame yourself, you question every moment you had together, wondering if it was genuine. You start asking yourself if that person – Dan or Harriet – ever really loved you at all. I mean, I'm sure she did. Not like Dan. Oh, Jake, I'm digging a hole here.'

'Not at all, and anyway, that's one of the things I like about you. You dig huge holes. You're open and honest and say what you feel.'

'Too much.' Poppy smiled at him and she brushed his lips with hers. 'Go on.'

'So, we were arguing and Harriet accused me of not being considerate and being moody. She was probably right, but I wouldn't back down. Then it came up – her sleeping with the guy – and she accused me of never being able to trust her again. She said I didn't want to trust her and I said that maybe she wanted to drive me away. Next thing I know she said maybe we should call off the wedding. I said "maybe we should." I didn't mean it and I hope she didn't, but I'll never truly know. She said she was sick of bloody St Piran's and my family and she wanted to go home.' He raked his hair back off his face. 'I should have stayed calm and not risen to the bait, but it's too late. It all happened in a flash. She said she was hot, and she was angry and wanted to go below to get away from me ... She ripped off her life jacket and she stood on one of the cockpit lockers to climb past me.' He let go of Poppy's hand and stared at the floor. 'Then the boom swung and the next thing I knew she was overboard.'

'Oh, Jake. That's horrible. I can't imagine.'

'I was frantic and tried to gain control of the yacht to make my way back to her but it was too late. She was unconscious in the water without a buoyancy aid. She'd been unconscious when she went in, so she never knew anything but I will always blame myself for that row.'

'Jake. I'm so sorry for this. It wasn't your fault, just bad luck and you said yourself that you had to move on.'

He took a deep breath. 'I have. I can't keep running and hiding and I'm ready to let Harriet go. Grandpa left the pictures hoping I'd stay. He stayed away when he knew you and I were ... getting on well.'

Finally, a small smile touched his face. Poppy had been worried that telling her about Harriet would drag him back down into the depths of despair.

'You mean Fen's been spying on us?' she said.

'And reporting back to Grandpa.'

'Oh, what a crafty pair.'

'I know, but I suppose I should thank them. When I came here to St Piran's and saw how beautiful it was and reconnected with it through Grandpa's paintings ... and ... I began to rediscover everything I left behind but that also meant facing up to losing Harriet. It was like I was right back there on that day when the lifeboat finally reached us. I was holding on to her once I'd hauled her onto the yacht and they had to tear her out of my arms. I've been holding on to her ever since, but in staying here and facing up to the past, I've finally been able to let go of her.'

His body relaxed as if he was physically letting go of the tension and pain. Poppy also felt as if she was letting go – of Dan and her bitterness – and embracing something new: new possibilities at the Starfish ... and with Jake. It felt like and putting on fresh clothes in bright colours.

'It's horrific to lose someone you love, and then, one day, when you realise that you feel happy again – in a new and very different place – it's terrifying. You feel guilty, as if you've betrayed them. That you've had to leave them behind twice. Once when they died and again when you live,' said Jake.

It was the most natural thing in the world to reach out and hold him.

'Believe me it was much easier to let go of Dan,' said Poppy, trying to ease his tension.

Jake smiled. 'Thank God for that. I was worried you might feel the same way as I did about Harriet. I didn't say anything before I left for Brazil. I deliberately put all that time and those miles between us, hoping I could escape from the way I felt, but the longer I was away, the more I missed you. I'm an idiot.'

'Yes, you are.'

He shook his head but was smiling again. 'I set myself up for that one, didn't I?'

'Yup. Carry on. I like it.'

'So, I still don't know if you're ready to start again, let alone with a brooding moody sod like me who spends half his life looking through a lens?'

'I think I could give it a try.'

Jake smiled. The sun was back behind his eyes, lighting their deep brown depths with warm rays. He rested his fingers on her cheek. 'I don't know exactly how this is going to work. I'll be away a lot, even if I do base myself on St Piran's ...'

Base myself on St Piran's. She let the significance of his words sink in but simply smiled. She didn't want him to realise how momentous they were. Not yet. Just in case he got scared and changed his mind.

'If you'll have me,' he added. 'I forgot to ask you that part.'

'You did. But my answer is yes.'

She leaned forward and kissed him. He leaned in too and at first, they simply kissed, just her mouth on his, slowly savouring the thrill of being in physical contact after so long apart. The kiss sent shivers down her spine. They moved closer and Jake folded his arms around her and she slid hers along his back. The warmth and closeness was joyous. There was no need to hide how she felt any more. Everything was possible. Even though she'd kissed him before, and enjoyed his body, it was different now they had nothing to hide from each other.

It seemed only moments before they were undressing one another and tumbling into bed, exploring each other again. Everything else – explanations, words, plans – could wait.

Later that day, Jake went to see how Archie was and returned to Poppy with the news that he'd spoken to Fen. Apparently, she'd been to spend some quiet time at the grave of an old friend and then walked the coast path for a couple of hours.

To everyone's relief, she was also coming home the next day.

The following morning, Archie went on his own to meet her at the St Piran's jetty, but after they'd had some time together, Poppy and Jake knocked on her door together. When she opened it, they were standing there hand in hand. The smile spreading over Fen's face when she realised that Poppy and Jake were together almost made Poppy cry.

Archie was inside, making a cup of tea and wearing one of Fen's aprons, looking like he belonged there. Leo was stretched out in the window, surveying his kingdom and his human vassals.

'It's not officially official yet,' said Poppy. 'We need as long as we can to enjoy being together before we go public.'

'Well, well, better late than never,' Fen said.

As Poppy and Jake walked back to the studio, Poppy couldn't help dwelling on Fen's lack of spark, despite their news. Poppy and Jake had tried to get her to talk more about the funeral, which had been for a friend Fen had known many years before but not seen much of lately. Fen hadn't wanted to 'dwell on it any more', she said, and was far more interested in hearing about how Poppy and Jake had got on and hearing about their plans for the forthcoming Low Tide Festival, next weekend.

She and Jake had respected this, but Poppy had spotted Archie patting Fen's back and giving her a sympathetic smile. At times, Fen had appeared to lose the thread of their conversation and when she made the tea, Poppy saw her gazing out of the window, frozen for a few moments.

She voiced her fears to Jake. 'Did you think Fen was OK? She seemed happy for us, but she looks very tired and I thought she was subdued.'

Jake nodded. 'Funnily enough, I thought the exact same thing. She wasn't her usual self. I guess it's to do with the funeral, and it must be depressing when you start to lose people the same age as you.'

'You're probably right. I know how draining and upsetting funerals are, even when you weren't super close to the person who's died. It's so horrible. I'm glad she has Archie back. That's bound to cheer her up and Leo looked like he was king of the world. He's happy that his humans are home.'

'Hmm. I thought he was planning his next assault on me. My trainer's never been the same since he decided to use it as his litter tray.'

They both laughed and walked hand in hand back to the Starfish, but despite her happiness, Poppy couldn't help worrying if there was something far deeper troubling Fen.

Chapter 33

The stepladder wobbled as Poppy looped new bunting over a nail on the veranda roof. Her heart rate jumped as she steadied herself. It wouldn't do to fall off and break her leg before the Low Tide Festival even started, but she had to have the Starfish looking its best.

Satisfied that the bunting was safely hooked, she climbed down to the decking and admired the pennants flapping in the late summer breeze. The mini flags in ice cream colours complemented the new paintwork beautifully and were a lovely backdrop for the display stock. In a couple of hours, the first influx of visitors would arrive for her first festival.

This year, it was to take place on the lowest tide of the year marked with partying, barbecues and general celebration. A steel band had been booked and beach cricket and boules tournaments organised. The Harbour Kiosk would wheel its mobile stand onto the sands to serve cold drinks and ice cream, while the Driftwood and Moor's Head had banded together to run a bar and seafood barbecue.

The festival marked one last hurrah before the weather started to turn and the nights drew in ever more quickly. Visitors had booked months in advance specifically to be on Scilly for the festival. Extra ferry services were bringing visitors from the other islands and they'd all have to pass by or very near the Starfish Studio. As it was Poppy's first Low Tide Festival, she'd employed Kelly to supervise the studio so that she could enjoy the height of the festivities with Archie, Fen and Jake.

With the studio in Kelly's hands, Poppy and Jake joined several hundred islanders and visitors on the sands. Slowly but surely, the waters retreated from the channel, gradually uncovering more and more of the seabed. Finally, only one small pool was left in the middle with sandbanks either side. Some people had already started walking from both islands and met in the middle with laughter and excited whoops. The food stands and entertainers had already set up on the sands at either side. The Caribbean sounds of the band filled the air. Soon there were several hundred people gathered, drinking and crossing between the islands.

Poppy and Jake bought fish tacos from the barbecue and amused each other with secret touches and looks. Every time his hand 'accidentally' brushed hers or he shot her a dark sexy glance, she tingled all over. It was almost impossible to hold a rational conversation with Jake by her side, knowing what they'd been up to for the past days in her bed at the studio. They'd spent the week together but as yet, no one seemed to have noticed.

Jake left her to take a few photographs, but Poppy still couldn't wipe the grin off her face as she watched him capture the festivities. The whole scene was bathed in the light bouncing off the water and creamy sand. She hadn't felt so happy for a very long time; perhaps never – *definitely* never. Last night, Jake had told her he loved her and it had felt natural to say it right back. She felt easy and comfortable with him in a way she now realised she hadn't felt with Dan. It was best for both of them that they'd split up, however painful it had been.

Maisie joined her with the buggy, leaving wet tyre marks in the sand. Baby Eloise was sleeping soundly.

'You look happy,' she said, with a shrewd glance at Jake.

Poppy tore her eyes from him. 'I am.'

Maisie raised an eyebrow. 'Any particular reason?'

Poppy couldn't resist it. 'Might be.'

'I'm very happy for you both. You deserve it.'

'Thanks.' She nodded at the makeshift bar where a handsome blond man was serving beers alongside the Moor's Head staff. 'Patrick looks busy.'

'He's in his element,' said Maisie. 'And so am I.' She looked down adoringly at the tiny bundle in the buggy.

Hugo Scorrier's dog, Basil, scampered past them, driven wild by the smells and scent of barbecued food. Hugo was chatting to Asha and didn't notice straightaway.

'Basil! For God's sake,' Hugo bellowed as his dog jumped up at the barbecue stall. 'Not the sausages!'

Basil ignored him and almost dragged the cloth off the stall.

'Basil! Come back here!' Asha's voice carried above the chatter and steel band.

Basil stopped dead. He trotted back to Hugo and Asha and dropped a sausage on her wellies.

'Good boy,' she said, patting his head. 'Go on, then. Just this one.'

Basil gulped down the sausage.

'He never does a damn thing I tell him. You must have the knack,' said Hugo and slipped his arm around her back.

'Bloody hell,' said Maisie. 'Thank God someone's taken on Hugo. The rest of us can relax. Right, I'd better be on my way before this one wakes up and gets all grouchy.'

A few people were gathered around Archie, who'd set up his easel and was painting. Jake was still taking photographs, leaving Poppy some time to take in the scene. She didn't think she'd ever felt so at home. She only wished her own family could be with her more often, but the season would be over by the end of October and she planned on going back for a longer visit – and taking Jake with her. She hadn't told her parents about him yet – that would cause a stir.

Fen joined her, a large gin and tonic in her hand. 'It's good to see them home, isn't it? And I'm so happy for you and Jake,' she said as they watched Jake and Archie at their work.

'Thank you. They both seem to have settled back in well, don't they? But how are you, Fen? So sorry that you lost a friend. Had you known her a very long time?'

'Since I was in my early twenties. It had been a long time since I'd seen her – Sheila – though.' Fen's voice broke. Poppy felt she'd touched a raw nerve.

'I didn't mean to make you unhappy.'

'You haven't. It's good to talk about her ...' Fen hesitated. 'I – I know you found those drawings.'

Poppy winced inwardly. How she wished that she and Jake hadn't uncovered this slice of Fen's private life. 'I'm sorry. It was the day we opened the drawer. We should have told you about them, but Jake didn't know what to do. We didn't want you to be embarrassed and ...' Poppy took a deep breath. 'I suppose we felt awkward too, even accidentally coming across something so personal.'

To her surprise, Fen smiled. 'You youngsters. I bet it was a shock to find out that a pair of oldies like us had a past.'

Poppy grimaced, then smiled to cover her awkwardness. She owed it to Fen to be open-minded and grown-up. 'That's our problem. I am sorry for finding them though.'

'Don't worry. Archie has shown them to me. In fact, he's framed one of them himself and it's in my bedroom.'

'Oh.'

'There's been enough secrecy and hiding things away. I think you deserve to know about those drawings.'

'I don't want to intrude, but if you want to tell me, I'm happy to listen.'

Fen touched her hand. 'Thank you. It might help a little to speak to someone who won't judge me. You see, I first met Sheila when she came to the isles in nineteen sixty-six. In those days, Archie ran painting courses to make a bit of extra money to support the family. I did some modelling for him. Ellie knew about it and seemed happy enough. At the time, although I had a crush on Archie, I kept it well hidden. Ellie was my friend and neither I nor Archie would ever have hurt her. I'd rather have died.'

So, Archie and Fen were in love. Poppy had always thought so, and Jake had told her Archie's side of the story but to hear it from Fen's own lips – it was so sad. 'Fen. I didn't realise ...'

'No. Some things are best left as secrets. I don't believe in all this sharing and baring your soul in public. Especially in those days and especially when you make a habit of falling for the wrong person. I loved Archie but, you see, I also loved Sheila.'

Poppy was stopped in her tracks. 'Oh ...'

'Yes. She and I hit it off right away. Almost from the first moment we saw each other, the way she looked at me wasn't like other women did. When I was modelling, it wasn't envy or disgust – Sheila liked me in the same way that Archie did. She was shy and the way she kept glancing up and looking at me, it was like a butterfly landing on a flower, so gentle and careful, but she kept on doing it. And I felt the same way about her.'

Poppy hardly dared speak, imagining what it must be like for Fen to speak of a love so private and personal and, back then, so illicit. Her heart went out to Fen. 'That's so beautiful. Did you get together?' she asked gently.

'Sheila was on the course for two weeks and we knew we didn't have much time, so I bit the bullet and let her know how I felt. I had the most wonderful two weeks of my life with her. We went on picnics and walks and took Archie's boat out. To the outside world, it was all innocent, because in those days, no one would have suspected we were anything but friends.'

'Did Archie know?'

'Of course, he did. Nothing shocks him and, bless the man, he was happy for me. He knew that the two of us could never be together and he was delighted that I'd found someone. But, of course, it could never be for me and Sheila. Not back then.'

Poppy's heart broke a little more. She guessed what was coming.

'Sheila went home and we promised to keep in touch. When she finished her nursing training, we vowed we'd get together and live together as a proper couple. We'd move to London or abroad ... We kept in touch for a few years and she sent letters and cards. I still have them in the cottage.' Fen smiled though there was sadness in her eyes. 'I keep them in an old box of Leo's Dreamies inside my wardrobe.'

Poppy let out a breath. 'So, the older drawing was for Sheila?'

'Yes. Archie wanted me to send it to her, but I never dared. It was a good job I didn't.' Fen sighed heavily.

'Why? What happened?'

'Sheila married a man she met at the hospital – a consultant – and her letters changed. They became the kind of letters that friends – acquaintances – exchange and when she told me she'd met "a wonderful man she was going to marry", I knew we'd never live out our dreams – perhaps I'd always known that. I wrote back and congratulated her and, after that, there were only birthday and Christmas cards with a scribbled one line, 'hope you're well' kind of thing. As the years went by, she'd always send a photo at Christmas, with her and the children – and the grandchildren – as if she wanted to remind me to keep my distance. Until last

Christmas.' Fen held up her hands. 'See these rings? The one on my left hand was from Archie, a couple of years after Ellie died.'

'It's beautiful. Not one of Minty's, I can see that.'

Fen smiled. 'I wouldn't have her stuff within a mile of my person. No, it was made by an artist on St Saviour's. And *this* one.' Fen pointed to the thin silver circle with its amber oval, on her right hand. 'This one came from Sheila. It arrived out of the blue in a jiffy bag last Christmas. There was a card with it, not signed but it said, "I'm sorry I wasn't brave." I knew who it was from and I also knew that something must have changed for her to have sent it. Turns out she had cancer.'

Poppy bit her lip. Her heart ached for Fen. 'I'm pleased she sent it to you, even though she was so ill. It's a beautiful ring. They both are and I've often admired them. She must have still cared about you very much. It's heartbreaking you lost her; I'm so sorry.'

Fen held out both hands. The rings glinted in the sunlight. 'Now, don't feel sorry for me. It wasn't our time.' Fen patted Poppy's hand, almost as if she was comforting her. What a brave, generous woman she was.

'I wish you could have been with Sheila, all the same.'

'Don't be heartbroken because I've had the love of Archie all my life, and in later years, his *full* love. That's more than some people do or they stay in a loveless marriage long after the joy has gone. You see, there are so many different kinds of love and ways of loving. I'm one of those people who doesn't see a man or a woman, or a label. I just see a person who I fall in love with or not. And there have only been two: Sheila and Archie.'

'But how awful for both you and Sheila, to love each other and not feel you could express it and to have to live a lie. I feel angry at the past, Fen. I want to go back and shout at people.'

'Well, you can't and you'll only eat yourself up with bitterness if you take that course. Times were different then. I hate to sound like an old fart, but you young people don't realise the freedoms you have and how precious they are. I know things are far from perfect, but you've far more opportunities to be who you are and love who you want. I kept my love life private. That's not easy, as you've found, especially in such a small community. I'm not an "ism" and I won't be labelled.'

'Oh Fen. I'd never label you or judge you.'

'You might not. You're young – you and Jake – and you're open-minded and you have a generous heart, but there are many who don't. Even if they didn't, I still prefer to keep things private, and so does Archie. So did Sheila. I don't blame her and I never will. She's gone now and her death and the funeral hit me hard.'

'I'm sorry you didn't have anyone to talk to about it. I wish I'd known,' Poppy hugged her.

'Thank you, dear. It was a shock and I was bitterly grieved when I heard.'

'And even at the funeral, no one knew how you'd felt about each other?'

'Gosh, no. Everyone thought we'd just been friends a long

time ago. Sheila lost her husband a few years back, but her two children and her grandchildren were there. Everyone was very kind to me, thanked me for coming, but to them, I expect, I was only another old codger who'd turned up for the tea and cakes.'

'I'm sure they didn't think that. When my grandad died, Mum and Dad were really touched and pleased that his friends had travelled so far to his funeral.'

Fen sighed. 'I wanted to scream out: "I loved her too and she loved me." Imagine if I'd done that over the sausage rolls and the scones?' Her eyes shone brightly.

'I can't imagine not being able to let the world know how much you love someone.' She glanced at Jake, brimming with relief that they'd finally decided to admit how they felt. 'At least Sheila knew you loved her.'

'Yes, and it makes me happier than I can say that you and Jake are together. You both deserved a fresh chance at happiness after what you've been through.'

Poppy hugged her again. 'That's lovely of you to say, but it's Jake who's truly suffered. I was devastated when Dan first went off, but now I think I had a very lucky escape. It was worth the pain to meet someone new.'

'Someone who's worthy of you,' said Fen. 'Now, let's not dwell on the bad times. Let's make the most of the party. Days like this don't come around that often and I don't mean the low tide.'

'Does Jake know about you and Sheila?' Poppy asked.

'I don't think so, unless Archie's explained, but you can tell him if you like. I'd be too embarrassed to speak to him myself, him being a young man – he's like a grandson to me, so you'd do me a service if you told him.'

'Of course, but what about you and his grandpa? Does he know about you two?'

'Archie's spoken to him about it and I think it's more than time that we stopped hiding how we feel.'

At that moment, Fen caught Archie's eye and he walked over, his stick sinking a little in the sand.

As Poppy looked on in delighted amazement, Fen linked arms with him and he kissed her on the lips.

Heads turned towards them. It was fair to say that a few jaws dropped.

'That's taken their minds off the tide!' said Fen in triumph.

Archie chuckled. 'Look at Trevor's face. And his wife's. Anyone would think we'd dyed our hair purple and walked out here in the buff.'

'Maybe we should,' said Fen.

'I wish we'd done it years ago,' said Archie, giving Fen another kiss.

Jake appeared, holding his camera in one hand. 'If two eighty-year-olds can do it, I think we could too,' he said and put his arm around her back.

Poppy turned and kissed him, the sun warm on her back, right there in the middle of the sand. When they broke away, they exchanged smiles and heard applause and whooping. Maisie raised her glass of fizz and mouthed 'way to go'. Fen, who was holding hands with Archie, waved at them.

'Hey! The tide's on the turn!' someone shouted.

The shout caught everyone's attention and they looked towards the channel, where the waters were covering the sand, filling in the hollows, shining in the sunlight, and slowly but unstoppably, joining together again.

THE END

Acknowledgements

The best part of writing a book is often the research, so I'd like to thank the renowned Cornish artist and former gallery owner, Heather Howe, who was a brilliant source of information on the art world and running a gallery. One of her gorgeous paintings of Cornwall now hangs on my wall. You can find her on Facebook here: https://www.facebook.com/heatherhoweart/

A big hand also goes to my author friend, Chris Stovell, who is an intrepid and keen (sometimes!) sailor and helped me with the yachty parts of the book.

Cat owners, Sue Robinson, Lindy Young and Janice Hume, had loads of anecdotes (especially the trainer incident, which happened while I was writing and instantly went in the book!). With my editor, Rachel Faulkner-Willcocks, having recently acquired two kittens, I was very lucky to have first-hand feline knowledge on tap.

I visited lots of galleries and chatted to many talented artist makers – none of whom were the slightest bit divaish. They included jewellery maker, Hayley White; Beryl Evans of Lichfield Society of Artists; and professional artist, Kara

Strachan, of the Art Loft, Curborough Countryside Centre. Textile artist, Philippa Day, was a big help and I must mention her canine companion, Jed, who has sadly now gone to doggy heaven. Hilary Ely has been my initial inspiration for this whole Scilly series and I couldn't manage without the support of Nell Dixon and Liz Hanbury, 'The Coffee Crew' and my bookseller 'bestie' Janice Hume.

I have (and it's now official) the best agent in the romantic fiction world: Broo Doherty of DHH Literary Agency. As for Team Avon – Rachel-Faulkner Willcocks, Katie Loughnane, Sabah Khan, Elke Desanghere and copy editor, Jade Craddock – after thirteen years in the business, I can tell you they're the absolute cream of the crop.

Last but most of all, I want to thank my family for their love and support through thick and thin – John, Charlotte, James, Mum and Dad and Charles. ILY xx

Nothing is simple, even in paradise. Will love bloom for the residents of the little Cornish Isles?

Available in ebook and paperback now.

Christmas has arrived on the Cornish Isles of Scilly, bringing mistletoe, surprises and more than a sprinkle of romance...

Available in ebook and paperback now.

Love the Cornish Isles series? Then why not take a trip to the Cornish cafe . . .

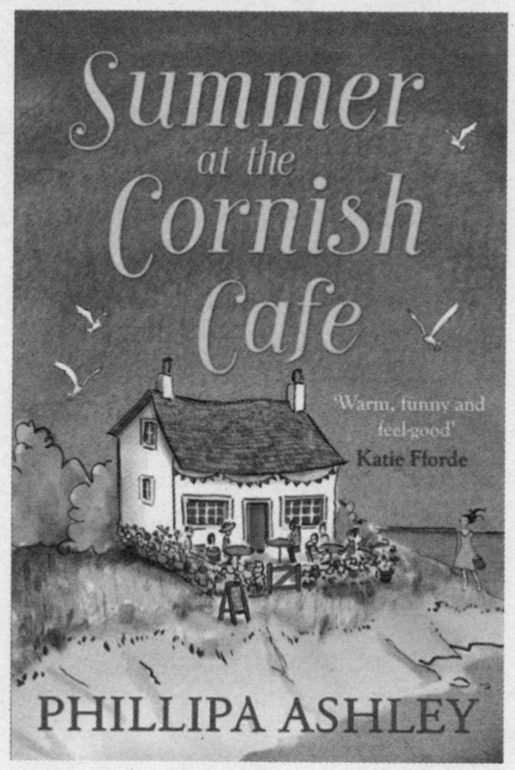

Available in ebook and paperback now.

As the seasons change, Dem and Cali's love story continues . . .

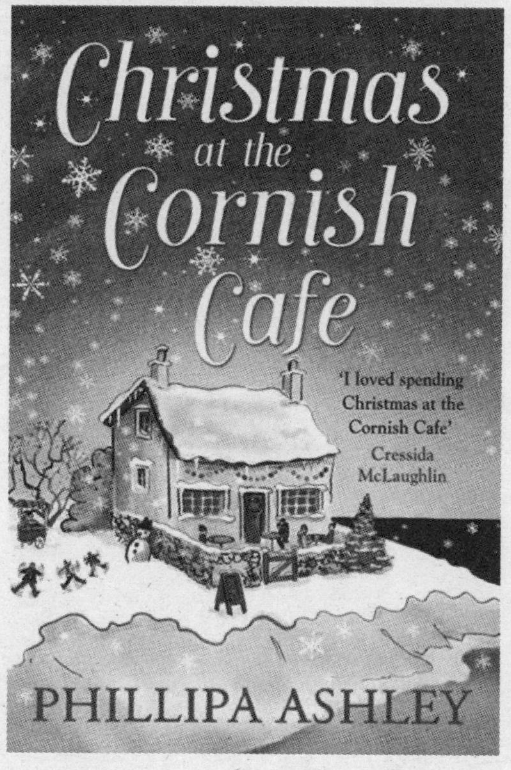

Available in ebook and paperback now.

Wedding bells are ringing on the Cornish coast . . .

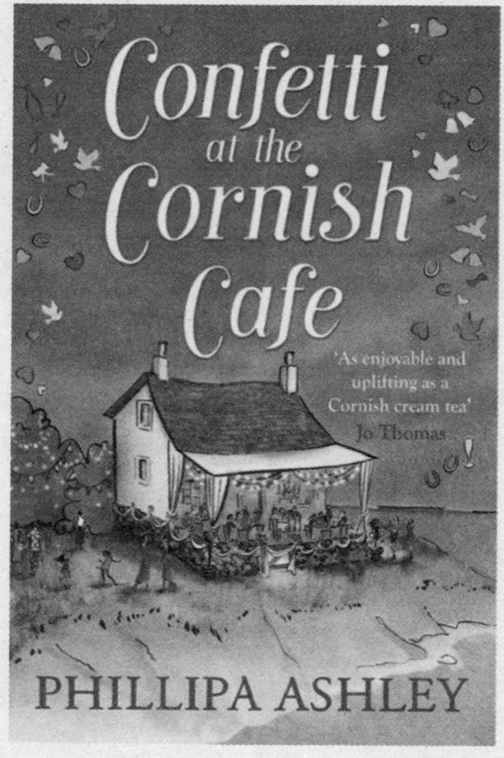

Available in ebook and paperback now.